the woman
he loved
before

Also by Dorothy Koomson

The Cupid Effect
The Chocolate Run
My Best Friend's Girl
Marshmallows for Breakfast
Goodnight, Beautiful
The Ice Cream Girls

the woman
he loved
before

DOROTHY
KOOMSON

sphere

SPHERE

First published in Great Britain in 2011 by Sphere

A CIP catalogue record for this book
is available from the British Library.

ISBN 978-1-84744-357-1

Typeset in Bembo by M Rules
Printed and bound in Australia by
Griffin Press

Sphere
An imprint of
Little, Brown Book Group
100 Victoria Embankment
London EC4Y 0DY

An Hachette UK Company
www.hachette.co.uk

www.littlebrown.co.uk

thank you to . . .

My wonderful family (including my fabulous in-laws). I love you all – don't ever change.

My agents, Ant and James. It's getting harder and harder to say something different about how amazing you both are. But you are. You know you are.

My publishers, Sphere. Jo, Jenny, David, Kirsteen, Caroline and everyone else who has been so supportive over the years, another HUGE thank you for all you've done.

My friends. I could get rather over-emotional on this page about how incredible you all are, but I'll keep it in till I see you in person.

Sally Windsor, for the additional research, and **Dr Sarah Marshall**, for the medical expertise (which I duly took creative licence with).

Matthew. Once again, none of this would have been possible without you. Love you long time.

You, the reader. As always, thank you for picking up my book – I really hope you enjoy it.

And, to G & B-B: Thank you for being you.

For My Little Angels

prologue

28th February 2003

Are you her? Are you the one he's with now? Is that why you've come looking for me?

If you aren't reading this letter fifty or sixty years from now then it's likely that I'm dead. Probably murdered.

Please don't be upset by that, it probably won't have been too much of a surprise to me – not with the life I have lived. But if you have these diaries because you came looking for me, and you were clever enough to think like me and find them, or even if you came across them by accident, please, please can I ask you a favour? Please will you burn them without reading them? _Please_?

I do not want anyone else to know these things. I wrote them for me. I know I should probably burn them myself, but it'd feel like suicide, killing a part of myself. And, in everything I've done, everything I've gone through, I would not kill myself so I can't destroy these diaries. Maybe you can.

I say 'maybe' because if you're with him then you'll want to know about him, you'll want to know if he really is dangerous and if he was the one to murder me, so, while I don't want you to, I can't blame you for reading on.

3

There's not much else I can add, except that I hope you do not feel sorry for me. I have lived a life and even though I knew great pain, I also knew great love. Some people can live a long, long time without ever experiencing that. I am lucky.

I wish you well, whoever you are.

Love,

Eve

chapter one

libby

When I think of Jack, I try to think of walking on wobbly legs after stumbling off the mini roller coaster at the end of Brighton Pier. I try to think of being fed puffs of sticky candyfloss while lying on a threadbare blanket on the pebble beach. I try to think of having handfuls of popcorn stuffed down my shirt in the front row of the cinema. I try to think of laughing and laughing until I'm doubled over and breathless, tears running down my cheeks.

'Libby, Libby, come on, wake up. Don't fall asleep yet.' The voice is gentle, nudging and slightly pleading.

I open my eyes and he's blurry. The man with the soft, pleading voice is slightly out of focus, and blinking doesn't seem to clear the view. My face is wet, and I'm dizzy, and I feel so cold. And it hurts everywhere all at once.

'Good girl,' he says. 'Try and keep your eyes open, OK? Try and stay awake. Do you know who I am? Do you remember me?'

'*Sam,*' I say, even though I don't think I am making sounds with my words. '*You're a fireman so you're called Sam.*'

He's a bit more in focus now, the blurriness is ebbing away and I can make out his features so I see his smile split the darkness of his face. 'Close enough,' he says.

'*Am I going to die?*' I ask him. Again, I'm not sure I am making sounds of my words, but Sam The Fireman seems to understand me.

'Not if I can help it,' he says, and he smiles again. If he didn't look so much like my brother, have the smooth contours of his face, his dark brown skin and bright, almost-black eyes, I could probably develop a crush on him. But that's what you're meant to do with heroes, isn't it? You're supposed to fall in love with them.

'*Is the car going to explode?*' I ask, more out of interest than fear.

'No. That only really happens in films.'

'*That's what I told Jack. I don't think he believed me.*'

'Tell me about him.'

'*Jack?*'

'Yes. You were telling me before.'

'*Jack . . .*'

When I think of Jack, I try not to think about the locked cupboard without a key that sits in the basement of the house that's meant to be our home. I try not to think of him curled up alone in the dark, crying as he watches old movies. I try not to think of sitting opposite him at dinner and asking myself when he started to feel like a stranger. And I try not to wonder when time is going to stretch its healing arms towards him and make him feel whole so he can truly open his heart to me.

'Libby, Libby, come on now. Tell me about your husband.'

'*Can you hear me?*' I ask Sam The Fireman, because I'm fascinated that he seems to be able to when I can't hear myself.

'I can lip-read.'

'*So you drew the short straw, did you? Got stuck with me.*'

'It's not a chore.'

'*Short straw. I said, short straw. You can't really lip-read, can you? You're just putting it on so you get to stay with the car. Avoid any heavy lifting.*'

He smiles again. 'Busted. Didn't realise I was so obvious.'

'*Obvious is nice sometimes.*'

'So: Jack?'

8

'*Do you fancy him? Is that why you're going on about him?*' I ask. '*I can put in a good word for you, if you want?*'

Sam The Fireman laughs. A deep, throaty laugh. 'I'm pretty sure I'm not his type. And I'm a one hundred per cent sure he's not my type.'

'*Ahhh, go on. You shouldn't be so closed off. He wasn't my type when I first met him. But look at us now: him with one dead wife and another on the way.*'

'You're not going to die, Libby,' he says sternly. He is cross with me all of a sudden. And I'm tired all of a sudden. I hurt all over, but especially one side of my head, and my nose. Actually, all that side of my body hurts and I can't move it properly. And I'm cold. I really want to sleep so that this pain and coldness goes away. You can't hurt in your sleep, can you?

'Libby, Libby, *Libby*!' he says again. 'Stay awake, please. Jack's waiting for you. He's refusing to go to the hospital until he knows you're safe. It's all going to be OK.'

'*You're a nice man,*' I say to him. He's so nice I don't want to upset him by telling him how much it hurts. He doesn't want to listen to me whining on. I just want to sleep. I just want to close my eyes and go to sleep—

'The lads are going to start cutting soon, Libby. After that, you'll go straight to the hospital where they'll look after you. OK? But I need you to stay awake while they're cutting. Do you hear me, Libby? Do you understand what I'm saying?'

'*I understand everything,*' I say. '*I'm the most understanding person on Earth – just ask Jack.*'

'There's going to be a lot of noise in a few seconds. I need you to stay awake while it's happening. OK?'

'*Stay awake.*'

The world is screeching, the car is screaming at me. It is being sliced apart, torn from around me and it is screaming out in agony. It wants the pain to stop, and I want the noise to stop. I want to sleep. I just want to sleep. I close my eyes and rest my head.

When I think of Jack, I try to remember the way we used to

9

sleep together: our bodies like two pieces of a living jigsaw, slotted so perfectly together the gaps looked like tricks of the imagination. I try not to think when I started to wonder, as we climbed into bed at night, if he wished for even a moment I was someone else.

When I think of Jack—

July, 2008

'I think you and this car are going to be very happy together,' Gareth told me. Gareth was one of those men who was your best friend when you were sitting in front of him, being convinced to part with your cash, but if you saw him in a pub or a club he'd not only ignore you, he and his mates – all of them old enough to know better – would take the piss out of you. Would judge your looks, your weight, your sense of dress, because you did not live up to the porn-star ideal he held in his head.

It was safe to say, having been in his company for forty minutes or so, I did not like Gareth.

I curled my lips into my mouth and managed a smile. I wanted this bit to be over. I wanted to pay the deposit, to give him my details and then to leave here – hopefully never to return, as I could get the car delivered after I'd made the rest of the payment by credit card over the phone.

My eyes strayed to the showroom window and to the Pacific-blue Polo sitting on the forecourt. She seemed to shine, to stand out among all the other grey, black, red and silver monsters out there. She seemed almost regal but demur with it.

Gareth was talking again so I turned back to him and forced myself to listen. I'd sort of lost interest in most things after slipping into the soft cream leather interior and taking her for a ride. My first car. I'd passed my test two weeks ago, and this was the first car I could see myself driving and that I could afford. I'd had to push for a good bargain because I had no other vehicle to trade in, but she was worth all that haggling.

10

'Now, Libby, do you want the interior and exterior treatment that will protect the car? It would be helpful with kids. Stops drinks and things spoiling that fantastic leather. And with living in Brighton, with the salty air—'

'Gaz, my man!' someone interrupted. I looked up at the interloper, standing inches from me. He was wearing large, black-lensed Aviator sunglasses inside. That was pretty much all I needed to get the full measure of him. The rest of him – his height, his wavy blond-brown hair, his well-groomed face, the thick gold band on the third finger of his right hand, and his body clothed in a Ralph Lauren shirt, Calvin Klein jeans, and Tag Heuer watch – were all inconsequential to the fact he wore sunglasses indoors.

Gareth jumped to his feet, his face overtaken by a grin, his eyes lighting up. 'Jack! Good to see you.' He eagerly held out his hand for 'Jack' to shake, excited by the chance to be touched by him. I'd seen some man-on-man crushes in my time, but this was so fervent it was embarrassing. I could imagine Gareth sitting home alone late at night, his phone by his side, waiting and waiting for that phone call where Jack invites him out to drink champagne and grope good-looking women.

'I need your help, buddy,' Jack said, warmly. If you didn't know better, you'd think 'Jack' genuinely liked Gareth when, in reality, Jack probably treated most people with disdain and mild contempt – it sat there plainly on his forehead and in the way he stood.

'One minute,' Gareth barely managed to throw in my direction as Jack slung his arm around Gareth's shoulders and started to walk him away from his desk.

'Gareth, I've messed up, again. I was wondering if you could get one of the lads to take the dents out of the Z4 – today, if possible. The regular dealer said next week, but I knew you were the go-to man to get it done today or tomorrow.'

'Yeah, sure,' were the last words I heard from Gareth as the pair of them wandered off across the shiny white and chrome showroom.

I spun in my seat and watched them standing by the large curved reception desk: Jack a full head taller than Gareth, his feet planted wide apart, his sunglasses in place while he made crude gestures in his chest area, obviously making reference to a woman's breasts. Gareth was lapping it up, his eyes agog, listening. I had taken the day off work to come here and buy this car. And Jack, who probably didn't even know what work was, had just wandered in and was getting his problem seen to straight away.

I looked out at my car again. My little beauty. I loved her, but not enough to be treated like this. There were plenty of other places much nearer to home where I could sit and be ignored before handing over a large sum of cash. Unfortunately for Gareth, while I'd got my debit card out of my purse and into his possession, he hadn't got around to swiping it through the machine. Which meant I could still walk away without losing anything but a little time. I stood up, plucked my driving licence and debit card from among the papers on Gareth's desk, shoved them into my bag, then hooked my bag decisively over my shoulder. Gareth could keep some other mug waiting; this one had waited long enough and she was off.

Shooting them both a look of pure contempt, I stalked to the door and pushed it open.

'Libby?' Gareth called after me. 'Erm, wait, I'll be with you in a minute.'

As my hand connected with the door I turned to him, and over my shoulder I shot him another contempt-soaked look and carried on.

Outside was hot but the air, laden with the promise of rain, weighed heavily on my shoulders. I inhaled and braved a last, longing look at my car before I walked slowly down the wide drive of the showroom and out onto the busy main road. I turned right, towards the bus stop. I was somewhere between indignant and sad: indignant at the way Jack had waltzed in and interrupted our chat without a second thought, and sad because my impulsiveness had stopped me getting the car I really loved.

Agh! I'd have to start my search again – after I'd run the gauntlet of bus, train and bus to get home. So much for my day off.

'Libby, Libby!' A man's voice called.

I didn't have to turn around to know who it was. Seconds later, he appeared in my path, which stopped me from walking. His sunglasses were still in place.

'I'm really sorry about that,' he said. 'I just—'

'Didn't feel the need to wait your turn because an insignificant woman was sitting there and you're so incredibly important your needs come first?' I asked.

He was shocked enough to strip his face of his sunglasses and stare at me. 'Not sure how to respond to that, really,' he admitted.

'Maybe there is no response, *Jack*,' I replied.

His face did a double-take: obviously people rarely answered him in this manner. 'Maybe an apology would be the appropriate response,' he offered.

I shrugged. 'Maybe.'

'I'm sorry. What I did was rude. I should not have interrupted your meeting, and I can only apologise for that.'

There was an unpleasant nuance to his apology: he had pitched it so that the words were technically correct, his tone of voice was contrite, but everything was smeared with ridicule. He was taking the piss out of me. He probably took the piss out of everything and got away with it because most people were left unsure of whether he was being sincere or whether they were being hypersensitive.

'Was that it? The best you can do? Wow, I hope you never have to apologise in your day job because you are rubbish at it,' I said. 'And if that was your idea of subtly taking the piss out of me then I feel even more sorry for you than I did a few seconds ago because you're even more rubbish at that.' I stepped around him and continued my journey towards the bus stop.

When I'd seen the beautiful little car on the forecourt, I'd been able to picture myself cruising along, the radio on loud, the windows wide open, my voice mingling with the singers on the radio.

Even being stuck in traffic wouldn't have been so bad because I'd be safe in my own little cocooned world. Now, thanks to his arrogance and my pride, I'd have to start looking from scratch.

And there he was again: Jack. Standing in front of me, blocking me from going any further.

'What do you want now?' I asked.

'Look, I really am sorry,' he said. 'As a result of my actions Gareth has lost a sale. It's not fair on him that my visit has potentially cost him his livelihood.'

'His livelihood?' I said, smearing my tone with his particular type of ridicule. It did not sit right with me, but this man clearly needed to be dealt with on his level. 'His whole *livelihood* rests upon the sale of one little car?'

'No, but it's not good to lose customers in this current economic climate. And he'll be doubly screwed if you go around telling people. That was all my fault. I'm sorry. Truly. Please can you give Gareth another chance? He's a decent man trying to make a living. I'm an idiot for messing around with that.'

'You'll get no arguments on that from me.'

'Please, will you give him another chance?'

The picture of me cruising along, window open, stereo on, singing out loud, danced across my mind. Gareth would be nice now. He'd stop trying to sell me extras and would want me to sign on the dotted line as soon as possible. And I did so love that little vehicle . . .

'You're always cutting off your nose to spite your face,' my best friend Angela often told me. *'I've never met a woman as stubborn as you. Even when it's not in your interests you'll do something to make a point. Sometimes, sweetheart, you need to go with the flow.'*

Car versus Tell this man where to go?

There really was only one option.

'She's still awake.'

'Awake?'

'Her eyes might be closed, but she's trying to speak.'

14

'Libby likes to talk.'

'You don't, do you, Jack? Not about anything that really matters.'

'Keep talking to her, it'll help.'

'Libby? It's me, Jack. I'm right here. Everything's going to be OK. You're going to be just fine.'

'I don't feel fine. I don't feel much of any—'

'What's the ETA?'

'About three minutes. We should have got a doctor to come to the scene.'

'They said there was no one available. Put your foot down. Oh, BP has just gone through the floor.'

July, 2008

Jack was sitting on the bonnet of a red car, chewing on bites of an apple when I had finally finished with Gareth. His long legs were drawn up towards his chest and splayed out at the knees, while he rested his elbows on his knees. I gave him a passing glance, a nod, then began towards the driveway.

'All sorted then?' he called at me, taking off his sunglasses.

'Yes. All sorted.'

'Good.'

Unexpectedly, the driver's side door of the car he sat on popped open, and a pair of bronzed, slender legs in a pair of Prada sandals stepped out. The owner of the legs slowly uncurled herself from the car and was, of course, beautiful: perfectly applied make-up, shoulder-length honey-blonde hair, a short, floaty Gucci number and a diamond-encrusted Rolex on her wrist. They could not be a more clichéd couple if they tried.

'Grace, this is Libby. Libby, this is Grace, my best friend's wife. She's here to drive me home while my car is being fixed.'

'Hi,' I said to her, wondering why he'd been at pains to clarify that she wasn't his girlfriend.

She smiled warmly, which wrong-footed me: in my job, I met women like her all the time and they generally behaved how Jack

15

behaved – as if the world revolved around them. 'Hello,' she said, the corner of her nude-lipsticked mouth turning up a fraction in slight amusement. If she wasn't his girlfriend, she probably liked the idea of Jack having to apologise. 'Pleased to meet you.'

'You too,' I said.

I nodded goodbye to them and then continued walking towards the bus stop. A minute later, he was in front of me again. He wiped the apple juice that had been glistening on his lips on the back of his hand and tucked his sunglasses in his top pocket.

'Is that it?' he asked.

'Is what it?' I replied.

'You and me, done and dusted?'

'Was there ever a you and me?' I asked.

'I thought there was a little frisson earlier. Something we could work on.'

'Frisson? You mean, you taking the piss out of me and me saying you were rubbish? *That* was a frisson? I feel really sorry for the women you go out with.'

'So this,' he moved his forefinger in the space between us, 'isn't going anywhere?'

'Where did you think it would go?'

'To dinner or a drink?'

'Jack, I'm sorry to say I don't particularly like you. Your clearly over-inflated sense of entitlement keeps bringing out the not very nice side of me. See? I would never normally say that to some-one – and believe me, I meet a lot of odorous people on a daily basis so I do know how to keep it in – but with you, I can't help it. So, no, I don't see this going anywhere.'

He studied me silently, his eyebrows knitted slightly together as his moss-green eyes held mine. 'At least tell me your full name.'

'Why?'

'So I can forever remember the one person who didn't fall for my charm, or lack thereof.'

The promise of rain in the air suddenly fulfilled itself, spilling out onto the world. This rain in early July was incredibly welcome: beautiful and calming. I lifted my face to the sky, smiling as the drops gently exploded on my skin. It was the enemy of my hair, would make me a frizzy mess in less time than it took to boil water, but I still loved the cooling touch of rain.

As I lowered my head, I saw on the horizon behind Jack, the large lumbering shape of a bus. It was going in my direction and I had to be on it if I had any hope of salvaging what was left of my day off. 'No, you can't have my full name,' I said to him. 'I know you'll just Google it, because you can't help yourself, and then you'll have to call whatever number you find because, again, you won't be able to help yourself. Believe me, it's better like this.' As I spoke, I ferreted in my bag for my one-day travel pass. Finally finding it lodged between the book I was reading and my umbrella, I pulled it free. 'Goodbye, again.' Without waiting for a response, I stepped around him to start running down the slick pavement for the bus stop.

'Libby!' he called to me.

I stopped, turned around. 'Yes?' I asked, pushing locks of my wet black hair off my face.

He smiled, shook his head. 'Nothing. I'll see you around.'

I shrugged. 'Anything's possible.' I turned and sprinted towards the bus stop, arriving just in time to get on.

Jack stood in the same spot and waved at me as the bus went past.

I gave him a wan smile then looked out of the front window to concentrate on where I was going, which was away from this place.

'BP's still dropping, she's extremely tachycardic.'

Why is only part of my life flashing before my eyes? What about everything else? Doesn't the rest of my life count?

'We need to get more fluids into her.'

Is my whole life really about Jack?

'I've lost her pulse!'

17

'Have you been keeping things from us, Libby Rabvena?' asked Paloma when I returned to the haven of the staff room after performing a particularly gruesome bikini wax.

I was still shuddering, hoping I wouldn't wake up tonight dreaming about it, when Paloma had stopped me in the doorway with her words. She was my boss: manager of Si Pur, the exclusive beauty salon for those who liked to experience purity from the inside out.

Standing beside her, like a row of white-uniformed, cleansed, toned and moisturised soldiers were Inês, Sandra, Amy and Vera, the other beauticians who, like me, lived to do nothing more than impart the Si Pur ethos. They were all looking at me with flawless, expectant faces, and I instantly drew back in apprehension. Those looks meant they were up to something, possibly planning a surprise of some sort. And I did not like surprises. I preferred to know what was coming, always.

'Not that I know of,' I said cautiously. I wasn't exactly living the most exciting life at the moment. The only thing that I hadn't told them was that I had lost my debit card yesterday, after paying the deposit on my car. Thankfully, I'd managed to cancel it before whoever found it had used it. I hadn't told them that because, well, why would I? I had told them about my car, which would be arriving sometime next week.

'Well, what do you make of this, then?' Paloma said and, almost as if they had choreographed it, the five of them stepped aside, revealing a bouquet of burgundy and cream roses.

I stared at the roses, all with lickably luscious, velvety petals, and at the expensive glass vase with a large red bow tied around its middle that they had obviously arrived in.

'Are those for me?' I asked.

'Yes,' Paloma said, not bothering to hide the naked jealousy in her voice. 'They've just arrived.'

'Right,' I said, perplexed. I could not think of a single person who would send me flowers, let alone ones as beautiful as these. I stepped forwards, and reached for the square white card with my name and the salon's address on the front that sat on its own metal holder in the middle of the bouquet.

'And who's Jack?' Paloma asked before my hand had made contact.

I wasn't surprised she'd opened the card, she did that sort of thing all the time. She made no secret of the fact that she thought she had first dibs on anything that came into the salon – even if it was sent specifically to one of us. It was a perk of management, she insisted to anyone who dared complain: you try doing her job on top of managing such a large salon for the money she made, she reasoned, it would make you realise that you deserved a little extra. None of us had been brave enough to point out that what she did was actually bordering on theft.

'Some man I met,' I said, slipping the card out of its envelope.

You wouldn't tell me your name, but I found this, so I took it as Fate. Call me. Jack. His number was at the bottom of the card.

From the envelope I pulled out my errant debit card. Ah. When I'd got my pass out of my bag, I must have dropped it. That was why he'd called me when I ran for the bus – for a moment he was going to return it, then saw it as too good an opportunity to pass up.

It was not Fate, it was me needing to organise my bag so things like this did not happen.

'You can't just say that! Where did you meet him. When? Who is he? How come he sent you flowers? Are you going to call him?' Paloma asked, straining to keep herself in check. She thrived on mysteries, the thought of one involving a man who sent flowers was probably driving her insane.

Paloma was stunning. She had thick dark hair that she wore in a sensible bun for work, a heart-shaped face, dewy dark-brown skin and long eyelashes that framed her chestnut eyes. She would love Jack. And he would probably love her. She might be less of a challenge than me, but she was on his wavelength: she had an innate sense of entitlement, and she was impressed by money and monied people. They would go together perfectly.

'You should call him,' I said, handing her the little white card. 'You'd love him: good looking, rich. Drives one of those sporty Z4 things and wears a Tag Heuer watch.'

She almost snatched the card out of my hand, stared at it wide-eyed. 'You really think I should?' she asked casually, while her eyes were desperately committing his details to memory in case I changed my mind.

'I do,' I said. 'You're his type.'

Once she had memorised his number, she raised her gaze to me and pursed her lips. 'What's the catch?' she asked. 'What do you want in return?'

Shaking my head, I went to the cleaning cupboard and liberated the jar of instant coffee we hid behind the bleach and washing up liquid. (If we ever had a visit from the 'so pure' people who owned the salons, they would probably die – after sacking us – to discover we didn't sip green tea and eat seeds all day in the purity of our staff room haven.) 'Nothing,' I said, going to the kettle and shaking it to see if it had enough for a cup. 'Oh, except maybe an invite to the wedding if it all works out.'

At the word 'wedding', Paloma's eyes suddenly lost focus and she began mentally trying on her – already chosen – Vera Wang wedding dress, placing her real diamond tiara on her head, and wafting the long white veil with Swarovski crystals hand-sewn onto it. It was obvious she would never invite any of us mere mortals to her wedding. She tolerated us because we were all good at our jobs, but she was treading water – the second she landed a handsome, rich husband she was leaving and not looking back. Once she hit her jackpot, she'd probably pass us in the street and pretend she didn't know who we were.

The more I thought about it, the more perfect she seemed for Jack.

'It's a deal,' she said with a smile.

20

Her hands reached out for the vase. 'But I get to keep the flowers,' I told her. Her manicured fingers hovered a few seconds longer around the base of the vase, before they were eventually – reluctantly – withdrawn. There'd be plenty more where they came from, she obviously decided.

Why is it so quiet?

And so dark?

And still.

A minute ago there was noise and sirens and people talking, and I think Jack was holding my hand, and everything was moving so fast.

At least the pain has stopped.

But I want to know why everything else has stopped, too.

Am I asleep?

Maybe I'm asleep. You can't hurt in your sleep. And all I wanted was to go to sleep before.

I want to wake up now.

Where is everybody?

Why am I suddenly alone?

'You're not alone,' *the woman's voice, as smooth and rich as velvet says.* 'I'm here. And I know exactly what you're going through.'

'Who are you?'

'Oh, come on, Libby, you know who I am.'

'No, I don't.'

'Yes, you do. You're a smart woman, that's why Jack's with you. Come on, you can work it out.'

'No, you can't be. You can't be—'

'We've got her back, but I don't know for how long. You really need to put your foot down or she won't make it.'

'I'll try, but there is so much traffic. No one is moving because there's nowhere to move to.'

'I'll keep pumping in fluids, but I don't know how long that's going to work.'

21

July, 2008

'That was very funny, giving my number to your boss,' Jack said to me as I approached my building.

He was leaning on the wall outside, holding a brown cardboard drinks tray with two white paper coffee cups slotted into the holes and a white bag perched between them.

It was eight o'clock. The world was bright, and London was, of course, already on the move: traffic was rolling past Si Pur's glass-fronted building at the bottom of Covent Garden, various people were heading towards buildings or the Tube station around the corner. I always came into work early because it meant I was less likely to have to do the late shift since I had the furthest to travel. I'd also been hoping to leave early tomorrow because my car was being delivered.

'Just happened to be in the area?' I asked him.

'No. I came to see if I could tempt you to sit on a bench and eat a croissant and drink a coffee with me. And to thank you for giving my number to your boss, of course.'

'She actually called you? She wouldn't tell us if she had or not.'

'She did.'

'And it didn't go well?'

'Not for me it didn't.'

'I genuinely thought you'd get on.'

'We did get on. It turns out we know quite a few of the same people, and she's funny, and intelligent, and if it wasn't for one little problem, I'd probably have asked her out.'

'Oh, right,' I said. 'That's a shame.'

'Don't you want to know what that problem is?'

I shook my head. 'No.'

'I'll tell you anyway: that problem is I'm interested in going out with you.'

'OK,' I said.

Jack's handsome face, which looked disconcertingly awake for the hour, did a double take. 'You'll go out with me. Just like that?'

'Yes. I will go out with you. Right now. I will go and sit on a park bench and eat a croissant and drink a coffee and we'll call it "going out" and then we can call it quits, OK?'

'What if you actually enjoy yourself? What if you decide that you quite like the attentions of the J-man and would like to see me again? How are you going to square that with—?'

'Don't push it. And don't call yourself J-man.'

'Got you. How about Soho Square?'

I liked early morning London, with the people, lives, and stories that made up the city's blood continuously buzzing under its skin, constantly moving it forwards. It was so different to early morning Brighton. Early morning Brighton was best experienced with a walk along the front, nodding to dog walkers and joggers and those who'd been partying all night. Brighton's blood flow seemed so much calmer than London's but I loved them both in equal measures.

'I feel like I need to be on my best behaviour or you're not going to finish your breakfast with me,' Jack said as we crossed Charing Cross Road and headed towards Manette Street.

'Why are you putting yourself through this, then?' I replied. 'There really is no need for it.'

'I find you intriguing. Not many people intrigue me.'

I'd been out with men like Jack before. Many, many times before because, it seemed, the beautician's uniform was a magnet for the type of man who wanted a girlfriend but not a woman. They wanted someone who would take care of their appearance, who would appreciate the gifts and the exotic trips, who would smile sweetly at the right moments, but wouldn't do things like have period pain, or hairy legs, or – horrors of horrors – expect to have their opinions and thoughts listened to. The last man I'd been out with, a diplomat for a small African country, had been horrified that the woman he'd met at a party who told him she was a beauty therapist turned out to have a degree in biochemistry and had once been a research scientist. I'd seen it on his face – he'd been expecting me to twirl my hair around my finger and sit there agog as he told me all about his diplomatic immunity and what things were like in his country. He didn't expect me to ask about the economic stability that indigenous fuel production could bring to his country (but I only did that because he'd been so presumptuous about me from my job title) and he couldn't get away fast enough at the end of the date.

Men like Jack did not want to go out with a real woman – they wanted the idea they had of what a woman was. That was probably why I intrigued Jack: I wasn't cute and cuddly, and every time there'd been an opportunity to become a 'lady' I hadn't taken it – I'd been nothing like the idea he probably had of womanliness in his head. That presented a challenge. And if there was anything men like Jack craved more than a demur woman, it was a challenging woman to tame.

At this time in the morning, most of the benches in Soho Square were occupied by people who had nowhere else to sleep; while the paths were littered with used condoms and spent needles. But I never let that bother me, those were cosmetic, inconsequential flaws – beneath them, Soho Square couldn't help being divine: a small, perfectly formed green jewel hidden and cosseted in the middle of a busy city. I often spent lunchtimes here, and I liked the idea of having breakfast here, even though it hadn't had a chance to get its game face on.

Jack balanced the tray on his lap and asked, 'Sugar or no sugar?'

'Whichever,' I said.

'I got one of each, so pick.'

'No sugar.'

He removed the white cup nearest to me and handed it over. 'Sweet enough already, huh?'

'Do you actually listen to the things you say?' I asked him as I uncapped the coffee and took a grateful sip of the warm foam.

'Not as much as I should. I admit that was a bit lame.'

'Were you just going to wait out there until I showed up at some unknown time?' I asked him. He picked up the white bag, which was now greased through with butter from the croissants, and held it out to me.

'No, Paloma told me that you often get in just before eight.'

'You asked her that?'

'Yes, I couldn't pass up the opportunity to ask as many questions as possible about you. She had nothing but good things to say. She thinks you're fantastic at your job even though being a beautician wasn't your first choice of career, and she suspects other salons are always trying to tease you away from her. She also told me you had a weakness for coffee and croissants, even though you know how they wreak havoc on the skin.'

'She said all that?' I asked, surprised and more than a little chuffed. 'That was so nice of her.'

'There was a lot of pride and affection in her voice when she spoke about you.'

'And she didn't mind that you weren't going to ask her out?'

'No. She has no shame – when I told her I liked you, she asked me if I had any single friends. I've set her up with Devin – he's American and rich. He'd love her.'

Vera Wang dress, here she comes, I thought affectionately and enviously. I admired Paloma for knowing what she wanted in life and love. I sometimes wished I was as focused as her. 'To be happy' was something I always aspired to. If I didn't like what I was doing, if it wasn't making me happy then I tried to do something else but somehow, at thirty-four, 'to be happy' didn't seem enough of a goal any more.

'Are you ambitious, Jack?' I asked.

I watched his face, symmetrical and smooth, with well cared-for skin and a healthy bronzed glow. He had incredible bone structure, and amazing eyes, while his lips ... There was no doubting how desirable he was and, sitting here, sipping coffee and eating pieces of croissant, he wasn't the person I had met in the showroom. He was normal. Considered, deliberate, contemplative. No question was answered without it being thought through. If I had met *this* Jack I might not have had such an aversion to him.

'Yes, in some ways. If I want something I go for it, if that's what you mean.'

'No, it's not what I mean. I'm asking if you know what you want in life.'

'Careerise-wise, family-wise, money-wise?'

'Yes. And no. I mean, are you working towards some big goal in life? In the big picture do you know what you want?'

He shook his head as he frowned. 'I thought I did. I thought I had it. But it didn't last. At that time, I thought what I wanted, what my big ambition in life was – wait for it – was to be happy.'

'And it wasn't?'

'No, it soon became apparent that happiness shouldn't be a destination in your life. It should be part of the journey of your life. Profound, I know, for someone as shallow as me, but take it from a man who knows: putting everything on hold to achieve the one thing you think will make you happy will actually mean that you're miserable along the way to getting there, and when you get there, you might find that the thing you wanted doesn't make you as happy as you thought it would. Or worse, you've completely forgotten how to be happy.'

'That really is profound,' I said.

'I do have gems of profoundness hidden in my shallows.' He ran his hand through his hair and I caught sight of his wrist as he moved: 8:35.

'Sorry, Jack, I've got to get to work.' I stood, scrunched up the paper bag. He stood too, a grand figure that slotted in perfectly with the quiet glamour of the park.

'I'll walk you back,' he said, his eyes scanning the park for a bin for our rubbish.

'That's kind of you, but no. I've had a nice time, despite my initial reservations, and you've given me something to think about, but I . . . I don't really want this to go any further. And if you walk me back, it'll feel like a date and it'll be awkward with whether you try to ask me out again. Let's leave this as a nice little interlude, OK?'

He said nothing for a moment. I could see he was trying to think of the right thing to say in reply because, to him, this was clearly not OK. 'You make me tongue-tied, you know. I'm sure it's not your intention, but I always have to think before I speak because I know you'll pick up on anything that's fake or double-edged in meaning.' He sighed. 'No. It's not OK that you want to leave things at this. But I'll call you and ask you again. Hopefully you won't put the phone down. You'll remember that little moment of profoundness I visited upon your life and you'll give me a chance.'

'Are you always this honest?' I asked him.

'Almost never,' he replied. 'But I will call you, ask you out again, because in my heart of hearts I'm hoping you're going to say yes.'

'Like I said last time, anything's possible. Bye.'

'Bye,' he replied and moved his intense gaze to my lips. It wasn't a particularly long look, but it was noticeable.

And it had me thinking about him, and happiness on the journey of life, all the way back to work.

'This is Libby Britcham, thirty-six, involved in RTA. Had to be cut from the vehicle. Suffered multiple contusions and lacerations to body, head and face, also possible concussion although was lucid and responsive at the scene. Could not make sounds while speaking, possible Aphonia from shock.

'Hypotensive throughout. She had PEA en route but responded to resuscitation and a further fluid challenge and we got her back after five minutes of resuscitation. She had two lots of IV epinephrine. She's had 900mls of gelofusine so far and two litres of normal saline, has a tender abdomen – looks like an intra abdominal bleed, probably spleen. Husband, Jack Britcham also involved in the RTA being treated in exam room two.'

'OK. Libby, can you hear me?'

Yes, I can hear you, I think at her, *there's no need to shout.*

'My name's Doctor Goolson. You're at the hospital. We're going to take very good care of you.'

27

There's that bright light being shone in my eyes again. Why do people keep doing that? Are they trying to blind me?

'Pupils responsive on both sides, set up the scan and get plastics as well as neurosurgery on standby. Get four units of O negative until we can cross-match. Also need a morphine IV here.'

August, 2008

I am so unfit! I thought as I forced myself to move forwards and chase after Benji, my nephew. He was five years old and pretty adept with a ball. It always seemed that whenever he came to stay with me for the weekend he was somehow gifted with even more energy than before while I was somehow less able to keep up with him.

He kicked his ball across the grass at Hove Park. I much preferred this park to the one near where I lived, but it only made sense to come here now because I could drive us here. Benji preferred it, too: it seemed more spacious and the greens were flatter, making playing football much easier.

I was in goal, standing between our two jumpers, but he'd kicked the ball and chased it in the opposite direction to where I was standing, heading closer and closer to the agreed boundaries for this game. If he went beyond the boundaries, I'd find it difficult to catch him up – he was that fast. I'd abandoned the goal to dart across the grass after him, calling to him to stop. Fear made me faster and I got to him in half my usual time. Just as I was about to reach out and grab him back, he shot me a wicked grin and turned around and started kicking his ball towards the now unprotected goal.

'Why, you!' I called, aghast that I'd been so tricked by one so young. I shouldn't be surprised, though. His father, my brother, was master of the double-bluff as well as being reckless and devious. He was a lone parent because his girlfriend – Benji's mother – had finally seen the light and had walked out, telling him he should try living her life while she lived his by going out to have some fun. I loved my brother, but he was not good boyfriend material – I'd been surprised that someone as seemingly intelligent as his ex had thought he was.

Running as fast as I could, I tried to get back to the goal, just as Benji kicked the ball straight down the middle of the two jumpers.

'GOAL!' he screamed then ran around with his hands in the air, as he'd no doubt seen his father do on many an occasion.

'You!' I said to him, scooping him up and spinning him around. 'You tricked me!'

'All's fair in love and football!' He laughed, his mahogany-brown face alight with pleasure. 'That's what Dad says.'

'I'll bet he does.'

A jogger who'd just run past on the path that snaked around the park reappeared suddenly and crossed the grass towards us. Jack. He was unmistakable, especially against this backdrop. He was sweaty, slightly red, his hair was damp and his grey T-shirt had a dark, V-shaped patch of sweat on his chest where flesh and cloth made contact, but he still had that 'togetherness' he always had about him.

'Thought it was you from a distance,' he said, unhooking his white iPod headphones from his ears. 'Knew it was you from up close.'

'Hi,' I said.

'Hi.' His gaze moved to Benji, who stared back at him undaunted and unafraid. 'Hi.'

'My name's Benji. What's yours?'

'Jack.'

'Are you my auntie Libby's boyfriend?'

'No,' Jack said. 'I'm sort-of a friend.'

'How can you be sort-of a friend? I only have friends or not friends, not sort-of friends.'

'Because even though I've met her a couple of times, she won't come to dinner with me, so we only sort-of know each other.'

'But why should she come to dinner with you if you're only sort-of friends and only sort-of know each other? I don't have my dinner with everyone I meet.'

Jack looked at Benji, then looked at me. 'You can tell you're related.'

'Because we look alike?' Benji asked, eagerly.

'No, because I have to think before I say anything to you.'

'Do you want to play football?' Benji asked. 'I keep scoring against Auntie Libby. She thinks I'm a sneaky little so-and-so cos I keep winning.'

Jack looked at his black runner's watch, and visibly tried to calculate something. Then he returned his attentions to Benji. 'I might stick around and score a few goals. But don't think I'm going to let you off because you're shorter than me – I know you're really a top player. Your auntie Libby can go in goal.'

'Oh, can I now?'

'Yes!' they both said at the same time.

'Right, well that's me told.'

Benji and Jack ran rings around each other: tackling, double-bluffing, stealing the ball. For the most part, they didn't actually need me because they spent so much time playing with each other, but when they did come towards me with a goal in mind, I did the obligatory throwing myself on the ground to try to save the ball.

After half an hour or so, Jack looked at his watch again. 'I really should be getting back,' he said to me. 'I'm having dinner with my parents.' He placed his hand on Benji's short, neat Afro. 'Thanks, mate, you've given me a good game. Shall we call it a draw?'

'*Nooo!*' Benji said. 'I scored six goals and you scored four.'

'Gah! I was banking on you not being able to count. Oh well, you're the winner. It was nice to meet you.'

'You too,' Benji said politely and shook his hand. 'I hope Auntie Libby comes out to dinner with you one day.'

'Me too, mate, me too. Maybe you can work on her for me.'

'Maybe,' Benji said.

Jack grinned at Benji then turned to me. 'Nice to see you, Libby.'

I nodded.

His eyes held mine for a moment, asking if I'd changed my mind, if I would go out to dinner with him. Despite what he'd said when we had coffee and croissants, he hadn't called me in the last two weeks but he was asking again for a chance. When I didn't respond, his upset spun a web of disappointment over his face, and he dropped his gaze to the grass, then turned away slowly. He headed back to the path, pressed an earphone into his ear.

He wasn't so bad. Twice now he'd shown me he wasn't so bad. The man I'd first met was so far removed from the man who'd brought me croissants and who'd played football with Benji. Maybe he wasn't like the other men I'd met, maybe he was worth a chance.

'Jack,' I called as he moved the other earpiece to his left ear.

Earpiece aloft, he turned to me questioningly.

'OK,' I said.

'OK?'

I nodded. 'Next Saturday, if you're free.'

He smiled, his expression a mixture of delight and shock, and nodded.

'Call me at work.'

He nodded again, waved to Benji and then began jogging back the way he'd come.

Benji and I watched him jog towards the park gates, but he wasn't completely out of sight when he jumped up and punched the air.

'Why did he do that?' Benji asked, turning his head up to me.

I looked down at him. 'Don't know,' I said. 'Just a strange man, I guess.'

'Suppose you're right,' Benji said. 'Can I get an ice cream?'

'Looks like a ruptured spleen, causing the abdomen to fill with blood. We're going to have to take her up to theatre straight away.'

I wish everyone would stop shouting. I can't hear myself think. Or remember.

'Page plastics and neurosurgery again, they're going to have to meet them up there.'

Please, stop shouting. It's not going to get anything done quicker, you know.

'Someone needs to tell her husband what's going on.'

August, 2008

We bounced off each other – putting aside the way we'd met – we chatted and teased and bounced off each other like we were old friends. He showed me glimpses of who he was or who he could be if you scraped away the shiny, gaudy veneer of a man who'd had life too easy. He was self-deprecating, and constantly asked me questions or tried to make me laugh. And my laughter was easy, it fluttered from my lips, having blossomed in my chest and my heart. He laughed in the same way.

He was impressed rather than disparaging that I worked as a beauty therapist, and he told me that he was a junior partner in a firm of solicitors in Brighton. I told him I'd moved to Brighton from London to go to university and had stayed because I couldn't imagine living in a place as big as London again; he told me he'd grown up in the Sussex countryside and to him Brighton and Hove were big cities. We shared our stories and our trivia and, as the night wore on, the atmosphere around us fizzed. I couldn't remember the last time I'd had such fun on a date.

We stood outside the restaurant in Hove after dinner, still talking, and he cautiously slipped his hand around mine and suggested I come back to his place, which was around the corner, to call a taxi home.

There was no expectation – no nudge-nudge, wink-wink double-talk – simply a genuine desire not to end the evening right then.

'Before you say or think *anything*,' he said as we turned into the road where he lived, one of the roads that lead down onto the seafront, 'I bought this place years ago, and when it was merely a shell. I have had to spend a lot of man hours and money getting it habitable. I am proud of it, but please don't think I bought it ready-done for the current million or so it could go for. I paid nowhere near that. OK?'

'OK,' I said as we stopped outside a huge double-fronted Victorian villa with cream-coloured render, stone steps that led up to the black front door, and a lower floor that was probably accessed from the inside. Every floor was studded with huge sash windows.

My head creaked around to look at him.

'I told you!' he insisted.

'I'm saying nothing,' I said.

The front door gave way to a wide internal porch with coat hooks and a sunken floormat, and another internal door made of glass, then a long, wide corridor with stripped wood floors, and a sweeping, breathtaking staircase. To the left of the front door there was a white console table with bowed legs beneath a huge gilt mirror. There was a door beside the mirror and further down the corridor I could see two more doors.

If he wasn't being economical with the truth, and he had bought this as a shell, then he had lavished a lot of care and attention upon it to get it back to its current glory, and to remain faithful to the period – from the cornicing and the ceiling rose to the dado rail and the cast-iron radiators.

I stood in front the mirror, waiting for Jack to let me know I could go ahead into the house. Instead of moving forwards, he turned, a mischievous grin taking over his face before stepping closer to me.

'May I smell you?' he asked, his green eyes dancing as he slowly manoeuvred me backwards until I was against the wall and he stood in front of me but wasn't touching me.

'*Smell* me?' I asked, taken aback.

'Yes. Smell you. Just your neck, if that's all right?'

I didn't see what harm it could do – I had thought he was going to kiss me, but if he wanted to smell me first then ... 'If you must,' I said.

'I've just ...' He buried his face in the nape of my neck, and suddenly, unexpectedly, I was overcome by the scent of *him*; his skin, slightly damp and salty, yet arid, with hints of something I couldn't place, swirled notes of a sensation up through my nose and directly into my blood stream. All at once, I was on fire. My body was aching and longing, bubbling and effervescing with the smell of ... of *him*.

'This scent has been driving me crazy all night,' he said, oblivious to what he had ignited in me. 'I've been having a mix of these incredible feelings because of that smell and I was wondering if it was you. And it is.' He pressed his nose closer into my neck, his body now touching mine. 'It definitely is.' The last three words moved his lips over my skin and I gasped as if in pain, pushing against the wall to steady myself. In response he came closer, his lips still on my neck. I gasped again.

He stood upright and stared down at me for a moment. 'You're so beautiful,' he whispered. He lowered his head, his lips aiming for mine and I closed my eyes, waiting for contact. When his lips did not touch mine, I opened my eyes again. 'So beautiful,' he repeated, then kissed the other side of my neck. Each kiss – soft and measured – injected more of him into me. I did not know this feeling, it was so ... *raw*. His hands moved down to my shoulders, under the lapels of my coat, pushing it backwards off onto the ground along with my bag. I was still intoxicated by his smell, the closeness of him, and didn't resist in any way. His hands skimmed down my body, over my ankle-length blue dress.

'Is this OK?' he whispered against my ear, his breath hot and laboured.

'Yes,' I managed to push out between my own laboured breaths.

'Do you want me to stop?' he asked.

Yes, I said in my head. *Yes, yes, yes, stop. Please stop.* I hardly

34

knew the man. But he seemed to know me intimately: he knew where to touch, where to kiss, how to fill up my senses. I knew I shouldn't be doing this but ... 'No. Don't stop,' I whispered. 'Don't stop.'

'I have to taste you,' he said, pulling away. His dark emerald eyes searched mine for a few seconds, looking for protest. 'I have to taste you,' he repeated, then he was on his knees, lifting my dress, tugging down my black knickers until they were around my ankles. Automatically, I stepped out of them and he immediately pushed my legs further apart. First it was his fingers – finding, feeling, filling; then his tongue – touching, tasting, teasing.

Within seconds I was whimpering; my knees trembling, about to give way; my body quivering, arching towards him as I craved more and more and more until liquid dynamite was exploding in my veins and I was clutching onto the wall, head thrown back, as moan after moan after moan of pleasure gushed out of me.

My mind still reeling, as he came to full height again, he took my hand, led me across the short gap to the mirror opposite then stepped behind me. 'See how beautiful you are?' he whispered in my ear. 'See?'

I glanced in the mirror, not paying attention to me, instead concentrating on him, how he had been transformed from the relaxed man I'd had dinner with to the man with this intensity and determination in his eyes.

'I want to fuck you,' he said into my hair. 'Can I fuck you?'

'Yes,' I whispered. 'Yes.'

I lowered my gaze from the mirror to the box of tissues on the table in front of me, listening to the jingle of his belt, the undoing of his top button, the opening of his zip, the lowering of his trousers, the crackling of a condom packet. Then his hand was gently urging me forwards until I was leaning on the table, and he was hitching my dress up, opening my legs, moving close ... And suddenly he was a part of me. His body followed where his scent had been. He curled his body against mine, his groans muted against my neck.

My eyes went up to the mirror again, to see his face, to see if it was for him what it was for me, but my gaze snagged on my reflection.

I was another person.

My hair was out of place and unruly, my body was bending forwards to allow a man to plough into me, my face was contorted with pleasure, my eyes were filled with an animalistic look. I was wild, wonton, uncontrolled. This person in the mirror was not Libby Rabvena. She was little more than an untamed beast. Sex had not done this to me. *He* had done this to me. And I had let him. I had *wanted* him to.

I immediately closed my eyes, scared to keep on staring in case that was the only reflection I would see of myself every time I looked in any mirror.

His movements became harder and he pulled away, standing up to grab tightly onto my hips as his urgency increased, his moans mixing with mine, both of us growing louder and louder until he cried out, a second or two before my cry, and we both became frozen as our pleasure rippled through ourselves and into each other.

Jack didn't withdraw straight away, he stayed with me for a few seconds, taking time to control his breathing, then leaning forwards to tenderly kiss the nape of my neck.

'That was incredible,' he said as he broke apart from me. I heard him grab several tissues from the box on the table and waited with my eyes closed and head bowed until I heard him stop moving. I stood upright, lowered my dress and turned away from the mirror before opening my eyes.

'That was incredible,' he repeated, then leant in and kissed my forehead. Before, the merest touch was a trip to an unsettling, almost feral pleasure, now it was a small, stinging blow of shame and guilt.

I managed a smile, then a slight nod. I did not know how to speak to him after what we had done. Words seemed inadequate.

'If you don't mind waiting here for a few minutes, I'll just get

36

rid of this,' he indicated to the ball of tissue in his hand, 'and then get some clean towels and a dressing gown so you can have a shower. OK?'

I nodded again. Inside, I was horrified – he expected me to stay? To *talk* to him? To act as if it was perfectly natural to have done that with a virtual stranger?

He looked at my mouth as if he was going to kiss me, or as if he needed me to remind him that I could speak, then smiled and kissed my forehead again. 'Really incredible,' he said. He stooped to pick up the condom wrapper. 'Two minutes,' he said, then disappeared up the stairs, taking them two at a time.

As soon as he was out of sight, I moved across the corridor, snatched up my knickers, then my coat and then my handbag. I stuffed the knickers into my bag, shrugged on my coat, and almost ran through the porch to the door. The lock was not like anything I had seen before, and I stared at it trying to work out what to pull or push or twist to release the catch, to set me free.

I heard the toilet flush.

I need to get out of here. I need to go, I thought desperately and began pawing at the gold latch, until something happened and the door clicked open. Closing the door quietly behind me, I ran down the steps as fast as I could in heels, then at the bottom turned towards the seafront.

I could hopefully hail a taxi on Kingsway. If not, I'd go up the road parallel to his to the taxi rank by Hove Town Hall.

As if sent from the gods, a yellow-orange taxi light came on right in front of me. I raised my arm and ran for it, praying he'd seen me. My heart skipped gratefully when he stopped and waited for me to get in.

'Devonshire Avenue, Kemptown, please,' I told the driver as I slipped onto the cracked black leather of the back seat and clipped on my seatbelt.

We didn't even kiss, I realised as the taxi driver pulled away. *We had sex but at no point did we kiss.*

That played on my mind the whole way home: I'd had sex, and I'd come away from that encounter with my mouth unkissed.

Where's that woman who wanted me to guess who she was? I haven't heard her voice since I came round in the ambulance. The way she said Jack's name, it was as if she knew him – intimately. Was she one of the women he'd been with before me? There was something familiar about her, though. And she spoke like she knew me. She said I knew her. Where is she? I want her to tell me who she is, because she can't be—

August, 2008
His car was parked outside my house.

I'd struggled up the hill with two bags from the supermarket, and turned into my street, and spotted a car like his sitting outside my building. 'Please don't let it be his, please don't let it be his,' I repeated in my head as I got nearer and nearer to home. I hadn't answered his calls last night, nor this morning. I wanted him to forget about it. To pretend it had never happened. Because that was what I had decided to do. It was all too unsettling that I'd managed to be like that, do that with someone I hardly knew, someone I hadn't even kissed. I always thought that sort of sex came from knowing someone properly, trusting them, being willing to explore your boundaries regarding sex and push them outwards together. I always thought that sort of sex came from being able to completely relax with a person, knowing they would still have feelings for you afterwards. I did not want reminding that our encounter probably meant nothing to him.

He was sitting on the steps outside my flat, legs wide open, elbows resting on his knees, sunglasses on his face. He'd morphed back into the man I first met, not the man who'd brought me coffee and croissants, who played footie in the park and who I'd had dinner with.

I stopped at the bottom of the stone steps and had to drop my heavy bags. Now that I had my car, I often drove to a bigger supermarket at the Marina or Homebush to do my weekly shopping, but I couldn't face the drive today. And there was no point in going the short distance down the hill in the car so I'd walked. Doing something physically punishing had been good for the body and refreshing for the mind after the confusion I'd been in since last night, but it was hurting now. I wiggled my fingers to get some feeling back and then turned them palm-side up and stared with interest as the blood returned to them and they went from an anaemic yellow to browny-pink again.

Staring at my fingers stopped me from having to face him.

'Well, I should probably tell you that I thought you were playing hide and seek,' he said. 'It wasn't until I actually looked behind the door in the dining room that I realised how ridiculous I was being.'

I stretched my fingers, clenched and unclenched my hands, watching as the ligaments and muscles moved in them.

'Was it really that bad?' he asked so softly I barely heard him above the sound of the seagulls and the voices, chaos and lives from the main road, St James Street, around the corner. 'I thought you'd—'

'I did,' I cut in before he said the word, but I still could not raise my gaze. 'I did, you know I did. And you know it wasn't bad at all.'

'Then why did you leave? I was expecting to wake up with you this morning.'

'I—I was ashamed of myself.'

'What on Earth for?'

'For doing that, enjoying it, when in the whole thing, I could have been anybody.' I managed to look up, to finally look at the man I'd had sex with the night before. He had taken his sunglasses off and his eyes were focused intently on me. 'It wasn't about me or us or a special connection we had, was it? I was simply another body to fuck, another hole to fill.'

It was his turn to look down, to confirm my suspicions that

39

he'd done that, in that exact same way, a significant number of times. I quailed inside, thinking of how many women had put their hands where I had put my hands and had opened their legs for him as I had done. I tried not to wonder how many of them had stayed, had used the towels and dressing gown he had gone to get for me, had been secure enough in what they had done to go back for seconds.

'Haven't you ever had one-night stands before?' he eventually asked, still with his eyes lowered.

'Yeah,' I said, looking down again. 'And with some of them I didn't realise they were going to be one-night stands until the person didn't call. But none of them have ever felt as . . . calculated and soulless as last night.' I undid then redid the blue jumper tied around my waist, which had been slowly working its way down my body. 'We'd had such a nice night, I thought I'd been proved wrong about you, then we did that. I couldn't stay and pretend it was OK with me because it wasn't. I . . . I was ashamed of myself.'

We both continued to stare at the ground, unable to say anything that would heal the situation.

'Do you want a hand with your shopping?' he asked.

I shook my head, still staring at the ground, scared to look up in case he saw the tears that were building up behind my face, and were already sealing up my throat.

I heard him get up and pause for a moment, probably to put his sunglasses back on. He came down to the bottom step, stopped beside for me for a second. 'I'm sorry,' he murmured.

I nodded. I knew he was and turning up here was a brave thing to do. If it hadn't all been so painful, I would have told him so. Instead, I stood still, my head bowed until I heard his car start up and drive away.

Tears slid slowly and continuously down my face as I picked up my shopping bags, ready to slip back into my life as if last night had never happened.

★

'We're going to have to go to theatre now, that bleed in her spleen seems to be getting worse and we need to get in there now if we're going to save her.'

Are you sure it's my spleen that's bleeding? *I think.* Because I've always thought that it's my heart that's too soft and easily damaged. I've always thought that maybe I was born with a bleeding heart.

October, 2008

I became a beauty therapist because I couldn't be a biochemist any more. Well, I could, if I decided that not eating or living with my parents were viable lifestyle choices.

I had emerged from university ready to save the world, hoping to find a way to make a difference. The research I had chosen to do wasn't anywhere near the 'hot topic' it had become now; at the time no one cared if the move towards using biofuels (things like soya and corn in place of petrol) would adversely affect the world's food resources and what we could do about it. And those who did care were not the people you financially got into bed with. So after a year of struggling to do what I wanted, I decided to stop. I didn't want to find a job that was nearly but not quite in that area because what was the point? I wasn't the sort of person who settled for second best, so I decided if I couldn't do what was my real passion, I'd find a new passion. And that lay at the other end of the scale for my qualifications – beauty. It still involved chemistry and biology, indulged my love of make-up and lotions and potions, but I could train to do it in under a year, could continually train in new specialities and I would get paid in the here and now.

The surprising thing was that I loved it. I mean, really loved it. I loved the chemical analysis of finding the right products for a person's skin, the science-like methodology of any treatment or process. I also loved seeing the results on people's faces when they looked in the mirror and saw what I saw when I worked on them – not the imperfections, but all the perfections that made up who they were.

Being a beauty therapist had many perks – being taken seriously by the world was not one of them. I saw the 'idiot' label flash up on people's faces when they spotted the beautician's coat. They thought I didn't have more than two brain cells to rub together, and that I sat around filing my nails and thinking about make-up all day. Who was I to shatter their illusions?

Who was I to point out that to be a successful qualified, certified beauty therapist you needed to understand the human body, understand chemistry and know how to successfully communicate with people? Who was I to explain to them that when you were faced with poverty or wearing a beautician's uniform, the uniform would win every time? Anyone who said they would rather starve than do a job like mine, hadn't been poor enough, hadn't had to make – more than once – the choice between food and heat. Choices like that focused the mind and hardened the heart to any sneers you might get from people who didn't know you.

Except possibly when you were crouched behind the life-sized wooden cutout of a female lifeguard holding a male swimmer at the entrance to Brighton Pier, clutching your bag to your chest and praying against hope that the man you had a one-night stand with nearly three months ago didn't see you turn and run here the second you spotted him coming towards you. When you were doing something like that, everyone looked at you as if you were strange, beautician's uniform or not.

I'd seen Jack several times in the past few weeks and I always ducked into a shop or crossed the road to avoid the possibility of having to acknowledge or – worse – speak to him, hoping while I did so that he hadn't seen me. This was the first time I'd had nowhere to run to, though, so had been forced to do this. Or to put my hands over my eyes like Benji used to do when he was two, because he thought no one could see him if he couldn't see them.

'I think you probably win the award for the most inventive way to avoid talking to me,' Jack said.

42

I froze, wondering if it was too late to try the hands-over-my-eyes thing. Slowly, I uncurled myself and stood upright. Jack and I sighed at the same time, both of us frustrated but for different reasons.

'Look, Libby, can't you just talk to me? It doesn't sit right with me that we don't speak when we've . . .' He didn't need to say it because we both knew what we'd done.

'Doesn't bother me,' I fibbed.

'It bothers me, a lot. I've seen you cross the street and throw yourself into shops to avoid me. I want to make things right.'

'There's nothing to make right. We did what we did and we just have to pretend it didn't happen.' I chanced a look at him. As I did so, I flashed back to his face in the mirror a moment before he told me he wanted to fuck me and I cringed, and refocused my eyes on wooden slats of the pier floor.

'But it did.'

'And for you it happened with a lot of other people – do you hound every one of them?'

'I have no need to because I still speak to them.'

'You mean, when you're in need of . . .'

'No!' he said sharply. 'I don't mean that at all. I mean we exchange conversation if we pass in the street.'

'Why is it so important that I speak to you?' I asked. 'What difference does it make to anything?'

'Why is it so important that you don't speak to me?' he asked, obviously thinking if he turned it round on me I might change my mind or something.

'I told you why: speaking to you, seeing you reminds me of something I'd rather forget. I'm still ashamed about what I did.'

He stood in silence for a while. 'Look, walk with me down to the end of the pier and while we walk, tell me everything that is wrong with what happened between us. I won't talk, I won't interrupt or try to justify myself, I'll simply listen, and you can purge yourself of that night. Hopefully it'll be cathartic, and if afterwards you still don't want to speak to me, I'll respect that. I'll walk past you in the street like you're a stranger. What do you say?'

'Libby, I'm going to be right here, waiting,' Jack tells me. 'I'm not going anywhere. You're going to be fine and I'll see you afterwards.'

October, 2008
'I've lost my bet. And won my bet as well,' Jack said to me, as we leaned on the railings halfway along the pier.

The length of the pier wasn't long enough to talk about what we were talking about. It was an unusually warm October, even this late in the day, so there was only a slight edge of coolness to the air, which allowed us to stand by the railings, watching the waters swirl below as we talked.

'Bet with who?'

'Myself. I bet myself that I would be able to get through this without doing something to mess it up.'

'You haven't done anything to mess up.' He had been impressively attentive while I had tried to explain how bad I'd felt that we'd had great sex that was so impersonal. Once I started talking, I realised that it was difficult to convey what I felt without bringing up the fact we didn't kiss. Theoretically, I could have kissed him (even though there didn't seem to be the opportunity) so, logically, it was my own stupid fault. But I was feeling distinctly illogical about it and had no idea why I was so hung up on a kiss. It was illogical, but vital. I still hadn't managed to get that across.

'I'm about to,' he said, and leant in towards me, his eyes closing as he came nearer. Millimetres away from me he paused, giving me the opportunity to move, then he continued and touched my lips with his. I closed my eyes as our bodies automatically moved closer and our lips crushed together. His hand slid into my hair, while the other rested on the base of my spine

44

as I slowly parted my lips to let his tongue carefully and tenderly slip into my mouth. For a few minutes, or was it seconds, our lips moved together and everything around us was still as we kissed. This was what was missing from that night. This was what I hadn't been able to articulate.

He pulled away first, then stood back staring at my mouth as he said, 'See, told you.'

'I repeat, you haven't done anything to mess up.' I was trembling slightly. I'd never trembled after a kiss before, but there really was something about Jack that touched parts of me that I didn't know existed.

He put his fingertips on his lips, as though checking they were still on his face. 'You're the second woman I've kissed on the mouth in over three years,' he stated. 'The other one was my wife. My late wife. She died three years ago.'

'Wife? You have a late wife? Why didn't you mention that when we went out?'

He looked down at his hands, twisting the simple gold band on the ring finger of his right hand around and around. His wedding ring. Of course! That was why it looked so incongruous with the rest of him and the way he dressed.

'Telling someone about your dead wife isn't exactly the best way to charm them, is it?'

'I guess not. Is that why you have sex like that?' I asked.

He kept touching his lips, almost as if they were tender, hurt, damaged from kissing properly after so long.

'Yes,' he replied. 'I could pretend that's only just occurred to me, or I could pretend that in my grief I'm not that self aware, but neither of those things are the case. Yes, that's why I have sex like that. I like sex, but kissing as we've just done would feel like I'm cheating on her. Cheating on Eve. That was her name. It's still her name, actually. Her name didn't change because she isn't here any more.'

'Sounds like she's still a big part of your life.'

'In some ways.'

'You could pay for sex, you know. I hear they have sex without kissing.'

He fixed me with a serious look as he shook his head. 'No, I couldn't. Maybe other men can, but I can't. Can you imagine me trying to strike up friendships with people who've only looked at me because I've paid them?'

'I suppose so. I've never really thought through the finer details of all that before.'

'Don't bother, it'll only upset you in one way or another if you do. I know it did me when I thought about it. I've done some appalling things in the last three years because almost everyone I know has let me get away with it, basically. At first, I genuinely didn't realise I was behaving badly because I was so consumed with grief, and everyone accepted that. As the fog cleared, I realised what I was doing and still no one said, "Enough, stop that!". So, I carried on. Getting that little bit worse each time to see if someone would say, "No". Not one person said it meaningfully until you.'

'That's terrible.'

'I know. And I do feel ashamed. But I know I would never stoop so low as to pay someone for sex. Or screw someone who I don't share at least some kind of real connection with.'

'There's logic in that, I suppose. But you really haven't kissed anyone else like that in *three* years?'

'Really.'

'So why did you kiss me?'

'Because it seemed like the thing I wanted to do most in the world. I thought, "If I don't see her again, at least I will have kissed her." I almost did when we had breakfast in the park, and that night in my corridor, but I was too scared. I can at least say now that I did. And it was better than I hoped it would be.'

'OK,' I said. It was better than I expected, too – I'd never been kissed like that before. I looked down at the water below us, wondering where we went from here. I liked him, that wasn't the problem. I simply wasn't sure if he was good for me. The way I was so rude to him, then the sex, then the trembling after kiss-ing . . . Jack was something different from anyone I had ever met.

'Libby, I know I'm arrogant, and I could pretend that my arro-gance comes from insecurity but it doesn't. It's a rather unattractive by-product of having had all the best opportunities in life and then a time period in my life when no one said no to me. But, I do have other qualities, at least I hope I do.' He stopped talking and I looked at him to find his eyes raised to the heavens, as if searching the air for where those qualities had been written down so he could recite them. He seemed to give up the quest and instead came back to talking to me. 'I like you, Libby. You're confident without being arrogant, and you're honest. And you make me examine who I am and how I present myself to the world. Few people can do that. No one has done that in a long time.

'And, you know, I've felt sick ever since that night. The sex was great, probably the best I've— but when you fled, I knew I'd done wrong. I knew I'd crossed the line. And your face when we were outside your house,' he rocked his fist into the hollow of his solar plexus, 'it got me there. Hadn't felt so bad since . . .' he shrugged almost in despair, 'since a very bad time with Eve. I'm sorry. I'm sorry for using you like that, and making you feel so bad.'

'It's all right now. I understand you a little better, so it's OK.'

He grinned at me and my whole body thrilled, the trembling starting again. We held each other's gaze, then at the same time we both decided to stare into the sea.

'How did Eve die?' I asked, refocusing on him.

The shrug he gave this time was different from the previous one; this one was defensive, and a little wary. 'To be honest, I don't want to talk about it. Kissing someone on the mouth, then talking about her is extremely unlike me – I'm not sure I'm ready to talk about why she's not here.' Another wary shrug. 'I'm sure you understand.'

I nodded. And we stood in silence for a few moments, allow-ing the sounds of the pier to fill the gaps between and around us.

'You can kiss me again, if you want,' I said, as much for something to say as a desire to repeat the experience. We'd never be able to get that back; we'd never repeat that experience because we would never again be the people we were ten minutes ago. He would never be the man who hadn't kissed a woman in the three years since his wife died; I would never be the woman who somehow managed to have sex with a man before she kissed him. What we would be is a woman who obliviously helped a widower to break through his fears and a man who was moving on from his wife.

Jack shook his head. 'I'm not going to push my luck.' And I smiled at him because I knew he meant he wasn't going to push his luck with trying to repeat the experience, not push his luck with me.

I want this to be over with. I want to skip to the end and to know that Jack is waiting for me, that the man I fell in love with is waiting for me, just like he said he would.

October, 2008

Walking to the station at six o'clock on an autumn morning was nothing new to me, but something I always did with a slight worry because it was dark. If I didn't plan to drive, then I couldn't take the car because I'd then be stuck with driving around trying to find an all-day parking spot close enough to make it worthwhile, which would also result in me missing the train.

Nothing had ever happened to me on this early walk, but there was always a first time. I'd been propositioned before – men had looked at me, walking the street at six o'clock, and had assumed I was out looking for business. I was never sure, in those circumstances, whether to be offended or flattered and always gave the men who did it a hard stare until they realised their mistake and drove away.

The headlights of a car approached and I was momentarily

48

blinded, but carried on as the car slowed and came to a stop. *Here we go*, I thought, *another man who should be at home in bed – alone or with his wife – not last-chance salooning it out on the streets.*

The driver's side window came down and the driver stuck his head out. 'Fancy running into you,' Jack said.

I blinked a couple of times, wondering if I was really seeing him. I hadn't seen or spoken to Jack in a couple of weeks – despite the kiss, and how lovely it was, I wasn't sure if taking up with him was something I should be doing. I liked him, there was no doubt about that, but I wasn't sure if he was good for me or not. I didn't always stick to things that were good for me – positively railed against it sometimes – but Jack was a different type of not good for me. He did things to my mind and body that I hadn't ever experienced before.

But it wasn't as if I could get him out of my head, either: every moment I had free would suddenly be crammed with thoughts of him. His soft lips, the gentle urgency with which they'd kissed me. The intoxicating smell of his skin. His moss-green eyes that would follow everything I said, then would meet my eyes so we could share a smile. It was driving me slowly and pleasurably insane.

'Jack,' I said, not being able to keep the grin from my face. He hadn't called me because he said he'd leave that choice up to me but had been pleased when I said if I saw him in the street I would talk to him.

'Off to work?' he asked.

'Yeah.'

'Do you want a lift?' he asked.

'What, to London?' I asked with a laugh.

'Yes, of course,' he said.

'No, a lift to the station would be more than enough,' I replied.

'OK, but a lift to London would be no trouble whatsoever.'

It wasn't until I'd clipped the seatbelt into its holder that I realised that him being out at this time probably meant he'd been out with someone and was coming back from her house. My stomach filled with liquid ice and flipped a few times. I did not like the idea of that at all. 'So, what are you doing out so early?' I asked, trying to keep my voice casual.

'I was on-call,' he said as he made his way through the dark Brighton streets. 'My client decided to break into his neighbour's house while they were away for a few days. Never mind the neighbour's high-tech security system and massive dog and the family member he had house-sitting for him. My client got a sound beating before the police picked him up. I wouldn't mind but this is the third time he's been caught this year. I've managed to get a suspended sentence – twice – for the man, but he's definitely going away this time. I didn't say this, but he's an idiot.'

The relief I felt that he hadn't been with someone else was a little embarrassing considering I didn't want to see him. 'Do you mind having to work such strange hours?' I asked.

'No more than you must mind walking to the station?'

'I usually get the bus.'

In the car, at that time of the morning, we were at the station in no time. 'Thanks for the lift,' I said, suddenly wishing it was a longer drive, that I had more time with him. It was the thought of Jack that I had problems with, I realised. The reality was really rather desirable.

'Are you sure you don't want me to drive you to London?' Jack asked, hopefully.

I wanted to say yes, but . . . 'No, no, I couldn't impose on you that way. I should probably catch up on my reading on the train.'

Disappointed, Jack nodded and mumbled goodbye before I mumbled goodbye, in return.

The station was, as usual, quite full for that time of the morning, swollen with those of us on our way to London and beyond, needing to be there early. I weaved through the crowd, feeling stupid. I should have let him drive me to London, it would have been a good way to spend time with him, to find out if the attraction I had for him was more than an enjoyable dinner and a few minutes here and there. I stopped walking and ignored the people who bumped into me, tutting before they stepped around me. Maybe it wasn't too late to go back out, see if he was hanging around? Maybe he would be waiting, staying there to see if I'd change my mind? I looked over my shoulder at the gaping exits. He'd offered to drive me; it wasn't as if I'd asked. And he'd clearly been disappointed when I said no. Maybe I should go back.

Are you insane? The voice of reason intoned in my head. *This isn't some romantic movie where you run outside and find him waiting for you, ready to sweep you into his arms. This is real life. Where real things happen. Like getting on the train and going to work.*

If there was anything in all the thoughts I'd had that morning, that was probably the truest. I turned back towards the barriers, towards the place I needed to go.

'Libby,' he said, suddenly in front of me. I stared at him in surprise, wondering if I was imagining him, if the other voice in my head that wanted me to go running out after Jack was conjuring up an image of him to make sure I didn't let this chance slip away.

'Jack,' I stated cautiously, not sure if I was talking to an apparition or the real person.

'I forgot something,' he said.

'What?'

Before I knew what was happening, before I could properly react, his arms were around me and his mouth was on mine, drawing me close to him, filling up my senses with the essence of him again. Unexpectedly, I swooned, my knees weakening and my body melting against him. I was scared as I kissed him back that when he stepped away I would fall over, feeling as weak as I did right then. As the kiss deepened and I slipped my arms around his neck, the world around us – the commuters, the announcements, the train engines, the murmurs of the morning – ebbed away until there was no one else in the world; the whole of planet Earth held only Jack and me, standing there kissing.

51

'I don't suppose you'd consider going into work late so we can have breakfast somewhere?' he asked immediately after we broke apart. We were both touching our lips, staring at each other in a muted but delighted shock. 'You know, to talk or . . .'

Trembling, as I had after the last time we kissed, I focused exclusively on him, not daring to wonder what the people around us were doing, if they were staring, grimacing or throwing disapproving glances our way.

When I didn't speak, Jack's gaze dropped to his feet, and his face twisted in disappointment.

'If I go in late, then it's not usually worth going in at all,' I explained.

He said nothing, simply nodded with his gaze lowered, the hurt of rejection written deeply in the lines of his face.

Watching the fall of his hair and his humbled body language, I was struck again by the effect he had on me. What *was* it? I was an ordinary woman. I grew up in an ordinary house in South London, with a postman father and a nurse mother. My life was unremarkable, especially after Caleb arrived. The whole world seemed to revolve around Caleb from the day he was born and I didn't mind. I loved my little brother and his dramas often became my dramas because I couldn't stand by and let him suffer without trying to help. In college I had a few boyfriends, but nothing special and it was the same after university, while studying for my Masters, and then when doing my PhD. In the years of my life, nothing extraordinary or special had happened to me. Not until Jack.

Not until this man, this man who could have anyone – who by all accounts had had lots of anyones – had begun to pursue me. His interest in me was so unexpected, and yet felt so right. I did not know why, but unlike anyone before him, he made me feel special, he made me feel like I stood out from all the women in the world. And he made me want to do lots of wild and crazy and extraordinary things.

'I could take the whole day off, instead?' I suggested.

Jack's face exploded with a smile that weakened my knees and, as if he didn't care where we still were, he reached out, pulled me towards him and kissed me all over again.

'You're going to go to sleep now, Libby. We're going to take care of you. Count backwards in your head from ten for me.'

Ten . . . nine . . . eight . . . seven . . . six . . .

April, 2009

We were breathless from laughing; wobbly and soaked through from splashing each other in the sea; slightly sick from feeding each other wodge after wodge of candyfloss.

After the kiss at Brighton Station, we were inseparable except we didn't sleep in the same bed. The last six months had passed in a haze of simple dates, glorious kisses and talking on the phone until the small hours.

Screaming and giggling, we ran and slipped as we made our way back to our blanket, shivering in the April chill.

'So, are you going to marry me or what?' he asked as we collapsed onto the shingle, fighting each other for a corner of blanket to dry ourselves off with.

I kept the blanket covering my face as I froze. Had he said what I thought he had said? After he waited for a reply in silence, I cautiously took the blanket away from my face to look at him.

'Did you just—?'

He nodded.

I licked my lips, the salt from the sea tingling as it dissolved on my tongue. 'How about we live together first?'

'How about we live together while we plan the wedding?'

'Marriage is a big commitment.'

'I know. And I want to make that commitment to and with you.'

'We're having fun, but . . .'

'But you'd marry me in a shot if we weren't having fun?' He

53

smiled that smile that had been making me feel something like drunk these past few months, and I felt all my sensibility and reason start to beat their wings as they prepared to fly away. Again.

'Marriage is for ever,' I said.

'I know that.'

'Are you serious about this?'

'I don't think I've ever been as serious about anything in a long time. Possibly in my entire adult life.'

What about Eve? The thought popped into my head. 'What about Eve?' The words popped out of my mouth.

Over the last few months, he'd talked about her, of course. Had mentioned her in passing but nothing major had been discussed, and I hadn't had the guts to ruin what we had by asking. I could have looked on the Internet to find out about her death, but that felt like violating his privacy and trust in me. If I wanted to know about her I should ask, not sneak around finding things out behind his back.

His gaze was unwavering, direct. 'I don't want this moment, this proposal, to be about anyone but you and me. Afterwards, when you've said yes or no, we can talk about anything and anyone you want. But not right now – this is about you and me.'

'And for ever.'

'And for ever.'

The wind blew across the beach, pushing the chill that had begun to settle upon me from my damp clothes closer to my skin. I shivered. Shivered, but did nothing to dry myself off.

He shivered too, obviously as cooled by the damp and air temperature as I was. 'I didn't mean to ask, by the way,' he said. 'It just came out, but the moment it did I knew it had because I do want to marry you. Not simply live with you, but make that permanent commitment.'

Something told me to take a leap of faith. To go with the flow and take that leap. It was the voice that had wanted me to run out of Brighton Station that time to see if Jack was still parked outside and to let him drive me to London. It was the crazy, idiotic part of me that I should probably ignore – but it was also the voice that spoke the loudest whenever Jack was involved. *Besides*, the crazy voice reasoned to the sane voice, *I can always change my mind at a later date, can't I? Can't I?*

'OK, yes. Yes, I will marry you.'

'And move in with me before the wedding?' he pressed.

I couldn't stop myself from smiling. 'Yes. And live with you before the wedding.'

For one moment I felt the world stand still, and I allowed myself the indulgence of revelling in doing something reckless and foolhardy because I was madly in love and I didn't have to worry about the consequences.

chapter two

jack

Almost everyone says they hate hospitals. I don't mind them so much – I hate them less than mortuaries, anyway. And cemeteries. When you point that out to people, they generally come around to your way of thinking. Or they shut up because they don't know what to say.

I am starting to hate this hospital. I have been pacing this corridor for an eternity and I'm no nearer to finding out whether Libby is going to be OK. She *has* to be, she's going to be, but I'd rather someone else confirmed it. Instead, they've been trying to keep me down in Casualty, asking me stupid questions, getting me to do simple memory tests and trying to get me to sit still so they can treat my wounds. Wounds? A few cuts and a little airbag burn are not wounds. Bleeding internally and externally, being so scared you cannot make sounds with your speech, technically dying in the ambulance; those are the results of real wounds, and those are the things that had happened to Libby.

Unbidden, the image of Libby twisted and trapped inside the crushed and torn pieces of metal that was once my pride and joy wells up in my mind and, as it has done since the crash, it rips a new hole inside my being. I'd tried to reach her, I'd wanted to stay and hold her hand, but the firemen said No. They were trained to be inside this sort of wreckage while they cut someone free, I wasn't. '*But you don't love her like I do*,' I wanted to say as two of them forced me back to the ambulance. '*If push came to shove, if it was a choice between you and her, you'd choose you. I'd choose her. Always.*'

This waiting is killing me. What can be taking so long? There was internal bleeding mainly from her spleen, they said, and the deep slices into her skin were as bad as they looked, they said. They seemed so certain and so sure of what was wrong and how to fix it, that I'd expected to have had an update by now. That they would have some idea if she was going to be all right. If she will get better and go back to who she was. I lean my head against the coffee machine and try to breathe. Try to take comfort in the fact that no news is good news and the longer they're in there, the longer they must be spending curing my wife.

'*Mr* Britcham, fancy seeing you here.' Her voice is the stuff of nightmares, her face is not much better. She is not ugly to look at, she is simply ugly to be around. They say beauty is only skin deep; ugliness, when it comes to this woman, begins at the core, slimes its way through every artery and vein, fills every organ then spills out to show the world who she really is.

I raise myself to my full height and turn to face the woman who haunts me. She is small and androgynous, a short brown bob compliments her beige skin, turned up nose and mean, circular eyes. My glare is probably expected because she smiles at me in response as she reaches inside her pocket for a notebook and pen.

'Ms Morgan,' I say.

'Detective Sergeant Morgan to you,' she says. 'Or you can call me Maisie if you want. We've got that kind of special relationship, haven't we, Jack?'

The plain-clothes policeman standing slightly behind her is as generic as she is, but I do not recognise him. He probably hasn't arrested anyone I've ever represented, but then they don't usually bother themselves with the small-time criminals I take care of.

'So, Mr Britcham, *Jack*,' she says, dramatically raising her pen and pressing the point into the notepad, 'do want to tell me what happened?'

'They've got you on a routine road accident?' I ask. 'What did you do to get demoted?'

'Sorry to disappoint you, Jack, but when I heard that it wasn't any ordinary accident because you and your wife were involved, I *had* to come and see for myself how you were going to explain away another woman dying by your side.'

She has a way of modulating her speech so that everything sounds sarcastic and condescending but, more than that, as if you're guilty of something she'll eventually find out about.

'She's not going to die.'

'Let's hope not, eh? Because it'd be pretty difficult to explain away two dead wives – both with only you as a witness – won't it?'

'There were plenty of witnesses and someone drove into us, not the other way around.'

'Hmmm, but it's odd, don't you think, how your airbag deployed and your wife's didn't?'

'The passenger airbag was faulty. I kept meaning to get it checked but never got around to it. I hate myself for that.'

'Did your wife know the airbag was faulty?'

'Yes,' I say through gritted teeth.

'A suspicious person might say this was an accident waiting to happen. Or should that be *fated* to happen?'

'If you've got something to say, Ms Morgan, say it.'

She shakes her head, twists her miserly little mouth and fractionally cocks an eyebrow at me. 'No, nothing. I just wonder if your second wife knows that being married to you should come with a health warning – something about a short life expectancy.'

'If you've got evidence that I killed . . .' I still find it hard to say her name. I try not to around Libby, but in general it is a name that causes a sob to swell in the back of my throat, a name that claws her memory across my tongue as I speak it. '. . . Eve, then charge me and we can go to trial. If you haven't then I'd appreciate it if you left me alone.'

'Ah, Jack, if I left you alone, you'd think you'd got away with it, and I can't ever let you think that.'

She wants me to lose my temper, she wants me to shout at her, to show her the other side of me. This is what she did during the interrogations last time: she would push and goad until I snapped. Then she would be in there, asking, 'Is this what happened? Did she wind you up about her past and you accidentally killed her? It'd be understandable, some women can drive a man to it. They do things that are just asking for a slap or two to keep them in line. Is that what happened? We'd understand if it was.' And even in my rage I'd tell her that I couldn't hurt anyone like that, especially not Eve. 'I love her,' I'd repeated over and over. 'I love her, how can you kill someone you love?'

'Are you going to take my statement about the crash or not?' I ask calmly.

She's a little peeved that I've ignored her last verbal dig. 'Why of course, it should make for interesting bedtime reading.' She flips over to a clean page in her book and again dramatically raises her pen. 'Go on, Jack, hit me with it.'

Behind her, I see the surgeon who talked to me briefly before he went in to operate on Libby coming towards me. He still has a surgical cap around his head and a mask around his chin, and his look is troubled. My heart feels like it has jumped out of a plane without a parachute and is freefalling from a great height.

I gather up my courage and step around the policewoman to go to meet him. 'Mr Britcham,' he says. I didn't realise until I heard him say my name that I have already braced myself for the worst.

libby

April, 2009

'Tell me about Eve.'

Since we'd officially decided to get married forty-eight hours ago, we had slept in the same bed twice. Curled up, facing each other, holding hands or stroking each other, our legs entangled. We touched, and held without the pressure or need to do anything more. We were currently in my bed, at my little flat, so I felt safe to ask. I could not have asked at her house, in her bed, reclining on the sheets that she probably chose.

'What do you want to know?' he asked, evenly, although every muscle in his body had tensed and he stopped stroking the length of my body with the flat of his hand.

'What was she like; how did you meet; were you happy? How did she die?' I shrugged, suddenly realising what a big subject I'd started on. 'I don't know, I don't know what to ask. It's just that I should probably know stuff.'

'Well, I don't know what I should and shouldn't tell you, so you'll have to give me a clue. Ask me questions and I'll try to answer them.'

'OK.' I nestled into the pillow, ready to watch him carefully for the answers to these questions even though part of me wanted to pretend she hadn't existed. I'd told him what there was to tell about me, and that wasn't very much – I had no one in my past that still held claim to my heart. That was why I wanted to pretend Eve had never existed, so Jack and I were starting this on an equal footing, both of us giving our hearts to each other knowing we'd never fully done that before.

Jack sat up, pulling the duvet to his waist, and resting back on the wrought iron headboard. His face was already drawing in, his eyebrows knitting together slightly as his eyes searched the mid-distance.

'How did she – Eve – die?' I'd taken a deep breath before asking that. It was the start of this new part of our relationship, and the end of the fun we'd been having. Reality had just entered our world.

He ran his hand through the blond-brown stands of his hair, his face drawing in tighter as he turned to look at me and forced a small smile upon his lips. 'You don't start with the small stuff, do you?' he said mirthlessly. He inhaled deeply, his whole upper body expanding with the movement, then deflating as he pushed the air nosily out of his mouth. 'She . . . No one knows for sure. I found her at the foot of the stairs in our house. Looked like she tripped on the bottom of her trousers and broke her neck on the way down.'

I placed a hand on his forearm, feeling at once the horror of that.

'No one knows for sure because I didn't realise I wasn't supposed to touch her. I was meant to leave her exactly as she was so the forensics team could come along and have a proper look and measure all their distances and go through all scenarios about how she fell, and how her legs were, and how her arms were, and what distance she was from the last step, et cetera, et cetera, et cetera.' He was gesticulating as he spoke. 'I didn't know this so, stupid me, upon finding my wife at the bottom of the stairs, I take her in my arms and I try to make her wake up and I talk to her, and I beg her not to do this to me, and I promise her anything if she'll just wake up. Then I beg God to let her live and I'll do anything, I'll even offer up my own worthless life if He just lets her live. Then I remember my mobile phone and call an ambulance and tell them to hurry because I think they can save her, all the while cradling her in my arms and imagining I can feel the warmth – the life – returning to her body. I didn't realise what I was actually doing was tampering with a crime scene.'

'Oh, Jack,' I said, sitting up to wrap my arms around him, pulling him in close. After a moment's resistance, he let himself go and rested his head on my chest, sliding down in the bed to allow me to comfort him. 'Oh, Jack.'

We sat in silence. I was trying to digest, process, the enormity of what he must have been through: finding her like that, trying to get her back, and holding her lifeless body until help came. But there was no help, no one could help, it was too late. It was simply other people arriving. More people to witness the tragedy that had befallen Jack and Eve.

'Everything about it was wrong. Eve wasn't clumsy, didn't ever fall over or bump into things, but then she always wore her trousers and jeans too long and she was always running up and down those stairs and it only takes one moment to trip. I don't know, but I still can't imagine her falling down the stairs for no reason.'

His body tensed again, and I couldn't see his face but I could tell it had twisted again in bitterness. 'The police couldn't imagine that happening either, so they launched a murder investigation.'

'On the strength of not being able to imagine her falling down the stairs?'

'Not only that. The upstairs looked as if it had been ransacked, there were what they thought were signs of a struggle, but no signs of forced entry, so they came up with the idea that maybe it wasn't an accident, that maybe she'd been "helped" down the stairs. Or maybe her neck was broken and she was thrown down the stairs to hide it. They couldn't tell, of course, because the body had been moved.'

A cold feeling began to edge, like a caterpillar on a branch, up my spine.

'They arrested me ten days later.'

'Oh God, Jack.'

He snuggled closer to me, thankfully seeming to take comfort in my presence. 'I didn't care. She was gone, nothing could bring her back and I stopped caring about anything. I answered their questions, but in a haze. I didn't even have a solicitor.' Stroking him, soothing him was the only thing I could do, but it didn't seem enough. 'I don't even know how long I was in there, everything was such a blur. My father came and put an end to it. He said if they didn't have any evidence then they had to let me go. They released me but said they were going to keep the case open.

'I was so angry with my father for making the torture end. I hadn't wanted rescuing; I had wanted to stay there, because, even though they were accusing me of something dreadful, while I was in there I wasn't out in the world where she was gone and I had to think about funerals and packing up her things and waking up to another day without her.'

'Your dad couldn't have done anything else, Jack, surely you see that? You're his son, he couldn't let you be subjected to that for a second longer than necessary. That's what parents do. Surely you can understand that.'

'Of course, I can understand. But at the time ... things have been so very difficult and complicated with my father for years. It's hard to explain to someone who hasn't grown up with a man like him as a father. I used to idolise him – he's so successful at everything he does – and I wanted to be exactly like him. But when I got to fifteen, and it came to the time where I had to prove that I wanted to be like him in every way, I couldn't do it. Since then he's made it clear that I'm not good enough, not manly enough in the way that he is. I can't do right in his eyes – I prefer football to rugby, I got "easy" offers for Oxford and Cambridge, chose Oxford when he went to Cambridge, but I didn't get a first. I followed in his footsteps into law but wouldn't let him help me get a job. That's why I was so enraged that with this – this thing that I was going through that he couldn't possibly understand – he had to come riding in to try to make things better again. He had to fix it and fix my pathetic life, as he saw it, in the process.

'I wanted to knock his block off but, at the same time, I wanted him – anyone, really – to look after me. I was so confused and angry. I didn't resist when he and my mother packed up some of my belongings and moved me into their home. They took over most of the funeral arrangements and told me what to do on the day, what to say, where to stand, who to thank for their condolences. I don't think of that day as Eve's funeral because it was nothing like she would have wanted.'

'In what way?'

'It was elaborate and showy, and because she had no family there were lots of people there she barely knew. They had sermons and readings and hymns when she'd never set foot in a church in her adult life. I was simply grateful I could play the grieving husband and not participate. I sat on the sidelines, dressed in black, nodding and shaking hands and accepting cups of tea.'

'You weren't playing the grieving husband, you *were* the grieving husband.'

'What I mean is, me being quiet in the background fitted in with their idea of what a grieving husband is like. Whereas in reality, being there was something I had to do. It wasn't my chance to say goodbye as it should have been – I did that much later, when I went to Bartholomew Square on what would have been our wedding anniversary and sat and watched people coming out after getting married. I watched them start their lives together, remembering that feeling. That was the day I said goodbye to Eve.'

'You got married in Brighton Register Office?'

'Yes. Like I said, she wasn't the showy type. We wanted a small wedding with minimal fuss. She wore a dress she'd had for years and the only two people there were Grace and Rupert as our witnesses.'

67

I was humbled by Eve. By the love Jack obviously had for her. By the way he wanted to suffer because she was gone from his life, and by the way they had obviously conducted their relationship: privately, quietly, intimately. I never would have thought that someone like Jack – someone who drove an expensive car, wore almost exclusively designer clothes, and had a big house – would have married in such a small, unassuming way.

Eve obviously did that to him – brought out the quiet side of him, brought out the side of him that I had fallen in love with. Eve must have been extraordinary.

Was I like that to him? Because he still had his ostentatious side. He still had moments when he wanted to be flash and play the big 'I AM' and it pulled me up short. It sounded as though Eve had been able to temper that in him: straight away or over time?

'What else do you want to know?' he asked, wearily. He did not want to say any more and I did not want to know any more because I was suddenly so scared by the love and grief he had for her. It was huge and it was unassailable; and it probably meant he would never have enough room in his heart for me. He would be constantly trying to fit me around the expanse that Eve still occupied.

'Erm, nothing,' I said. 'Well, not nothing. I mean, this is big stuff we've talked about, so how about we talk again another time?'

Jack lifted his head, studied me for a few seconds. 'Are you sure? I don't want you to feel as if I'm hiding things from you.'

'I don't think you're hiding anything from me. It's just this is getting a bit intense: maybe we should take a step back.'

He was up on his knees in an instant, frowning at me. 'Are you saying you don't want to get married?'

Was that what I was saying? I hadn't consciously meant that, but now he'd broached it, maybe that was what I was hinting at. I was starting to think that perhaps he wasn't ready. You don't get over that kind of love in three years; you probably don't ever get over it. Why would you want to marry someone when your heart belonged to another?

'Maybe we should date for a bit longer? There's no rush is there? We should carry on dating and—'

'I've only been in love with two women in my life,' he interrupted. 'Eve and now you. They're different types of love, because you're different women. But, Libby, make no mistake about this: I love you and I want to spend the rest of my life with you.'

Breathing deeply, a slow steady in and out, I looked down at the valleys and hills that our bodies made in my white duvet cover.

'I can't pretend Eve didn't exist,' he said, 'in the same way that I can't pretend that you're not the most important person in my life right now. I love you as much as I love her. *Loved* her.'

'I know bugger all about long-term relationships, and I know nothing about marriage having never been in either, but I do know I'm—'

'Scared that I don't love you as much as I loved Eve? That I won't be able to love you as much because I'm still in love with her?'

I hung my head and nodded, ashamed at how petulant and childish that sounded when repeated back to me. I hated sounding so needy, so unsure of myself.

'I promise you, she is the past. You are my present and my future. I can't rewrite my past, and I wouldn't want to, but,' he came closer to me, took my hands and waited until I raised my head to look at him, 'I love you.'

It was different this time when he said it. He'd said it before and it was a wonderful thing to hear, but this time there was a new element – a reassurance that in his heart I had the greater part. In every part of him that felt anything, it was me he felt it for. This time, I couldn't mistake what those three words meant: 'You. Only you.'

I nodded my understanding.

'Will you still marry me?' he asked through his huge grin.

I nodded again.

His beam took over his entire face. 'We're going to be so happy, you'll see. I promise you, we're going to be so happy.'

jack

The first time I *noticed* Libby was a few minutes after I started talking to her. It was after she told me that I was rubbish at apologising and I was rubbish at taking the piss out of her.

She'd intrigued me by walking out of the showroom when I interrupted her car purchase, but it was the way contempt curled her lip and raised her eyebrow while causing her nostrils to flare that got that kick going down below. She didn't notice me scanning her body as she stormed away from me: the slenderness of her legs in jeans sloping up to the neat curve of her bum; the firm, fullness of her waist and chest; the gentle shape of her neck disappearing under her masses and masses of shiny, straight black hair.

When Libby glared at me, resolutely refusing to be drawn in by my second apology, I saw her all over again and felt an unfamiliar boom, as powerful as a bomb exploding, in my chest. It was the explosion of something I thought had died a long time ago. I *liked* her. And, at that time, I did not like many people. I was not capable of liking people, especially not women, especially not in a non-sexual way. I was consumed by a selfishness and arrogance that I didn't dare let go of until I found a new persona to hide behind. I suddenly had a reason to want to be someone else because the woman in front of me would accept nothing short of a personality transplant.

'You'll get no arguments on that from me,' she replied when I said I'd been an idiot for messing about with Gareth's sale, and I knew there and then I had to change. Grace had been telling me for months that I couldn't carry on indefinitely doing what I was doing – screwing women and then saying I wasn't ready for a relationship but that I wanted to be friends. Grace was right, of course, but I hadn't heeded that until Libby stood in front of me and told me she didn't like me.

I suddenly felt like a teenager in love with the best-looking girl at school – desperate to get her to notice me; eager to be given a chance.

I sit by her bed now, watching her sleep her drug-induced slumber, holding her right hand between my two hands as if in prayer. I want to pray for her and for us, but I fell out with God a long time ago, so it would be churlish to go back to Him now – especially if He answers in the way He did last time, if He lets the woman I'm married to die.

'Libby, my beautiful, beautiful Libby,' I whisper into the hush of her hospital room. The whole of the left side of her body is bruised and swollen, huge sections of her face and head are covered in dressings. She is wounded and hurt, battered and almost broken.

From a distance she is a mass of bandages and damage, but closer there are pieces of her that are as they were before.

The curve of her jaw on the right side of her face is untouched. I noticed the bone structure of her features and jaw when she lifted her head to catch the rain as the sky opened on that July afternoon – I'd wanted to reach out and trace my finger along the outline of her face.

Her full, rounded lips don't have any marks from the crash either. I'd wanted to kiss the flakes of croissants off those lips when we had breakfast in the park, and again that night as we stood in the hallway but I'd been too scared of where that might lead so I stupidly started 'the routine' on her instead.

Her chestnut-brown eyes, with their large, black pupils, are closed and untouched and they are my most favourite part of her. So much of what she's about to say begins in her eyes. And I carry the scars of the look in those eyes when I went to see her after we first had sex. She hid her gaze from me until she made me confirm that I regularly seduced and fucked women in my hall – then her eyes had exploded with an agony that had pierced my heart. I thought I'd felt every kind of pain there was to feel three years before, but in that unguarded moment she taught me different.

Her forehead – the place I'd kissed her after sex – is mostly untouched.

Every part of her face, damaged or not, is perfect, a reminder of the process – the heady, exhilarating, gut-wrenching, humbling process – of falling in love with her.

I want her to wake up. I want her to wake up and to speak and to tell me everything will be OK. That's unfair, I know. It should be the other way around, it should be me being strong and resilient, promising in word and deed that we'll get through this. How can I, though, when she is lying in a hospital bed looking like this?

chapter three

libby

I have been unconscious for twenty hours. Or so I've been told.

I have woken up in a hospital room surrounded by equipment and with a sense that nothing is real. I feel so disconnected from the world around me and from the body I'm in. I'm not sure if it's pain or if it's the painkillers, but I keep wanting to touch things to make sure they are solid and real, but at the same time I'm scared to do so in case they aren't. In case they melt away or go spongy at my touch – then it would mean I am still asleep. Or never going to wake up.

My parents, Angela, Grace, Rupert, Caleb, Benji, and Jack's parents – Harriet and Hector – are waiting outside while the doctor and Jack piece together what has happened. So far they have told me that I was unconscious for twenty hours instead of the planned twenty-four because once they'd reduced the drugs keeping me asleep, I woke up; I lost a lot of blood, and needed a fair amount before and during surgery; I underwent surgery to repair my ruptured spleen, which was a complete success; I have a hairline fracture of a rib on my left side and severe bruising on the others; I have severe bruising on the left side of my body that will get better over time; the crash had been caused by a man using his mobile phone who wasn't paying attention so mis-judged the space he had to do the crazy manoeuvre he tried.

What they are actually telling me is that I am lucky to be alive. And I keep bursting into tears.

My weeping doesn't last very long, but every time I cry the doctor stops talking and waits for me to calm down, to snuffle up my tears or allow them to dry on my face, because I cannot touch anything – least of all myself – in case it is not real. In case I am not real.

They are keeping something from me, I can tell. I don't know what it is, but it is something big. I think I can still walk because if I tried to move my legs they would; I know I can speak because I told the doctor my name and the date when he asked.

I wish they would tell me what is wrong. Thick vines of fear are quickly taking root in my mind and body, and will soon grow out of control and I'll find it almost impossible to think or breathe.

I wish, too, that Jack would hold my hand, stand nearer, look at me more. He is so distant, removed, while standing right beside me. If this was real I would be able to feel the heat from his body. Maybe he isn't here. Maybe he isn't real. Maybe that is what the doctor is keeping from me. Maybe he died.

Panicked, suddenly, not caring if the world is spongy and unreal, I reach out an aching, heavy arm to touch him. He is as solid and real as anything can be right now. He is warm, not like a ghost would be. And he flinches. Instinctively, automatically, he flinches at my touch, pulling away slightly. I stop listening to the doctor and shift as much as I can to look at him, to try to understand why he would not want me to touch him.

'Jack?' I say.

'Libby?' he replies, turning to me. He is trying to control his face, he is trying not to breakdown. This is about her. About Eve. About me almost doing to him what she did.

One night, about three months after we decided to get married, he got so drunk he could barely make it to the bedroom in my little flat. When he collapsed fully clothed on the bed, he started asking me to promise I wouldn't die first. If I had to die, I was to let him know so he could finish himself off and not have to live without me. 'I can't,' he said, 'bury another wife.'

He's probably been holding in the terror that he would have to go through that all over again.

'Nothing,' I say, easing myself back onto the pillows propping me up. 'Nothing.'

Jack nods and returns his attention to the doctor.

My husband is scared, and hurt, and angry with me too. He had taken my silent refusal to make him any such promise as agreeing that I would not die first. And now, of course, I have nearly broken that promise.

'The final thing I wanted to talk to you about was the lacerations you suffered to your head and face,' the doctor says gently.

'OK,' I say, resolving not to cry this time. Jack's hand suddenly finds mine, making me jump, and the fear squeezes me so tight I can't breathe.

'There's no easy way to tell you this, Mrs Britcham, but you sustained rather extensive damage to your scalp, meaning we had to shave away a significant proportion of the left side of your hair in order to be able to repair the damage.'

My hair? My free hand goes up to my head, but there is a bandage around it and I cannot feel any shaved areas. In fact, I can still feel the soft black strands that make up my hair. I run my fingers through them, and they feel real, they feel like they have not been damaged or shaved. Maybe he is being melodramatic and they only had to take away a small part, which, with clever styling, I can hide until it grows back.

'There has also been some damage to your face, ostensibly on the left side. We expect you to make a complete recovery from these injuries, and the surgeon who worked on your face did the best he could to not leave a trace, but there will be some scarring.'

'How much scarring?' I ask cautiously. This is the point where I usually burst into tears, but I do not feel like doing that at the moment. I feel like throwing back the covers and running around, looking for a mirror.

'They were very serious injuries and, as I explained, quite extensive.' Extensive injuries did not result in 'some' scarring.

I look at Jack. He is staring at the doctor, trying to control his face, trying not to cry. Now I know why Jack hasn't looked at me: he knows how bad it is.

'I need a mirror,' I say to the doctor.

'I don't think that would be helpful right now.'

'I need a mirror!' I say, desperation and fear making my voice rise.

'Tomorrow,' the doctor insists evenly. 'We'll be removing your dressings then, so you will be able to see your injuries then.'

Tomorrow? Do you have any idea how far away tomorrow is when something like this has been dropped onto your shoulders?

'I'll send the nurse in to teach you how to manage your pain relief. Try and get some sleep, Mrs Britcham.'

'Thanks, doctor,' Jack says as the doctor leaves the room.

I reach up to the left side of my face, feel the sticky dressing covering a fair portion of it. Most of my face feels thick and swollen and tender. More than a touch causes needles of pain shooting through my face and scalp.

'Is it bad?' I ask Jack.

Slowly, as though he can't avoid it any longer, Jack finally turns to look at me. 'I don't know, I haven't seen anything.'

'But they think it's bad, don't they?'

He suddenly comes down to my height, enclosing my hand in both of his, as though trying to protect as well as comfort me. 'No matter what, we're going to get through this together,' he says. 'Everything's going to be all right.'

I nod, knowing that he doesn't believe that any more than I do.

libby

I've never thought of myself as ugly.

By the same token, I have never really looked in the mirror and seen myself as outstandingly beautiful. It often amazes me that other people do. That they can make such firm judgements on themselves – especially the ones who aspire to be models – by simply looking in a mirror.

I am looking at myself in the mirror, and I am seeing myself for the first time.

I am not ugly.

My black-brown eyes are surrounded by whites that are threaded and veined with red. My nose is wide and flat, my skin is an even-toned dark brown that has always been easily invigorated with a little foundation. My forehead is gently curved, my chin is small and unobtrusive. My lips are wide and full.

I am not ugly. A little tired looking, maybe, but that is not surprising considering the last forty-eight hours. But I do not fundamentally look any different. This is who I am. This is who I have been my entire adult life. And I am not ugly.

Until I allow my eyes to properly focus, to stop the Libby in the mirror from being a slight blur, then I can see who I am now. Today. This minute.

On the left side of my face, from my ear to about a quarter of the way up my hairline, and then straight back to the nape of my neck, I have no hair. Instead, I have a bald, brown scalp with a jagged, blood-red scar that is held together by thick black stitches. That's where my head collided with the partially open window causing the skin to split open, like the skin of a tomato peels apart after it has been in boiling water.

From the middle of my nose to the middle of my cheek, running in a straight tangent, is another dark-red line, but this one is thin and has tiny, careful stitches that are the work – apparently – of a master surgeon. This scar is from where a piece of metal – probably from the car's roof – sliced across my face as we were crushed against the lamppost.

The left side of my face is scattered with scratches that will fade to nothing over time. These are from flying, shattered glass.

I am lucky that the force of the crash didn't cause the open window to crack my skull; I am lucky the metal didn't scrape a bit higher because it could have hit my eye; I am lucky I was wearing a seatbelt so that the internal injuries were limited to my spleen; I am lucky I had a fireman to talk to me and keep me awake, to stop me falling into a coma I probably never would have woken up from. I am lucky to be alive. I am lucky.

That's why huge, gut-wrenching sobs keep quaking my body but escape as small gasping whimpers; that's why my eyes are swimming with tears that don't fall. I am lucky. Everything I am seeing in the mirror means I am lucky to be alive.

'The repair work on your face has been very successful, so with the right after-care the scarring should be minimal,' the doctor explains gently as the nurse takes the square mirror away from me. I don't need the mirror any more, the image of myself – changed and branded – is clear in my mind, burnt like a holographic image onto my eyelids. 'And your hair will grow back around the areas that are damaged on your scalp,' he adds, even more gently.

When the nurse removed the mirror, Jack's hand took its place. 'You can wear a scarf or something around your hair until it does,' he adds, helpfully. I change my gaze to him, realising that he's known me less than three years. He doesn't know me as having anything other than long, straight black hair. He knows I have my roots re-straightened every eight weeks, but he doesn't know how long I searched for a hairdresser who wouldn't damage my hair, rip me off, or keep me waiting for hours. He has no idea that I spent years travelling all over London, sometimes further afield, looking for the right hairdresser. He has no clue that even when I moved to Brighton I had to keep going to London to see my hairdresser until I happened to meet Angela, a mobile hairdresser who was fantastic and professional.

He doesn't understand what it means to be a black woman trying to have her hair looked after properly. Which is why it is easy for him to say I can wear a scarf or something until my hair grows back – he has no idea that it will take maybe a decade to get it back to this length.

'When can I go home?' I ask the doctor, ignoring what Jack has said because this is not the time to try to explain it to him.

'You're making excellent progress, so I should think you could be home in a week or so.'

'OK. Thank you.'

'Thank you,' Jack echoes as the doctor nods and leaves the room.

I am lucky to be alive, I tell myself as the nurse fusses around me, straightening the sheet, making sure that my pain medication dispenser is close to hand.

I am lucky to be alive.

I am lucky to be alive.

I am lucky to be alive.

I am going to keep saying that to myself until the horror that is bubbling up in my mind goes away. *It doesn't matter what I look like, I am lucky to be alive.*

Before I know it, before I can stop myself, my shoulders are shaking and I'm breaking down again. This time not so quietly, not with any of the dignity I have been trying to maintain.

'Oh God, Libby, don't cry,' Jack says, desperately. 'I'm sorry, I'm so sorry. I wish it was me that was hurt and not you. I'd do anything to take your pain away. I'm so sorry.'

'I know, I know,' I say. 'I just . . .'

'It's going to be OK.' Jack easily fills the gap where my words have failed. 'It's going to be OK, that's what the doctor said. We'll get you the best care, a nurse at home if necessary. You'll be better in no time and you'll hardly be able to notice the scarring, especially once your hair starts to grow back. Time will fly by and we'll get you well again. It's going to be OK, I promise.'

I let him speak because he needs to. He is feeling guilty, and scared. I know Jack, I know he'll be terrified that I'll hate him for this, that I'll always blame him because I'd reminded him more than once to have the airbag seen to. 'You do realise that my little car is probably safer than yours to drive right now?' I'd told him. And he'd meant to get it done, I know he had. I don't blame him.

I am crying, not only because of what I have seen in the mirror, but also because I still feel so disconnected from every-thing. I can touch things, and they are real, but I can't say the same about what is going on in my head. I think things, I remember things and I do not know if they are real, if they hap-pened. In the ambulance, I heard a woman's voice who spoke like she knew Jack and she knew me. Before the fireman, I was awake – I think – and I was trying to tell Jack something impor-tant.

Between what I know and what I remember, there is a huge gulf that is terrifying me. I do not know what it is that is sitting at the edge of my memory, but it is trying and failing to get my attention. It is, however, making me scared.

'What happened?' I ask Jack. 'After the crash, what happened?'

'After the crash, they cut you out of the wreckage and brought you here,' he replies, staring at me with his dark emerald eyes, they remind me sometimes of green velvet, so soft and deep you want to feel them on every part of your body.

'I mean after the crash and before the fireman, what happened?'

Jack kisses my fingers where he has linked them through his. 'You don't remember?' he asks, his eyes now cautious and guarded.

'No, it's gone. I remember—' The violence of the car being rammed shudders through my body and I close my eyes against it, feel the jolt, then the falling sensation as the world around me is lifted and—

Jack's hand tightens around mine. 'It's OK, it's OK.'

My eyes fly open and I'm in the hospital room with Jack; I'm safe.

'I remember the moment of the crash, and I remember the fireman,' I say when my breathing has slowed and the terror has moved away. 'But something else happened and I don't know what.'

'It's not important now,' Jack says. 'All that's important is getting you better.'

'Something happened. Tell me what it is,' I ask, almost begging. I don't like not knowing, I don't like to think that I was conscious and doing something, saying things that I have no memory or knowledge of now. The days of drinking to that point are way behind me, and this is different, anyway. Back then there was enjoyment; this is like staring into your past and seeing nothing but a gaping black hole, ready to gobble you up and trap you there, disconnected from everything. 'Tell me, please.' The edge of that black hole is creeping closer.

'Nothing happened. We were both a bit shaken up, and you were incredibly brave while they were cutting you out. Nothing happened, I promise you.'

Jack is looking at me while he speaks but the pupils of his eyes dance around, never settling for too long in one spot. Is that because of my scars or is it because there is something he can't tell me?

'Do you want to see people?' he asks, changing the subject,

85

which allows him to change his line of sight – to the door, beyond which my family and friends are waiting. They saw me when I was unconscious, they saw me with the bandages on, now they'll see me with my newly carved up face and scalp. I'm not ready for that. I'm not sure I'll ever be *ready*, but right now I definitely am not.

'No,' I say, 'tell them I've gone to sleep and I'll see them at home.'

'OK, beautiful,' he says, automatically. The word stings my skin, scrapes inside my ears, rubs salt into my scars. He could barely stand to look at me, how am I supposed to believe what he just said? He kisses my forehead, the most undamaged part of me. 'See you later.'

'Yeah, see you later,' I reply.

As he reaches the door, I call, 'Jack?'

He stops and turns to me, a smile on his lips. 'Hmm?' he asks.

'You would tell me if something happened, wouldn't you?' I ask.

He nods. 'Yeah, of course. Yes.'

chapter four

libby

There are eight stone steps from the pavement to the front door. It's going to take me a while to climb them unaided.

Although I am not in constant pain any more, it is still hard to walk without the fear of tugging apart the stitches in my abdomen, or feeling something pull inside making me worry about the damage I'm doing.

I stare at the steps – smooth and curved at the edge of the treads, an ordinary grey stone – that I have walked and run up many a time. Not this time. This time, I have to wait for Jack to help me, just like I've been doing in hospital all week – I have to wait for someone to help me to do the most basic of things: go for a wash, get to the toilet, brush my teeth, wash the undamaged parts of my face without the aid of a mirror. And I've had to put on a happy face for my visitors.

The visits were short and pleasant enough, but I always had to let them know that I was 'O' 'K' with what had happened; I was focusing on the positives of being alive; and I wasn't dwelling on the hair thing, the face thing, the recovering from major surgery thing. After each visit I would sag against my pillows and will myself better so I could go home and at least not answer the door if anyone came who I didn't want to see.

The taxi driver has left my bag on the top step. Jack is now standing with him up there, paying.

The hospital made it clear that I was going home in a car or in an ambulance – the taxi was the lesser of two evils as the *thought* of an ambulance brought on panic attacks. We sat in the back of the taxi, not speaking, his hand wrapped around mine, while my petrified body did not move, and I kept my eyes closed to avoid seeing any other car that came near us. I'd been extremely relieved when we pulled up outside our house. Our home.

I'm scared to go inside.

When I was lying in hospital, I was desperate to get out of there, to be at home and, now, 'home' is where I'll have to start again. I'll have to be me with this face and this hair in the place where the other me lived. That's a terrifying thought.

'Your parents, Angela, Grace, and my parents wanted to have a welcome home party,' Jack had told me as he wheeled me to the waiting taxi, 'but I told them you probably wouldn't want that. Not right away. I hope I did the right thing.'

'Yes,' I'd said, 'that was the right thing.'

Jack puts his wallet into his back pocket, opens the outer door, then the inner door, to put my bag inside.

'Good luck,' the taxi driver says as he passes, an unexpected blessing from a stranger. 'Take care.'

How many people does the taxi driver wish good luck? I wonder as I watch the man I married descending the steps to help me. *Random people, hospital returnees, or damaged people who look like they need it?* I suppose I am all three.

A smile overtakes Jack's face as he stands in front of me, and I smile back. All of this would be so much harder without him. I don't think I'd have coped as well, would have had some good hours in among the hours of despair, if I didn't know he was there with me all the way.

May, 2009

'So you're Elizabeth,' Jack's mother said as we stepped over the threshold. She was beaming, with her arms stretched out in

90

welcome. She wrapped her arms around me, hugging me close, surrounding me with that soft, intoxicating, talcum-powdery smell of a woman who takes pride in her appearance and has almost always had the money to do so. She had never ploughed her way through the bargain bin in her local supermarket for the right shade of eyeshadow. She was elegantly attired: a fawn-coloured silk shift dress under a cream, cashmere cardigan; fawn court shoes on her feet, although this looked like the type of house where visitors usually took their off shoes. Her light brown hair, streaked with strands of silver, was cut into a stylish bob, and she had gold and pearl earrings in her ears.

She clutched me tight, checking I was real perhaps, then stepped back, her hands slipping smoothly down to take my hands.

'Let me have a look at you,' she said, and gave me another wide, genuine smile. 'You're nothing like I expected. My son wouldn't tell us a thing about you. But you're beautiful.'

'*Mother,*' Jack said.

'Oh, shush,' his mother said, jovially. 'You should be grateful that I like her. How many young women complain about having a mother-in-law who doesn't like them? Many, I would wager. But Elizabeth, you have been such a tonic for my son.' She moved back a little further, still holding onto my hands. 'He has been like a different person since you started courting. I never thought I'd see him laugh, or take an interest in life again . . .' All four of us in the corridor, not least Jack's mother, were horrified when her eyes began to mist over with tears.

'You must excuse my wife. She does come on a bit strong sometimes,' Jack's father said, coming forward. 'You're embarrassing the poor girl. You'll frighten her off.' He held out his hand and his wife immediately let my hands go to allow me to shake his. 'Hector,' he said. 'Pleased to meet you.'

Jack had inherited his father's frame, height and self-possession. I was sure there were very few people on Earth who made Hector feel insecure. Jack had mentioned in passing that his dad still went to the gym and played golf – it showed: his skin was smooth and unblemished, while most of his thick head of hair was neat and disconcertingly shiny.

'I'm very pleased to meet you, too,' I said, sounding prim and proper. I hadn't intended to, but it had come out that way.

'While my wife might have been a bit overwhelming, it *is* a pleasure to have your company today, Elizabeth. My son has been very circumspect, some might even say evasive, about you.' He shot a pointed look at Jack, who lowered his head. 'I see absolutely no reason for that. You are most welcome in our home.'

A little churning began in my stomach, the butterflies of nerves at meeting them, but also the anxiety by the fact I'd have to tell them that my name wasn't Elizabeth. They were both being so nice, so gracious and welcoming, how could I say it now? I realised with a start that Jack didn't know it, either. The man I was about to marry didn't know my full name. *And you've managed to convince yourself you're not rushing into this?* I berated myself.

'Are we going to spend all our time in the hallway?' Jack asked.

'Of course not, of course not,' Harriet said. 'Come in, come in.' Hector let go of my hand, which was still tingling from the firmness of his handshake, and Harriet immediately hooked her arm through mine and began to lead me along their hall towards the living room. Since I'd walked in, one or the other of Jack's parents had kept hold of me – almost as if I might disappear or run away. Maybe that's what happens to a family after someone dies: they cling to anyone new in their world. I actually thought it would be harder, that they would look at me with suspicion and disdain – they would question my motivations for being there, while showing their slight disgust at me daring to try to replace the person they lost.

'Now, Elizabeth, you must tell me all about what you've got planned so far for the wedding. I'll be as involved as you want. I would love to take over because I don't have a daughter but I'm sure your mother is already doing that.'

'Umm, not really. Jack and I haven't really talked about what we want from the wedding. We thought it best to meet each other's families first.'

'That is sensible,' Hector said.

'Who wants sensibility when there is love and romance involved?' said Harriet with a smile that was practically a wink.

Their living room, like the rest of the house, was huge. I could fit my whole flat in there twice over with room to spare. The walls were a pale sage green topped with high, white ceilings, and many display cabinets and sideboards lined the walls, as did pieces of ornate, elaborately pretty furniture that were obviously expensive antiques. Jack came from money, I knew that, but this house drove the point home that we were different, we had different experiences of the world.

I sat on the sofa nearest the fireplace and was surprised that Jack immediately sat on the arm of the sofa, laid his arm along the back of it and rested his hand lightly on my shoulder. I liked being near him – having his warmth and scent right next to me was one of the best things about being his lover – but this was different; odd. Almost a forced show of solidarity, as though marking out his territory, but also showing that we were A COUPLE. Maybe his parents weren't as cool about us getting married as they made out. Maybe they were waiting to be convinced in some way that I wasn't simply the rebound girl, and that he wasn't rushing into this. The twirling in my stomach intensified. Jack not knowing my name was hardly a ringing endorsement about our knowledge of each other.

'Tea, Elizabeth? I baked some scones this morning. Hector is desperate to try them with the clotted cream he brought back from a business trip to Devon last weekend. I think I also have some homemade strawberry jam left. Last year we had such a wonderful crop of strawberries that I managed to make pots and pots of it. Which was a good thing because this year's crop wasn't quite as successful. Can I tempt you?'

'Yes, that would be lovely,' I said.

'Make it a coffee instead of a tea, please,' Jack said as his mother turned towards the door. 'Libby only drinks tea in the evenings. And she's not that keen on strawberries, she finds them too tart on her palette. But you've got some marmalade, haven't you? She loves that. Even though it's not really done with scones. I'll have the same, if that's all right.'

I'd always known that Jack noticed the details, but this was astounding. *How does he know all that? I'm sure I've never told him those things explicitly.*

Harriet beamed at her son, saying, 'Of course, darling. Oh, Elizabeth, you should have said. We don't stand on ceremony here. Hector, can you come and put the coffee machine on? Is filter OK for you?'

'Perfect, absolutely perfect,' I replied, quickly.

'Right, what's the matter?' Jack asked sotto voce the second his parents were out of earshot.

'What do you mean?' I replied.

'Every time one of my parents says your name, you tense up.'

My eyes widened in alarm.

'No, my parents haven't noticed, I can just feel it. I know you, don't forget. And I can feel when things aren't right with you. What's wrong?'

'My name isn't Elizabeth.'

'Oh, my parents are old fashioned, they'll get used to calling you Libby in time. I'm sure your parents do the same.'

'No, Jack, you don't understand. Libby is short for Liberty. My birthday's the sixth of March, which is Ghana Independence Day, so my parents called me Liberty.'

'Oh,' Jack said, thinking the same thing as I was: we were getting married and he didn't even know my real name.

'Do you want to tell them when they get back?'

'*No!*' I said. 'I'm actually going to change my name by deed poll on Monday so I never have to admit to them that when I became engaged my fiancé didn't know my real name.'

Jack laughed and a multitude of stars started to light up in my chest. That was why I was marrying him – he could do that to me with something as simple as laughing. Did it really matter if he didn't know my full name?

'If you can bear it, I'll put my mother straight when we get home.'

I shrugged. 'Fine by me, although Elizabeth isn't such a bad name – just in case you don't get around to telling her.'

He grinned again and I smiled back at him, happy that we were in this together.

'Will you be OK if I nip to the bathroom?' Jack asked.

'Of course,' I said, relaxed now that someone else was in on the secret.

'Right back,' he said and pecked a kiss on my mouth before leaving. I took the chance to look around properly. Their living room, although big and impersonal, was crammed with photos of their family. They weren't the kind you'd stereotypically expect a rich brood to have on display – all stuffy poses and formal dress – they were happy images, showing many, many moments of the private, contented life they shared. My parents had a few photos on display, but most were in albums or boxes in the loft – like most people, they didn't have the acres of space to show off all the pictures they had.

On the edge of the white marble mantelpiece above the large, ornate fireplace, one picture in particular captured my attention. In a simple silver frame, about five by seven inches, was a photo of a laughing couple holding hands, in a shower of what looked like snow but was actually confetti. The man was in a plain grey suit with a pale blue tie, the woman was wearing a gorgeous pink gown. From this distance, I could make out that her skin glowed without foundation and her unusual blue eyes still stood out without the help of mascara, shadow and liner. She was more than beautiful, she was divine, almost celestial. I was transfixed by the image: their body language, their faces were mesmerising – I didn't think I'd ever seen two people look so happy; joy seemed to radiate from every part of them.

I'd never seen Jack smile like that. And yet, in that photo, it seemed he used to do it easily, naturally, regularly. *When he was with Eve.*

My eyes returned to the table in front of me moments before Jack's parents returned to the room. 'Elizabeth,' Harriet said, sitting on the sofa, while Hector placed the tea tray in front of us without rattling a single piece of crockery. 'Have you thought about dress styles? Are you a strapless sort of a woman, and will you be going for the full skirt?'

'I'm not really sure,' I replied. 'I have to confess that I'm not one of those girls who has always had the idea of the perfect wedding dress in her mind.'

'Nonsense,' Hector said, jovially. 'Every woman has the idea of the perfect dress for her wedding, even if it's not a traditional kind of wedding dress.' He affectionately patted Harriet's knee and she laughed a little in response. 'Or so I'm told.'

Not traditional like Eve's, you mean? I thought. 'Oh, dear,' I said, laughing along, 'I really have let the side down. I'll build a time machine as soon as I can to go back and have a quiet word with my younger self.'

Hector and Harriet both laughed while Harriet set about transferring the crockery to the table before she started pouring the tea and dispensing the scones.

Jack's not the only person still a little hung up on Eve, I thought. I kept wanting to look back at the picture of the woman I was constantly worrying I could never match up to. Not that I needed to see the image again, it was traced with indelible ink onto my mind's eye – obviously the same ink that her memory was written with onto the hearts of all the Britcham family.

Jack comes down the steps and I reach out to lean on him to go up the stairs. 'I think I can do better than that,' he says, and stoops to scoop me up in his arms, gentle enough to not jar anything.

'What are you doing?' I ask, laughing softly.

'Carrying you over the threshold, of course.'

'Of course,' I say.

And he does, just like he did every day for a week after we were married.

jack

Libby is compliant and unmoving in my arms, so different from how she usually is when I pick her up. She usually screams with laughter, telling me to put her down and swearing all sorts of revenge if I drop her. She's lighter than usual, but that is because she hasn't eaten much in the past week.

One of the things I love about Libby is her appetite, the way she'll attack any meal put in front of her like it is her last. She's a tidy eater, but an enthusiastic one. She told me that for the first year of her PhD she lived on soup, bread, beans, Gari that her mum sent her from London, and homemade Ghanaian stew. 'You can make most things taste nice with a few herbs, but God I got sick of having to make do. Now, I buy the most expensive foods I can afford and I never let them go to waste because I know what doing without is like.'

The past few days have stripped her of her appetite; all she can manage is a little soup.

I carry her into the drawing room, to show her what I have done down here. I continue to hold her in my arms, as she casts her eyes about the room. I have moved most of our bedroom downstairs: the chest of drawers where I have neatly folded her most regularly worn clothes; the portable television and DVD player; the bedside tables with their crystal base lamps and on 'her' side the picture of Benji and me sitting in the park after a particularly muddy game of football; as well as the two huge heart-shaped rugs that she brought from her other flat. I've even put hooks on the back of the door to hang up our dressing gowns. The only thing not moved from upstairs is the bed. It is new. I had to go from shop to shop to find it, but it is a replica of the iron-framed bed she had in her flat, the first bed we made love in. I bought it to remind her that I love her, that, no matter what, I cherish every moment of being with her.

Before Libby moved in, Grace had bought us a baleful of new linen, and Libby's friend Angela had bought us an airing cupboard's worth of new towels – both of them had said they were early wedding presents. I'd called Grace to thank her and to ask her why she'd bought them when she knew we had enough linen to service a medium-sized hotel.

'What woman wants to sleep on the sheets the last woman bought?' she replied, scathingly. 'New bed, new linen.'

'New bed?' I'd asked.

'Tell me you've got a new bed and you don't expect Libby to sleep in Eve's marital bed?' Grace replied.

I thought about it: Libby had slept over a few times in the time we decided to get married, but she was always keen to stay at her flat where she said it was warmer and she had all her things around her.

'God, you're thick sometimes,' Grace said.

'Is that why she keeps suggesting she brings her bed with her?' I asked Grace.

'Yes, idiot.'

'Why didn't she say?'

'Erm, let's see, why didn't the woman you're marrying, who loves you with every fibre of her being, want to upset you by suggesting you get rid of something that reminds you of your wife that died? Hmmm ... I don't know, you'd think she'd simply come out and say something like that, wouldn't you?'

'I had no idea,' I confessed to Grace. 'It didn't even cross my mind.'

'Try to think about things from her perspective, eh? She's on shaky ground because you've done this before and she, like the rest of the world, can see you get irrationally upset whenever Eve is mentioned. Just give her a fighting chance, eh?'

I'd suggested to Libby that we start from scratch; that we go out shopping for bedroom furniture together, and maybe buy some other bits and pieces for the rest of the house as well. The sheer relief in Libby's eyes said everything I needed to know about whether Grace was right or not.

I made the effort for a while, I tried to think about Libby, tried to show her in word and deed that I was always thinking of her first, but I've let that slip over the last year or so. I don't pay as much attention, I shut her out and turn away from her when I should turn towards her. This bed is a sign that I want to undo that. A new bed for another new start, if she'll have me.

Reluctantly, because it means being apart from her, I place her gently on the bed and stand back.

She smoothes her hands over the cream duvet, and stares long and hard at the bedpost. 'You bought a new bed,' she says.

'Yeah, I thought it'd be easier for you down here, rather than trying to negotiate the stairs. It seemed fitting to get a new bed.'

Her eyes fill with tears, and I feel that kick of pain in my head and chest that I always feel whenever Libby is hurt. 'It's like the one I had in the flat,' she says.

I nod, unable to speak as I watch her wipe away the tear that has just fallen from her eye.

'Thanks,' she says, finding a smile for her face. 'Really. I've been so scared, you know, of coming back and things being different and not being able to settle again at home.' She looks around the room. 'But this is probably the best thing, isn't it? It's something new and we can share it.'

I nod at her. Carefully, she eases herself backwards onto the bed, and reclines against the pillows, the agony of movement evident in her eyes and on her face.

'Do you want a cup of tea or coffee?' I ask her.

'No,' she says with a small shake of her head, 'I'm fine. I might try to sleep for a bit.'

'OK,' I say. 'I'll wake you for dinner.'

'OK,' she says. 'Or you could come and lie with me for a bit?'

My face relaxes into a smile as I realise that she really doesn't blame me for what happened. I go to the bed, so grateful for the chance to hold her, while pushing away the guilt that I haven't told her everything about the crash.

chapter five

libby

This is not who I am.

I am not like this. I don't care about looks, I know that beauty comes from within, I know that hair length, and weight and the smoothness of your skin is not as important as the person you are. Yet, I can't seem to stop it. The thoughts, the feelings, the pain that drives me to be like this, to be sitting in front of a mirror with tears falling silently from my eyes as I float in a sea of despair.

I am still Libby. That jagged line that snakes its way from my forehead to the nape of my neck has not stopped me from laughing out loud whenever I find something funny. The scratches that fleck my face like gravel scattered carelessly across a path have not stopped me from flicking over when the adverts start on TV. The line that diagonally bisects the left side of my face has not stopped me from loving to wake up to the sound of seagulls shrieking and calling like overzealous market vendors.

None of these marks, these superficial things, can change who I really am. Who Libby truly is. Which is why I shouldn't be crying right now. I have not changed.

And when Angela, reflected in the mirror, holding her scissors and waiting for me to give her the nod, starts cutting I still won't have changed.

I am only looking at the long strands of my black hair and

saying goodbye to the person I am with them because I am probably still in shock about the accident.

It is not because I am scared I will look ugly and unlike me without my hair.

I close my eyes and nod.

'Are you sure about this, babe?' she asks. 'We can try to work with what we've got, you know.' Angela has stunning skin and heavenly hair. She is as dark as me, and her complexion is smooth and unblemished. She has long, thin dreadlocks, which are kinked and wavy all the way to the middle of her back. She looks like a woman, she looks like a real woman.

'Please, just do it.'

She is gentle, she is careful as she hacks away my hair but I do not open my eyes. I can't watch. I can't see myself in the mirror, and I can't watch her hands in real life as she works.

Once she stops, I can hear her changing implements. 'Next stage, OK, babe?'

I nod again, not opening my eyes. I tense at the sound of the clippers being started, the buzz filling the fragile silence with such foreboding. I try not to recoil, force myself not to scream as the cold metal shears touch my head. It doesn't take long for her to remove the rest of my hair.

But it takes a lifetime for me to open my eyes.

To look in the mirror and see the woman I have become.

jack

My heart stops when I see her. She is bald, the only things on her scalp are the line of the scar and the stitches holding it together.

She stands in the hallway anxiously and nervously picking at her fingers, looking so much like a little girl who has been caught doing something naughty and is awaiting punishment.

'Your hair,' I say, 'it's gone.'

She nods, and then the tears fill her eyes. I stride down the hall to her and rest my hands on her shoulders. 'I'd rather have nothing than a bit that's all right,' she says.

'I think it looks fantastic,' I say, and she blinks at me in surprise.

'Really?' she asks.

'Yes. There are very few women out there who can pull off something like this, and you're one of them.'

'Really?' she asks again, her body sagging in relief.

'Yes. And the most wonderful thing is, I can see all of your beautiful face.'

'So I don't look awful?' she asks.

'No, you could never look awful,' I say, then pull her close.

Her words rattle in my ears: *I'd rather have nothing than a bit that's all right.*

I hope that's not true. I hope with all my heart that's not true.

chapter six

libby

'Mrs Britcham, we won't keep you long,' the policewoman says. She's plain clothes and has a plain-clothes officer with her that she hasn't bothered to introduce. It's all a bit much for giving a statement about a 'normal' accident.

And I really don't like them being here.

I wanted to keep all the crash stuff away from the house, but no one seemed interested in asking for my version of events during that week I was laid up in hospital with nothing else to do but answer questions, even though they'd talked to Jack. Now, at home, when I'm trying to do that thing called 'moving on' they're here, dragging me back. I feel as if I am being interrogated, as if I have done something wrong by wantonly sitting in a car that got hit. Jack is on the other side of the room, leaning against the dining table, even though the police officer asked him to leave. He looked like he was going to unquestioningly do it until I'd asked, 'Why does Jack need to leave?' She didn't have an answer so had said if he had to stay, then could he please not interfere in the questioning. If I didn't know otherwise, I would have thought I was being interrogated for some crime, not being asked to recount for the record what happened.

'Can you tell us, in your own time, what occured on the day

of your "accident"?' she asks. She adds a strange weight to the word accident that ignites a niggle inside.

'I don't remember much,' I reply as the male officer scribbles on a notepad. 'I remember Jack and I were talking and then we were hit and I remember seeing the wall and lamppost coming towards me. And then I was talking to a fireman. That's it.'

'And what was your husband doing at the time you were hit?' she asks.

'Apart from driving the car?' I sound facetious, but I don't really understand the point of the question.

'Was he driving erratically, too fast? That sort of thing.'

I close my eyes, try to remember what was happening before that moment. I open my eyes. 'We were talking, and then the car hit us.'

'Talking, not arguing?' she asks.

'If we were arguing, I would have said we were arguing.'

She looks pointedly at Jack. 'As we both know, it's not always easy to say what we mean if we feel under pressure.'

'I don't feel under pressure, and Jack and I don't really argue,' I reply. Which is true. We generally don't have anything to argue about – our main bone of contention is Eve and we simply don't talk about her, and if we try we end up not talking at all.

'Not at all?' The police officer, Detective Sergeant Morgan, asks.

'No, not really. We don't have anything to argue about.'

She nods sceptically and makes a note in her notebook for the first time. She's trying to talk to me woman-to-woman, but it's not working because I get the impression she does not like women. Or men, for that matter. But there's something uncon-ventional in all of this. My eyes go to Jack, to the way his rigid body language and unblinking glare are directed at her, and then my eyes go back to the policewoman. Jack and Detective Sergeant Morgan know each other. How though? She doesn't look like the sort of person whom Jack would have had enough of a connection with to seduce, but then things might have been different when they met. There might have been a spark between them.

I reassess her, now that she might have slept with my husband. She doesn't make the most of herself. She's done her make-up all wrong: that brown lipstick does not go with her natural colouring. If I was talking to her, I'd advise her to go for a foundation a little less orange-beige and little more bluey-pink in undertone. On her lips I'd advise a stronger red lipstick – not bright red, but maybe burgundy red, then on her eyes with one coat of black mascara during the day, and two coats in the evening. Her current make-up job makes her seem mean. But then maybe I am being generous – maybe it isn't the make-up, maybe she looks mean because she is mean. Jack wouldn't have slept with her, I decide. She's far too unpleasant a person. So why does she have an axe to grind with him? Because she clearly has one.

'What were you talking about before the crash?' she asks.

'About what it was like when Jack and I first met. I think I was saying that he wasn't irresistible to all women, thankfully, and he was asking me why thankfully, and as I was about to reply we got hit.'

'So he'd asked you a question? Did he look at you while asking it?'

'Not that I remember,' I reply.

Like a hungry dog thrown a bone, she leaps on this statement like the piece of evidence that she's been waiting for: 'Are you saying you're not sure if his eyes were on the road when the accident occurred?'

'I'm sorry, I don't understand the point of these questions,' I say to her, redoing her make-up as I stare at her. Maybe she's doing the same to me, maybe she's visually removing my scar and putting hair on my head. 'Wasn't it the other driver who was breaking the law by being on his mobile phone and trying to turn out onto a busy road without concentrating? I was looking in the direction the car came from and I didn't see it, how would Jack? And if he did, what would he have been able to do?'

113

Detective Sergeant Morgan's plain brown eyes stare at me as if I have sworn at her. Then she starts calculating how to get to me, how to upset me. The axe that needs grinding has clearly been extended to me.

'Maybe we should move on,' she says, diplomatically. 'What do you know about the death of the first Mrs Britcham?'

I draw back inside, wondering where this has come from. *Is this how she plans to get at me? To accuse me in the death of Eve?*

'Nothing,' I reply, quickly, in case she takes any hesitancy as me trying to conjure up an alibi. 'Nothing at all. Why, do you think I had something to do with her death? Because I didn't know her and I didn't know Jack at the time.'

'But you did know that the airbag was faulty in your husband's car, didn't you?'

A sickness is starting to whirl around my stomach. What is going on? 'Is that illegal?' I ask. 'Should I have not got into a car that I knew had a faulty airbag? Am I going to get arrested for that?'

'No, no, I'm not saying that at all.'

'Then what are you saying?' I ask.

She throws a look in Jack's direction, obviously wishing he wasn't there. This is all too much. I've had enough already of people talking to the right side of me, of them avoiding my scar with their looks and their conversations, of them avoiding my hairlessness in the same way. I don't need it from a random stranger who is trying to blame me for something I couldn't have stopped.

'Can I ask you something?' I ask her, and before she can answer, I continue, 'Why are you asking me these questions? What has Eve got to do with anything? For that matter, what has our conversation before the crash got to do with it? The other man went into us. I want to know why you're being like this.'

Detective Sergeant Morgan sighs, a bit too dramatically for someone as unemotional as she is. 'Mrs Britcham, I don't like doing this kind of thing,' she says, when she clearly does, 'but I have to investigate when a second person close to a murder suspect is hurt in suspicious circumstances. And I'm sorry to point this out, but your husband nearly killed you.'

My heart grows cold. 'Did he?' I'm alarmed and it shows. 'When?'

I'm wracking my memories, trying to work out when he tried to do that. I look at Jack, who is glaring at her like he did before. If he did try to kill me, then he's being very languid about it.

'With the crash,' Ms Morgan replies.

I frown at her. 'But someone went into us.'

'I know,' another of her dramatic sighs, 'but you were most hurt because your airbag didn't deploy.' Oh, that's who she is. She's the police officer who questioned him when Eve died. She must be.

'So you think Jack was driving around hoping someone would crash into us and I'd be killed when the airbag didn't work?' I ask, trying not to sound patronising. '*Really?*'

'It's just as plausible as asking us to believe that Eve Britcham died from simply falling down the stairs.'

'Oh, right,' I reply, because I do not know what to say.

The silence in the room stretches and stretches, and I'm supposed to end it, I think. But I'm not inclined to do so. What am I to say to this half-baked accusation and unnecessary line of questioning?

'I'm sorry I had to put that thought in your head,' Detective Sergeant Morgan says.

'No, you're not,' I reply quietly. 'You want me to be upset; you want me to be suspicious of Jack. What I don't understand is why.'

'I don't want you to be suspicious of Mr Britcham, I simply want you to know what you're dealing with. There is a reason why we haven't closed the case on the death of Eve Britcham and why the coroner recorded an open verdict.'

'And there's a reason why you had to release him without charge,' I reply.

'It's not that simple, Mrs Britcham. When we were investigating the background of Eve Britcham, or Eve Quennox as she was known before her marriage, we came across a lot of information that made us suspicious of Mr Britcham. Let me put it this way: if my husband found out some of those things about me, I wouldn't be surprised if he snapped my neck and threw me down the stairs to hide it.'

My gaze shifts to Jack, and my stomach flips to find he is no longer glaring at Detective Sergeant Morgan with all the resentment he must feel towards her – instead he is staring at the ground, his arms folded tightly across his body, his hair falling forwards, his body language like a weeping willow, reaching towards the ground for comfort and relief. He's not angry; he's holding himself together. He is trying not to crumble.

'Things like what?' I ask, returning my focus to her. I hate that she's got my attention, and that Jack seems to be falling apart at this. What has she said that would do this to him?

'That's not for me to tell you,' she replies, satisfied now that she has finally managed to needle me and awaken my curiosity. Because both of those things lead to being suspicious of Jack, which is clearly what she wanted all along. 'I just want you to be careful. I'd hate for you to have another accident.'

If I had another 'accident' – preferably a fatal one – she'd be on cloud nine. She'd be right there waiting for me to be declared dead so she could slap handcuffs on Jack. She is more than a mean person – she is nasty, conniving and cruel. I curl my lips into my mouth to stop myself from telling her what I think of her. And from telling her that if I didn't know for a fact that Jack didn't kill Eve then she could easily have destroyed me with what she has done today.

'Can you leave now, please?' I ask Detective Sergeant Morgan.

'Of course,' she says, solicitously, clearly happy that she's got to me.

'I have to put cream on my wounds and take my painkillers,' I add. 'That's what I have to do now. I'd show you out, but I find walking really difficult as my left leg was very badly bruised, as were a lot of my internal organs. The doctor who took the stitches out of my head said I should try to avoid stress or upset, so you'll understand why I'm not that keen on thinking about having another accident.' Ms Morgan swallows and I can see a tiny flash of guilt in her eye. Her unnamed companion eyes her up with distaste, obviously not impressed with her timing, either. 'But it's OK, now that you've done your best to put the idea into my head that my husband's probably a killer, and told me you'd hate for me to be hurt – or possibly even killed – I'm sure I'll be fine. I'm sure this won't set back my recovery at all.'

She says nothing as she leaves, but the policeman gives me a sad smile and I know that he doesn't agree with what she has done, nor does he believe Jack is a killer.

Jack doesn't move until we've heard the door click shut behind them. Then, when he is certain we are alone, he raises his gaze to me and our eyes slot together. The smell of burning rubber, the lift of the car, the sound of crunching metal swell around me and I feel all my internal organs contract painfully in response. I force the memories away, but our wary gazes stay linked.

'I'm sorry,' Jack says, tiredly. 'I should have stopped her.'

'I don't think anything could have stopped her,' I reply. 'She just has this ability to make me feel . . .'

'Guilty?'

He nods. 'Even though I didn't do it,' he says. 'I didn't kill her.'

'I know,' I say. 'It never occurred to me that you did. I know you couldn't.'

I want to ask about the rest of it. About what it was in Eve's past that could possibly have led to them thinking he did, what it was about what she said about Eve that took him from being angry and indignant to being scared and shaken. But I can't. That is an Eve conversation. And, of all the Eve conversations we are never going to have, this is probably the least likely of them all to happen.

'Can you get me my painkillers, please?' I ask him.

'Of course,' he says, standing up. 'Of course.'

Once I am alone in the living room, I close my eyes. It's easy to get the image I have of her up in my mind, to see that smile, that sparkle in her eyes and that pink dress.

What secrets did you have, Eve? And should I try to find out about them?

chapter seven

libby

'You know how it is, Sis,' says Caleb, my brother, throwing his hands wide while his face is the picture of 'this is bigger than all of us'. He does and says that far more than any adult should. Despite how he behaves, he *is* an adult – with a son. And now, apparently, a dog.

I shake my head. 'No, I don't. I can promise you, I really don't.'

I'm pretty sure most people wouldn't understand how you could blithely pull up outside someone's house with a dog and ask them to take care of it for you because in the rush to prepare for a holiday you booked *six months ago* you forgot to make arrangements for the dog. They're en route to the airport, by the way.

Who does this to two healthy people, let alone one who is recovering from a car crash? Oh yes, that's right, my brother.

'Ah but, Sis—'

'I'll give you "Sis",' I say to him. 'Why are you taking advantage of our good nature?'

'I'm not,' he protests, genuinely horrified that is what I think he is doing. 'There's no one around to look after the dog. Benji wouldn't let me leave him with anyone, and you know how much he trusts you, so what am I supposed to do? Leave the dog on his own?'

'You could have simply picked up the phone to call and ask me in advance. You do know how to use a phone, don't you?'

The words have no sooner left my mouth when my brother's phone starts to ring. He reaches into the back pocket of his jeans and removes it, peering at the screen. 'I've got to take this,' he says and immediately pushes a button and puts the phone to his ear. 'Yeah?' he says, his tone dripping with honey.

He is tall, my younger brother, and good looking, and a charmer on so many levels.

'Uh-uh,' he says into the phone, as he paces the floor of my kitchen. I look out of the window into the small patch of garden that this house has. Jack is playing with Benji and the dog, Butch. It's cute, a brown fluffy ball with black patches and a small, narrow face that looks like it is constantly trying to make sense of what you're saying while keeping inside all the secrets it is has learnt from its time on Earth. It's not the dog I object to, it's the lack of warning – actually, the outright deceit. I have spoken to my brother at least three times in the last few days, and he has not at any point mentioned the dog. I should have known that there was something odd about the fact he only called when Benji was asleep. *Because Benji would have told me.*

I look over at Caleb as he uh-uhs into the phone.

Moving stiffly, because it is still difficult to walk with the pulling sensation and with pain sparkling at my nerve endings, I go to him and snatch the mobile out of his hands, put it to my ear. A woman is talking.

'Love, he's not worth it,' I say to her and hang up before slapping the small, silver rectangle back into the palm of his hand.

'Libby!' he almost roars. 'That was my bank manager!'

'Really? So why's she calling you on a Saturday? Not enough days in the working week to talk to you?'

His glower is one that would be guilt-inducing had I not known him all my life. He is a laugh, and I do adore him, but he is known for taking the Michael. His glower slides seamlessly and effortlessly into a sulk. Anyone looking at us now would think he was a teenager being told off by his mother. But he is a father. I often think he forgets that. He loves Benji and is responsible when he has to be, but I think the thought of what he has to do all the time scares him, so he decides to check out and leave it up to our parents or me to sort out. I mean a dog, *really*!

'Caleb, you've not really been fair on us, have you?' I say. 'What would you do if I turned around now and said we can't look after him? That we're off on holiday ourselves?'

He looks alarmed. 'You're not, are you?' he asks, then doesn't wait for an answer before saying, 'Nah, course you're not. You wouldn't be going nowhere with your hair like that.'

Automatically, I raise my right hand, run it over the smooth curves and bumps of my scalp, avoiding the scar. He hadn't seemed to notice when he pulled up and came into the house. Benji's eyes, however, had widened and he'd said, 'Wow!' with a massive smile on his face. 'You're soooo cool Auntie Libby.' Then he'd rushed around to the back seat of the car to get the dog out.

Caleb's phone starts to ring again, this time the one in his inside jacket pocket. Of course my brother has more than one phone; I'm pretty sure he has more than one name when dealing with the various women 'friends' he has. At least with Jack, I always knew that he used his real name with every woman he slept with. Caleb reaches for his phone.

'If you answer that phone, I will not only chuck it down the toilet, I will pack up your dog and send you all on your merry way. Do you get me?'

He hesitates, not sure if I mean it. He studies my expression for a few seconds, and comes to the conclusion that I mean it.

'Ah, Sis, you know what it's like,' he says again, ignoring his phone to pull out a chair and sit down heavily. 'Benji's wanted a dog from time. The boy ain't got no mother. How can I say no to him?'

'I don't care about the dog,' I say. 'It's the not telling me part that I object to. You constantly make decisions that involve me and then expect me to go along with them. How is that fair?'

'Sorry, Sis,' he mumbles, as if he means it. On one level he does; on most other levels he is only saying that to get the bollocking over that bit quicker.

'Jack has to go back to work on Monday, and I can't look after a dog – I can barely walk across the room, let alone take him out for walks twice a day. How are we supposed to do this without any advance warning?'

'Sorry, Sis.'

'You're not though, are you?'

'I am!' he insists, with conviction.

'Even if I believed that, and it's a very big "if", please tell me how I'm supposed to do this? And what about paying for him?'

Caleb has the audacity to look around the room, telling me with his eyes that money is no object to me. He's not the only one who thinks I hit the big time when I married Jack. Paloma, who is still planning her wedding to Devin, actually started headhunting for replacements within hours of me telling her we were getting married. She had been horrified when I told her I was going to carry on working. Most people thought I'd give up my job and stay at home, when in actual fact I could think of nothing worse if I wasn't staying home to look after our children. I kept my job and went to London every day like I did before I got married. I still put money towards the mortgage and pay my share of the bills.

'The world doesn't owe you anything,' I say to Caleb. 'And neither do Jack or I. If Butch is staying for four weeks, you need to pay me.'

'I'll sort you out when I get back,' he says.

I click my fingers in front of his face. 'Focus! Focus! Remember who you're talking to,' I say. 'I'm not one of the "bank managers" on the phone, I am your sister. I know you, remember? There's a cashpoint up the road, you can draw some money out there.'

'I've used all my cash limit up for today.'

'OK, then you've clearly got it now.' I hold out my hand.

'I've used it all on petrol getting down here,' he says quickly.

'Do I have to search your pockets?' I say. 'Because you know I will.'

'Ah, Sis, man!' he says, reaching into his inside pocket and pulling out a wodge of notes. Far more than his daily cashpoint limit, that's for sure. He peels off a couple of twenties and holds them out to me.

I stare at the purple notes in his right hand, and then at the bundle in his left hand. My hand reaches out and snatches the bundle from him. I take off six notes, as well as the two in his other hand, then give the rest back to him.

'That's our holiday money!' he complains, watching anxiously as I roll up the notes and tuck them down my cleavage. I've never done that in my life, but I'm pretty certain my brother will not rummage around my bra to get his cash back – even he has standards. 'What are we supposed to do now?'

'I don't know, but you might have more of a clue if you stop thinking I'm going to spend my life bailing you out.'

For a moment I think he is going to say 'It's not fair!' and throw himself on the floor like he used to do in the supermarket when he was four. I stare at him as I used to then: with wide-eyed awe that someone that small could cause such a fuss. After seeming to seriously consider whether the floor-based tantrum would work or not, he grudgingly shrugs.

'I'll go say goodbye to Butch,' he concedes.

In the garden, Jack is flat on the ground, covered in grass and dirt, while Benji stands on one side, trying to get Butch to hop over Jack to him. 'Here, Butch,' he keeps saying, patting his thighs with his hands. Butch meanwhile is very much engrossed with chasing his little brown tail in ever-more fervent circles.

I love Benji's unfailing optimism, I admire Jack's enthusiasm for these sorts of things with Benji, and I adore Butch for being so clueless. (And for having probably one of the most inappropriate names of all time.)

'OK, mate,' Caleb says to Benji, 'we need to hit the road. Say bye to Butch and everyone.'

Benji abandons the game, leaps over Jack and scoops Butch in his arms. Butch doesn't protest and is obviously used to Benji's hugging. 'Bye, Butch. Please look after Auntie Libby. She's well cool.' He squeezes Butch again. 'And Uncle Jack's cool, too.'

Caleb goes to Butch, too, but doesn't hug him. He rubs the patch of fur between his ears. 'See ya soon, Butch.' Then Caleb moves to Jack and slaps his palm into his so they can shake hands in a manly fashion, while Benji throws his arms around me, butting his head in my abdomen and nearly causing me to pass out from the pain. 'See you soon, Auntie Libby. Butch is nice. He'll look after you.'

'Thank you,' I say to him. 'You have a nice holiday with your dad.'

Benji then goes to high-five with Jack, while his father comes towards me. Caleb is gentle as he wraps himself around me for a hug. He's always surprising me with his hugs. Even if I've torn a strip off him for being selfish and a bit of an idiot, just before I leave he'll grab me and hug me and say goodbye.

'All right, Sis,' he says to me. 'Take care of my boy Butch, and take care of yourself.'

'I will,' I say. Butch stops chasing his tail and sits on the grass, watching patiently as Benji and Caleb go. I'm actually more surprised than not that he doesn't raise his paw and wave at them. As they disappear around the side of the house, Butch turns to me and cocks his head to one side. He's sizing me up, I realise. He's seeing if I meet his standards. Eventually he seems to resign himself to the fact that, up to scratch or not, he's with me for now, and does the doggy equivalent of a shrug by shaking himself once, then he wanders towards Jack. Probably to see if Jack is a better option.

'Well, you aren't that much of a catch yourself, mate,' I say to him.

'Are you starting a row with a dog?' Jack asks, still reclining on the grass.

'No,' I say petulantly.

Jack's face twists up into a smile that is a half-laugh of incredulity and despair, which he gives me whenever he thinks I'm being unreasonable or outrageous.

I have to look away, my face twisting into a smile too. He's usually right when he treats me to one of those smiles – I am being unreasonable or outrageous or ridiculous.

'I'm going for a lie-down,' I tell him, still trying to fight my smile.

'OK,' Jack replies.

I shuffle my way into the house knowing that he is never going to let me live this down.

jack

Never being able to have children with Eve is one of the things that used to haunt me. Many, many things haunted me, but that is the one that left the deepest furrows of pain in my heart.

I've never told anyone that. It's not the done thing, is it? Men aren't supposed to be broody – they're supposed to want to plant the seed of a son in the bodies of as many women as possible and be satisfied.

They're not supposed to feel jealous as they stare at other men who are rolling around on the grass at the local park with their children, or strapping their kids into carseats in the back of big, ugly cars, or watch them struggle to control their offspring in supermarkets. They're not supposed to feel a gut-wrenching agony as they watch other men do the things they can't. I didn't simply want children – I probably could have found someone who would have been willing to do the baby thing – I wanted them with *her*. I longed to see the sparkle of her eyes in the eyes of a child; to have that infectious laugh of hers coming out of a baby's mouth as I tickled them; I wanted to hold a child in my arms and look at it and see her and me, our genes combined to make another human being. When it came to me, six months after she died, that that would never happen, I put my fist through the back door. All these little things kept coming to me, all the 'I'll nevers', but that was the worst one after never seeing her again. Then I hated myself for saying we should wait.

She'd wanted to start trying almost as soon as we got married, but I'd said we deserved to enjoy the time we had together before we settled down properly. 'What's the big rush? It's not like we're going anywhere. We've got the rest of our lives together,' I said, with the ignorance and the arrogance of someone who thinks death is for other people. I didn't realise what I meant was, 'We're going to live for ever, we can get around to that whenever we like.'

I grieved for the children we'd never have almost as much as I grieved for Eve.

Butch's barking cuts into my thoughts. I'm taking Butch for his first walk along the seafront, just as I thought I would take my child in a pram at some point. Butch likes me to talk to him, to tell him about the buildings we pass, the beach huts, the statute, the things out to sea. Whenever I stop talking and lapse into silence, consumed by my thoughts, he stops walking then sits down to bark at me.

'Look, Butch, I've got a lot of thinking to do,' I say to his upturned face. 'I don't have time to give you a guided tour of Hove and Brighton.'

In response he hangs his head low, as if hurt that I'm telling him I don't have time for him. Would I have done that to my son or daughter? Would I have been too busy at some point to play with my child and then would have regretted it in years to come?

'OK, OK, enough with the look. I'll do my best.'

Butch's head springs up and he gets to his feet and starts walk-ing.

'Places of interest,' I say to him as he trots along on his skinny Yorkshire Terrier Cross legs, careful not to strain too much on the leash in case he misses something. 'There, on your right, is the bit of beach where I accidentally proposed to Libby.'

I proposed to Libby because I wanted to do the baby thing with her. After splashing each other in the sea and laughing and running back to our blanket, I realised as she dried her face off, still gulping with laughter, that how I felt about losing the chance to have babies with Eve would be twice as bad if I didn't get the chance to do it with Libby. I had been shown how short life was, how quickly it could be ripped away, so what was I waiting for with regards to the sea-soaked woman laughing in front of me? What would I tell myself if I didn't watch her grow gorgeously ripe with our baby? If we didn't become sleep-deprived and snappy with each other as we tried to navigate the stormy seas of parenthood together.

Butch treats me to a growl – of approval or not, I can't tell. I stop walking and he does too. 'And what's that supposed to mean?' I ask him indignantly as he looks at me over his shoulder. 'I did it because I love her. I would have proposed properly you know with dinner or something inventive, but for some reason it happened there. And, you know, I wanted to spend my life with her, to have kids with her, so it came out in a rush. Admittedly, she didn't say yes straight away, she sort of argued, but that's Libby all over.'

Butch looks at me with his big brown eyes, and realise I'm doing what Libby did earlier – I'm talking to him like he's a human, behaving as if he can understand and (more importantly) judge me. It'd amused me that this little creature had, within minutes of being around her, brought out the side to Libby I love – that unreasonable wildness that makes being with her a challenge, and never boring. She pushes my boundaries and never allows me to 'get away' with being a spoilt, rich boy who's had too many advantages in life. She tries on so many levels to get me to open up and talk about what troubles me, even if I'm not sure I want to. And, most of all, she trusts me. She didn't even consider for one moment that DS Morgan's accusations were true, that I had murdered Eve. I could tell in the way she was confused by the questioning and so outraged that Morgan even suggested it.

A cupful of shame trickles its way through me. Libby trusts

me, and I have lied to her, cheated on her almost. Not with my body: with my heart. I'm not sure how to get back from where I have arrived at because if I tell her, as I know I should, it will be over.

Butch starts to bark again, obviously unimpressed with the way the walk and its accompanying conversation is going. I watch him, seeing the good he can do Libby. He can help her back to who she was, help her to get over this initial shaky period and return to herself. And if she's herself, maybe she won't hate me as much if she finds out the truth. Maybe she'll be more understanding than she would be at the moment.

'I think I'm going to like having you around, Butch,' I tell him.

He doesn't reply. He's far more interested in the pitch-black Scottie dog prancing along the promenade towards us. I watch Butch watch the Scottie dog and remind myself that I haven't ruined my chances of having children, just yet. Not if I'm careful and if I try to keep everything together. Not if I keep the most important parts of what really happened after the crash under wraps.

libby

'Eve, Eve,' Jack cries out. 'Eve!'

'Jack,' I say gently, shaking him carefully.

He doesn't stir, simply continues to writhe in bed, his eyes scrunched shut, his face twisted in whatever agony he is trapped in inside the dream. 'No, Eve—'

'Jack,' I say more forcefully, and shake him harder. It's awful watching him so knotted up and immersed in something so painful.

'Huh?' he replies, his eyes flying open, his face and body immediately unclenching. He pulls himself upright to sitting, his chest heaving, his heart no doubt racing. 'What happened?'

'I think you were having a nightmare,' I reply, easing myself up also.

His eyes lose focus as he trawls his memory for what he was dreaming about. 'I think I was dreaming about the crash,' he eventually says.

'You were calling for Eve,' I say. He reacts in the same way he always does to me saying her name: he stiffens as though I have cussed him, as if I have used a forbidden word and mortally wounded him in the process. If I was saying, 'Adam and Eve' he would not have a problem, I suspect. It is the conjuring, the meta-physical calling of her, that he finds hard to assimilate.

'Was I?' he asks absently, his body still tense from his reaction to my saying the forbidden word.

'Yes,' I say, careful to not sound accusatory, 'several times.'

Jack shakes his head, scrunches his lips. 'I don't know what that's about. I could have sworn I was dreaming about the crash.'

I notice he hasn't looked at me, but that might mean nothing. Or it might mean something. Just like it might mean something that he almost fell apart when the policewoman talked about Eve's past. It's sometimes difficult to know with him what is significant and what isn't. So mostly, I just let it go. 'Right,' I reply. 'Right.'

'It's still dark out,' Jack says, looking at the night surrounding the shaded window.

'Yeah,' I reply. 'We've only been asleep about an hour.' I haven't had my nightmare about the crash, yet; the night still has that joy to unfold. 'Were you having these dreams when I was in hospital?' I ask him.

'Not that I remember,' he says.

'OK.' There's no point pushing anything that might become an 'Eve conversation', there never is. It always ends the same way: Jack, quiet and withdrawn, curled up tight in his shell; me, floundering, not sure if I should stop talking or should keep going to get to the bottom of it all. I snuggle down under the covers, and turn on my side towards the window, away from Jack.

Sometimes, living with him is like being told to hold my breath as a matter of life and death – but never being told when to let that breath out. So I don't know what to do for the best. To let out that breath and suffer the consequences or to keep holding on no matter what it does to me.

Sometimes, I am scared to breathe around Jack because it may be the death of our marriage.

'Goodnight.' I haven't got the energy to decide what to do, to pick my words, to try to draw it out of him. We've both been hurt and shaken and damaged by the crash, and then again by that policewoman's visit – if this is how it's manifesting itself in Jack, all I can do is not add to his pain and confusion by not pushing him to talk. All I can do is withdraw and leave him to sort it out on his own.

'I love you,' he whispers suddenly, unexpectedly, curling himself around me. He's gentle, careful, trying not to put too much pressure on my bruised body.

'Love you, too,' I whisper, shaken. He never does this after an 'Eve' moment.

He presses a kiss on the nape of my neck and whispers it again against my skin, as if trying to brand the words on my body. For the first time ever, after an 'Eve' moment, we are bound together instead of miles apart in the same place.

February, 2010

From the doorway of the living room, I stood in my pyjamas and watched a black and white version of Rex Harrison speaking to Margaret Rutherford. There was no sound to the old movie that was playing in the lounge. The lights were off so the images from the screen cast dancing, bouncing shafts of light all around the room.

Jack sat perfectly still on the sofa with his back to the door, to me. He must have heard me come down to find him, but he did not move. I went to the sofa, where he continued to sit stock still, clutching the remote control in one hand, his gaze fixed on the television screen.

'Jack?' I whispered, lowering myself onto the sofa beside him. 'It's the middle of the night, come to bed. You've got an early start tomorrow.'

The light suddenly illuminated his face, showing me the tracks of his tears, tears that were still drizzling out of his eyes. My heart grew still and cold, terrified of what had done this to him.

'Jack? Are you OK? What's the matter?'

'This was her favourite Noel Coward story,' he said, his voice a series of low, barely controlled sobs.

I turned to the screen, I liked *Blithe Spirit*, too. It was witty and clever and absolutely silly.

'She thought it was Coward's best work,' he continued, his voice trembling under the strain of his hurt and tears. 'God, I miss her. I miss her so much.'

This was the first time he had given away a little piece of who Eve was as a person rather than as simply the woman he was married to. The first time he had revealed she had likes and dislikes just as most humans did. 'Oh, sweetheart, of course you do,' I said, moving to put my arms around him, to hold and love him through this.

He recoiled from me, as if I meant him harm. 'I need to be alone,' he said, still staring at the television screen, obviously willing me to go away. 'Please.'

I stared at him, horrified. Why didn't he want me to help him? To hold him? I didn't know her, but I loved and cared about him. I'd do anything to help him through this pain. I thought I'd made that clear, I'd thought that was what he wanted, why we'd got married. I thought the whole point of marriage was that we were in it together – any problem we had, we could face it together.

'OK,' I said, my heart feeling as if it had been twisted in barbed wire, caught and stuck, pierced in several places. *Please don't let this be the start of what I think it could be,* I thought as I left the room. *Please don't let this be the start of Eve coming between us.*

jack

I have this recurring dream that I walk into my bedroom and Eve is sitting on the bed, wearing her pink wedding dress, her knees pulled up to her chest, arms wrapped around her legs, and her hair falling like waves over her arms as she rests her head on her knees. Her sobbing fills the room and the room seems to shake in sympathy with her distress.

'God, Eve, what's wrong?' I ask, unable to get too close to the bed because her sorrow is like a wall around her. I want to reach out to her, but she will not be consoled.

'Oh, Jack,' she sobs in reply. 'How could you? How could you fall in love with someone else? How could you marry her? Don't you even care that I'm not here any more? Don't you love me?'

Originally, my eyes would fly open at that point and I'd be almost sick with guilt, my heart galloping in my chest. Libby would be cradled in my arms and I'd have to untangle myself, gently easing our bodies apart so as to not wake her, then I would roll away, to the other side of the bed, face away from Libby while I tried to blot out the sound of Eve crying in my head.

Over time, the dream progressed. It slowly became more and more detailed, intricate, damning. I wouldn't wake up at her accusation, I would instead be standing in front of her, pleading with her to understand.

'Of course I care that you're not here any more. Of course I love you.'

'So, why did you have to fall in love with her? Sex doesn't mean anything, love means everything.' And her sobbing would escalate, filling every part of me with a searing, twisting pain.

'Eve, I'm sorry, I'm sorry. I don't love her,' I'd say. My mouth running away with me, desperate as I was to make her stop crying. 'Eve, Eve! Eve, no! I made a mistake, I should never have married her. I don't love her.'

It would work, Eve would stop crying and her red, swollen face would finally lift from her knees and she would look beyond me to the doorway. 'See? I told you,' she'd say.

I'd turn and find Libby standing there, watching me. She'd look at me with understanding and a sadness that was heart-piercing in its hopelessness before she turned and began to walk away.

I've been having this dream again since the accident. Libby dreams about the crash, I dream about this. Like her, I wake bathed in sweat, shaking, harried. Unlike her, I also wake up with another piece of my soul sliced away. Now, I'm apparently calling out to Eve.

I wish I could explain to Libby what Eve's death did to me, how it's there almost everyday. But I can't vocalise it without telling her everything. And 'everything' is not something I can talk about.

But not telling her is taking its toll on her.

She's so very fragile now. The changes not visible to the eye are the things that knot me up inside: Libby is fretful, jumpy, uncertain. I watch her, and I can see nothing but confusion in her eyes, in her actions. Sometimes it's as if she doesn't even remember how to do everyday things like put water into the kettle or open a tin of dog food because she is not sure she is doing it properly.

The ache I feel when I watch her trying to be normal when she is only just holding herself together is like nothing I have ever felt before. When Eve died, it was easy to let myself go and grieve, I did not have to keep what I was feeling in check because it would hurt her: Eve didn't know. With Libby, after the dream has dragged me into the real world, I lie awake, staring at the ceiling, recounting all the ways I've let her down.

Before the wedding, we moved into her little flat in Brighton because the house was being redecorated. Buying new bedroom furniture had turned into a desire to make the place ours. I suggested a new colour for the walls and new carpet and she had asked me if I was sure. I wasn't – it was like painting over the time I had spent there with Eve – but I had to push forwards, to make my life with and about Libby. She'd wanted us to paint it ourselves, but the enormity of the task especially when we were planning a wedding meant she had to let me get decorators in.

Meanwhile, we bedded down in her flat, small and cosy with nowhere to run to if we felt like we were getting on top of each other. It was perfectly claustrophobic; a confined time I had never spent with anyone I loved before. I watched her sleep, I watched her pad to the tiny bathroom next to her bedroom, her pyjamas creased, her hair tied up in a scarf, rubbing her eyes and murmuring curse words at the time of day. I lay in bed and through the wide-open door noted with loving care her mannerisms as she spooned porridge with tinned milk into her mouth while standing over the sink in the kitchenette at the end of the living room. I grinned every time she called to me to enjoy my lie-in because staying at her flat meant my walk to work was only fifteen minutes away. I loved the way she flopped onto the sofa when she came home from work, the way she'd smile at me if I said I'd make dinner, the way she would try to stay awake past ten o'clock but would always end up drooling on my shoulder and protest when I forced her to bed. 'Stop watching me,' she'd say all the time, a little smile on her face because she was watching me too.

'I can't help it,' I'd reply, 'I'm fascinated by you, in love with you.'

'Well, go be fascinated and in love with the TV. I'm trying to sort out this spot, it's not easy with you watching.'

A week before the wedding, while I was wide awake and watching her, she reached up and stroked my cheek with her eyes closed and I kissed her mouth, and for some reason it was going to be then. We hadn't even come close to it since *that* night, but it was now because I was undressing her, she was running her hands over my body, making small sounds of pleasure at the back of her throat. Just before I pushed into her, I heard her murmur something. I wasn't meant to hear – it didn't even sound as though she was aware she had said it; it was a thought in her heart that had accidentally tumbled out of her lips.

We fell asleep curled up like we usually did, but what she said stayed with me.

'Please don't break my heart, Jack,' she'd whispered.

I won't, I silently replied. *I couldn't.*

I have.

I should tell her, put her out of her misery and confusion, allow us both to move on from where we are in a more honest place. The good times we have together are wonderful, and the bad times are usually brought about by me trying to spare her feelings by keeping quiet about Eve.

I'm not sure she would mind, but I am scared to take that chance, terrified of her hating me properly. If she never remembers what I did after the crash, then I'll never have to see another woman I love look at me with hate in her eyes.

libby

As usual, Jack is on the other side of the bed when I wake up again, sweaty and shaking from my nightmare about the crash, but unlike usual he is reaching out for me, his arm outstretched, as though he couldn't help moving away, but he's doing all he can to stay as close to me as possible. I close my eyes and try to force myself back to sleep. Maybe the crash has had a good effect on us, maybe now that we know what we have to lose we're going to be more open with each other. Maybe – hopefully – this is the start of the rest of our lives together.

libby

'Butch, there's nothing down there for you. I promise.' He's at the cellar door, scrabbling away, damaging the paintwork. I probably should get upset by that sort of thing – Jack would normally – but I really don't care. There are bigger, better things to worry about, I suppose.

This dog, a Yorkshire Cross, apparently, has been with us five days and when he isn't lounging in his bed in the hall, he is desperately trying to get into the cellar. Anyone would think he'd buried a bone down there for safe keeping and wants it back.

Butch stops scrabbling at the door, turns then sits down and looks at me. He's fed up.

'I've told you, no,' I reply to him.

He barks.

The doorbell interrupts this moment of conflict and I think for a moment of ignoring it. Pretending I'm not in and letting the person go away. But it won't be a cold caller, someone I can legitimately ignore, it'll be someone I know who will ring my mobile and ring the house. If I don't answer, they'll ring Jack, and he'll come charging home to rescue me, even though it's his first week back in the office after the accident. That's if the ambulance, police and fire brigade haven't already been told to break in.

'This isn't over,' I tell Butch as I move towards the door.

'Ding-dong, Grace Clementis calling.' She is glowing; the very picture of a woman who takes her beauty seriously. She is holding up her Louis Vuitton case, in which she keeps her manicure set. Before the accident, Grace had been using me as a cheap beauty school because it is one of her passions.

'It's like God answered my prayers in more ways than one,' she said when I met her again, this time as Jack's girlfriend. 'Jack gets together with someone lovely and she's a beautician. I must have been so good in a former life.'

I stare at her, wondering if she really wants a lesson right now. I can barely walk, can barely hold a thought in my head – giving her a beauty lesson isn't necessarily the last thing I want to do, but it's pretty far down that list.

'I'm thinking your nails have probably been neglected these last two weeks. So what you need is someone to give you a professional manicure. And ta-da,' she twirls, 'here is one such professional.' In her real life, she is head of a marketing department of a major bank.

I say nothing. What is there to say that won't be rude and hurt her feelings?

'Thing is, lovey, I'm not leaving until I get to paint your nails, so we can do this hard way or we can do it the harder way.'

She smiles as I step aside to let her in. Butch is in his basket in the corridor and raises his head to look at her. He gives her a welcome bark. She smiles and says, 'Hello, boy, aren't you a cutie?'

He barks her a happy reply, then looks disparagingly at me before contentedly laying his head down on his paws and closing his eyes to go to sleep. I marvel once again, as I often do, at how Grace can charm virtually anyone.

'What was Jack like after Eve died?' I ask Grace.

We're sitting at the kitchen table, Grace's tools spread in front of us, a rainbow of nail colours to my right. She's been working in silence, concentrating as she's massaged my hands – the left one still slightly tender from the accident – with luxurious hand cream, then used nail varnish remover to prep my nails for the basecoat.

The basecoat brush in her hand halts its progress from the base to the tip of the nailbed on the forefinger of my left hand, and her lowered head dips a fraction more.

She hesitates then gathers some composure before she starts to paint again. I've never asked her about Eve before, I've never felt the need. But Jack calling out to her in his sleep is starting to get to me. Mingled with the things the policewoman told me and I'm starting to feel very down. I thought I was moving forwards, getting better, but I seem stuck, unable to shake the feeling that Jack is keeping something from me. He's not himself and I want to know if this is how he responds to trauma or if there is something else eating away at him.

'What do you mean?' she asks.

'I mean, what was he like, how did he react? He's told me he didn't behave very well, but what does that mean exactly?'

She halts the brush again. 'It means he became a different person.'

She raises her head, the blanket of honey-blonde hair she had twisted around the base of her neck to keep out of the way of my nails falls gently back into place by her face and shoulders. I envy her hair. Not just that, I envy her the ability to hide behind her hair if she so chooses. And even more so, I envy her for looking like a woman. 'He was almost finished by Eve's death. It was like he'd been ripped apart and it was only his skin keeping him together. He was permanently angry, he would rage and lash out at everyone – I really don't know how he kept his job. He drank non-stop. I tried to reach him – we all did – but nothing we did would sink in.'

'So, what happened to make him stop?'

She stares into space for a moment. 'I'm not very proud of this, so ... Well, basically, about six months after she died, he went on an all-day bender then *drove* to our house. Rupert went through

143

the roof. I've never seen him so angry, because Jack had not only put his life at risk but the lives of every person on the street. He was scared, too, that Jack would destroy himself, but at that time he was so furious he refused to let Jack stay with us. Rupert bundled Jack into the back of our car and then dropped him off here. I said I'd stay to make sure he was all right; Rupert couldn't because he was still too angry.

'As far as I was concerned, that was it. Jack was going to kill himself and I was going to lose another friend. When Jack woke up and found me in tears he thought I was crying about Eve and started trying to comfort me. I told him I was crying because it felt like he had died too and that, the way he was carrying on, it was only a matter of time.

'And to that, he said, really nastily, that he didn't see the point in living any more. At that moment, I stopped being scared and became incredibly angry. Here was I – and everyone who knew him – trying to help him and he'd all but decided to do away with himself. None of us mattered, just Eve. I told him he was a selfish bastard and left. He turned up later that day to collect his car and to apologise, but I wouldn't even let him in the house. I stood at an upstairs window and threw his car keys at him and told him to ... to fuck off out of my life so it wouldn't hurt so much when he finally did kill himself.

'He was really shocked because that was the first time I'd ever turned on him. He admitted that he'd been selfish, and I said he was all talk and I had to see real change before I became his friend again.'

'Did you mean that?'

'I don't know,' she admits. 'I wanted to. I wanted to shock him out of the state he was in, but I don't know how long Rupert and I could have kept it up. He made the choice, thankfully, to stop the drinking and the rage.' She shakes the bottle of basecoat vigorously between her thumb and forefinger. 'I think he realised he'd hit rock bottom because we were threatening to cut him off. If he'd chosen to carry on, God knows what would have happened.' She shudders and grimaces at the thought. 'He didn't change overnight, you understand, or even become a better person, he simply stopped doing dangerous things. He behaved badly in other ways until you put him in his place. But that, I could handle.

'I'm just glad he stopped before he'd killed or maimed someone in his—'

Grace's cheeks almost explode with scarlet. She uncaps the bottle, dips her head, this time not moving her hair aside but instead using it as a veil to hide her face while she goes back to the manicure. 'I'm sorry,' she says.

'It's OK,' I reply, and it is. The accident wasn't Jack's fault, despite what thoughts and doubts that policewoman had tried to plant in my head.

'Did you ever meet Detective Sergeant Morgan?' I ask Grace.

'*Her!* That ... I hate to speak ill of the law, but she ... She tried to get all sorts of information about Jack out of me. Trying to find out if he was violent, if he could have killed Eve. I soon put her straight. Even if he was violent, she went about it in such a ham-fisted way that if there was anything to tell – which there wasn't – I would have kept it to myself.' Grace pauses in painting and looks up at me. 'Hang on, how do you know about her?'

'She came to take my statement about the crash, but what she was really doing was trying to tell me that Jack murdered Eve and I was probably next on the list.'

'I hope you told her where to go,' Grace says, more outrage in her voice than shows on her face. There's something in the way she drops eye contact while shaking her head at the audacity of the policewoman that unsettles me for a minute or two.

'Of course,' I reply, watching her not look at me.

'She's got some nerve, I'll give her that.'

I can tell the conversation is over from the way Grace slips into silence as she works on my nails. Every stroke she paints onto my nails smoothes on a temporary coolness that shivers a pleasant thrill through me. I watch the brush, flattening out as it moves, covering and protecting my nails from the colour that is to come. I suppose it must be awful to think of your friend being painted as a killer: it's obviously not something she wants to talk about. I don't want to, either, I'm more interested in Jack and the effect Eve had on him.

'What were Jack's relationships like before Eve?' I eventually ask.

'Before Eve? There was no before Eve, I thought you knew that.' Grace is ready to move onto my right hand but pauses as she reaches for it over the table and stares at me. I return her gaze blankly. 'You didn't know?'

'Know what?' I ask.

She keeps her hand covering mine, as if she is about to deliver some terrible news. 'Jack was a virgin when he got together with Eve.'

'*I want to fuck you. Can I fuck you?*' Jack says in my head. That memory often unspools in my mind: the carefully modulated demand in his voice; the way it mingled with his body pressing close to mine; the manner in which he phrased it to make sure he had full consent; his impeccable timing so I had already orgasmed and was more likely to comply ... those were the actions of an expert. Not a—

'You seriously didn't know? I'm not being funny, but what do you and Jack talk about?'

'All the wrong things, apparently. He was really a virgin before Eve?'

Her hair bobs forwards and back as she nods and I wish she would stop it. I wish she would stop having hair that moved. I wish she would stop having hair right in front of my face. 'When Eve died and he started to get himself together, it seemed like all he lived for was to have sex with lots of different women. Before Eve, he wouldn't, didn't. He was waiting for the right woman to take that step with; he always said he had to be completely in love before he had sex.'

'And that was with Eve,' I state.

Grace moves her slender shoulders up and down. 'I guess so. She wasn't a virgin. She was like the rest of us, had at least one notch on her belt. I think it's all his father's fault.'

What does Hector have to do with anything?

'Have you decided on a colour yet?' Grace asks, fanning her fingers over the pots she has carefully set out on the table.

'Red,' I say absently. My mind is still trying to process this new information about Jack. Was that why he was obsessed with her? Most of us still have a soft spot for our first love, and for the first person we ... For Jack that person had been one and the same and he married her. No wonder he couldn't let her go completely.

'Why would it be Hector's fault that Jack was a virgin till Eve?'

Grace stops looking over her colour collection, instead her eyes examine me with surprise and incredulity. 'You two really don't talk much, do you?' she says.

You have no idea, I think at her. 'Not about stuff like this,' I admit.

'Well, I probably shouldn't tell you, but I can't see what harm it'll do since it was such a long time ago. But when Jack turned fifteen, on his actual birthday, his father took him to an upmarket brothel in London and told him to pick a girl.'

'That's *horrible*,' I whisper, once the initial shock has allowed me to speak.

'It gets worse. When Jack couldn't because he was too scared and pretty freaked out, Hector angrily told him off for humiliating him and then wouldn't speak to Jack for a week.'

My hand flies up to my mouth.

'Oh, I know,' Grace says. 'Can you imagine what it's like for me? I've known Hector my whole life, and to find out something like that. It made my skin crawl then and it makes my skin crawl now. He and my father are really good friends so obviously that set me wondering ... which made me freak out, so I had to stop thinking about it.'

'God, you poor things.'

'It really messed with Jack's head. While I can never be certain that my father did anything like that, Jack had proof that his father cheated on his mother. He had to decide whether to keep quiet or risk destroying his family by telling Harriet. All of that on the shoulders of a fifteen-year-old. It's no wonder he didn't want to go near a woman until it was right.'

'I had no idea.'

'Well, you wouldn't, would you? No one looks at a man like Hector and thinks he ... Anyway, Jack staying a virgin was also the perfect revenge on his father because it became this big thing in Hector's social and business circles that he had this good look-ing son who wouldn't "act like a man", whatever that is. Hector was always making dates for Jack and introducing him to women, but Jack wouldn't play along. He had the last laugh on that score.'

'I danced with Hector at our wedding.' *He had his arms around me at our wedding.* I'm trying not to think of all the times I had physical contact with Hector but failing, and that's the main one that keeps coming to mind.

'He insisted on dancing with me at my eighteenth party and at my wedding, which was just blergh! Eve was the smart one with them semi-eloping, eh? She got to avoid all that.'

'Hmmm,' I reply, my mind reeling. The first time I met Hector I actually liked him better than I liked Harriet. I thought Harriet was a bit odd, a bit over the top with how happy she was that Jack had fallen in love again and with how cool she was about being involved or not in the wedding arrangements, when clearly she wanted nothing more than to be involved. Hector was polite and friendly and affable, and he'd come across as the sort of person you'd want Jack to grow into. I couldn't have been more wrong.

'OK, now, back to your nails. Which colour?'

'I told you, red.'

'Red? I have fifteen different reds – you're going to have to be more specific than that.'

'I don't know, Grace, I'm not functioning on full power. I can't even decide whether to wear a bra or not most days and that's kind of essential – this is not. So I'm sorry, I can't decide between the different shades of red. I don't care.'

'You don't care? You wash your mouth out, young lady. I'm not letting a little accident rob you of your beauty duties,' she says sharply. 'Angela and I are going to get you back to your old self in no time.'

'You've talked to Angela about me?'

'Of course!' she says. 'You're our friend: we're going to do whatever it takes to get you well.'

'I am well.'

Grace's eyes, a light blue with hazel flecks, fix on me and force me to stare back at her. 'You know what we mean.'

I immediately drop my gaze. I know what they mean. I thought I was getting better, but Jack's dreams and the police-woman's visit have knocked me back a bit. Or maybe it was a natural comedown, something that would have happened when the reality of my situation fully hit home. I feel so frustrated. I want to grab myself by my shoulders and scream at myself to snap out of it, to stop what I'm doing, what I'm feeling, to *pull myself together*. But I would be shouting at a woman deafened by the horror of what she sees in the mirror, defeated by the fear that the reflection will always be the same, petrified by the knowledge that something like this could have laid her so low. I want to be well, but I cannot see how at the moment.

I reach down, my hand aiming for a nail polish pot. I pick up a dark red. Dark red, like the colour of my scars when they were two days old and I saw them for the first time. 'This one,' I say, holding it out to her as a peace offering, a white flag of surrender so she will leave me alone.

Her cheeks dimple with the smile that moves across her face. Her eyes, as insightful and probing as Angela's, tell me quite clearly they are not fooled. But she'll accept my symbol, for now.

chapter eight

libby

'I'm sure I speak for us all,' Hector says, holding forth from his place by the fireplace, 'when I say that we're extremely happy that both Liberty and Jack are here with us today.'

Around the room, our gathered friends and family nod and murmur in agreement. Everyone is here: Mum, Dad, Grace, Rupert, Angela, Angela's husband Spencer, Paloma, Sandra, Inês, Amy and Vera, Grace's parents, Harriet and, of course, Hector. A few people from Jack's office are also here, as is Rachel, Jack's assistant. Caleb and Benji are still on holiday, as is Jeff, Jack's brother, and his family. I sit on the sofa opposite the fireplace, holding onto Jack's hand as he sits beside me.

'I'm sure you're all as relieved as I am that they're both on the mend,' Hector continues.

For some reason, he has appointed himself the one to do this, to be the leader and to make a speech. In the past, this would not have bothered me but, knowing what I know, I feel a little sullied by it all, as if he is infecting us with the filthiness and shame of his actions. Which is ridiculous, I know, because until it was brought up I had no need to be disgusted with Hector. He was simply Jack's father who was no less or more likeable a person than many of the other people I have met since I became involved with Jack.

'I hope you will join me in raising a toast to Liberty and Jack, and to the wonderful life they have ahead of them,' Hector ends.

'To Libby and Jack,' most of the people in the room chorus, apart from Jack and me. He squeezes my hand in reassurance and I lean into him in reply. We both wear painted on smiles for everyone here. This is all a bit too formal for both of us. When Harriet and Hector suggested a small gathering so that people could all see us in one go and so that we wouldn't be plagued by a stream of visitors, I'd envisaged them and Mum and Dad, maybe Jeff and his family. I hadn't realised they meant all these people, and I hadn't realised they intended to get so much food made and sent over. It was all very not us.

I'd felt awful when I realised yesterday that this was what was happening, because I knew Mum and Dad would have liked to have been involved, and also because it meant facing more people than just close family looking the way I looked. The sentiment was lovely, and their hearts were in the right place, but I'd have preferred a tiny gathering of only our nearest and dearest.

I have a scarf around my head but it is too soon for make-up, so have had to brave people looking like I do. I'd kind of hoped to blend into the background, to sit in a corner, with my face partially hidden and let Jack get on with it. Hector has put paid to that. He's drawn attention to me. The problem is, of course, that he can now do no right in my eyes.

Thankfully, people seem to be entertaining themselves, many of those who don't know me well are keeping their distance and only look at me when they think they can get away with it. Which, in the grand scheme of things, when the alternative is having to carry on a conversation where they're trying not to stare at my scar, is the best option.

'Liberty,' Mum says, with a serious tone, sitting herself down next to me when Jack gets up to refill our glasses. I know she's either going to try to get me to go to see her pastor about praying over my scars to heal them quicker or, worse, she's going to say, 'Why don't we go shopping in London this week for wigs?'

My heart and body sink. 'Mum—' I begin.

'Mrs Rabvena,' Angela says, suddenly appearing from nowhere, 'I was thinking of asking you about the church you go to in London.' She sits down on the other side of my mother, ready to throw herself into the line of fire for me. That's why she is my best friend. 'Can anyone go, and do they do the special all-day services for Easter and Christmas?'

Mum is torn for about thirty seconds between persuading me to go along with her plan to make me look like a woman again, and finding another convert for her church. They are probably thirty of the longest seconds of her life but in the end she chooses God over harassing me.

I'm watching Hector. I'm looking for any hint that he visits or has visited prostitutes. Or that he letches after other women, because I have never before felt uncomfortable around him. I'm trying to see if I can catch him surreptitiously looking at Paloma or one of the other girls I work with, or Grace or Angela, or the wives of the women that Jack works with, or even Rachel. Nothing, absolutely nothing. The only time he notices them is when he's talking to them. Maybe Grace got it wrong?

My eyes flick over to Grace, who is mercilessly questioning Paloma (as she did at our wedding) and probably has her sights set on the other girls for professional beauty secrets. Every so often, I notice that her gaze goes to Hector and, whenever it looks as if he is going to be on the same side of the room as her, she manoeuvres the person she is talking to away from the area, or she ends that conversation and moves to talk to someone else. It's quite obvious, now that I know, that she is avoiding him. That he does indeed make her skin crawl. She hasn't got it wrong.

'How are you, Libby?' Hector is standing in front of me, then he is bobbing down to get to my height.

'Oh, I'm ... I'm fine,' I say, wishing that Mum was harassing me about the wig now, because at least I wouldn't be talking to him. I don't know what to say; I don't know how to act. It's like walking in on someone having sex – which happened to me with

155

my flatmates a few times when I was at university: you can never really get that image of them out of your head. I hadn't seen Hector do it, but the image of him handing over a wad of notes before . . .

'It's good to see you looking so well,' he says, his face and voice full of genuine concern. 'Jack was very worried about you.'

I find Jack with my eyes across the room as I say, 'I know. It's been difficult for both of us.'

'I'm glad you're on the mend. I'm sure it'll be no time at all until you're at full strength and back at work.'

'I hope so,' I say. 'Although I'm not really looking that far ahead at the moment.'

'I understand.'

I spot an empty plate on the table: this is my way out of this conversation. It's all a bit much for me. I put my hand on the arm of the sofa and lever myself upright, just before Hector offers to help me. 'I'll put this in the kitchen,' I tell Hector, seizing the plate. 'Then I'll be right back.'

'Yes, of course,' Hector says, standing and towering over me.

Without looking back, I move through the room and out of the door, managing to breathe a little once I am away from the living room.

In the kitchen, I slide the dish onto the side and tell myself to breathe. It's not as if Hector has done anything to me. It's not as if he had taken me to a brothel. But the idea that he could take anyone to such a place, let alone his fifteen-year-old son, is one of those things that I find it hard to ignore. Hard to reconcile with the man who put his hand on the small of my back and wrapped his other hand over mine and whirled me around the dancefloor to . . . I can't remember the song. How was I to know two years later I'd be trying to remember the tune we'd danced to so I could make myself feel even more sick?

I close my eyes and try to stop the world spinning so fast, and to give my stomach a chance to settle.

'Are you OK?' Harriet asks, causing me to jump and my eyes

to fly open. I immediately turn to the side, and move the plates together, concentrating on piling up the empty dishes. They clink together, the noise suddenly magnified in the quiet of the kitchen, even though there are voices and music in the other room.

'Yes, yes, I'm fine,' I say, trying not to sound flustered. I don't want to look at her, I don't want her to see disgust or the pity I feel for her on my face.

'Are you sure? You seem very nervous.'

'Oh, it's . . . it's . . . this is the first time we've had people over since the . . . erm . . . accident. Just a bit overwhelming. You know how it is.'

'Here, let me help,' she says, and starts stacking plates up for me.

'Thank you,' I say, and move away from the sink to the table.

'You really should rest,' Harriet says.

'You're probably right, but it's hard with a house full of people.'

'Would you like me to ask them to leave?'

Harriet is a lovely person. That's why it kills me that Hector did that to her. And it sounds as if that wasn't the first time. I shudder inside at the thought of it. *Does she know? Does she know and tolerate it, or is she completely clueless?*

I force a smile at her. 'Secretly? I'd love it if you did. But it's not fair; they've come all this way to celebrate the fact that Jack and I are still here, so I shouldn't really wish for a bit of peace and quiet, should I?'

My mother-in-law smiles at me conspiratorially. 'Libby, if you knew the number of times I've thought the same thing at parties at my home . . . It's expected, though, of a top businessman's wife to be the perfect host. I'm a little envious of you sometimes that you haven't allowed yourself to become simply Mrs Jack Britcham, if I may say that.'

'But Jack's nothing like his father when it comes to that world.'

'No, he isn't. But he could be, because the Britcham name means so much in the circles he works in.'

157

'God, do you think Jack feels a bit wronged that I still work and have my own life?' *Did Eve slot into that world so much better than me?*

Harriet beams at me, and it kills me inside again that she's been so ill-treated – whether she knows it or not – by Hector. 'I think it's a credit to Jack's character that he has managed to find not one but two wives who have their own lives.'

'Oh, God, sorry, I've just realised how that sounds. I don't mean you don't have your own life, I just mean—'

'I understand what you mean,' Harriet interrupts. 'And I'm not offended. I have my own life, but it is one that is based around my family and my husband. There's nothing wrong with that choice, just as there's nothing wrong with your choice. That's what I like about the modern world: choice. We all choose what we have to live with.'

My hand automatically goes up to my hairless head: the choice I'd made because of the choice another person made. My loss because of someone else's decision to be selfish and stupid. This is why I am not enjoying the party – it's not something I would have *chosen*; it's not the sort of party I would have thrown. And this isn't a party, it's the wake that would have happened if we'd died in the crash.

'Actually, Harriet, would it be really awful if I asked you to get rid of everyone?' I ask. I don't like to feel weak and powerless: I don't like not being in control of my life and my destiny. I don't like having my choice taken away from me.

'Not at all, Liberty,' Harriet says, her eyes loaded with concern. That's a look I don't like seeing, because behind the concern there is also pity. 'Not at all.' She pats my hand on her way out of the door.

'Are you OK, beautiful?' Jack asks after everyone – including Harriet and Hector, who respectively stayed behind to clear up and talk to Jack – have gone. I heard Mum kicking up a fuss about staying to help tidy up but Dad wouldn't let her – he said they needed to get back to help an elderly neighbour. Poor Mum had been so conflicted, but when Dad actually got up and went to get his keys, she, thankfully, chose the neighbour – and needing to be up early for church in the morning. I couldn't have withstood another conversation about getting a wig. A wig was not on the agenda, and that was a choice I *had* made not based on that driver's actions.

'Just tired,' I say to Jack, allowing him to assist me in easing myself down onto the bed.

'Here, let me help,' he says, and gently tugs off my shirt, which I've been struggling to remove. I've left it too long between painkiller doses and my muscles are starting to protest at not being properly soothed, and so movement is hard. I'd known it was time for a dose of painkillers, but I couldn't risk leaving my hiding place in the downstairs shower room for them – not when the goodbyes would then have lasted longer than the party. Gently, Jack takes off my T-shirt. 'Lie back,' he says, taking my hands so he can help me lie down.

Leaning over me, his scent fills my senses as he undoes the button of my jeans and unzips me. 'If I didn't know you better, Jack Britcham,' I say, drowsy with pain, 'I'd say you were getting some kind of cheap thrill out of this.'

He smiles sadly at me as he gently takes off my jeans and then stops to look over my body. I know what he's seeing because I looked at my body this morning, too. My skin is black, blue, purple and yellow all along my left side. The bruises radiate outwards towards the centre of my body like paint spilled onto brown paper. Those are 'multiple contusions'. My ribcage is still taped up to support the hairline fracture of my rib. I have the scar from my spleen operation, which is slowly healing, and other smaller grazes and scratches, most of which have scabbed over.

I see him swallow the lump of emotion at the back of his throat, as he tries to stop his face from crumpling with tears. This is why I've mainly undressed for bed alone, to spare him this sight knowing it'll rip him up inside.

'Do you want your bra on or off?' he asks, even though his

159

chest is starting to heave as he tries deep, slow breathing to control himself.

'Off,' I say. I can't wear it for too long during the day because it digs into me and aggravates the bruising.

Tenderly he removes that too, and then has to press his lips together to stop himself letting out a sob at the bruising on my breast. 'I'm so sorry,' he says quietly as he reaches for my pyjama bottoms.

'Shhh,' I whisper. The aching is spiralling slowly but surely into intense pain, and it's hard to talk, hard to breathe. 'It's all right. I'm all right. It's not your fault.' I close my eyes and am no help at all as Jack dresses me in my stripy pyjamas.

'Libby, Libby,' his voice says gently while his hand strokes my face. 'Come on, sit up, take your tablets, and then we'll go to bed.'

'It's early,' I say, allowing him to prop me up. 'You can stay up.'

My hand feels weak and not really connected to my body as I move the two tablets in my palm to my mouth. I spill a little water as I raise the glass to my mouth and Jack has to steady me. Tablets taken – although the jerk of my head to get them down was probably not a good idea – Jack moves me to my side of the bed, where he has pulled back the covers, then lays me in place.

He covers me up, then stands in front of me as he quickly strips.

'You're gorgeous, you know that,' I say as my eyes flutter open and closed like the up-and-down movements of a bird's wings. 'Course you know that, everyone knows that.'

The last thing I remember is feeling Jack's arms around me as he snuggles up behind me and carefully wraps his arms around my body.

'I'm sorry I hurt you,' he whispers in my ear before the pain and the tablets take over and move me away from Jack and from consciousness.

chapter nine

libby

The door to the cellar is barely open before Butch has darted past me and scampered down the stairs.

'Oi, you!' I shout after him as he is swallowed up by the black-ness down there. 'If you fall down in the dark and hurt yourself you'll get no sympathy from me.' We both know that's not true. He's left extra special 'presents' in both my and Jack's shoes and he's managed to simper his way out of trouble. I'd be devastated if he was hurt.

I switch on the light and suddenly I can see down into the cellar. The noise of Butch's paws on the stone rises up the steps at me. It is pretty nice as cellars go: the floor has been relaid, and the walls damp-proofed and painted white, even the old fireplace is restored and fitted with a Victorian black iron surround and grate. The cellar actually extends underneath all of the house, but the other chambers have been bricked up and nothing done with them. It's also the only place in the house that I'm usually too afraid to visit.

By the time I have stiffly negotiated the stairs, Butch, who has been trying to get down here for over a week, is in front of the old wooden cupboard pushed in the corner right at the back of the cellar up against the wall. His black and brown white-topped paws are almost a blur as they scratch away at the cupboard doors.

It's because of this cupboard that I have braved the cellar, and Butch seems more desperate to get in than I am. The doors of the cupboard are a smooth, pale wood with a keyhole at its centre, holding the two doors together. It is locked, and apparently there is no key.

A huge wave of disappointment swells inside me as I remember that the conversation about this cupboard was the first time I realised that Jack not only could but would lie to me. A month after we were married, when I'd had no problems going down into the cellar, I had been down here looking around and obviously couldn't fail to notice the large, locked cupboard so naturally asked Jack about it. He'd looked at me a little vacantly and said, 'Oh, that old thing? Is it still there? Had forgotten about it, to be honest.'

'What's in it?' I'd asked.

He'd shrugged and glanced back at the TV, seeming even more vacant than he had been a few minutes ago. 'Just stuff, bits and bobs.'

'Aren't you even curious?' I'd pressed.

'No, not really. Don't even know where the key is.'

Like a door slowly being opened to shine light on the other side, it dawned on me why he was being so vague. 'Does it have Eve's stuff in it?' I asked gently, and he flinched like he always did when I said her name.

He took a while to answer, instead staring at the window as if he wished he could open it and fly away. Slowly his head moved up and down as he whispered, 'Yeah.'

'Right,' I said.

'Sorry,' he said.

'It's fine. I don't want you to get rid of her belongings if you're not ready. It'd just be nice to know, seeing as I'm living here now.'

He nodded. 'Yeah, you're right. Sorry. I'll sort it out soon.'

'When you find the key, of course.'

He turned his head to look at me, and I stared back at him

because I did not want him to think he'd got away with that lie. He didn't need to lie. All he had to do was tell me, I would understand. 'Yeah, when I find the key.' He went back to watching the window, and I curled my feet up under me on the sofa and went back to watching the television while reading the newspaper. We hardly exchanged more than a handful of words for the rest of the night.

Nearly two years later, the cupboard is still full and locked, and my aversion to the cellar, which began right about then, is still in place. Because of the way he'd been so secretive about it, it felt like Eve was down here. Buried here. While I always seem to 'feel' her around the rest of the house, and often feel like an intruder when I walk into some rooms – especially the ones that haven't been repainted and re-carpeted – down here it is as if I am walking on her grave, and any second now her hand will reach up out of the earth and grab hold of my ankle.

That thought has me climbing back up a few of the stairs, further away from the cupboard, closer to the escape route. But I need to see if I can get into the cupboard to find out what's inside, if it will give me any insight into their marriage.

Automatically, I glance back at the door at the top of the stairs (*what if it swings shut and the key somehow turns itself?*) before I gingerly place a foot on the solid, stone floor of the basement. I pause, waiting for Eve's hand to appear and to reach for my ankle. Nothing happens so I go over towards the cupboard, causing Butch to flee, knocking aside a few boxes, bumping and rattling both the large wooden wine rack and the fireplace, then darting past me to another part of the cellar. He's made a bit of a mess, caused a lot of dust to fly up which makes me cough, which in turn makes my ribs ache, but I'm not going to give up.

Grace's revelation about Jack being a virgin before Eve set me on the road to thinking about why he was still obsessed with her. And with the dreams, with the way he won't talk about her, I have to find out what is going on. Why he can't let her go. Because, as I am having to admit, all roads lead to Eve. They

165

always have, they always will. So maybe I can find out what I need from this cupboard. I have tried the Internet and there is nothing except a few small mentions about her death, and nothing at all about her before she became Eve Britcham. I could ring the policewoman and ask her, but I'd rather die than give her that power over Jack or me, so I have nothing to lose by seeing if this cupboard is unlocked.

It might be. Jack might have been down here recently, going through her things. He might be taking them out and finding comfort in them, trying to capture notes of her perfume, or holding items and replaying the memories, or even re-reading love letters. If it were me, and I had lost him, I would do the same. I don't think I'd be able to completely let go. If he has gone through her belongings recently, he might have forgotten to lock the cupboard behind him. Failing that, I could maybe convince him that I'd got hold of an axe that went out of control in my hands, cleaving the doors apart in the process. Or even that I tripped and accidentally pushed it over, thereby breaking it apart in the fall.

The keyhole can't be that strong a lock, but it's enough to show any attempt to break into it. The doors have no handles, probably not put on when it was constructed, so you need the key to unlock it and then to lever the doors open. They are still locked. Of course they are.

Butch is still sniffing around the rest of the cellar, searching for something. 'Go on, Butch, find me the key,' I tell him. 'It's here somewhere, I'm sure of it. Go on, Butch, you can do it.'

Butch stops what he's doing to shoot me a dirty look, then goes on about his business. 'Yeah, I know, I was being ridiculous,' I say.

I look around at the brick walls, painted white, the flagstones laid on the floor, the ceiling also painted white with a single light bulb at its centre. There are shelves on two of the walls, and the tall, mahogany wine cupboard is near the steps. Butch is focusing his attention there, sniffing, scratching at the flagstones. Cobwebs line the place, most of them dusty and ancient-looking as if the spiders that made them are long gone. There is dust covering most things.

Well, that was pointless, I think to myself, as Butch knocks over another box. *Might as well tidy up.* Most of the boxes are white document boxes where Jack stores old paperwork. Over the last couple of years, my stuff should have been moved down here, but it never felt right, what with it being Eve's place, so I keep my bank statements and things up in the office. These boxes are too heavy for me to lift, not unless I want to open up an internal wound, so I push at them.

As I am pushing, I notice that Butch has knocked the semi-circle back plate of the big iron fireplace, so that it is leaning backwards. It is only pushed into that position when a real fire is burning, to let out the smoke.

'You're such a messy pup,' I say to him as I go to it, hook a finger in the hole at the top of the semi-circle to pull it back into place. As I do so, my finger touches something crinkly and plastic-feeling. Confused, I remove my finger and push the plate a little further back so it is closer to horizontal than vertical, then look into the cavity beyond.

On the ledge inside the fireplace wall I see a flash of white in the pitch black. A thrill of excitement and surprise bolts through me. *What is this?* My mouth is dry and my heart is racing as I slowly lower myself to my knees and peer into the blackness.

It is white, but I can't really see what it is too clearly. Without thinking through the consequences, I reach in and my hand touches plastic. It doesn't crackle under touch, so it must be old and disintegrating. Carefully, I take it out.

It is a carrier bag, an old flimsy one from a shop in London the name of which I don't recognise, but it has the old 01 dialling code on it, and is covered in debris that has fallen down the fire-place. It is coming apart in my hands, leaving pieces of white and dirt on my fingertips. I unwrap it, the plastic falling to pieces until I come to another plastic bag, thicker this time. It is racing green in colour with no writing on it, and it has weathered the time in its hiding place much better so it's easier to open it up to its full size and pull the contents out. Inside is a thick bundle, about A5 in size, wrapped in black velvet and tied up with a pink ribbon.

This stops me in my tracks. Someone has gone to a lot of trouble to hide this bundle; should I be opening it? Should I really look? Shouldn't I give it to Jack since it was probably his house when it was placed here?

But if I give it to Jack, there's a chance he'll never tell me what it is – he'll fob me off with tales of lost keys and not remembering.

I turn to Butch, to ask his advice, and find he has gone. Abandoned me to return upstairs, probably for a lie down. Or maybe he could see the way this was turning out and wanted to escape while he could.

Sitting on the dusty floor, among the white boxes and beside the cupboard, I stare at the item in my hands. I probably shouldn't do this. But then, what have I got to lose? My husband? He's slipping further away from me with each passing day. My certainty in the world? That went the moment that driver made his choice.

Just do it, I order myself and, before I can change my mind again, I pull apart the ribbon and unwrap the thick black velvet.

I gasp when I see what's inside, and it's quickly clear I have just made the biggest mistake of my life.

jack

I wonder what would happen if I told her? If I told her what had happened directly after the crash, what I did, I wonder what would happen. Would Libby forgive me? Would she turn me away? Or would she think about it and then reject me?

'Libby,' I say to her over dinner.

She is distracted, has been all evening since I came home and I'm a little scared that she has remembered. Or that she is on the way to remembering. It'd be better if it came from me, surely? It'd have less sting, would cause less upset if I told her first. Like all the little secrets that Eve didn't tell me straight away – if I'd found out for myself, rather than hearing them from her lips, things would have been a whole lot worse than they were.

'Hmmm?' Libby raises her head from staring at her dinner plate and stares at me as you would a stranger who knows your name but you're not sure how or why.

'I, um . . .' *Tell her, you idiot, tell her now. Do it quickly and she'll thank you for it.* She blinks those big, liquid brown eyes at me, her bisected face an unreadable blank. 'Are you OK?'

She nods, then returns her gaze to the plate in front of her, moving food around with her fork.

I can't do it. This is not the time to do it. Butch comes to me and snuggles against my legs. He knows it's not the right time, too. She has something on her mind and it could be because she knows, or it could be something completely different. Whatever it is, it's not the right time for me to do this. To come clean and smash up what we've got.

libby

I have Eve's diaries.

The Eve. *Her* diaries. The best insight into her I am ever going to get. And I know it's wrong. It would kill me if someone found then read the mad ramblings of my life that I put down into a diary.

Also, she asks in the letter she left at the top of the diaries to burn them if she's dead. But then . . .

For the past two days, I've been cleaning and dusting as much of the cellar as I can, while I've been turning over in my head what I should do, scared of what I'll find if I read them, terrified of what will happen if I don't.

What do you do when you've got the answers to all your questions in your hands, but to read those answers would be betraying someone you've never met? Someone who never did a thing wrong to you, so why should you violate them so?

'*I would read them, personally,*' a voice says. It's a voice in my head, of course. But it is also the voice of the dark-haired woman in front of me, sitting on one of the stack of boxes, wearing a pink dress with several lines of sequins down the front. '*You want to find out about me, so there you are: the perfect opportunity.*'

I stare at her. She is exactly like the picture I saw of her on her wedding day. She is radiant: her long, shiny dark hair loose

171

around her shoulders, her eyes big and soft and an unusual not-quite blue – almost indigo. Her skin is flawless and without make-up, her mouth is a perfect bow and striking without lipstick. Her dress is the perfect fit, almost as if it was designed and made with her in mind. She looks like that because that's the only picture I've ever seen of her.

When I first read the letter on top of the diaries, it seemed as if she was talking directly to me – I was not reading, she was sitting in front of me, telling me what was on the page.

My gaze wanders down to the diaries, to the letter. The top diary is a reporter's notebook and the rest of the diaries evolve over time from reporter's notebooks to bound books to a beautifully soft, suede-like, blue diary.

'*Are you her?*' she asks me, just like she did yesterday.

I say nothing, continue to stare at the words on the page, hoping they will blur under my scrutiny and disappear.

'*Are you her?*' she repeats. '*Are you the one he's with now?*'

Slowly, I nod my head. Yes, I am. I am the one he's with now.

Once I do that, she seems to settle back and starts to speak. And I let myself listen.

chapter ten

eve

28th February 2003

Are you her? Are you the one he's with now? Is that why you've come looking for me?

If you aren't reading this letter fifty or sixty years from now, then it's likely that I'm dead. Probably murdered.

Please don't be upset by that; it probably won't have been too much of a surprise to me – not with the life I have lived. But if you have these diaries because you came looking for me, and you were clever enough to think like me and find them, or even if you came across them by accident, please, please can I ask you a favour? Please will you burn them without reading them? Please?

I do not want anyone else to know these things. I wrote them for me. I know I should probably burn them myself, but it'd feel like suicide, killing a part of myself. And, in everything I've done, everything I've gone through, I would not kill myself so I can't destroy these diaries. Maybe you can.

I say 'maybe' because if you're with him then you'll want to know about him, you'll want to know if he really is dangerous and if he was

175

the one to murder me, so while I don't want you to, I can't blame you for reading on.

There's not much else I can add, except that I hope you do not feel sorry for me. I have lived a life and even though I knew great pain, I also knew great love. Some people can live a long, long time without ever experiencing that. I am lucky.

I wish you well, whoever you are.

Love,
Eve

7th December 1987

My name is Eve Quennox. I am sixteen.

I used to live in Headingley, which is in Leeds, with my mum, but now I live in London. It's a long story about how I came to London, but I'm here now and I'm going to make the most of it.

My mum used to be my best friend. She's not any more. And I don't call her 'Mum' any more. We fell out two weeks ago and after that I couldn't think of her as 'Mum', only the person who gave birth to me, my mother. But, before that, she really was my best friend.

My dad died of a heart attack when I was five years old. I still remember him a little bit. I remember that he used to laugh a lot and my mother used to laugh a lot when he was here.

I used to live next door to my Uncle Henry and my Aunt Mavis. They weren't my real aunt and uncle, but I called them that because they had known me for ages and ages, and they knew my dad. Earlier this year they both died. Uncle Henry died of a heart attack, too, and then a week later Aunt Mavis died. I heard my mother ask the doctor if Aunt Mavis had died of a broken heart and he said yes. I was really sad when they died and then things just got worse and worse at home, mainly because of my mother's new boyfriend, so I had to leave.

176

I didn't take much with me. I took the green bag Uncle Henry had given me when I was nine. He had been in the army, it was one of his prized possessions, and he had given me it. I took a few of my clothes, but not many. I took my red-bead rosary that Aunt Mavis had given me, I took my post office savings book, and from one of the photo albums in the drawer at the bottom of the wardrobe I took a small picture of my dad, my mother and me. It was my favourite picture of the three of us. We are standing outside our house, I'm about two-years-old, I have on a blue cord coat with fur around the hood, blue tights and black, shiny shoes. I've got a white hat on my head and white mittens on my hands. I'm holding my mother's hand. She's wearing a long black winter coat and a furry black and white leopard-print hat with a black peak. I'm also holding onto my dad's hand. He's dressed in a suit and has a long black coat on, too. We're all smiling for the camera but, if you look closely, you can see that my parents are looking at each other from the corners of their eyes, grinning at each other. They're in love. That's what love is about. I've always believed that that's what love is about. Not what my mother had with her new boyfriend.

I don't have a boyfriend at the moment. I had one, he was called Peter and I really, really, really loved him. We even made love. I liked all his family and I could go to his house to get away from my mother's new boyfriend, but then Peter's dad lost his job and the only one he could find was in Canada. We both cried and cried when he had to leave. My mother came with me on the bus to the airport and slept on the floor of my bedroom that night because I was so upset. Peter and I wrote for a while, but it wasn't the same and the letters took so long to arrive that in the end we just stopped. I still love him, though. I think I always will.

I took Peter's letters with me when I came to London but I burned them the first chance I got because I didn't want anyone else to read them. That's why I have to be so careful with this diary. I don't want anyone to find it.

I left everything else behind because I had to leave quickly two weeks ago. I told my mother everything, all the stuff I'd been keeping secret for two years and I thought she believed me. I thought she was going to make her boyfriend leave. But she didn't. He was sitting there at the breakfast table the next morning, so I just packed up and left. I saw my mother a couple of times, but she wouldn't make him leave, so I realised I had to get as far away as possible.

So, anyway, here I am in London and starting this diary. One of my old teachers told us once that if we wanted to be a writer when we grew up we should start by keeping a diary. She said we should practise writing every day and that we should write down conversations with the speech marks, like they have in books. That would give us an idea of how people talk.

I don't know if I want to be a writer. I like to read but I don't know if I could ever write a book. I thought starting a diary might be good for me to get my thoughts down when I don't have anyone to talk to, and to record what happens next in my life.

I was quite excited as I got the bus to London. I'd spoken to Dawn who I'd been friends with in fifth form in school until her family moved down here. She has her own flat and has said I can sleep on the sofa until I get a job and my own little place.

It's dead nice here. I'm living in somewhere called Kentish Town, which is really near a massive park called Regent's Park. Dawn works most nights in a club in town, so she's out a lot and I've been signing on at temp agencies all around London. I haven't had much luck since I don't have any qualifications beyond O Levels and I'm not that good at typing. I'm too young to work behind a bar and I don't have any experience of waitressing. Some of the agencies are nice about possible cleaning jobs, but no one's really that keen on employing me because I'm so young. They think I'm going to leave when school starts again even though I've said I'm not going back to school. I'd love to go back, but to do that I'd have to move back home – there's no way I could get my own place and not work. Everything is so expensive down here!

I've asked Dawn to ask if there are any cleaning shifts going at her place but she's always forgetting. She comes in dead late and sleeps most of the day. She always looks wrung out, even after she's been asleep until the afternoon.

I try to help out as much as possible – I clean up and make food, which I buy. She doesn't like to eat much because she says in the bar where she works it's all about looking good to make sure you get the best tips.

I'd be lonely if I wasn't so excited about seeing London. I get the bus right into the centre sometimes and then just walk about, looking at places, marvelling at how BIG everything is. It's so full of people and the buildings are old and gorgeous. I expected everything to feel dirty but it doesn't. The roads and the constant traffic feel like the blood in your veins; the people on the pavements are like a secondary circulation system – the lymph system. I remember reading about the lymph system in a book I got out from the library – it's much slower, much closer to the skin than your normal circulation system but just as important. I love being able to launch myself into the stream, the circulation, and to move along with and be moved along by it. I love feeling a part of it and then, when it gets too much, when I want to stop moving, I can just step out, sit in a park, sit in a square, sit at a bus stop until I'm ready to join it all again.

I need to find a job soon, though. I'm going through my savings really quickly. I give Dawn some cash towards the bills and stuff, and she says she's fine, she doesn't need it, but I feel bad. I like to pay my way in the world, that's something my mother taught me. She made me pay for all my trips to the cinema with Peter so he wouldn't ever think I owed him anything. So even though Dawn doesn't want my money, I give it to her all the same. It's only fair.

So, that's me up to date. I'm in London, 'the big smoke' people call it. I like it here. I think I'm going to stay, as long as I can get a job. Fingers crossed.

Love,
Eve

PS Sent my mother a postcard saying that I was OK and in London. I didn't tell her where, but I didn't want her to worry. I almost wrote that if she ever got rid of her boyfriend I'd come home in an instant, but I didn't because I didn't want to hurt her any more. And I wasn't sure if that was true. I'm not sure I could ever leave London now, if I'm honest.

12th February 1988

I've got a job!

It's all happened so quickly, I can't quite believe it. I was sitting in Dawn's flat getting ready to go out for a walk when the phone rang and it was a woman from one of the smaller agencies I'd been to. She was older than my mother and seemed really nice and concerned about me when I went to see her.

She's dead posh and said on the phone, 'Eve, darling, I've got a client who is an old friend who is in desperate need of someone to do some filing and photocopying at her little business in King's Cross. I said I had just the person. Do I? Are you free right now?'

'Me?' I said to her, wondering if she was talking to me.

'Yes, darling, who else would I be talking to on the phone called Eve? You're not on drugs, are you? I can't abide people who take drugs.'

'No, I'm not on drugs.'

'Well, darling, grab a pen and write down the name and address of the company, then get yourself over there straight away. And, darling, make sure you wear a nice suit. Ophelia, that's the name of your contact, but you must call her Mrs Whitston, can't abide sloppiness. If you do well today, there's every chance I can persuade her to keep you on.'

I didn't have a suit, and I didn't have time to buy one, so I had to borrow one from Dawn, who was still in bed in the bedroom. I didn't want to wake her up, but I had to go to this job interview even if I only had the slightest chance of getting it.

After taking down the address, I told her I'd be there and that I wouldn't let her down, then hung up. I knew Dawn would understand, so I crept to her bedroom door and opened it a crack.

The first thing that hit me was the smell. It was so strong and overpowering – it smelt like booze, I think, and something else. As if something had been burning. I didn't have time to work out what, I just focused on the wardrobe at the back of the room. Her bedroom floor was littered with clothes, damp-looking towels – she always *always* had a bath when she got in – as well as books, magazines and upturned shoes. She was like a face-down naked starfish in her bed with her arms spread wide and her face smooshed into the pillow, her long brown hair obscuring most of her face. I crept across the room, avoiding as much of the stuff on the floor as I could. In the wardrobe, I found more clothes – she probably wouldn't have been able to fit all the clothes she owned in it – but a lot of the stuff hanging up was bikinis or posh spangly underwear. I stared at them for ages, wondering why she would hang them up and leave most of her other clothes lying on the floor.

But I didn't have time to wonder for too long. I spotted a black skirt suit and a white shirt and unhooked them from the rail, then carefully made my way out again.

I left her a note in case she woke up before I got in, and then I left.

The job was working in a small accountancy firm not too far from Dawn's flat. I did everything they asked – photocopying, making tea, putting invoices in envelopes, going to the post office – and at the end of the day they said I could come back again in the morning. Mrs Nixdon, the woman from the agency, was so happy with me and said that they were very hard people to please, so if they wanted me back I must have done something very right. My official job title is Office and Admin Assistant, and I actually love it. I only have one person above me – the office manager called Maggie – and she's really nice and easygoing. She said to me that if I worked hard, I might be able to get a day release to go back to college and take my A Levels, especially if I think I might want to become an accountant.

So, I've been working there for over two months – Dawn said I could have all her suits as she wasn't ever going to use them – and, now I've got a job, I can start looking for a place of my own. All the walking I've been doing has been really helpful because now I know little pockets of London really well and can take my time looking for somewhere to live.

Dawn's been fantastic. She's seemed more tired than usual recently and stays in bed later and later, but she keeps saying how pleased she is for me. 'I'm so glad one of us managed to get a happy ending,' she keeps saying, then she'll collapse into fits of laughter. But I don't think she's being mean; I really think she means it.

So, that's me. A proper job and everything.

I wrote to my mother again, told her about my new job and that I was going to be looking for somewhere to live, but I'd still be at Dawn's for a while. I sent her card and a Marks & Spencer gift voucher for Christmas and got nothing in return. Not even a card. She didn't reply to the letter about the job, just like she hasn't replied to any of my other letters and postcards. I was wondering for a while if she was getting them or if her boyfriend was throwing them away. But I've written to Rhian from school as well and she said that when she ran into my mother, she had been raving to Rhian about the great time I was having in London. She can talk to other people about me but not to me. Sad, huh?

Never mind. Maybe she'll call or write when I get my own place. She could even come and visit if she came on her own. I don't think I could go back there again. This is my home now. I really am happy here.

Love,
Eve

31st March 1988

Just got in from a night out with the people from work.

It's so nice to work with people and to earn money. I sometimes forget that I'm only sixteen because they're all so nice to me and they treat me like I'm one of them. We went out for a meal in Chinatown, and Dominic, one of the partners, was dead nice and sat next to me and told me what everything was on the menu. It was so tasty. I've never had proper sweet and sour pork before.

So nice to come home to my own place. Dawn was great, but towards the end she was just so unpredictable. She'd sleep all the time and then would be grouchy and grumpy when she got up. She seemed to have a permanent cold and was sniffing all the time, but thankfully I never caught it. She was always pale, too, and sickly looking.

My place is a flat on the main road in Caledonian Road, near King's Cross. I was lucky because one of the people at work knew someone who needed to move really urgently but she couldn't unless she found someone to move in. The rent is dead cheap considering I have a living room, a smallish bedroom, a little kitchen bit at the end of the living room and – get this – a bathroom with a bath and a shower over the bath. It's not perfect, and a little damp, but it's mine. The windows are huge and I can climb out of the bedroom window onto a small roof terrace with a railing around it where I can see for miles over London. It's great because in the summer, when the mornings and evenings are light, I can walk to and from work. All the furniture is a bit old and lumpy or grubby, but I got some good cleaning stuff and the place scrubbed up a treat. The landlord was a bit unsure about having me as a tenant and he made it absolutely clear that he wouldn't take anyone on benefits, but I had the deposit and a month's rent in advance saved up so he said it was OK.

How many other sixteen year olds get to have a place to themselves in London? Not many, I bet.

Wrote to my mother again and told her. But haven't heard anything back. Doesn't mean I'll give up, though. She has to talk to me sometime. In a way, it's not such a bad thing that what happened happened. I'd never have moved down here and experienced all this if I hadn't left when I did.

Love,
Eve

Lots of worry and gossip going on at work at the moment.

There are rumours going round that the partners are selling their business to a larger firm. No one knows for certain, but Ophelia and Dominic are out all the time 'in meetings' and Maggie is doing almost all the correspondence nowadays. I'm not allowed to see any of their letters or go to any of the meetings. 'You'll be all right,' Beatrix said to me the other day. She's one of the junior accountants. 'They'll always need admin doing. It's people like me that have to worry; the bigger firms will have their own people they're training up.'

Haven't written to my mother for a while, don't want to worry her. Saw Dawn the other day. She was getting into a car with a man who didn't look like her boyfriend, Robbie. It was dead weird because the car pulled up a little away from her and she walked up to it then got in the back. He drove a little further away and then stopped. It looked like the man turned around in his seat to talk to her, then he drove off again. She looks so thin. I know she didn't eat much before, but now it looks like she doesn't eat at all. She didn't see me and, in a way, I'm glad. I'm not sure she'd want me to see her looking like that.

Hope all the work stuff turns out to be a storm in a teacup, as Aunt Mavis used to say.

Eve

Well, it's happened. Ophelia and Dominic made the announcement yesterday.

They gathered us all around and Maggie had been out to buy us some sparkling wine – I was allowed a small glass – and they told us they'd sold the business to a large accountancy firm based in The

City. They call the place where all the businesses and money markets and the stock exchange is 'The City'.

Everyone was shocked but not very surprised. We all clapped and smiled, but EVERYONE was worried about their jobs, you could tell. Despite what Beatrix said, I'm worried too. I think I'd be stupid not to be.

Ophelia told everyone it was a very exciting move and that we should all do our best to make the transition as smooth as possible because we would be moving to The City. She thanked us all for our hard work and said we should pat ourselves on the back for helping to make the company such a success that a company as prestigious as the one that bought us out wanted us.

I didn't want to say anything but I wasn't sure if anyone else had noticed that Ophelia didn't tell us at any point that there wouldn't be any job losses.

Please God, let me keep my job.

Eve

25th June 1988

Why does everything go belly up just when you think it's all going so well? We moved offices, and Maggie and I were really involved with it all. We had to do most of the organising because even though the company had been sold they still had to get on with every-day business. Lots of people were calling in 'sick' – meaning going for interviews – and we'd been picking up the slack, as Maggie called it.

Anyway, we got the move done and everything and we were all really pleased. Maggie and I had been trying to talk to Ophelia about our jobs but she just kept saying she'd look after us.

We had to apply for our jobs again. The big firm had their own office manager and lots of assistants, so Maggie was going to have to take a demotion – which she had to apply for – and I was going to have to apply for a job that another girl on trial was also doing.

That was two weeks ago – Ophelia kept saying she'd done her best and her hands were tied when we managed to get to speak to her. Neither of us got our jobs. Maggie was so hurt because she'd worked for Ophelia for years. I didn't think I'd get the job because everyone knew the other girl. I worked really hard and was always first in and last out, but it made no difference.

So there I was, with no job. Maggie was too upset to say anything much. I could tell she wanted to give Ophelia a piece of her mind but couldn't because she needs a reference from her.

I've gone to a few job agencies and they've been more positive than last time now that I've got more experience and a nice reference – which is what I think Ophelia meant when she said she'd take care of us. But it's not as if she had anything bad to say, is it? I mean, she couldn't exactly write, 'Sits on her bum all day eating chocolate and burping,' could she? I ALWAYS worked hard. So did Maggie.

The thing is, everyone keeps telling me there's a recession on and employers are making do without temps and aren't really taking on new staff. I could go and sign on, but then I'd lose this flat because the landlord told me absolutely no benefits. I've got enough for next month's rent but I need to get a job fast.

About the landlord: I am soooooo stupid! I rang to tell him that I'd lost my job but I could pay the rent and he was over here like a shot – literally, less than an hour later he was at the door. He wanted to check the place over, which was fine – I haven't done anything to it. In fact, I'm quite proud of how nicely I've kept it. I've even cleaned away all the mould and painted the bathroom again. He looked around and didn't say anything really. Then he sat down next to me on the sofa and asked me what happened with my job. I told him, like the idiot I am, pouring my heart out to him and he was so sympathetic.

'It tough out there, Eve,' he said. 'I no envy you trying to find a job. But I sure you get something.' I don't know where he's from but my favourite thing about him is his accent and broken English.

'Thanks,' I said.

Then, the next thing I know, he's only got his hand on my knee, hasn't he? I mean, really! And then he says, 'In meantime, we come to some kind of arrangement?'

And I said, like the idiot I am sometimes, 'What sort of arrangement?' while trying to get his hand off my knee without offending him.

And he goes, 'Bunk-up or two once a month – rent sorted.'

Honest to goodness, that's exactly what he said! Well, I wanted to tell him where to stick his bunk-ups but I couldn't, could I? I need a place to live, so I said, 'That's very nice of you, but I've got a couple of interviews lined up for tomorrow' – I hadn't at all – 'so I wouldn't want to put you out.'

'Ahh, well,' he said, not at all bothered, 'you change mind or want extra cash, let me know.'

He seriously expected me to call him for a 'bunk-up' so I could pay my rent. I'd rather live on the street.

Why is it all so hard sometimes? Everything was ticking along really well and now this. Which means my home's in danger. And the landlord expects me to – urgh!

OK, I'm going to be more positive. I'm sure it'll all turn out all right if I get out there every day and look for a job. I don't for one second want to be in a situation where I start thinking about his offer.

I wonder, though, how many of his other tenants have taken him up on it? Urgh, the thought of his belly jiggling away and his fat hands on your skin . . . I've only ever done it with Peter, and that's because I loved him.

It's weird to think that some people not only do it when they're not in love with someone but they do it to make money or to pay their rent. Weird and sad. I could *never* do that.

Might ring Dawn and see if she can get me any cleaning shifts at her place.

Eve

PS With everything that's been going on, I'd completely forgotten it was my birthday today. My mother forgot as well, it'd seem, and you'd think if there was one person who'd remember it'd be her. Happy Birthday to me.

libby

Butch, who has been sitting patiently beside me on the floor of the cellar, suddenly cocks his head then scampers to his feet, as he does every evening when Jack comes home.

Is it really that late? I think as Butch bounds up the stairs to go and wait for Jack to come in. I don't have time to tie the diaries back up in the ribbon, only to wrap them in their velvet cloth, return them to the plastic bag and then to replace them in the fireplace. I need to be careful because if I don't put them on the ledge in the fireplace and they fall onto the floor I won't be able to get them again without having the whole surround removed.

From upstairs the sounds of Butch's happy barking floats down and I pull the fireplace plate into place. Then, thinking quickly, I grab a bottle of wine and start to climb the stairs.

Jack's waiting for me at the top with Butch happily running in circles around his feet.

'Are you OK?' Jack asks.

'Yeah, fine, why do you ask?' I reply, avoiding eye contact and moving away from the cellar door.

'You don't usually go down to the cellar unless absolutely necessary,' he says, still puzzled.

I hold up the bottle of red I'd grabbed. 'I thought I'd get us a bottle of wine to go with dinner.'

'Can you drink with your tablets?' he asks.

'Probably not,' I say, 'but I can watch you.'

Jack stares at me and I stare at him. My heart is racing in my chest. I've never really kept anything from him before; I've always been honest and open. This doesn't feel right, but it's necessary because Jack won't tell me anything about her. And with each night that we spend in the same bed, with him thrashing about and calling for Eve, the more I believe that he is hiding something about what happened during or directly after the crash. Actually, the more I *know* deep inside that it isn't trauma that is giving him nightmares: it's guilt.

We continue to stare at each other, both of us obviously with something to hide.

chapter eleven

libby

I wake up in my bed upstairs, and for the first time in months, I am not in pain. It doesn't hurt to shift even a little in bed. Stretching my arm out, I can feel the normal, natural pull of muscles reordering themselves after a night of sleep.

I throw back the covers and smile to myself as again there is no pain. The months have flown by and my body is healing itself. A funny fluttering on my forehead reminds me that my hair has grown back. Yesterday, Angela straightened it for me and it reaches my ears now, and covers the scar. I don't need to look in the mirror to be reminded that the scar across my face looks like nothing more than a faint thread vein, and is virtually invisible to anyone who isn't looking.

The radio or television is on downstairs and as the delicious, intoxicating smell of cooking bacon and eggs wafts up to me, I remember that Benji and Butch are here to stay. The smells and the chatter draw me towards the kitchen.

At the big range cooker, a woman is cooking my porridge with the berries and apple pieces. On the wooden worktop beside the cooker, the empty porridge box gapes open and the last packet is half-crumpled. There's none left for me. Jack and Benji are leaning over the open paper, checking the football news.

I go to the woman at the cooker. 'That's my porridge,' I say to her. 'And you've used it all.'

She turns to me, the large waves of her dark hair moving like a whisper as she smiles with her perfect mouth and unusual blue eyes. She is wearing my black pyjamas with the floro-pink piping and 'I AM DIVINE' emblazoned in clear rhinestones across the front. Jack bought me those pyjamas on our first Christmas together. 'Sorry, Liberty,' she says regretfully. 'This is my porridge.'

'No it's not, it's mine. No one else likes it, only me.'

'Liberty, stop fighting it,' Eve says to me. 'This is my porridge, just like this is my house, and that is my husband and my nephew. You don't have anything any more because you died, remember? You need to let go now. You'll be much happier on the other side.'

I look to the table where Jack is nodding at me, as is Benji – except it's not Benji, it's another boy. He is Benji's age, but he is white with the same dark hair as Eve. I look to the dog basket beside the kitchen door and a cat sits there instead of Butch.

'I'm dead?' I ask Eve.

'Yes,' she says, gently. 'You're the woman he was with before. I'm the one he loves now.'

'But you're dead,' I say to her.

'No, you are. You were in that hideous crash, remember? You were in a coma for a while, then you slipped away. Jack met me a few years later.'

'OK,' I say to her because she sounds so convinced. And if the other two are nodding and the cat is staring at me, I must be wrong and she must be right. They can't all be mistaken, can they? 'If you're sure . . .'

'Why don't you go back upstairs and lie down? It'll all come to you and you'll realise that I'm right.'

'OK,' I say, and go back upstairs to the bedroom. At least it's still my bed in here. I climb back under the covers, pull them over me and snuggle down into the mattress. I close my eyes and go back to being de—

I open my eyes to find Butch staring at me with his little doggie head on one side. I'm sitting at the dining table in the living room having fallen asleep with my head on the notebook in front of me. I lever myself upright, ignoring the shooting pains in my torso. *Stupid* could be my middle name, falling asleep like that in my condition.

Butch is still staring at me with furry interest.

'What, was I whimpering again?' I ask him.

He lets out a little growl-bark.

'You know what?' I tell him. 'You try being dead in your own life in a dream and see how much whimpering you do.'

Butch stares at me a bit longer then turns and walks away, padding into the kitchen for a slurp of water.

Ever since I found those diaries, I haven't been dreaming about the crash; I've been having this dream, about Eve. I haven't looked at the diaries in a few days, instead I scrawl things down on pieces of paper, snatches of things I think I remember from the crash to see if they will jog my memory. It's almost as if Eve is taunting me with the dreams because I haven't had the guts to go back; she is reminding me that this is all, essentially, about her and that if I want to move forwards, I need to find out more.

I'm a little scared of those diaries, if I'm honest. They are reminding me of things I'd rather forget. I know exactly what it's like to have no source of income and to be terrified of losing your home, your dignity, your place in the world.

When I began my PhD, my supervisor had been very supportive of the subject I was proposing, especially because it hadn't been studied at the university before. We were both confident that I would find outside funding, that some companies would be interested in it. Very few were and the ones who were . . . I had one meeting with one person from a company that seemed keen, and the same thing happened to me that had happened to Eve with her landlord – I found myself with a man's hand on my thigh, offering the funds to do whatever I wanted if I was 'friendly' to him.

I'd stared into his blue-green eyes and his face – which I had thought wasn't unattractive when we'd sat down in the meeting room to discuss my proposal – and felt revulsion as his hand edged a little higher up my thigh. Outside the room, on the other side of the door, were hundreds of people, but inside the room he felt safe enough to do this.

'Are you serious?' I'd said.

'Research, and the funding to do it, is a serious business,' he'd replied. 'We, the potential sponsors, all need something to sweeten the pot, and you, the applicant, need to stand out from the crowd.'

Reading Eve's description of that moment with her landlord had churned me up inside. Had reminded me that in that split second I had asked myself, *'Is this what I need to do to be able to get what I want?'* before I took his hand away, thanked him for his time and left.

I realised on the way home that I'd have to stop doing my research if the only person interested in backing me wanted sex from me first. I was scared of what choice Eve had been forced to make.

It didn't sound as if she could go home and she was so close to the wire with money: what choice did she have? I didn't want to read those diaries in case Eve had been forced to go the other way, and I would have to face up to what could have happened to me if I'd chosen to have sex to survive.

But I'm being drawn back to the diaries. I have a feeling in the pit of my stomach that the answer to all my problems – from Jack's calling for her to my memory loss after the crash – are within the relationship that she and Jack had. *Have.* Because it's not over, and I need to know why.

I return to the notepad. Once I've finished jotting down everything I remember, I'll think again about the diaries. Because they are a path I'm still not sure I want to continue down.

libby

'This is all your fault, you know.' I say to Butch. 'If you hadn't been scratching at the door, I wouldn't have remembered the stupid Eve cupboard was down here and I wouldn't be doing this.'

He lets out a lazy, unbothered sound without even raising his head. He's very good at adapting to the person he's with. When he's with Jack, or even Benji, he's full of life and can't stop moving, barking, jumping – with me, he is very slow and considered. Most of the time, wherever I am, he is too, almost as if he is watching over me. I wouldn't go so far as to say he liked me, but I get the impression he feels responsible for me.

I suppose it's nice to have the world's most cynical dog watching your back.

I've brought a cushion down here for comfort, and a small clock so that I know when I need to finish reading by and I don't have a close shave like last time.

Feeling uneasy about it still, I unwrap the diaries and pull out the one I was reading.

Flicking through the pages for where I was, I notice that she's back, sitting on the document boxes. She's still wearing her dress, her feet and arms are bare, but this time she is resting back on her arms, while her legs swing over the edge of the box as you would if you were dangling your feet at the end of a pool.

'*Where were we?*' she says, that rich, smooth sweetness in her voice making me touch the scar on my head. I feel so lumbering and grotesque beside her, even though she is a figment of my imagination.

She watches me as I remind myself what I look like, and shakes her head. '*When will you get it, Libby?*' she says. '*It's not about you. It's all about me.*'

I say nothing to her. Instead I concentrate on finding my place in the diary.

'*Oh, yes, that's it. I'd just lost my job, I was running low on money and I was going to ring Dawn to see if they had any cleaning shifts at her place.*'

eve

Went to see Dawn today. I rang her to see how she was doing and to ask about the job. She sounded so far away and disconnected on the phone I thought I'd go over, since I haven't got anything else to do.

Had such an awful shock when she eventually opened the door. She was like a skin-covered skeleton, and her face was hollowed out with huge dark circles pressed under her eyes. Her face lit up when she saw me and I felt really bad that I hadn't been in touch all this time, especially when she had clearly been ill.

'God, Eve, you look so different. Did you have a wash or something?'

Her pyjamas were hanging off her and her indigo dressing gown – which used to be mine – was off one shoulder and almost dark with dirt. She obviously hadn't washed it since I'd left.

'Yeah,' I laughed. 'That, and I grew up a bit.'

'Ah, must try it myself one day. The washing, not the growing up – that's just not for me.'

She lay on the sofa – which had been my bed for months – and I made us tea in her tiny kitchen. It was all clean and neat, and there was tea in the cupboard but no milk. That was fine because, for lots of us, I think things like milk were becoming a luxury.

199

I sat on the end of the sofa, pulled my legs up under me. I wanted to ask her what had happened, what was wrong, but I didn't want to force her to talk if she didn't want to. God knows she was patient and kind when I wanted to talk about what had happened at home, and she never pushed me when I would clam up, my throat and mouth glued up with tears and sadness.

'You all right, then?' she asked, and smiled at me with her mouth closed. I knew why: when she'd laughed before I'd seen the grey and black devastation that was her teeth.

'I suppose. Like I said on the phone, I'm out of work again. I'm so gutted.'

'Yeah, me too. The out of work thing.'

'Oh God, really? Sorry, didn't realise. When did that happen?'

She shrugged. 'Not sure. Just remember waking up one afternoon and thinking I couldn't face another night of shaking my bum in some guy's face just so I could get enough cash to score. So I never went back.'

'Oh,' I said. I suppose, deep down, I knew what Dawn did and I knew why, but because she'd never told me, and I'd never officially asked, I pretended she really did work behind the bar in a club, that she liked pretty, spangly underwear and that the sickening smell from her room was the weird incense she burned. It was easier thinking that than thinking about the alternative.

If she was no longer stripping and obviously still hooked on drugs . . .

My mind went back to the day I saw her getting into that man's car. *God, surely not*, I thought. 'How are you getting by?' I asked her, because while I didn't want to know I could tell Dawn wanted to talk. And after all she'd done for me, the least I could do for her was let her talk.

'What do you think? I let men have sex with me for money.'

The first thing that came into my mind was my landlord – his face, his chubby hands, and his wobbly belly. Had he paid someone like Dawn? Had he paid someone like my friend to have sex with him because they were so desperate – for drugs or not to be thrown out onto the street?

'God, I'm sorry,' I said to her.

Her face creased up into a smile. 'What have you got to be sorry for?'

'I'm just sorry that you need your drugs so much that you do that,' I said, feeling a bit foolish at not having anything more suppportive to say.

'Eve, never lose that, OK? Never become so . . . beaten down by the world that you lose your ability to feel compassion for someone like me. When I don't really deserve it.'

She was my friend, how else was I supposed to react? Was I meant to tell her she was disgusting and stupid and that I wanted nothing more to do with her? If I was, then something was wrong with me because I couldn't do it. I couldn't bring myself to think that way about her. Not when her stripping had given me a place to stay for all those months and she'd been so lovely to me and given me her suits. It wasn't easy living with her at times but it'd been better than sleeping on the streets, I think anything would be better than sleeping on the streets, which is what I'm facing now.

'What was it like?' I asked her. 'Stripping?' *Was it really that bad? When it made enough money to allow her to live in this expensive area of London and to support her habit for so long, could it have been that bad?*

'It was OK but after a while you see the same old faces, and the same old expressions, and it gets boring on top of everything else. You're kind of dancing on autopilot, you're not really giving it your all, which is what you need to do if you want to earn lots of tips. But, you know, some of the girls loved it. They said it made them feel powerful that men would come in to pay to watch them dance. I thought it made the men seem pathetic and me in the process.' She shook her head. 'But I needed to get my fix, so I did it. But it's easy money if you're desperate.'

I was desperate, had very little money left, but the question was, 'am I that desperate?' Two months, or even two weeks ago, I would have said no. Now, I couldn't say that with such conviction.

I wanted to ask her about the sleeping with men for money, but I didn't dare.

'It's better than what I do now in some ways,' she said. 'What I do now is real desperation, but then again it's more money for less hours and I don't have to give anyone their cut, like I did at the club.'

'You have to give the club a cut of the money? I don't understand.'

'All the strippers work for themselves and you have to pay the club to be able to dance there. Which means, every night, you have to make enough to pay the club their fee, and then anything on top of that you get to keep. Sometimes, if it's a slow night and the other girls are more bolshie and desperate than you, you won't make enough to cover the fee so you go home making a loss.

'That's why what I do now is better in some ways. I always make a profit if I get a punter.'

'Don't you mind?' I asked her. 'Don't you mind doing it with someone you don't care about?'

Dawn's eyes drifted away as she thought about it. 'Dunno,' she said eventually. 'Never really thought about it. I sort of fell into it. A man who recognised me from the club saw me in the street and asked me if I did "extras". I thought, Why not? and followed him to his car. It was all over really quick and I'd made a hundred quid. I just kept on from there, really. I rarely get that much now. It doesn't feel like sex, not like it did with Robbie. It's just letting someone stick his thing in you.'

From what I remembered with Peter, sex was more than that. But what did I know? I'd only done it with him.

'Can we talk about something else? I'm bored of this now,' Dawn said.

'Yeah, course.'

I stayed for another hour and we chatted about all sorts of things, but the talk was constantly punctuated with Dawn's hacking cough. As time wore on, I could see she was getting jittery, and she started to get all clammy, the grey of her face deepening, while her eyes kept going to the wall on the clock. She was getting close to the time when she needed a fix, so I thought it best to leave her.

She hugged me at the door and said it was nice to see me. I said it

202

was lovely to see her and I meant it because underneath it all, she was still Dawn. I offered her some money – I had twenty pounds in my purse – and I saw her eyes widen as she stared at the battered purple note. I could see how much she wanted to take it, but something stopped her. 'Nah, thanks Eve, you're really sweet, but taking money off you would be like taking the food from the mouth of a puppy. Thanks.'

'Are you sure?' I asked her.

'No, of course not. But please put it away before I do take it and I feel worse about myself tomorrow.'

I can't stop thinking about her. She seems so fragile, I don't know how much more she can take before she permanently breaks. I wish there was something I could do to help her, but I can't even help myself right now.

Something good has got to happen soon, hasn't it?

Eve

17ᵗʰ September 1988

Ah, another day, another diary entry.

It's been a while, though, hasn't it? Three months. And everything is so wonderful again. Hahahaha! I can't believe I'm lying to my diary. What will I do next? Try and hide from my reflection in the mirror?

Well, at least I'm still in my flat, and I didn't have to 'bunk up' with the landlord to stay. I swear he actually thought I would. When I rang him to tell him I had another job he sounded quite disappointed.

I've also started smoking. I tried it when I lived with Dawn, and I've got a real taste for it now. It's something to do to pass the time and to calm me down. So, what am I doing? Guess. Yes, I got another job as an admin assistant for a big accountancy firm. Well, that's what I told my mother in my last letter to her.

The truth is I'm now doing what Dawn did. I'm a stripper. But I don't just take my clothes off, I dance for men with virtually no clothes on.

Time ticked away from me and while I got the odd day's temping work here and there, it was getting closer and closer to the time where I would have to pay my rent and I wouldn't be able to pay it. I couldn't sleep for the worry, and I spent all day every day feeling sick.

I even considered going back to Leeds, but the thought of living under the same roof as 'Uncle' Alan, my mother's boyfriend, waiting for the day he would corner me and rape me was too scary. Because I know even then he'd find a way to convince my mother it hadn't happened. I could have gone back if I'd known my mother believed me, or even if Uncle Henry and Aunt Mavis were around still because they'd known what was going on and had me over at theirs whenever possible. I almost wrote to my mother to ask her if she'd consider asking him to leave so I could come back, but her face when I told her what he'd been doing to me and the way she'd believed him over me stopped me.

So, I went to the Job Centre to find out about signing on. But when I looked in the local paper and *Loot* for flats or studios, even the ones that took benefits people were just too expensive. I thought about moving out of the area, but the only places I could afford were so far out, that I'd be isolated and find it harder to get into town to get jobs. I tried shops, cafés and cleaning, but nothing. Now my office experience worked against me because they all thought I'd leave the moment I got an office job and they didn't want to take that risk. They said it to my face: I was a gamble they couldn't afford to make in a recession.

So, I was desperate. When I went to see Dawn I knew I was desperate, but I didn't know if I was as desperate as she must have been – then came the day when I realised I was. I was desperate enough to at least give it a try. I'd almost given Dawn a call to ask her advice but then thought better of it. She had her own problems and I knew she'd try to talk me out of it.

I looked in the local paper and the *Yellow Pages* for any clubs in the area and found there was one about a fifteen-minute walk away.

After memorising the address, I changed into my best set of underwear – just in case they wanted me to take some clothes off – then I pulled a comb through my hair, put on some lipstick and mascara, and left before I could change my mind.

I kept my head down and walked quickly to the club, every step taking me nearer to where I would change my life, but I knew I had to do it. It was that, the streets or going back home. This was the least worst option. Well, that's how it felt.

The club was down a backstreet that I had never been near before. It was quite desolate even in the middle of the day. At night it must have been like walking around an industrial desert. The club had two huge black iron doors, thick bars on the windows and obscene graffiti decorating the walls outside. Hanging above the left door was a sign that said 'Habbie's Gentleman's Club' in unlit pink neon; the name was also painted on the right door in the same lettering.

My legs almost turned themselves 180 degrees on my body to walk away, very fast, but my brain was in charge so I raised my hand and made a fist, then knocked. I almost ran away again in the moments it took for the door to be opened, and then I actually took a step back to run when the tallest, widest man with the thickest neck I'd ever seen opened the door. 'Yeah?' he asked through the slabs of muscle that were his face.

'Are there any jobs?' I asked, my voice sounding pretty normal considering I was terrified that this man could snap me in two just by breathing too hard in my direction.

He stepped back, jerked his head to mean, 'Come in' and I realised that he could murder me and no one would know what had happened. I hadn't told anyone I was coming here. Still, I stepped in and found myself in a long, wide corridor with an unmanned pay booth to my right, and a grubby carpet that seemed to lead down to somewhere there was music. There were stairs to my left, going up to the depths of hell – at that moment, I felt like I'd stepped into whatever place was lower than hell.

'Down there,' he said and waited for me to walk ahead of him.

He reached above me to open the door and I found myself in a huge expanse with a bar that stretched from almost beside the door to the other end of the room. In front of me was a stage with shimmery curtains behind it and at its centre a huge, thick poll going up to the ceiling. There were tables around the room, with three or four chairs around each one. With the lights up, you could only occasionally see the little shiny squares of the glitter ball as it turned above my head, but you could clearly see the grubbiness of the place.

'Wants a job,' the big man said to another guy who I had only then noticed sitting at the bar. He was young and good looking in an odd sort of way – dark, slicked-back hair and friendly features but really unsettling eyes and a mouth that looked like it sneered instead of smiled. He was wearing jeans and a burgundy Fred Perry top, and had on a massive gold watch and massive gold rings on most of his fingers. Beside him on the bar was a short glass with an amber liquid in it.

'How old are you?' he asked.

'Nineteen,' I replied, lying. People didn't ask your age unless it really mattered that you were over eighteen.

'Yeah? What's your date of birth?'

'25 June 1969,' I replied, quick as a flash, then raised an eyebrow at him. It was cheeky and pushing it, but I got the impression he wouldn't believe me if I didn't give him at least a little attitude.

'You don't look it,' he said.

I shrugged. 'I know. It's always made life easier, with not paying adult fares,' I lied again. I'd never do anything like try to get away without paying the right fare.

'Got any experience?'

'No,' I replied.

'And you think you can do this job even though you've got no experience?'

'I'd like to try. I like to dance.'

'Take off your clothes.'

Inside I turned to jelly. But I couldn't let him see that. From looking at him, I could tell that any weakness would be punished. I forced my fingers not to shake as I quickly undid the buttons on my denim jacket, and slipped it off. He and the big man were both staring at me, and revulsion slithered through me as I realised men like them and more would be looking at me like that every night if I got this job. I pushed that thought away, then closed my mind to all thoughts of how wrong this felt.

When I was young, I saw the life story of the famous stripper Gypsy Rose Lee. She was really shy the first time she got up in front of an audience but she carried on despite her terror as she sang 'Let Me Entertain You' in front of a group of men who were wanting to see flesh and bumping and grinding. Right then, I tried to be Gypsy Rose, I conjured up the look of terror and defiance she had on her face as she carried on singing even though the men in the audience were laughing. I kept that scene in my mind and suddenly, without remembering quite how, I was standing in front of them in only my pink bra and pink knickers.

Their eyes ran over me just as closely as their hands would have, feeling and touching every line, lump and goosebump.

'Not bad,' the man at the bar said. I realised that I didn't even know his name but here I was without any clothes on in front of him. 'Stomach's good and flat, tits a nice shape. Turn around, let me see your arse.' I turned around, still with 'Let Me Entertain You' in my head. 'Hmmm, not bad. Bend over.' I hesitated. 'Open your legs and bend over,' he repeated and I swallowed hard and did as I was told. 'No, right over, as far as you can go. Put your hands on your knees if you have to . . . That's right. Now look at me.' The last thing I wanted to do was look at him. I did not want to look at anyone right then. I twisted my body slightly and did it. 'That's it. Now smile.' He nodded. 'Yup, that'll do.' The pair of them weren't looking at my face: their eyes were groping my bum. 'Stand up now.'

I stood up and turned around. I wasn't sure how much more I could take, but this was what the job was about, wasn't it?

'Take it all off,' he said casually, removing a cigarette from the packet beside his glass.

'Everything?' I asked, the bile starting to slither through me again.

'You got a problem with that?'

'No, I was just wondering if I have to do that every night.'

'Nah, usually just the top. I need to see down below to check you isn't . . .' He turned to his mate and they both grinned together at their private joke, 'you know, carrying anything extra down below.'

What? I thought.

It must have showed on my face because the big man said, 'That you ain't a fella.'

'Oh,' I said. 'But I'm not.'

'Yeah, that's what they all say, love. Don't always make it true,' the big man said.

Let me entertain you, I sang in my head as I did what they wanted.

'Definitely a girl,' the man sitting down said as he stared at the lower part of my body with his head on one side while lighting his cigarette. I hoped for a moment that he'd singe his eyebrows on his match, but he didn't.

'Yeah, definitely,' the big man said, staring down there, too.

The guy at the bar spun away, picked up his drink and took a swig. He was suddenly bored by me. 'Shave your legs, shave your minge and you can start tomorrow.'

I stood, naked, cold, exposed, listening to him, not knowing if I should get dressed yet or what. 'OK,' I said.

'You could sound a bit more enthusiastic. I'm taking a risk with you. Your tits and arse are OK, but you aren't experienced. My punters don't like being test-runs for inexperienced girls.'

'I mean, thanks for the opportunity,' I said, still not knowing if I could get dressed or not.

'Get your kit on, then,' the big man said.

'Come in tonight, see how things are run,' the man at the bar said. 'Talk to the other girls, find out about the fees and the rules. Make sure you do, cos if you break 'em, you're out.'

He waved his hand to tell me it was over, I was dismissed. He stopped his glass halfway to his lips. 'What's your name?'

I almost said 'Gypsy' but didn't think I could get away with it. I wasn't going to tell him my real name, and the film that had been on the TV when I left home earlier came into my mind. 'Honey,' I said. From *A Taste of Honey*. I'd been on the verge of tears watching it – the scene where Josephine is forced to leave home because of her mother's boyfriend scraped far too many raw nerves for me.

'Honey,' he repeated. 'That's good. You've got that sweet and innocent look about you. And I ain't got any other Honeys on the books. Go on, get out.'

And that was it.

On the way out, I saw another woman on her way in. She was incredibly tall and incredibly beautiful. She smiled at me and I smiled at her. 'Are you new?' she asked.

'Yeah,' I replied.

'Well, I'm Connie and I'm working tonight if you want to come back and ask me some questions. I've been here donkeys.'

'Oh, thank you,' I said, grateful to her. I wasn't looking forward to having to befriend other people to find out my job description. I was learning not to trust people after what Ophelia had done. 'Can I ask you something now?'

She nodded, her large, slightly hooded eyes staring at me intently and kindly.

'What's a minge?' I asked.

I could have died when she told me. She also told me to get it waxed rather than shaving because it lasts longer and doesn't itch as much when it grows back.

Really tired. Don't know if I can write any more right now. Feel a bit worn down by it all. No wonder Dawn used to sleep half the day away. I'm sure it wasn't just from the drugs. It takes it out of you in a whole different way to normal work. But more about that later. Right now, I just need to sleep.

Eve

I've been a dancer for over a month now. Isn't that great? I work six nights a week and earn more money than I did as an admin assistant, so I can afford luxuries like keeping the lights on when I have a bath, or buying more than one loaf of bread a week. I was poor before, when I worked in the office, but that was fine because I had the idea in my mind that I could possibly make a career out of it. I could maybe become an office manager or even do as Maggie suggested and go back to take my A-Levels and train for a profession. Even if it wasn't accountancy, I could do something.

Now, I have more money – enough to live on, enough to get by – but I'm not sure where I'm going after this. I still apply for jobs, but it seems a bit pointless now. I'm hardly going to put this down on my CV, am I?

It's not so bad, really. I think the second night was worse than the first. The first night I was nervous. I'd watched the other girls, I'd seen how they approached the men, how they smiled and chatted to them, subtly moving their bodies so the men became almost hypnotised by them and wanted to have them dance for them. I watched the way they came close to sitting on the men's laps but would never touch – that was the main rule, NO TOUCHING – and how they would get nearer and raunchier to the men towards the end of a song so the man would eagerly pay more for the dance to continue. There was the pole, which everyone has to have a go on during the night but which the girls weren't that keen on because being up there meant less money.

Some of the stuff the girls did on the pole I just knew I could never do. It was physically demanding so I figured that I'd have to use it as much as possible to incorporate into a dance routine and hope I was so rubbish they would take me off it after a song or two.

Why was the second night worse than the first? The first night, a little bit of me was hoping I would be told to go away and never come back. I didn't want to be standing in front of a man who had his legs wide open, and had his hands clenched on his thighs as he did all he could to stop himself touching me. My first routine was for a young good-looking guy who was on his own and wearing a grey pinstripe suit. He came in alone, sat away from the other men at tables and ordered drink after drink while staring at me. Other girls went over to him but he turned them all down, just stared at me, and eventually I went over to him.

'Would you like me to dance for you?' I said to him. My voice was different because I'd been practicing all day. I'd been getting into the role of Honey. She walked differently to me, she talked differently, she danced differently. She was different because she could take her clothes off in front of people she didn't know whereas I would always have a problem with it.

He nodded. I'd got a new thing to keep in my head – the money I would make from a dance. I focused on the twenty quid I would get and kept that figure in my head. I put a wall around my mind, so I wouldn't think about what I was doing, and on that wall in huge numerals I would see '£20'.

The song came on and I danced, doing what I'd seen the other dancers do and adding some of the things I practiced at home. When the song ended, he gave me a five-pound tip and then looked through me while I put on my bra and dress. It was virtually the same the whole night and at the end of it I was told to come back again the following night. I got some cash in my hand, from which they'd taken the fee for being there, and the owner – Adrian – patted me on the bum for doing so well and said he'd see me the next day.

The second night was worse because I knew that was it. I was there for a while, I was there until I got another job and with the world as it was, still in recession, that other job was not going to be coming around soon. So as I put on make-up like I'd seen the other girls do, and got ready to go out there, I felt a sickness I hadn't felt since I'd come up with this crazy plan. This was my life, this was what I'd chosen to do. I had chosen to wear the persona of a fantasy girl so that the real-life one could carry on living in this world. And for the foreseeable future, that was what I was going to have to do to get by.

One bath wasn't enough to remove the smell of smoke and booze and sweaty expectation that had wound itself into my hair and ground into my skin, but eventually I felt OK again. I felt like Eve again.

I just had to leave all that to Honey.

As I went to sleep that second night, I couldn't help thinking about Dawn. About which came first – the drugs or the dancing. What had she told herself to get through every day of doing that? And how much longer was she going to be alive?

It's second nature now, of course. It only took a couple of weeks for me not to have to concentrate on being Honey when I get up there to dance. Now, the second I walk through the doors of Habbie's I switch into being Honey and I switch her off the second I leave. That's what is so good about having her: I don't have to bring my work home with me because the person who does it, is just a figment of my imagination.

Eve

18th October 1988

Every day I walk past this shop. It's just an ordinary little clothes shop. But it's got this dress . . .

It's not the sort of thing I'd usually like, and I can't ever afford it, but I have to stop every time because it's so beautiful. That's not the word. It's more than that. Breathtaking, like people say, you know, about the places they see on their hols. It takes my breath away, and I can't *not* look at it. Sometimes, even if I'm nowhere near there, I go and have a look. It should be mine. I want it to be mine. I've never had anything like that, anything so pretty and so classy. It's this incredible shade of pink.

It's tight at the top, around the boobs and to the waist, with a delicate scattering of sequins down the front and a tie around the middle. Then the skirt falls in waves. Each strap goes up and branches out into a V, but it's not too revealing because it's got a little panel across the centre. In the window, they've got this big net skirt underneath it, but I wouldn't wear it like that – I'd just let it flow around my legs, right down to my shins.

I want it.

I want it so much it's difficult to breathe, sometimes. I stare at it long and hard, looking at the stitching, the detailing, the depth of the hem, the spacing of the sequins, the way light falls on the gentle folds of the fabric. I'm always looking for imperfection, something that will hopefully put me off, make me love it a little less.

It should be mine. But where would I wear it? What would I wear it for? I don't go anywhere. Just to work and then back again. I sit in this little flat, and I watch the telly, or read a book from the library, or I smoke cigarettes. It'd be silly to buy it. To spend all that money just to sit in wearing it.

I want to stop loving it, but I can't.

Kind of sounds like how I feel about my mother.

Eve

Had a moment today. The first time ever.

Bit shaken afterwards.

Man grabbed me into the alleyway beside the club. He came out of nowhere. I was walking past, thinking about the shower and bath I was going to have when I got home, when I felt the hand on my arm, another one in my hair, and I was being dragged into the narrow gash of the alleyway, unspeakable things squishing and squelching, crunching and crackling beneath my feet. I was winded as the hands slammed me against the wall, and hundreds of stars exploded behind my eyes.

A second or two later I felt a hand, as thick and clumsy as a ham, close around my throat, and fear crept into me. I realised what was probably going to happen to me.

'You liked it, didn't you, bitch?' he said right up at my face, not bothering to hide his. 'When you were on top of me, you liked it. You wanted more.'

On top of you? I thought. And then, through the dim light, I saw the shadows and contours of his face. He didn't stand out, they never stood out. Not really. Not unless he was especially ugly. Or stench-ridden. Or rough with his hands. Or had flashed a particularly big wad of cash to try to get as many girls as possible vying for his attention. Most of them were quite ordinary, and I wouldn't know them if I tripped over them in the street. This man wouldn't stand out if I tripped over him in the street, or if he slammed me against a wall, wanting more than he had paid for. Wanting the extension to the lap dance he probably begrudged shelling out for.

I stared at his face, wondering if he was one of the ones who had touched me. The ones I pretended were special so I let them touch me so that they would stay and spend their money with me. Or was he one of the ones I could tell wanted to touch but would move on after a song or two, wanting to clock up as many girls as he could so he could leave feeling like a big man?

'You're not like the others,' he said to me, his voice low and rasping with his sick excitement. He didn't look like a thug, more like the normal blokes I used to see on my way to work every morning – the ones who would stumble in with their mates following a few after-work drinks, looking for a laugh.

This man wasn't laughing. 'Tell me you wanted more,' he said, shaking me slightly.

I stared at him. Not defiant, but mute with fear and shock. Was I that good an actress? Did he really believe that?

'Come on you dirty little whore, tell me you want more!'

Are you talking to me? I wondered.

One hand still around my throat, the other started to move lower, down into my trousers, his thick fingers, with their jagged fingernails clawing at my skin, trying to get inside me.

Started screaming then. Started to shout and scream and fight back. I didn't care that his vice-like grip around my throat was tightening because I was still managing to make noise. He was telling me to shut up, snarling it at first, then shouting and, although he was stronger, I was managing to fight him, keeping him at bay.

'Oi, get off her!' A voice suddenly cut through the scuffle of noise we were making, and he was being hauled away from me. 'Get off her! What do you think you're doing?'

And suddenly my attacker was scrabbling around on the filthy ground, trying to get his footing again.

'You don't treat women like that,' my saviour said.

'She ain't a woman, she's a whore, mate,' he spat at my saviour as he got to his feet. 'She gets paid for it. She likes it rough.'

'Just get lost,' the second man spat.

'You ain't going to get nothing for free mate,' he said. 'So I wouldn't bother.'

'Piss off!' the other man snarled.

My attacker scuttled away, leaving me with the second man.

'You all right?' he asked.

I nodded, still a bit too shaken to speak.

'You should be careful around here, you know, because of that club. No decent woman is safe to walk the streets, they're constantly being mistaken for strippers,' he said. 'I wonder if the tarts in there think about the danger they put other women in?' Then he looked at me, really looked at me, and he stopped talking because he saw my make-up and my big hair and he realised that I wasn't a decent woman. I was one of those tarts.

He shook his head, disgust on his face. 'You should be careful.' Then he walked away.

The second man actually hurt me more than the first one.

But it's true isn't it? I'm not a decent woman. No decent woman would do what I do.

God, I hate myself sometimes.

Going to stop signing my name as Eve. What's the point? I know who I am.

Dress was gone from the window.

Felt sick.

Rushed inside shop, heart racing. Just couldn't believe it. Someone had bought it after all this time. It's only a small shop that people call boutiques. The woman who ran the place looked me up and down.

'Can I help you?' she said, dead snotty.

I was like something nasty and smelly to her, but I didn't care. I only cared about the dress.

'The dress from the window,' I said to her, out of breath with anxiety. 'Is it gone?'

Her mean eyes flicked over me again, up and down, quick and disgusted. 'Someone, a paying customer, is trying it on, although what business it is of yours I don't know, I'm sure.'

'I wanted to buy it,' I said, giving her a bigger hold over me, giving her a chance to act even more snotty and superior and snide.

'It's a designer original, costing well over four hundred pounds. Do you really have that sort of money?' she said, not adding that she fully expected me to try to steal it. I would never steal something as incredible as my dress. I would never steal, full stop.

'Yes,' I said, trying to be brave.

The corners of her mouth twitched because she was going to start laughing at me. I felt the tears trickling down my throat and rushing like a fast-moving stream to my eyes. I did not want to cry in front of her. The metallic whoosh of curtain rings being pulled back filled the gap between us and we both turned to the small changing booth at the back of the shop. Out stepped a woman wearing my dress.

It felt like she was wearing my wedding dress, and she was going to marry my groom because of it. It was like she had skinned me alive and was wearing my skin. The pain was immense, and like nothing I had felt in so long. She had something that should be mine and she could afford it. She could buy it whenever she liked. While, I . . . I would always be on the other side of the glass, looking in at things like this. I would always be on the wrong side, because I did not deserve to have nice things.

'You look absolutely divine in that!' the saleswoman said brightly, more for my benefit than hers. She wanted me to know that she knew I was scum. She left the counter and walked towards the woman in my dress, shutting me out, telling me to leave, I was not welcome here. 'I absolutely insist you buy it.'

'It's a little out of my price range,' the woman replied.

'Don't worry about that, we have some very reasonable discounts and payment terms for our favoured customers,' she said loudly, because she was actually talking to me. 'Leave a small deposit and you can pay the rest off over a month or so.'

'I wasn't aware you did things like that,' the delighted wearer of my dress said.

'As I said, we do for our most favoured customers.'

'Oh God, should I? It is a beautiful dress, it does look lovely on . . .'

'It certainly suits someone like you. Very few people can get away with wearing something this beautiful. It wouldn't suit just anyone.'

'Oh . . . it is lovely.'

No, it isn't! I wanted to scream at her. It is not lovely or beautiful or any of those pathetic, lowly, unworthy words you're using. It is divine. It comes from the place where the sun gets its rays, it is made from the cloth woven from pieces of rainbow, it was sewn by angels, it is so much more than beautiful or lovely. It is perfection.

I turned away, ripping my eyes from what was happening in front of me. I could not watch her buy something that she did not have full appreciation for, not when I would love it much more. This was what it would feel like to watch the man you love, have given your life to, marry someone else. I never wanted to feel like that again.

I knew the woman who owned the shop would be smiling as she watched me leave in the mirror, feeling superior and satisfied that she has seen off scum like me. I never did anything to her, but still she took great pleasure in putting me in my place.

I walked home in a daze, feeling like I'd had the fight kicked out of me. Didn't realise how much that dress had given me purpose.

Focus. I didn't seriously think I'd buy it but, I suppose, the possibility that I might had kept me going. The possibility that I might one day own something pretty, something nice – like the other girls who I used to work with and who I pass all the time in the street – kept me from going completely insane. Kept me from questioning why I haven't tried harder to get more temp work, instead going back to Habbie's night after night, coming out smelling of the foul creatures who walk in the door, and barely being able to look myself in the mirror.

I suppose the dress has been a sign that I was capable of changing my life. Of doing better. Of being 'normal' again.

Going to bed now. Will phone in and say I've got my period. No point in getting up tomorrow.

Love,
Me

29ᵗʰ November 1988

Hadn't been past the shop in weeks. No point. Still hurt that someone else had the dress – *my* dress. And I was still smarting from how that stuck-up bitch treated me.

So, guess how I reacted when I finally had to go past the other day – otherwise I'd be late for work – and it was there again. The dress. My dress. Back in the window on the shiny faceless mannequin like it'd never been taken off and tried on by that woman. The shop was closed, so I couldn't go in, but I did stop, even though I was late, and stare at it. I stared and stared, then I reached out and touched the glass, imagining I could feel its soft folds through the window, the vibrations of its divinity gently flowing through me.

This was my second chance. My chance to show that bitch, and my chance to prove to myself I could do better. I could own something perfect.

I gently took my hand away and then had to run the rest of the way to work. I knew what I had to do. I knew that I had to do anything ANYTHING I could to get the money to buy that dress. ANYTHING.

chapter twelve

jack

Sometimes, being in Brighton feels like being in London, surrounded by lots of people all looking different, all with their busy lives. I've stayed a few nights in London, I've lived in Oxford and in Brighton (and now I'm settled in Hove) and I'll never grow tired of the ability to hide in plain sight. It feels even easier to do in Brighton because the best bits aren't as spread out as they are in London.

Walking through the cobbled streets of North Laines, I feel anonymous and free, like I am Jack Britcham again. I am a man in my thirties, who has his whole life before him. I can do whatever I want, whenever I want to. Nothing can hold me back. Among the crowds I am merely another obstacle in the road to step around, another being who happens to be in the same city at the same time as the people passing by. I am not important. I like not being important. I often crave being no one. In my world, with the people I know, being no one is not an option.

Set up on the corner of Gardener Street and Church Street, right before the road narrows into a claustrophobic alleyway flanked on both sides by shops, a street-seller's stand catches my eye. He has a perforated board leaning on an orange plastic milk crate with neat rows of crystal hearts. Some are smooth and clear, others are almost brutally cut with visible facets, others still are smooth but with roughened surfaces. They are striking in their simplicity, the way they catch the light, their myriad colours like droplets of the entire colour spectrum, dripped onto the board. They're cheap, but incredibly beautiful in a way I rarely see.

Tucking myself in to avoid disturbing the crowds trying to get past, I stare at them, transfixed. The seller is probably my age, wearing a grubby, mustard-yellow wax jacket with a straggly, fair beard and sunken eyes. His fingers are exposed in green fingerless gloves and his nose is red as if permanently cold. 'Make them all meself, mate,' he says with a thick London accent, then loses interest in me and returns to rolling a cigarette. I've been hypnotised by these glass gems.

Libby would love one of these. At least I think she would. I have been wandering around Brighton trying to find the perfect gift. Everything I have seen that I think she would love is too expensive for her to enjoy. Other men, I'm sure, would be envious of me having a wife with modest tastes. She likes beautiful things – she knows instantly the label of something and if it is a fake or real – but she rarely indulges in said items. She cannot bring herself to spend that money – even if she doesn't say it aloud, I can see she is thinking, *That's nearly a month's mortgage payment*, when confronted with buying non-essential things. *If I couldn't pay my bills because of this, what would happen?* She always has to contextualise it to see if it is truly worth what she would have to pay for it.

When we were first married, I said to Libby I'd pay for her to go back and finish her PhD if she wanted. She'd smiled at me, her face lighting up as it creased with joy. 'Thank you. Thank you so much for the offer,' she said. 'But no, that ship has sailed. I'm a beauty therapist now. I was actually saving to go back but now I don't really want to.'

'Because you're scared you won't be able to catch up?' I asked.

She shook her head and said, thoughtfully, 'No, because I'm a beauty therapist.'

'Well, we could finance you opening your own salon down here in Brighton or Hove,' I suggested.

Again, she smiled that smile of pure delight, her joy dancing in her eyes as she looked at me. 'That's a brilliant offer, Jack. Thank you, but no.'

'Why not?' I asked.

'I'm just not that ambitious.'

'You're incredibly ambitious and motivated, you have passion and drive.'

'I think what I mean is, I don't have the type of ambition that will make me do anything at any cost to get what I want. I couldn't finish my PhD because I didn't want to be beholden to the people who would finance my research. I don't want to open a salon with your money because I don't want to be indebted to you.'

'I'm your husband; it's our money.'

'Morally, legally, maybe yes, but in here,' she put her hand to her head, 'and here,' she lay the flat of her hand over her heart, 'it's your money. You earned it or were given it way before you met me.'

'But that's crazy,' I told her.

'Maybe, and I'm sure I'd feel differently if we had children. But right now, when it's just you and me, I still think of that as your money. Now we're together, anything we earn is our money.'

'Still crazy.'

'I've been poor, Jack. I've seen what the need for money, the desperation for it, can do to people. You have very few choices when you're desperate for money, and so far I've managed to avoid being forced into making those choices.

'And, yes, if I'm honest, there was something else I wanted to do when I went into beauty therapy, and that was to start my own line of beauty products. But it's something to work towards, not something that should be handed to me on a plate. What's the point of doing something if you know that you've got someone to rescue you if you fail? I like to work hard at something and then to reap the rewards. I take pride in what I do. What's the point if I know my rich husband will bail me out if I mess up?'

That made me think of my complicated relationship with my father. Hector was always trying to get me to rely on him. He didn't like that I did things without consulting him first – he liked (*needed*) to be in control. He was always giving Jeff and me money, telling us we could come to him if we had problems, never letting us stand on our own two feet – which meant our successes and our failures were nothing but reflections on him. I'm always having to temper and hide my battles to be out of my father's control because my mother is so keen for us to be a close family. I often fear it would break her heart if she knew how much I hated him most of the time, and just why he thought so little of me. I often look at my father and see everything I hate about being a man, and then I look at my mother and remember I would never want to hurt her.

Eve was very much against my father's attempts at control. She kept saying we shouldn't accept financial gifts from my parents but I found it hard to say no because I knew how much it meant to my mother to be able to help Jeff and me. Eve found a way to get the point across by donating the ninety thousand pounds he gave us from the sale of one of his properties to a women's refuge and a homeless charity. I would never have had the ability to do that but afterwards, when I told him where the money had gone, my father had stopped giving us money.

I want to buy Libby a glass heart. They are not too expensive, they are beautiful, but I am not sure if it is the sort of thing she would truly like. Eve would have loved one, I think. I'm not sure. The pair of them become mixed up in my mind sometimes, to the point where I do not know which one likes what, and which one doesn't. They were/are both unimpressed by money. They both liked/like beautiful things. They both make my heart beat in triple time. But they are not the same. They are different in many, many ways, but at times like this I forget which is which. Who is who. The subtleties that make a person who they are, that make a woman the person I fell in love with, are sometimes so blurred I am scared to speak to the woman who I am married to.

I am scared that I will credit Libby with something that Eve said or did or liked, and she will never forgive me.

My eyes are drawn to the cloudy clear heart at the centre of the board.

My fingers close around it, unhooking it from the board and encasing it in the palm of my hand. The blood pumping through my body seems to focus on this hand and it feels as if the heart is beating in my palm. It is alive and well and beating.

Even if Eve would have loved this, I'm sure Libby will like it, too. And what else can I give her after everything she has been through except this: my imperfect heart.

eve

I spoke to Connie today, asked her about how to make more money so I could buy that dress. I didn't tell her what is was for, I doubt anyone would understand why I *needed* a dress – I just told her I needed more money as soon as possible. She stopped leaning forwards to see herself more clearly in the light-bulb surrounded mirror in the dingy backroom laughably known as the dressing room as she applied make-up. Connie turned on her swivel chair to me. Connie's the only person at work who I trust, really.

She's been dancing for a while, and is so sanguine with it. She isn't as bitchy, and snidey and bitter like the rest. She's got an incredible body with long, smooth bronzed muscles. She's Amazonian in stature anyway, but in her heels and with her hair all teased and clipped back, she looks like a goddess. The men flock to her, almost as if they long to be crushed under the spikes of her heels, to be tamed by her. She seems so oblivious, immune to it. She doesn't become someone else to go out there. She is Connie out there in front of the dribbling men, and she is Connie in here in the dressing room, and she is Connie outside of work. I am Honey in here, I am Honey in front of the men, I am Eve out of work.

226

'What do you need money for, sweetie? If that's not too personal a question,' she asked, her head on one side, her dark, sultry eyes examining me. She kept her voice low so that no one around could hear.

I shrugged. 'I just need it.' Someone as immune to the effects of dancing as she was would not understand what I needed the dress for; how it would help me.

'Not for a man, I hope?'

I shook my head. 'Nothing like that. I'd never do this sort of thing for a man.'

'Never say never,' she said ruefully, wisely. 'So you need to make more money? Well you can start doing private dances, you know, in the VIP rooms. Tell Adrian and the others that you'll do them and they'll start to push the men who're into that to choose you for a dance.'

'Do I do a normal dance in there? Just a bit longer, maybe do it naked?' I asked.

Connie stared at me long and hard, as if asking herself if I was really that naïve. I'd never done VIP dancing before and I'd never been that curious about it. I usually made enough to pay the club fee and to cover my rent, food, bills, etc. I came, I did, I went. No need to get involved in the other stuff.

She sighed. 'Honey, in the private rooms the rules that they pretend to stick to out front don't really apply. You know out front we make them think that if we let them touch us it's something we do just for them? In the back, they get to touch you. They get to wank off while watching you dance, they get to finger you, they get to touch your tits, they get to make you play with yourself, you have to wank them off if they ask for it, some girls suck them off and—' She stopped talking, stared at me with dismay, obviously halted by the horror on my face. 'I really don't think private dancing is for you.'

'But I need the money,' I insisted.

Connie began to chew on her lower lip, smudging lipstick on her teeth – it was the first time I'd ever seen her unsure of herself. 'OK, but you have got to toughen up. If you show any type of weakness in there, they'll eat you alive. I mean that literally. Some of the scum that come in here will force you to finish them off with your mouth if they think they can get away with it. One girl was raped in one of those rooms with the bouncers stood outside, because she was too scared to scream. Then the wankers who run the joint put pressure on her not to report it cos they could lose their licence. They slipped her a wad of cash then basically told her to fuck off. And the bastard who did it? He actually tried to come back a couple of times until all us girls refused to dance for him and the managers barred him.' She shrugged. 'Probably doing it somewhere else.'

I put my hand over my mouth. 'Why do you still work here?' I asked her, knowing I couldn't work somewhere knowing a friend had been raped while I was there.

Connie's rueful, wise smile returned to her lips and she turned again to the mirror, picked up her blusher brush and started on her cheeks. 'I need the money.'

I spun on my chair to the mirror, too. Looked at myself. My hair backcombed to stand on end, my eyes heavily made up in black, brown and blue to stand out, artificial eyelashes, blood-red mouth, and glowing cheeks. Around my throat a gold, sparkly dog collar. I needed the money, too. I needed the money to be Eve again.

'I wish you wouldn't,' Connie said, still applying her make-up. 'I know you're going to anyway, but I wish you wouldn't do it. I remember the first time I saw you and I knew then you shouldn't be here. You're not meant for this type of place, Honey. You're not hard enough. In years to come, you'll look back and start to hate yourself for this.'

'Is that what you do?' I asked her.

'I hated myself long before I came here. This place just gives me another reason to justify the hatred.'

'I need the money,' I said again to myself as much as to her.

'Don't we all?'

I need the money, I need the money, I need the money. I kept repeating that to myself after my shift when I asked Adrian to let me do some private room stuff.

'Are you sure?' he asked, obviously surprised. In the time I'd been there I hadn't shown any interest in anything other than doing my shifts, collecting my cash and going home.

I nodded. *I need the money, I need the money, I need the money.*

'The punters will love it: a bit of new flesh in the back. You'll get a bigger cut, too. Just let them know what you will and won't do before you get down to it. You're going to love it,' he said patting me on the bum. 'The way men will be gagging for you, you're going to love it.'

I need the money, I need the money, I need the money.

8th December 1988

I did a private dance for the first time today.

He wasn't repulsive or drunk. He wore a suit and he seemed pleasant enough. He also had on a wedding ring. For some reason, that upset me. I had to avoid looking at his hands.

I had to sit astride him naked, moving to the music, while he put his hand, the one with the shiny gold wedding ring on my lower back, the other hand he used to get himself off.

I've had three baths since I've come in but I can still feel his right hand rubbing against me as he moved it up and down, and I can still feel the gold band of his lifelong commitment and fidelity to someone else against the skin of my lower back, almost burning where it made contact.

I've put the notes from tonight's wages into the virtually frosted-over icebox of the fridge because I can forget about them there. I cannot bear to think about them right now. In fact, right now, I'm going to have another bath.

19th February 1989

I walked into the dress shop today with a bundle of money burning a hole in my pocket. I had earned every single one of those notes. A 'new girl' for the VIP room is, apparently, a very popular thing for the regulars and for those who often do it elsewhere. They think that it will be easy to get me to do 'extras' for very little, that I can be swayed to 'go all the way' for the price of a dance, or that they can convince me that they can be helpful and show me the ropes in return for a discount or a freebie.

'You have got to toughen up,' Connie had said and so that's what I did. While at first I was a little nervous and found myself having to dig deep to go through with it, I found the thought of being ripped off by these men – especially the ones with shiny gold wedding bands – even more terrifying. The first time I danced for them, they always tried it on. 'Desire does that for twenty quid less,' they'd say. And at first I didn't know what to say so I would tell them I couldn't do it for that amount, but would allow them to bargain me down a little. Then I got wise. I'd say, 'Oh baby, that's such a shame, I was looking forward to dancing for you. But if you want Desire at her prices you wait here, I'll get her for you.' Their egos always had them paying me what I asked.

I never did anything purely sexual – no blowjobs, no handjobs, no sex – and in a way I was able to not feel as bad about that. I did charge a few of them the price of five dances to let them touch me down there for a few seconds at the end of a song, pretending that I liked it and that I wished it could continue for free after the last bars faded out.

It was so odd that they believed it. That they genuinely thought that I would look twice at them, let alone get naked with them, if I wasn't being paid. A part of me did feel sorry for these men, wondering what their story was that made them so *deluded* that they thought I liked it. That I could possibly even consider fancying them when they had walked into a place to pay to be turned on. Most of the time I stopped myself from feeling. I let a man run his hands over my breasts before he began fiddling with the zip on his trousers to start finishing himself off while I gyrated in front of him but the wall I had been building up since I started in this job just thickened around me. I hated being a part of it, but always I kept the words, 'I need the money' in my mind. My feelings were walled off, my thoughts were focused.

I had earned every single penny of the notes in my pocket, all stored up in the freezer so that I wouldn't have to think about them. Now, that extra cash was about to be used, to buy what I had needed it for. It would seem ludicrous to anyone who didn't understand – that I would do all that just to buy a dress – but I *needed* it. There was very little I had in my life that I needed – there was stuff I wanted, there was stuff all of us wanted, but I needed this dress to make myself feel . . . real, I suppose.

The world I lived in, the things I did, made me feel unreal. I was so often disgusted with myself and when I stopped being Honey, when I stopped pretending that I didn't see anything wrong in what I did, I was confronted by the fear that I would disappear. Honey would take over, little by little, and soon I would walk out of the club and would not return to being Eve. I would walk away as Honey, Honey would return to my flat, Honey would take off her clothes, Honey would get in the bath, Honey would scrub herself clean, Honey would sit in a dressing gown with wet hair and smoke cigarettes while staring into space. Honey would eventually climb into bed and go to sleep. Then Honey would wake up in the morning and go about the day as Eve would.

Every day it got harder and harder to come back to who I was. It would take longer to stop being her and start being me. I needed this dress, this thing that Eve loved to look at. With the dress, with Aunt Mavis's rosary, Uncle Henry's kit bag, and the photo of my parents and me when I was two, I was collecting more and more things that meant something to me, to *Eve*. *Things* that meant I was real. I had things to ground me here, so I was less likely to disappear.

The discreet shop bell intoned as I pushed the door open. The bitchy woman who had made me cry looked up from the jumper she was folding on the counter, a smile ready for the valued customer who had stepped into her exclusive haven. She recognised me, it showed on the frowns of her face, but for some reason her lip did not curl into a sneer and her eyes did not narrow. Maybe she wanted to wait until I was right in front of her before she tried to take me apart. But she couldn't now, could she? I had money, I was as good as her. No matter how much she did not want to, no matter how much

231

better than me she thought she was, she was going to have to sell me that dress.

I was trembling slightly, but the money in my pocket gave me courage to keep walking.

'Yes?' she asked when I stopped in front of her, the counter separating us.

'I'd like to try on the dress in the window,' I said. I sounded polite and confident.

'Of course,' she said.

I couldn't help but draw back a little in surprise. I had expected to have to get the money out of my pocket, to show her that I wasn't wasting her time and that she had no reason not to sell me the dress.

She finished her folding, then moved from around the counter and walked calmly towards the window. She stepped up onto the window display and unzipped the dress, pulling it carefully over the top of the headless mannequin. A burst of a song from the movie *Mannequin* exploded in my head, 'Looking in your eyes, I see a paradise . . .' I went to see that with Peter on one of our dates. I think it was before we did it for the first time. We sat holding hands in the front row, my heart almost bursting with what I thought was love. I think what love is changes over time, as you grow older, learn more, do more. I remember my love for him changed so much after we had sex. I felt like I was his, he could do no wrong and I could feel no pain. For the time we were together it felt like there was nothing that could hurt us or tear us apart. And then he was gone from my life.

With the quality of the material, the dress was quite heavy as I lifted it off the small wooden hook in the dressing room at the back of the boutique. I took my time to step into it, and then zipped it up under my arm almost reverentially. It was so soft against my skin, as if it was stroking me, hushing me wherever the material made contact, and once I was secured in, the waves of comfort that it brought were incredible. Tears came rushing to my eyes, and stung my throat. I felt like I was being hugged, being loved and swayed in someone's gentle arms.

I braced myself for the saleswoman's scorn and pulled aside the

232

curtain to step out to see the mirror. She had the phone receiver pressed to her ear and was looking towards the front of the shop as the saleswoman listened to what the person on the other end of the phone had to say. I crept out, my feet bare as I didn't have the perfect shoes for this dress, and moved to the mirror.

My hand flew to my mouth and I had to physically hold back a cry as I saw myself properly for the first time. I did not look like the person I thought I was. I did not look like Honey. I did not look like anybody I had been since I had walked out of my mother's house all those years ago. I looked like a grown up woman, someone who had learned the hard way to stand on her own two feet. But I also looked fragile and delicate and peaceful. The dress made me glow. This was probably how women felt when they got dressed on their wedding day. They felt like the prettiest woman in the world.

'The colour compliments your eyes,' the saleswoman said. I hadn't heard her approach and had no idea how long she'd been standing there because for the first time I had been completely focused and absorbed by me. I glanced away from my reflection to look for her snidey expression but it was not there.

'You look beautiful,' she said thoughtfully. 'You really deserve to have that dress. It wouldn't look right on anyone else.'

I continued to stare at her in the mirror, wondering where the venomous woman was. The woman who had so hated me for merely crossing the threshold.

'I was unkind,' she said to my silence. 'And you still came back. This dress must mean a lot to you.'

I thought of all the things Honey had done to get me enough money to buy this. It meant . . . it meant enough to come back. I couldn't really speak to her, because I was scared that she would turn on me.

'I'll wrap your clothes up if you'd like, because I think you should wear it home.' She knew that I had nowhere to wear it, that this would probably be the first and last time I got to feel like this. I smoothed my hands and fingers over the skirts of the dress, a thrill running through me every time my skin made contact. It was not warm outside but she was right: I did not want to take my dress off.

The saleswoman went to the dressing room cubicle and returned with my clothes, handing me my jacket and trainers, then taking my jumper and jeans and socks to the counter. I slipped my trainers onto my feet, and then pushed my arms into my jacket. Even these ordinary items did not dull the beauty of the dress or diminish how I felt in it.

'That's £225,' she said when I finally went over to the counter.

My fingers paused in reaching for the bundle of notes in my pocket. 'You told me it was £400,' I said.

The woman coloured up, her eyes full of shame. 'I was extremely unkind,' she replied.

Bile swelled inside. I would not have had to do so many stints in the VIP room if . . . *No, don't think I about it*, I told myself. I had the dress, that was all that mattered. I handed over the money and tried to push everything else out of my mind.

Outside the shop, I paused for a moment, enjoying the rush of being a woman in an inappropriate dress with the whole world at her feet. I could do anything I wanted to: this dress had given me super powers; I could go out and save the world.

Instead, I went to a café and bought a coffee. I sat in the window and stared out as I waited for my drink to be brought over. This was the life that Eve, the one I saw in the mirror, had thought she'd have. It wouldn't matter if she was alone, she'd just find peace in the craziness of the world.

'I love your dress,' the waitress said as she placed the white cup with froth on top in front of me.

'Thank you,' I replied.

'Is it from the shop round the corner?' she asked.

'Yes,' I replied.

'I used to drool over it,' she said. 'But I could never afford it, not in a million years. It looks so good on you, I doubt it would have suited me anyway.'

She smiled at me, and a bubble of tears gathered together in my throat – she was being nice to me. In London, most people didn't have time to be nice unless they wanted something from you. In my job, most people didn't bother being nice to me because they were paying me to make them feel good.

'Thanks,' I replied.

Her smile deepened and she put her head to one side as she looked me over. 'It gets easier you know,' she said.

'What does?' I asked.

'Life.' She shrugged. 'It gets easier and simpler, I promise.'

I thought about that statement for a long time after she had left, why she had said it to me and if it was true. My life had not gone like that. It had got more complicated and more difficult the longer I lived in this world. What if she was right, though? I must be due a big dose of simplicity and ease. I must be about to come into a bit of luck that would have me living the life of a normal seventeen-year-old sometime soon.

She waved to me on my way out and, as soon as I was clear of the window, I ran all the way home. I did not want her to come after me, to ask me questions, to maybe force me to take back the tip of one hundred and seventy-five pounds I'd left for her. I couldn't keep that money. I'd had enough of trying to forget it existed. I had done what I needed to do to get my dress, and I wanted the rest of that money gone. And I wanted it to go to someone who would appreciate it for being cold hard cash, who wouldn't know it was the symbol of men using my seemingly willing body to get their kicks.

I'm still wearing my dress. I don't want to take it off. If I take it off, I know that I'll be stripping my body of Eve, too. In my mind, I can see myself as the woman in the mirror. I'm going to hang onto that image and feeling for just that little bit longer.

It's not like I'm hurting anyone, is it?

Me

17th March 1989

Something nice happened today.

I was in the supermarket, picking up a few bits, and worrying on how I was meant to fill in a tax return – because I'm self-employed apparently and I have to do that and work out how to pay the tax people what I owe if I owe them anything – when I bumped into someone.

A man. I looked up at him briefly then went bright red because I recognised him from the club. I put my head down but he said, 'It's Eve, isn't it?' And I breathed a sigh of relief because, you know, if he had been at the club then he'd think my name was Honey.

'Do I know you?' I asked him.

'Ah, shame! I thought you'd remember me. I'm Elliot. I work at the company that bought out the place you worked for. I was a junior accountant then, well, still am.'

He was a bit taller than me, but not much. He had wavy brown hair and nice brown eyes. He was in a navy blue suit but the top button of his white shirt was open and the tie was a little undone.

'Oh, OK,' I replied, not really knowing what to say. But I was getting a butterfly feeling in my stomach – the longer I stood here, the better looking he got.

'I was gutted for you that you didn't get the job. You were much better than the girl they employed. Joke was on them in the end because she ended up getting sacked for stealing.'

'Really? Is there a job going then?' That would have been fantastic.

'No, this was a while back. They've got someone new now.'

'Why didn't they call me? I did apply for job,' I said, feeling slighted. I worked really hard for them.

'It's all a bit different there now. Ophelia got pushed out within a couple of months. But lots of people said it served her right after what she did to you and especially to Maggie. You know her and Maggie had been friends since school?'

'No, I didn't know that.'

'Yeah. My company just wanted Ophelia's high-profile clients and not her. They basically made her life a misery until she left. Dominic wasn't far behind, he could see which way the wind was blowing and left too. They've both started their own businesses from scratch with no real clients and rumours about how badly they behaved.'

Wow, what goes around really does come around. I actually shivered a little to think that Ophelia was in a similar situation to me. Couldn't see her getting up and dancing around a metal pole though.

'Do you fancy a drink sometime?' he asked, out of the blue.

'Sorry,' I said, 'I've got a boyfriend.' I crossed my fingers in my head as I said that, obviously because I don't like to lie. But I couldn't go out with him when I was still a dancer.

'Of course you have. Girls like you aren't single for long.'

'Girls like me?' I asked, suddenly defensive. Just because I took my clothes off didn't mean I slept around.

'Pretty girls.'

'Oh.'

'Look, here's my card. If you and your boyfriend split up, call me. And call me if you need any help with any accountancy stuff. I may not be able to help, but it'll be a great excuse to see you again.'

'Do you have a pen?' I asked him.

He produced a blue Bic biro from his inner pocket. I turned his card over, and wrote my number on the back. 'If you hear of any jobs going, please can you give me a call?' I handed him back his card. 'I remember the work number, so I know I can call you there.'

He nodded and smiled. 'Great, it's a deal.'

I walked home on cloud nine. He was going to bring me good luck, I could tell. And he did. Earlier, a regular gave me a hundred-pound tip.

Yes, one hundred pounds! I mean that NEVER happens. All the other girls were dead jealous but I didn't care. I didn't flash it around or brag about it, but it made the rest of the night fly by because I knew I'd made enough to pay the house and I didn't have to go flat out to earn as much.

I actually came home with a smile on my face. See? If you wait long enough and try hard enough, something good is bound to turn up.

Night, night.

Love,
Me

libby

On my pillow is a small package of pink tissue paper, tied up in an ivory ribbon with a card slipped between the lines of the ribbon.

That's probably why after dinner Jack did nothing more than ask me if I needed a hand to get my tablets from the bedroom before he took Butch out for a final walk.

I sit heavily on the bed, and stare at the package. Jack likes to give me things, presents, tokens of his love. They're always beautiful, sometimes expensive, but most of the time, I'd rather have him. I'd rather have him talk to me, share with me, rely on me. I'd rather our relationship moved below the surface when it comes to the almighty Eve.

Except, it's becoming harder and harder to keep thinking of her negatively. The more I learn about Eve, the more I start to feel for her, and if I start to feel for her then I start to understand why Jack is still so obsessed with her.

I desperately need for her to be a bitch. I need for her to have had some sort of nefarious hold over Jack so that I would be able to look into the future and see that once the hold is broken, he'll completely give himself to me. But learning what she had to do for money, to pay the rent, to feel connected to the world . . . it tears me up inside. Almost as if I knew her. That could have been me. I could have slept with someone to get funding, I could have done what I heard a couple of the other women doing their masters and PhDs did and become a stripper to make ends meet. I walked away but that could have been me. It *was* Eve.

I reach out for the package and it is deceptively heavy for an item so small. Pulling apart the ribbon and then the paper, I find at the centre a heart. About two centimetres from top to bottom, it is clear crystal with swirls like waves of a pure white mist trapped and frozen in time at its centre. A tiny hook attached at the V of the heart has a black leather thread looped through it.

It's like nothing he has ever bought me before.

Curious, I pick up the card and remove it from its envelope.

I love you. J x

I gather the heart to me again, hold it gently in my fist and place it against my chest as I lie back against the pillows.

I'm going to stop reading the diaries. It's intrusive and now I know a little more about her, I don't want to intrude on her space any longer. And what I am doing is betraying Jack, too. I should ask him, talk to him, *make* him tell me about her. I know that's possible now he's given me the gift of his heart. I've never felt I've completely had it before.

chapter thirteen

libby

We're at the traffic lights at the bottom of Eleventh Avenue on the seafront, and a car pulls up beside us. He's in a red Ferrari and has 'cock' written all over his face. He revs his engine to get Jack's attention, obviously keen for Jack to feel intimidated in his 'little' Z4.

I roll my eyes and immediately say, 'Don't, Jack.' I place my hand on his forearm to calm him. It's the sort of thing that winds Jack up enough to burn the idiot at the traffic lights, except he wouldn't be able to and he'll become frustrated and angry.

'He's a wanker,' Jack says almost without moving his lips or ungritting his teeth.

'Out of the three of us sitting at these traffic lights, I think we all know that. But you'd be the bigger wanker if you do something like race him. Is your ego really that fragile? And imagine if someone decided to run out across the road just before our traffic lights changed to green and you hit them? How would you feel in hurting someone because you let that twat over there wind you up?'

The Ferrari engine revs again and I can almost see the hairs on the back of Jack's neck stand up in animosity.

'You know, I often wonder how someone like him walks with that giant phallus protruding from his forehead,' I say.

Jack takes his eyes off the road and laughs. 'Is that what you said to Angela about me after our first meeting?' He returns his eyes to the traffic lights.

'I couldn't possibly answer that question, Mr Britcham, on the grounds I could incriminate myself.'

'Ohhh, you're a harsh lady!' he quips.

The lights mutate to amber, and in the second amber slides into green the Ferrari roars away from its spot at the lights, while Jack pulls off at normal speed. Gratifyingly, the camera at the top of the lights flashes at the Ferrari man.

'Bet he feels even more of a dickhead now that you didn't race him,' I say.

'Oh no, Mrs, you're not getting off that easily,' Jack replies. 'What did you say to Angela about me after our first meeting?'

'We're married, what difference does it make now?' I ask.

'None, but I still want to know. What did you say?'

'I told you, I didn't mention you at all,' I say. 'You didn't really register on my radar until you turned up with coffee and crois- sants. And even then it was the croissants and coffee that piqued my interest.'

'Oh, Oscar Wilde had it so right – it really is better to be talked about behind your back than to not be talked about at all.'

'Don't take it so hard,' I reassure. 'It really was nothing personal.'

'I can't believe you were so indifferent to me,' he wails.

'Not every woman finds you instantly irresistible, thankfully.'

'Why thankfully?'

'Well, I don't want every woman fan—'

The bang from somewhere to my right comes first, a fraction before the car is swept aside as if swatted by an angry giant. The screech of wheels fill my ears, my stomach falls at the lifting of the car; then there are the rough yellow sandstone bricks of the wall, and the solid muted grey of the lamppost hurtling towards me—

I open my eyes and I am in my bedroom, being held by a sleeping Jack. I am sweaty and shaky; my heart is racing, running, galloping away from the nightmare that was a reality. My breathing is erratic and scattered, my chest hurts trying to keep oxygen in.

I'm probably crying, I feel as if I am. I feel as if I am back there, trapped in the wreckage, wedged beside a lamppost, my face is stinging and wet.

I couldn't make a sound when I spoke; I kept losing chunks or slivers of time. But I kept trying, I kept calling his name, to see if he was OK. I just needed him to be alive and OK.

I think I'm suffocating. Jack's suffocating me. I'm trying to breathe but he is squeezing the breath out of me by holding me. Not caring if I wake him, and ignoring the pain that ignites my nerve endings, I push him off me and sit up in bed and instantly my breathing improves, my heart slowing with every passing second that puts distance between us.

'Libby?' he asks, resting up on one arm. 'What's wrong?'

I turn my face away, I don't want him to look at me, nor I him. I want to be as far away from him as possible. Everything is wrong, I want to say. 'Nothing,' I say, 'just a dream.'

'Oh, love,' he says, moving towards me. It's my turn to shy away from him. All those times he's done it to me, now I'm doing it to him. It causes him to sit up, a frown on his face. He does it again – reaches for me – and I can't stand it, I can't stand to have him act like this, to act like everything is OK and everything is normal when he has been lying to me. Since I asked him about the crash back at the hospital, he has lied to me. He knows what happened directly after the crash, when we both came round, he knows what he did. I pull away from his reach, and slip out of bed.

'I need to get a glass of water,' I say.

'OK,' has barely left his lips before I am out of the room and fleeing down the corridor to the kitchen.

I sit in the dark, staring at the surface of the table, watching the imperfections in the wood make themselves into images.

This is because I decided to stop reading the diaries, isn't it? I ask the great beyond. I decided to give Jack another chance, to move on and to maybe talk to him, and instead I'm given the true answer to the question he answered with a lie when I was in hospital. I now know what happened. I can now name that emotion that has been driving my need to find out about Eve. That emotion that is thumping through my veins, crawling over my skin like a million biting ants, sitting at the back of my throat like a pool of acid.

I am feeling betrayal, wrapped like climbing ivy around a huge monolith of jealousy.

jack

I think Libby knows what happened after the crash and that I lied to her about it. The way she fled the bedroom last night and didn't return until I had fallen asleep, the way she was so quiet and reserved this morning, the way she skipped her daily row with Butch about whether he really expected her to bring his food and water to him in the corridor, by simply doing it, she tells me she knows.

Even Butch sat up and looked suspiciously at her, then at the food, sniffing it to see if it was all right.

'I'll see you later,' Libby had said after she'd put breakfast on the table, without once looking in my direction. 'Have a good day.' She didn't even wait for a reply before leaving me alone in the room.

She knows, so it's only a matter of time until it's all over.

libby

Growing up, I don't remember feeling jealous. Not the true emotion of jealousy, the type that sinks its poison-tipped claws into your heart and feasts on the reason centre of your mind, while staining who you are with its filthy, indelible green ink. Jealousy is like a drug more addictive and rewarding than anything known to human kind. Its effects are instant, bolting through you faster than light, and switching you into that heightened state in an instant.

Once you are there, ensnared, doped up by this thing called jealousy, you see chances for a 'hit' everywhere.

The way Jack moves the cup to his lips then dips his head to take a sip of hot coffee – did he do that with Eve or did she know when to serve it to him so it was the perfect temperature for him to drink in comfortable gulps? The way he forgets where he's put his keys – did he always do that or did Eve have a system whereby he never had to look for them? The way he smiles – did he always smile like that or did he always smile at Eve knowing he could *never* love anyone else like he loves her.

Because that's what it comes down to, isn't it? That's what fuels my jealousy and what gives it a hit every moment of every day – can he truly love someone else like he loves her? Can he truly love *me* like he loves her?

The answer has been staring me in the face since the moment I had sex with him in his corridor: no. He might want to, but he can't. Or won't. It doesn't matter which: the reality is, he doesn't.

In the empty kitchen of this perfect house, I sink to the ground and clutch the plate I have just cleaned and dried to my chest as if it is a teddy bear that will offer me some comfort. My whole life with him has been a lie. I have fooled myself into thinking that he was capable of loving me. He can't because he still loves Eve. He thought he could share his heart with two people, dividing it up so we both got our fair share. But it is not that simple: if you were giving two children slices of cake – you would give the older one the biggest piece. They are bigger, have been around longer so they deserve the bigger portion. The younger one can't compete – no matter how much she tries – with the length of time the older one has been around.

I have the smaller piece of the cake that is his heart.

Every time I close my eyes, the vision I first awakened to moments after the crash comes into focus, and I am transported back there, to the smell of burning rubber and twisted metal, to the agony of moving, the constant wetness running down my face and down my body . . .

I'm not in so much pain for some reason, the agony is receding like the tide going out, but I feel cold. I'm always cold though, so it's probably nothing to worry about. I can move my right arm, so I reach out towards Jack. I feel the solidity of him, then I feel him move and relief and gratitude sweep through me.

'Jack,' I say. 'Are you OK?' But I'm not making noise with my words, I am speaking without sound.

'Eve, are you OK?' Jack asks, his body moving a little more under my hand. 'Sweetheart, please tell me you're OK.'

'I'm not Eve,' I say soundlessly.

'Eve,' he continues, because he can't hear me. 'Squeeze my

arm if you can hear me.' I don't squeeze his arm because I am not the woman he wants me to be.

'Oh God, Eve. I can feel your hand on my arm, please tell me you're all right. Please. I love you, I can't live without you.'

'I'm not Eve,' I try to scream at him, but that makes the pain rush back into my body.

Blackness.

'Libby, Libby?' Jack brings me round. 'It's OK, it's OK. We've been in a crash, we're going to be OK. I think we should try to get out before the car explodes.'

'That only happens in the movies,' I say, but of course he does not hear because I am not making words that can be heard; the words I make stain the air like letters written quickly and point-lessly on water.

'Help's on the way. You'll be OK. It's all going to be OK.'

Blackness.

'Libby, Libby, wake up.'

I open my eyes again and there is man I do not know sitting where Jack was a minute ago. He is dressed like a fireman. I decide that his name is Sam.

'Can you hear me?' he asks.

'Yes,' I say.

'Good, good. I'm Bill, and I'm a fireman.'

'I like firemen,' I tell him.

'Well, that's good. Think of me as your own private fireman.'

'OK,' I say.

'We're trying to get you out of here, but it's complicated because the car is at an angle and too close to a lamppost for us to use the cutters yet.'

'Fine. Don't mind me, I'm going to go to sleep for a bit.'

'No, Libby, don't go to sleep. You mustn't go to sleep.'

'Why, will Freddy Kruger get me?'

'No, he isn't real.'

'Spoilsport. Please let me go to sleep.'

'No. Tell me about yourself, tell me about your husband.'

'Jack? When I think about Jack …'

Blackness.

My eyes snap open, in case I become trapped back there, in case I have a black-out like I did then, when there is no one here to wake me up.

It's not that he called me Eve. He was in shock and confused and probably terrified. That I can understand and almost dismiss – if it wasn't for his reaction when he found out I was Libby. He was concerned and scared, but there was none of the begging, none of the 'I can't live without you's. For all he knew, I could have been dying and he didn't even say, 'I love you.'

libby

I'm trying to keep my head down as I walk to the doctor's surgery. I have a floppy, peaked cap on that hides the scar on my
scalp and if I keep looking down fewer people will see my face.
I'm walking as quickly as possible but that's pretty slow when
you're in as much pain as I am in. I couldn't have got a taxi. I just
about managed in the one that brought me home from the hospital and now the thought of being in a car again actually makes
me feel physically sick.

I know it was an accident, and cars aren't dangerous – the
people behind the wheel are – and I should get into a car soon
because the longer I leave it, the harder it will be. I know all of
the logical arguments, I've told myself them over and over
again, but still I can't do it. And why should I when I have one
perfectly good leg and another perfectly damaged leg to carry
me wherever I need to go? In this instance, an emergency
appointment with my GP. They had a cancellation and said
they'd let me have the slot. The air feels odd against my skin:
it's warm but fresher than I remember the air being. I go out
into the garden for a few minutes every day, so I haven't completely forgotten what fresh air is like, but this is different. It's
fresher, purer, despite the pollution, despite the carbon dioxide
expelled by the people around. I've given and had quite a few

oxygen treatments in my time and they never felt as cleansing as this air does.

I need to open all the windows in the house, let this air through the place, sweeping away in its path all the dust, cobwebs, stagnancy and, of course, *Eve*. We painted it, re-carpeted it, refurnished it, even brought some of my stuff over, but – as I often feel – she is still there, hanging on, clinging on to her house, her life, her husband.

The pain I felt before, a band of fire around my middle, squeezes tight again. I'd had it while sitting on the kitchen floor thinking about Jack, and I'd nearly blacked out. It'd struck again as I crawled across the floor, Butch sitting in the doorway watching me, to get to my phone on the kitchen table. I'd been fine once I'd got the doctor's appointment, but now it is back.

I stop in the street, cradle my middle in my arms and take a few deep breaths. In, out, in, out, in, out.

'You all right, love?' someone asks.

My body quakes at the horror of someone speaking to me. I haven't spoken to anyone other than Jack, Grace and Angela face to face for over a week now. I lower my head further. The man wears stonewashed jeans and big workmen boots. I don't know what else he is wearing because I can't raise my head even a little in case he sees my face.

'Fine. Just going to the doctors,' I say.

'Is it far? Do you want a hand?'

I shy away from him. 'No, I'm fine. I'm fine. Thanks.'

Then my feet move me onwards, towards someone who can help and who can make this all go away.

'How can I help?' Dr Last asks.

'I need some more painkillers,' I tell her.

'OK,' she says, spinning to her computer screen and typing in my details. 'You're on quite a strong dose of Co-codamol as it is,' she then says after reading what the computer tells her.

The computer may be right, the dose may be strong, but it's

not strong enough: the tablets aren't working. 'They're not work-ing. I need something stronger,' I tell her. 'It hurts.'

'Are you in pain constantly?' she asks.

'Not constantly.'

'What sort of pain is it?'

'Earlier, it was around my middle, sort of chest area. It was so bad I nearly passed out. It's a kind of clenching pain.'

'What were you doing at the time?'

'Nothing, I was just thinking.'

'Did the pain get better or worse when you moved?'

'It stayed the same.'

'So it's a new type of pain to the one you had as a result of your injuries?'

'Yes, no. I don't know really. I only know that it hurts.'

'How long have you felt the tablets aren't working?' she asks.

'Just today, when this new pain started. I think I need some-thing else.'

'I'm concerned that after two weeks on a medication you're starting to feel it isn't working.'

'They aren't. They used to make me feel better, now they don't.'

'Feel better emotionally or physically?'

I knew what she was getting at, and I wasn't falling for that. 'Physically, of course.'

'Painkillers aren't meant to make you feel physically or emo-tionally better,' she says. 'They are simply meant to stop the pain. If you're needing them to feel better in either way then there may be something else going on here that needs to be addressed.'

'I just want the pain to stop,' I say.

'You've been through an enormously traumatic event—'

'I know!' I tell her. 'I know that. I just need the pain to go away.'

She stares at me and I know what she is thinking: Liberty Britcham is mad. I know because I am thinking it too. This hys-teria and panic is not me. I am usually balanced and unflappable but, at this moment, I do not recognise myself.

254

'I'm sorry,' I say. 'I shouldn't have raised my voice.'

'Do you have a support network?' she asks kindly.

'Yes,' I tell her. *No*, I tell myself. I have people who care, people I can rely on, but they can't support me because I can't tell about the dreams I have about Eve, that I have her diaries, that I've realised that I have made the biggest mistake of my life. I shouldn't have got involved with Jack, let alone married him. He wasn't ready. I was stupid to go along with it because I loved him. Who was it that said love isn't blind, it's stupid? They were right. And I've been the most stupid person on Earth.

'Would you like me to refer you for some counselling?' she asks.

I shake my head, wipe away a tear that has been crawling down my cheek. 'I'll sort out a private counsellor,' I say. 'I don't know what's wrong with me. It's not like anyone died.'

'In a way, they have,' the doctor says. 'The person you were before isn't here any more. You're probably still in shock and emotional pain because your world has been shaken. It's not surprising that you seem to be focusing on your physical symptoms rather than face the emotional impact.'

'OK, thank you, doctor,' I say, although I don't know why I am thanking her when she hasn't done anything; she hasn't given me anything to take away my pain.

'Come back if you want that referral. If the pain returns we'll look again at your prescription.'

I nod at her and leave her room. Walking is difficult with the ton of bricks that are now sitting on my shoulders.

'Mummy, look! That woman's got no hair!' a small child calls out as I walk through the large waiting room to leave. I left my hat in the doctor's room, having automatically taken it off when I sat down.

I feel the eyes of everyone in the surgery swing towards me, the ones to my left obviously seeing my scar – a thick, black greasy-looking scab sealing the pieces of my skin together. Their eyes probably flick away with disinterest almost straight away, but I can

255

still feel their collective gaze crawling over my head. I should go back for my hat but that would mean staying here for a second longer than necessary. And anyway, I won't be needing it again, because after today, I won't be leaving the house until the day I'm strong enough to leave Jack.

libby

'*I'm glad you're back,*' Eve says from her place on the document box. '*I missed you.*'

My eyes focus on her for a moment and I can tell she isn't being snidey. She isn't the snidey, bitchy type.

'*You were at that bit where I'd just met Elliot in the supermarket and I got a hundred-pound tip? Remember?*'

I nod at her. I can do nothing but remember nowadays.

eve

25th June 1990

Have just had the best birthday.

I knew things would get better, and they have. After the last two birthdays being 'just another day' x2 without so much as a card or phone call from my mother, I thought that this year I was going to do something different. I wasn't going to sit at home, waiting and waiting for a card that probably wasn't going to come.

I've written loads to my mother, probably a letter a week, and I get nothing in return. I wish I could stop myself but she's my mother – she was my mum – how can I just give up on her? She might have given up on me, but I can't do it to her. I love her. Still.

Yesterday, I did something that I've been ashamed to write about. I rang her. I picked up the phone and I rang her. Actually, I've been calling a lot but I hang up after the first or second ring because I'm too scared to speak and I wouldn't know what to say. If I speak to her, I'd probably say I want to come home, but that place isn't my home any more. I'm not her little Evie any more. And how could I go back when her boyfriend was probably still there? But yesterday I got the courage to stay on the phone after more than two rings. My heart was in my throat and I was shaking as I waited for it to be answered.

'Hello?' said a man's voice.

258

I started shaking even more – horrified that he was still there, and even more horrified that I hadn't thrown the phone down rather than speak to him.

'Hello?' the man said again.

'Who is it?' my mother called from the background and I had to hold back a sob. I hadn't heard her voice in so long, I hadn't been connected to my mother in this way in a lifetime.

'Don't know, but they're still there!' the man called back. Into the phone, he said, 'This is your last chance: hello?'

Still clutching the handset, I closed my eyes and let the tears fall, holding my hand over my mouth so I wouldn't give myself away.

'Here, let me have that,' my mother said and suddenly she was there, as clear as day, speaking into the phone. 'Hello, this is Iris Quennox, how may I help you?' she said politely, obviously thinking that his phone manner was putting the person off.

'I love you,' I mouthed into the phone, speaking without words, wanting to be heard but too frightened of the consequences.

'Hello?' she repeated.

'I think about you every day,' I continued without speaking.

'Eve?' she said.

'And I miss you. I miss you so much it hurts.'

'Eve?' the man said. 'You think that's Eve?'

'No,' my mother said, 'but I can't think of anyone else who would call without speaking.'

'Bye,' I said. 'Bye, Mum.' Then I hung up and spent the rest of the night crying.

I'm ashamed because I should have spoken to her properly, I should have said something. Letters are easy, aren't they? But at least now I know she's well, she's all right and that if he's around still then she's probably happy in her own way. And, maybe, one day she'll want me back.

Anyway, to avoid moping today, I decided to go to the seaside. I mean, how crazy is it that since I was young I've never once been to the seaside? On the way to the Tube station to get the train to

Victoria, I bumped into Elliot again. Remember him? He worked at that company I should have got that job at all those years ago and I bumped into him in the supermarket a while back. He looked older and a bit more worn by life, but he seemed cuter than I remembered. Maybe because in those days I was so focused on getting a new job and didn't really notice much of anything else. Or maybe it's because I've seen the ugly side of human nature and anyone who is removed from that – who isn't a bitch trying to harm me on the dancefloor or a man who is trying to get me to fuck him for free because he is *that* special – seems to be unique and rather lovely.

'Gosh, Eve,' he said, looking genuinely pleased to see me. 'Can't believe I haven't seen you in all this time.'

'Yeah, me too,' I replied. 'Are you still at Hanch & Gliff?'

'Yeah, for my sins. And you?' he asked. 'Did you find a job?'

'Yup. I'm not sure it's what I want to do for ever, but it's a job.' I shrugged. 'It pays the bills, keeps a roof over my head.'

'I know what you mean. I still haven't worked out when exactly I decided that being an accountant was a good idea.'

I, of course, knew exactly when I decided it'd be a good idea to become a lap dancer. That's what I am, by the way. Looking back over these pages, I never had the guts to name what I do, but I am a lap dancer. Saying I'm a stripper implies that all I do is take my clothes off to titillate men, or that I take some pride in what I do, when in reality I get as close as I can to simulating sex because some man has handed over a couple of notes. Yes, some of the girls I work with still say they are in control because they get to turn a man on, they get to turn him down if he is repulsive or if he is rude to them. 'True control,' I always want to say, 'is in being able to be proud of your job and not have to make excuses for how you're seen.' And, of course, what's the point of thinking you're in control when the man on the other end of the cash thinks he is?

'Look, sorry, Elliot, but I've got a train to catch. It was nice seeing you.'

'Where are you going?' he asked.

'To Brighton. I fancy visiting the seaside.'

'Could I come with you?' he asked. 'It's my birthday and I'd love to have a reason to bunk off work.'

I thought about it. It seemed to be Fate because we have the same birthday so I said yes, and we went. And we had the best day ever.

We ate fish and chips, we walked on the beach, we put coins into the slot machines, we bought sticks of rock, we drank beer outside on the Pier and then at the end of the day we kissed each other's faces off on the train platform.

On the train, I fell asleep on his shoulder while he stroked his hand through my hair. That was the best part of the day, I think. I got to experience the touch of another human being and it was gentle and kind and loving without demanding anything I wasn't willing to give.

That's where love starts, isn't it?

17th December 1990

I've been seeing Elliot for almost six months now.

My whole life has changed the most in the last three months. He's moved in and he's begged me to stop lap dancing. His job is good enough to support us both, so I don't have to work. To be honest, while I've wanted nothing more than to give it all up, I didn't feel right about it. I don't like not being in command of my own destiny.

But it was nice to have someone love me so much he didn't want me doing those things, didn't want other men staring at my body and salivating over it night after night. He didn't condemn me and the choices I'd been forced to make, but it horrified him that I'd done it for so long. 'But you're so clever, how can you do that?' he kept asking.

And I had to keep telling him that taking your clothes off for money did not mean you were stupid or unintelligent. In some ways it was a sign that you were pretty shrewd because you knew that no matter how deep a recession the country was in, sex would always sell. *Always.*

In the end, I could see the pain in his eyes, the sorrow that just the thought of what I did brought him and I knew I couldn't do it to him any longer. I wished, actually, that I hadn't told him. That I'd just said I served drinks behind the bar instead of doing that stupid Eve thing of being honest.

So I gave it up and picked up bits and pieces of temping and cleaning – I was now more employable because I had massive holes in my CV that proved I had no aspirations that would tempt me away from a low-paid job. Every day, I see more and more that dancing for money is exactly like every other menial job, except with these other jobs I don't have to take my clothes off. And that made cleaning and photocopying and answering phones and entering data far superior occupations. I just hated the loss of power, by which I mean, of course, the loss of money. The whole thing with my dress taught me that once you have money, you have power and people respect you. It might not be ideal, it might not be how it should be in a perfect world, but it is how it is in the world I live in.

When I agreed to stop dancing, I asked, in return, that Elliot give up smoking weed and occasionally taking coke. But he replied that it wasn't very often that he did it, especially the coke, and it's better for him than going out and getting bladdered every night. Which is true, I suppose. I don't like drugs, though. After what they did to Dawn, I don't like being around them and I don't like the idea of Elliot taking them. But he seems to have it under control and I have to trust him to know what he's doing.

So, here I am, back where I started but worse off, I suppose. I have money saved, but I pretend that is not there. I remember Aunt Mavis once told me to always have a running away fund. She said, no matter how much you loved a man, always have a stash of money that would get you as far away from him as possible in an emergency. As it turned out, the first time I had to use that money was to get away from my mother and her 'boyfriend'. I have managed to put enough aside over the years to top it up again. That's why I didn't use that money for my dress. I needed to have enough money to get away if I had to.

Why am I worse off? Because I have much less money I can freely spend – I have to ask Elliot for cash if I don't get any work, and that makes me uneasy.

But I can't complain too much because I have someone who loves me. That's something I couldn't have fathomed happening when I first came to London and especially when I started dancing.

I like the way I can write that down . . . I have someone who loves me. That makes me smile.

Love,
Me

11th March 1991

When will I learn? Pride comes before a fall. Always. I took too much pride in the nice life that we had and now, three months later, we've fallen.

What has happened? Well, today Elliot, came home from work and told me that he'd been sacked. And it was all my fault. He didn't say that, obviously, not until I dragged it out of him.

Basically when I came in after the cleaning shift at the local gym he was already sitting on the sofa. The television was off, which is how I knew something was wrong, and he was just staring into space.

'What's wrong?' I asked him, not moving too far from the door because I had a feeling I would want to run out the second he told me what had happened.

His glazed-over eyes finally found my face and he looked devastated, as if all the stuffing had been kicked and kicked out of him. He was still in his suit but his tie was undone. 'I've lost my job,' he eventually said. So much time had ticked away between the moment I asked and his reply that I had been on the verge of asking again.

'Oh God, how? What's happened?'

'They gave me some bullshit, but I can't believe it's happened.' He

263

sounded distant, as if his faith in the world had been seriously shaken. I remembered how I felt when it happened to me and I hadn't even been there that long.

I crossed the room to the sofa and sat down beside him, aware that I still had the fug of ammonia and bleach and chlorine around me. I snuggled up to him – put my arms around his middle, rested my head on his chest, pushed my body as close to his as possible. I was trying to take away his pain, to absorb it into my body. His heart was beating so fast in his chest I was scared it was going to stop suddenly. 'What happened? They can't just sack you, can they? Aren't there laws about this sort of thing?'

He slowly stroked his chin and was silent again for a long time.

'Can you take them to court or something? What's that thing called – an industrial tribunal? What about that? Won't they be able to help you?'

He shook his head. 'No, they can't help. No one can.'

'But why? I can't believe you're not even going to try. They can't do this. You're a great employee. And if you don't fight it, how are you going to get another job?'

'Maybe I'll do something else. There's no point trying to get another job in accountancy, not once they've finished with my reputation. And I was getting bored of it all, anyway.'

'No, you weren't! You love your job. And what on Earth are they going to do with your reputation? You've done nothing wrong.'

'Let's just drop it, Eve. I'm really not in the mood. They're a bunch of wankers and I'm best off out of it.'

'But I don't understand,' I said. 'Please tell me what's happening. I won't be able to sleep for worrying about it.'

He sighed and my heart sank to my ankles. I knew then it was something to do with me.

'Phil called me into his office. Asked if I was seeing you. I said yes and that we lived together, were even talking about getting married someday.' My heart skipped a beat because we hadn't talked about marriage but it was obviously in his head. 'And he said did I know that you were a lap dancer.'

My heart, which had been so lifted a minute ago, started to sink again, falling down to my stomach, then began freefalling towards my toes.

'I said that you used to be, but you weren't any more. And he said did I know that you also did extras in the back rooms? And I said you didn't and he said you did. He said you'd once given him . . . he said you'd gone down on him. I said you wouldn't do that. And things got out of hand and one thing led to another and I punched him out.'

'Oh my GOD, Elliot!'

I sat up and looked at him, horrified. The fact this man Phil lied about me was nothing compared to the fact that Elliot had fought him to defend my honour, as tainted as it was.

'Don't, don't. I feel awful enough as it is. But at least I got him to admit you didn't go down on him.'

'They sacked you.'

'Said I was lucky I wasn't being charged with assault. But I'll be paid until the end of the month, so that's something.'

'Oh God, Elliot, I'm so sorry.'

'It's not your fault.'

'But I feel responsible. It's not true, though, you know that, don't you? I never did any of that. Other girls might have done, but I didn't.'

'I know, Eve, I know. That's why I got so mad at him. Bastard. He's lucky they dragged me off him when they did.'

'What a mess,' I said.

'Yeah,' he replied.

We both sighed desolately and sat in silence for about an hour. I don't know what he was thinking about, I was too scared to ask in case he was thinking that he should have known better than to get involved with someone like me. I was going from thinking about what had happened to wanting to hug him because he was thinking about marriage. Then I would start to worry about money. I had given up my job because he could support us. But if we didn't have that . . .

I'm not sure what we're going to do, to be honest. After our hour of silence on the sofa, neither of us felt much like eating so he had a couple of smokes (won't let him near my bed with cigarettes, let alone

265

weed – which I've noticed he's doing a lot more of) and I smoked a couple of cigarettes and we both went to bed.

He eventually fell asleep and I've been sitting here, writing in this, hoping the answer to our impending money problems will present themselves. None have occurred to me so far. I don't know, I feel sick when I think about our situation. I'm not sure I can go back to lap dancing. Although I miss Connie and some of the girls, and although I miss the freedom the money from it gave me, it was still – at the end of the day – being ogled and groped by strange men night after night.

Elliot wasn't that keen on me working in bars but, now that he'll be at home during the day for a little while until he gets a job, he might not mind not seeing me in the evenings. Well, even if he does, there's no way around it, is there? We need the money.

What a mess.

Me

14ᵗʰ October 1991

I would laugh if it wasn't all so … something.

I can't quite find the words to describe what is happening sometimes. It often feels like I am living someone else's life and that the real me is off somewhere at university, watching comedy shows, getting drunk in the college bar and becoming all political. The me that I get to live with, the one with the boyfriend who has been out of work for six months, wakes up to find the electricity has been cut off and then a few minutes later there are bailiffs on her doorstep because the electricity bill she thought was all paid up wasn't and they need the money in cash right then or they're coming in to seize stuff. By stuff they of course mean the furniture that belongs to the landlord, my rubbish TV that works when it feels like it, my stereo that is clearly of the same mind as my TV, and my collection of clothes that are mostly fit to be binned, apart from my beautiful dress. I gave them all the cash I had after they explained I would have been sent letter after letter after letter about this, and that I would have had phone calls too.

And then, working on instinct, I picked up the phone to discover it had been cut off, too. So I got dressed and went to the phonebox down the road and I called the gas people to find out if they'd been 'keen to make contact' and of course they had. The same with the Poll Tax people, the phone people, and – oh yes – the Waterboard. The only person who wasn't chasing me for money was the landlord but that's because I pay him myself. Everything else is 'sorted out' by Elliot.

So, this me that isn't living it up as a student decides to draw out almost all of her savings to pay off all these people and, when her boyfriend returns from wherever he's gone, she will tell him he has to find a job, even if it is one he thinks is beneath him – such as working behind a bar – because they have nothing left and they can't afford to support his quest for the perfect career any longer.

Then I have to actually go into the bank after the machine eats my card and I find that I am overdrawn by one hundred pounds. Obviously that can't be the case because I had nigh on two thousand pounds in there the last time I checked. I had saved that from dancing in Habbie's, and saved some from the cleaning and admin work. How could it all be gone and then some?

'Could your card have been stolen?' the nice cashier behind the counter asks, obviously seeing my distress.

'No,' I tell her, 'there's only one card to my account and it's just been eaten by the machine.'

'Could someone have been using your card without your knowledge?' she asks, almost as concerned as I am.

Why it took this nice lady's concern to have it dawn on me, I have no idea. I thanked her for her time, took my printed out statement and walked out of the bank. I walked the streets until I arrived at a park and I sat on the bench and I stared into space and I wondered how my life, which at one point seemed so settled and lovely, was now down the toilet?

When it was dark, and no answer arrived, I headed home and I found him reclining on the sofa, his mouth full of crisps, the TV on, the lights off and not a care in the world upon his head. The electricity people were surprisingly good at turning the service back on after I cried on top of paying them their cash. I sat down beside him and I waited and waited until an advert came on because it would be rude to interrupt, wouldn't it? And this is what happened:

Him: You all right?
Me: No, not really.
Him: Why?
Me: The bailiffs showed up today to take away our stuff because we hadn't paid the electricity bill.
Him (Switching off the TV): What? The bastards! I'll be on the phone to them tomorrow and kick seven types of hell out of them. They've made a mistake, I've paid it.
Me: Oh, right. Well, you're going to be very busy tomorrow because the gas people, the council, the phone and the Waterboard have all made exactly the same mistake. Strange, isn't it?
Him (Sitting up): Eve, I can explain.
Me: No, don't worry about it, I'll sort it. I've got a bit of money saved for emergencies, I'll go get it tomorrow and pay everything off.

And he just sat there and stared at me. Then he nodded, as if that was a good idea, as if it was even possible.

Me: Oh, wait, I can't do that, can I? Because you've already emptied that account and left it a hundred quid overdrawn.

He stared at me, his eyes growing smaller and darker with every passing second. 'I had just as much right to that money as you did,' he said angrily. What he had to be angry about, I didn't know.

'Really, how did you work that one out?' I replied, calm to his anger.

'Who's been supporting us for the past year? While I was out at work and you got to sit at home on your arse all day, who was

268

bringing in the money? And all along you had this secret stash in an account I knew nothing about.'

'I haven't stopped working since you made me give up dancing,' I said, just as calmly. 'And I always made enough to pay the rent, or didn't you notice?'

'Well, I paid for everything else. Do you know how hard that is? Do you have any idea the pressure I felt under?'

'What, you mean the pressure I've felt under for the last seven months? Or the pressure I'm going to feel under because I've got to find a way to pay all these bills and don't even have the fall back of using my savings to cover them?'

'How do you think I managed to pay the bills all this time I've been out of work?'

'But you haven't paid them. They haven't been paid for the last two quarters. And you must have been hiding all the bills, the red letters, the final demands, the court letters, my statements. Everything. So, the only thing I can ask is, where's my money?'

'It wasn't just your money.'

I ignored that because I had never dreamed of asking for access to his accounts, or asking him how much he had in the bank, and it would never occur to me to take it without asking. 'Where is it?' I asked again. I was strangely calm considering we were facing financial ruin.

'I spent it.' He was defiant. Staring at me as if I had done him wrong, not the other way around.

'On what?'

'On stuff.'

'Elliot!' I said, sharply. 'I am not your mother and you are not my teenager. We're both adults. Tell me what you spent my money on or find some other idiot to prop you up while you smoke hash all day and plot world domination from the sofa.'

The surly look on his face fell away and suddenly he was Elliot again. 'I . . . I owed some people some money. Some bad people who were going to reposition my kneecaps if I didn't pay them back with interest.'

'Money for what?' I asked.

'If I hadn't lost my job, I wouldn't be in this mess,' he said, turning it back on me.

'You mean, if you hadn't resigned from your job, you wouldn't be in this mess?' I replied.

Oh yes, he resigned. On one of my cleaning jobs, I'd met one of the girls who used to clean for Hanch & Gliff. She asked me how Elliot was getting on since he'd quit. I'd said was that the official story because he'd had a row with one of the partners? And she had put me straight: Elliot had been regularly fucking up clients' accounts, as well as turning up late in the mornings, being back late from lunch (if returning at all), and had been caught with coke on more than one occasion. Because of all this he'd been given his second – and final – written warning. He'd refused to accept it and instead resigned.

I didn't even get that upset that he had constructed such an elaborate lie to cover his back because I was so relieved that I hadn't been the cause of his job loss. And I didn't bother saying anything because it wasn't worth the argument. But I knew that's why he couldn't apply for jobs anywhere else – his reputation would have proceeded him.

He blinked at me a few times, stopped in his tracks by the realisation that I knew. 'Are you calling me a liar?' he snarled.

'No, I'm asking you what you owed money for.'

'I don't know!' he said, exasperated that I wasn't going to be sidetracked. 'Stuff! I owed Zed money for the stuff he'd given me. And a few others for some bets I'd placed. I was trying to get us out of this hole of debt we're in. I've been trying to win it back.'

'Why didn't you try earning it back, or did that seem too much like hard work?'

The slap he delivered stung a little but not as much as it probably should – not since I was still numb from the shock of seeing all that I'd worked for gone.

I immediately slapped him back, twice as hard. 'Don't push your luck,' I snapped at him. 'You don't steal from me and then hit me, too. OK? I'm not that girl.'

270

He sank back in his seat, his face drawn in, obviously not sure what to do next. He was probably wondering if he should hit me again, up the violence, or if he should leave it.

I stood up. 'I'll try to sort out the bills in the morning, but you have to get a job or you have to leave. Those are the two options left for you. And, to be honest, right now, I don't care which one you take.'

Quite wisely, he's decided to sleep on the sofa tonight. Thankfully, I had my post office book with my diaries so it's well hidden, and it's had about two hundred pounds in there for the past few years. So, I still have a running away fund, but nothing else. That makes me nervous. I'm going to call tomorrow and hopefully sort out the bills and will see if I can get some evening and afternoon shifts cleaning because that's more regular than office admin. I've not been very successful so far with the bar work because I have to be up so early to go cleaning, I'd never sleep if I got another job late at night. I really don't know how we're going to cope. I know I should throw him out, but it's just not in me right now. He has no one else and we made a good team once, didn't we? For quite a while it did seem to be Elliot and Eve against the world. I *loved* him once.

God, if I'm honest, I think I love him still. If he could sort himself out, and I really think he can, then we'll be all right – both financially and emotionally.

Me

15th January 1992

Things are a bit better.

I knew he could sort himself out and he has. He has a job now. He went out the day after the bailiffs called and found a job on a building site. First it was doing the labouring, then he had a few chats with the foreman and was allowed to look at the books. He's been doing the books ever since. It pays next to nothing, but it's better than nothing.

He hands three-quarters of it over to me, and keeps the other quarter to do with as he pleases. The money he gives me goes towards the payments to every utility company we owe money to. It took me a while, but after a few calls and tears and promises, they all agreed to let me pay off the outstanding balance in instalments. We are stretched so tight it's hard to breathe sometimes. I often have to choose between eating and buying cigarettes and often choose food because if I can eat it all, Elliot can't share it with me. Then I feel mean because I can see he is trying.

I hate him for what he's done, but I still love him for the man he was. That doesn't make sense, but is love about sense? I love Elliot for being the man who cared enough to want me to stop lap dancing; who I used to snuggle up to at night and share my dreams with; the man who made me feel like I was a whole, complete person after all those years of being leered at for my breasts, my bum, my barely covered fanny by the patrons of Habbie's. I might be stupid, but I still believe the real Elliot, the Elliot I love, is still in there. He just needs to get through this bit and he'll come out the other side as him again.

Me

5ᵗʰ April 1992

My landlord has put up the rent.

I suppose he's been fair: he hasn't put it up since I moved in and it's a prime area. I've seen in the papers how much he could be getting for this, even if it is just a mangy one-bed flat. He came round and told me, and was really nice about it. He didn't even ask for 'favours' to make up the shortfall. He explained it was just business and he'd be sorry to lose me as a tenant, especially since I'd kept the place so nice, but he wanted the going rate for it and I had first refusal.

So, that's it. I have been sitting here with a spread of bills in front of me, a piece of paper with all the figures noted down and how much I can get coming in and there is no way I can get them to balance.

We've been living on the breadline as it is. Elliot keeps falling off the wagon and getting himself beaten up because he can't pay his debts, which meant so much time off work, he's lost his job. He is out there looking for another one, but without his money there's been no way for me to pick up the slack. I don't give him any money, we can't afford to eat anything more than toast most days, and I've given up smoking because I can't afford it. I walk to wherever it is I'm working, and often leave the house at four-thirty, when it's still dark in winter and barely light in summer. I walk quickly through the streets, feeling displaced from the people who are mainly coming home from big nights out. When I could afford the bus, I would get on the first one and would be surrounded by loads of other cleaners, most of them not speaking English, off to our offices all over London. Walking, I feel alone and that's probably not helped by the fact my situation feels so lonely and desperate. When I walk past rows of houses – some with their lights on, others with their lights off – I often wonder how many of the people inside are so poor they cannot afford to eat, how many of them feel trapped by a man who they used to love and want to love again. Even if they haven't been where I am, there must be so many people who are one pay packet away from being here.

Money, it's always about money. I hate it. I actually hate money. Money isn't the root of all evil; the love of money isn't the root of all evil; the NEED for money is the root of all evil. You need it, and without it you are no one and you will sink without a trace.

I keep thinking about Dawn, and how she gets by. She lives in a much better – more expensive – place than I do, she supports her drug habit, and she still survives. But what she has to do to make that money . . .

I've got three weeks to come up with the rest of the rent or I – we – will be homeless. I will have to fend for myself out there on the cold streets when I can barely fend for myself with a roof over my head and a job. And once I'm out there, how will I get off the streets again?

I'm not even going to bother talking to Elliot about it. We've barely spoken since he last got beaten up. I occasionally buy him cigarettes because without them, he picks at the furnishings until they fray. All he can do all day is sit on the sofa and watch television. I often hear him crying, although what he has to cry about when we are where we are because of him is anyone's guess.

I've called Habbie's and a few other clubs and they haven't got any space for another girl.

And I've called estate agents, who tell me I'll need a month's rent in advance, plus a month's rent as a deposit and that, nowadays, a lot of people are doing credit checks. Of course, my credit rating is shot to pieces thanks to Elliot's behaviour with the bills, and I don't have the money required for the deposit and month's rent. I've looked for places further out, which will be cheaper, but then I'll have to find a job closer to wherever I move to because I won't be able to walk there. And most people won't take anyone who isn't working. I am stuck. I AM STUCK. I AM STUCK. I AM STUCK.

Maybe I should just get a train back to Leeds? Maybe my mother will take me in? I'm not a teenager any more – if Alan tried anything, he'd get a knee between his legs and a smack in the mouth. But it's not like she's replied to any of my letters. And it's not like I've actually forgiven her for choosing him over me.

It's not like I can get over the fact that even when she thought it was me on the phone, she didn't bother to write or ring to find out.

God, what am I going to do?

As Always

10th April 1992

I'm just back from seeing Dawn.

She's looking so much better than the last few times I've seen her. She's been in rehab and has kicked the habit 'for now' she said. She's put on weight, her skin is better, her hair is looking less lifeless, although the same can't be said for her eyes. Even though they're not as glassy as they were, they still have that dead look to them, as if Dawn is not at home any more.

'Is it really that bad?' I asked her after we'd done the obligatory small talk about how each other was.

She sighed, stared at the worn circular rug that now sits between the settee and the coffee table, and didn't say anything for a while.

'Yeah,' she said. 'It is. I tell myself it isn't so I can still do it, but it is.' I didn't need to tell her what I was asking about. She looked me over in the same way that Connie did when I asked her about working in the VIP rooms at Habbie's.

'Think of the worst sex you've ever had,' she added. Immediately, a night with Elliot a couple of weeks after he'd stolen my money and I'd been too worn down by everything to reject him came to mind. 'Times that by about a million and you'll come close.

'Now think of the best shag you've ever had.' Elliot didn't come to mind, Peter did. Nothing will ever get over how special that was, probably because when I first slept with Elliot, I was already so jaded about men and the way they looked at women's bodies that I held back. After Peter and I got over our nerves, we loved being together physically and emotionally. I loved him being close to me and inside me. That was the best, without doubt. 'Now, that's how you have to pretend it feels like every time you do it if you want them to come back, which is the way you make money long-term.'

'I wouldn't want to do it long-term.'

'No, I didn't either. But now I don't really know how to do anything else.' (On my way home, I realised that was the scariest thing out of everything she said.) 'Do you really need to do this, Eve? Really?'

'I can't see any other way out.'

'And what about Elliot? What's he doing?'

'Sitting around, smoking, feeling sorry for himself. He keeps getting beaten up for getting drugs on the slate. I'm surprised anyone will give them to him.'

Dawn's eyes darkened and her face twisted with disgust. 'Elliot is bad news, Eve.'

I've thought that so many times and then I think about the Elliot I used to know, the Elliot I fell in love with, and I can't even think about letting him go when I know he can be that man again.

275

'Why don't you move in here, until you get yourself sorted? I know the sofa is old and a bit lumpy, and it might feel like a step backwards, but it's better than the alternative, believe me.'

'I can't, Dawn. I couldn't sponge off you again. And I have so many debts that I need to pay off. I've tried a few more dancing clubs, but no one's hiring these days because of all the new restrictions. And besides . . .' I didn't want to say it, but we both knew I couldn't leave Elliot. I couldn't abandon him when he was so low.

'Eve, cut him loose. He's going to bring you down with him if you're not careful. It's only a matter of time before the people he owes money to will turn their attentions to you.'

'I can't, Dawn, you know I can't. What sort of a person would I be if I abandoned him when he's down?'

'You're too nice, you know?' She shook her head. 'I hope he appreciates it.' She shook her head again. 'Look, if you have to do this, try not to end up on the streets. You're good looking, smart. If you dress up nice you can maybe work the hotels. Try the ones down in King's Cross and Paddington. That's where the men with money go. I'd say try escorting, but the agencies take a massive percentage and that's the last thing you want when you're in dire need like you are. Hang around the hotel bars – the men who use whores always seem to know who we are. I can't do hotels: I look too obvious and the staff throw me out.

'And also, don't have a set rate. Have a vague idea of what you'll charge, but look at the man who's offering and price accordingly. No point doing it for fifty with a man who carries five hundred in his pocket as loose change.' I was grateful to her for the tips. I was grateful to her for not trying harder to talk me out of it because it probably wouldn't have taken me much to cave in and not do it.

What she'd said about not knowing how to do anything else scared me because it reminded me of how disconnected I am from the world again. I haven't read a book in so long, and I used to love reading. Now all I do is get up, walk to work, clean, come home, worry about money and sleep. I hardly look at my beautiful dress any more; I have nothing new to remind me who I am; I do nothing

276

pleasurable to remind me I am more than just a machine trying to make money to pay off debts.

What if I do this thing and even more of who I am is erased away until there is nothing left?

The Person Living This Life

I told Elliot what I am going to do. He said nothing, although his mouth started to quiver as if he was going to start crying again. And I knew that I could not spend another night comforting him. It's all too much as it is – where is my comfort while I am trying to fix this? Where is the person to throw their arms around me and tell me that everything would eventually be all right?

He didn't cry, although his brown eyes, eyes that I had once been so enchanted by, did become wet.

'I'm sorry,' he eventually said.

Fuck off, I said in my head. 'I know,' I said with my mouth.

And that was the end of that, I suppose.

Me

libby

I can hear the house phone ringing upstairs. I want to ignore it, but it could be Caleb, I've tried to call him a number of times to tell him he has to come and get Butch, or find someone else to look after him, because as soon as Butch is taken care of, I'm going to find somewhere else to live.

I understand now why Jack has been so keen not to tell me what happened directly after the crash: it shows that he doesn't really love me. He has just been going through the motions. His reaction to finding out it was me in the car and not Eve was like the difference between a family member and a colleague being at death's door – with one you'd give anything to make it all right, with the other you hope as much as you can it'll be all right.

I place the diaries on the ground. Jack won't be around for a little while longer: I'll talk to Caleb and then come back.

I get to the phone just in time.

'Yo, Sis, what's up?' His voice is crackly and far away because he is far away.

I have some money saved so I could possibly find somewhere to rent, or I could bite the bullet and move back in with my parents. It's not ideal, but it's got to be better than being in Eve's house with Eve's husband.

'You need to come home,' I say to him.

'Why? What's happened? Is Butch all right?'

'Yeah, he's fine, but I need you to come home and get him or find someone else to look after him.'

'What do you mean?' Suddenly the line is clear, I can hear his voice. Suddenly he is bothering to speak to me properly, probably by doing something as basic as putting the phone to his ear. The ten messages I've left saying to call me obviously haven't told him that something could be wrong.

'We can't look after Butch any more, so you need find alternative arrangements,' I say.

'Hang on, Sis, what's happened?'

'I just need you to come and get Butch or tell me what to do with him.'

'If it's a real emergency and you can't look after him any more, then you can take him back to my house. The person I've got house-sitting will look after him, no problems.'

'The person you've got house-sitting? You mean, all along there's been another option and you forced your dog on me?'

Silence.

'OH MY GOD! What is wrong with you? Why have you guilt-tripped me into looking after your dog when there was someone else to do it all along?'

'Cos you need him. Butch is feisty and good-hearted like Benji and you need someone to look after you. I know you always feel better around Benji, so Butch is the next best thing cos, Sis, you ain't in a good place. I knew it when I walked into that hospital. And your voice on the phone told me you was sinking, so I thought he could stay with you to help sort you out.'

My brother, the most selfish man on Earth, did that for me? I cover my mouth with my hand for fear I'll start sobbing.

'Look, take Butch to my house if you want, but he's good to have around. Even if he a bit feisty.'

'OK,' I say. 'I'll, erm, let you now what I decide to do.'

'All right, Sis. Hope you're feeling better. I'll call you soon.'

'Yeah,' I say as he cuts the line.

When did I stop taking care of myself? I wonder. When did I become so immersed in Eve's life that my own seemed so secondary and unimportant? Because it has, clearly. I've been scrabbling around finding out about her, trying to work out what Jack was keeping from me, but I haven't thought about me, about my recovery, about what I need to push forwards. If I'm not well, how can I move on from Jack? If my life is so dependent upon what he is feeling, about him not talking to me, about unpicking the life of the woman he loved before me, then where am I in all of this? What will happen to me when her life is revealed? What will I have left to live for? I'm not keen on going back to work because that would mean a wig and heavy make-up for months, and having people stare while they try to work out what exactly is wrong with me.

Right now, I have nothing. I need to start rebuilding my life. That doesn't mean finding out about Eve; it means finding out about me and where I go from here.

'I need to get a counsellor,' I say. I need someone to help me find out who I am now I don't have my other life any more.

Butch's barking makes me stop staring at the table and focus on him.

'You think I need a counsellor, do you?' I say to him.

He simply stares at me.

'Right, I'd better put those diaries away and then come back and find the number of someone to talk to.'

Butch gives a satisfied bark, as he meanders back to his basket.

jack

Libby hadn't started dinner when I came in, but she was sitting at the kitchen table, in the dark, waiting for me. Unlike usual, Butch didn't scamper up to greet me. He stayed in his basket until I got closer to him, then he raised his head a little and let out a little whine of solidarity.

I pulled out the chair opposite hers and sat down.

She was staring down at the tabletop and didn't acknowledge me for the longest few minutes of my life. It reminded me of the minutes before the ambulance crew pronounced Eve dead. I knew what they were going to say, but I'd been holding my breath and willing them not to say it. I was doing the same with Libby, holding my breath and willing her not to say it.

'I hope you don't mind if I stay here a bit longer until Caleb comes back for Butch and until I find somewhere to live.' She was trembling as she spoke.

'Where will you go?'

'I don't know, probably to my parents' house,' she said quietly. 'Paloma has said she'll keep my job open but I'm not sure I want to go back to all that. I don't know, it's a big old world out there. I'll find something.'

'Yeah,' I said.

'I'd like it if we could still be friends,' she said.

281

'I don't want to be your friend, I want to be your husband,' I replied.

I saw the agony of those words rip through her. 'I know you want to, but you can't, can you?' She stood up. 'Because in your head, and everywhere else it counts, you're still married to her.'

Running has always been a way to get rid of tension, to help clear my mind, it isn't working now. Like the night Eve told me something that blew my world apart – I ran and ran for hours that night, and I still could not get it straight in my head.

Libby leaving me is bad enough, but having to face the possibility that she is right, that in my mind and in my heart I'm still married to Eve, would mean I have been so unfair to the one person who has been nothing but wonderful to me. Libby, not Eve, helped me to become the man I am today, and in return I've betrayed her.

libby

Eve is curled up in a foetal position on the boxes today, and she can barely lift her head to look at me as I open one of the diaries.

I know I'm not meant to be doing this, but I can't stop reading about her. She was faced with a hideous choice about what to do to sort out her problems when I had to stop reading last time.

I know how she feels. Finishing with Jack last night was one of the hardest things I've ever had to do. But staying with him, living like this, as someone who would always be second best, would have destroyed me in the end. I know what I am like, and – just like with my career as a biochemist, as with my hair – I would rather have nothing than something that was all right. I thought he loved me as well as still loving Eve but he doesn't. And I deserve better. Everyone does.

Eve deserved better than Elliot, but she was lucky: she got Jack in the end. And, I guess from the way he feels about her, that she was the best for him.

chapter fourteen

eve

13th April 1992

'Can I buy you a drink?'

'Yes, if you'd like.'

'Glass of white wine for the lady, please. Beer for me.'

Quietly: 'Are you working?'

Just as quietly: 'Yes.'

Even quieter: 'How much?'

'BJ, seventy-five; hand, fifty; full, two hundred.'

'Greek?'

'A grand.'

'Without?'

'Two grand.'

'One-fifty for full?'

'One-seven-five.'

'Room 214. Ten minutes.'

'OK.'

The wine is left untouched. In the room, the clothes come off slowly, teasingly, just as they used to in the club. The act is not unpleasant: there is touching and licking but no kissing. The dressing part is quicker than the undressing – then the realisation that money wasn't taken upfront.

Ten twenty-pound notes are handed over – twenty-five pounds as a tip – and the bathroom is used to tidy hair, brush teeth, check make-up. A wave goodbye and a promise to do it again sometime.

That was my first time. Honey's first time. The second time was worse. It was much the same as the first time, but – like the second night as a dancer – the second time tells you that this is the path you have chosen and it is going to be very hard to get off it.

I cried in the bath earlier. None of them had been awful to me; none of them had been hideous; they all paid and gave me a tip; they were all perfectly nice afterwards; I came home with six hundred and fifty quid – but still I cried.

I cried because I did not want Honey to do those things any more than I wanted Eve to. I cried because I should have stayed at home in Leeds. I should have let Alan rape me because if I had, I wouldn't be in this mess. I wouldn't be letting perfectly nice men, almost all of them with wedding rings on, hurt me in ways I did not know I could be hurt, and ways I cannot describe.

E

6th May 1992

Every night I sit in front of the dressing table with my make-up in front of me.

I start with cover-up stick, to hide the blemishes – the patchiness of my skin, and the spots that have become red and inflamed, as well as the dark circles under my eyes. Then I move to foundation. I use a brush not a sponge – Connie taught me that you wasted less make-up that way. I stroke it onto my skin, moving with the contours of my face, then sliding down to my neck making sure it is the same colour as my face. I go right up to and just behind my ears, to make sure that it looks natural, even though I am applying a lot. I have to apply a lot to get me through the night, and right through everything I have to do. I then set my foundation with powder, dusting it on with another thick, many-bristled brush. And then dusting some onto my lips to prepare them for lipstick. I use a black pencil to line my eyes, then a blue shadow to cover my lids. I then go back over the lines around my eyes with the pencil, then I stroke on mascara to make my eyelashes stand out.

I outline my mouth with a browny red, then I fill my lips in with a pale, tawny-red lipstick that won't stain a man's face or body. I blot with a tissue, then colour in again. Finally, I unclip my washed and dried hair and let it fall in loose waves to my shoulders.

I pull on the dress – usually black, short and tight – that is laid on the bed, then step into black stilettos. I pick up my bag (with condoms, two spare pairs of knickers, pressed powder, eyeliner, hairbrush, lipstick, toothbrush, mirror and keys) and return to the mirror, where Honey is looking back at me.

'Hi, Honey,' I always say.

I leave the bedroom, and walk through the living room to the door. Eve's boyfriend, Elliot, sits on the sofa, watching TV and smoking cigarettes. He can afford to now that Eve gives him money. He says something that sounds like 'Be safe' and Honey ignores him. Outside of work, Honey would never speak to someone like him and just because he's Eve's boyfriend doesn't mean Honey has to speak to him. She closes the door and walks the distance along the dingy corridor and down the stairs to the front entrance then steps out into the night. The air is usually cooler in the evening, and she breathes it in, allowing it to sear through her, scorching and strengthening her lungs, giving her the power to go out there and do what she needs to do to earn money.

Every night I go through this ritual so I can look in the mirror and see Honey before I leave. When I was dancing, Honey would only appear in the mirror at the club. It helped to separate the two. I've found that if Honey – confident, practical, aloof – leaves the flat and Honey returns, Eve does not spend the night crying. Because Eve is at home, in bed with a book or in front of the television immersed in *EastEnders* or *Corrie* while Honey goes out to work.

I've stopped crying now. And that's all that matters.

I have stopped cleaning altogether and instead I become Honey, in other words 'work' during the day as well as at night.

I was meant to phase Honey's work out, meant to stop, but since I've paid off all the debts, I have become addicted to the freedom of the money – and the ability to be myself.

I didn't count on that, did I? Now that I am able to earn in three or four hours what I earned in a day or two of cleaning, I can do things like read books. I can visit the library and I can even *buy* books. They are no longer a luxury that I cannot justify. I can spend the afternoon walking around areas of London I am curious about, and I have even begun to save money.

Somehow – I'm not sure how, really – I have started giving some of the money I make to Elliot. He's better now so he could work, but he doesn't. It's almost like I am paying him now to allow me to do this. If that makes sense? It doesn't really to me, but I do it.

Part of it is to do with my new-found freedom. I think deep down I feel guilty that I am not tied to working all the hours God sends because I have sex with other men, and yet I cannot bring myself to do it with him. It's not even the Eve–Honey split. I could pretend to be Honey the times that Elliot comes on to me, I could slip into that role and do it, but I don't *want* to. I don't want to have sex with Elliot. I feel guilty about that, so I suppose I am paying him off. Paying him to leave me alone. I pay the rent, I pay the bills, I buy the food. In the purest sense, I suppose he is my pimp because he is living off my earnings. In the real sense, he is someone I share a flat with, a bed with, but not a life with.

If he did not come back one night, I would not mind, I would not really care, but it's not in me to throw him out. We live separate lives and that suits me.

Obviously I hide my money well. I hide it separately from my diaries because if one thing was discovered, at least I would still have the other.

My life isn't perfect, or even good. It is . . . different. Better.

I wish I didn't have to do what I do; I wish that I wasn't having sex to finance a life where I am grateful that I am not desperately unhappy; I wish I had a life where I was happy. But for the likes of me, poor girls without any qualifications on paper, this is one way to make it through life.

Right now, not having to worry about money is the better option. Better even than the threat of being arrested, the threat of being harmed by a punter, the threat of finding out one day that Honey has taken over my – Eve's – life.

Me (Whoever That Is)

14th February 1995

There were two of them.

The first one got me up to his hotel room by accepting the price without bargaining, the other hid in the bathroom, with the knife.

They didn't want anything except my money, and I gave it to them without arguing. I usually hid it in the ripped lining of my bag and I told them where to look, all the while my eyes fixed on the blade resting on the apple of my right cheek. My heart, too scared to beat, was cold and still in my chest, my breath came in short, slow gasps.

They made me undress to prove I wasn't hiding any cash anywhere, then they threw me naked outside the room. Thirty seconds later, laughing loudly, they threw out my dress, my jacket, my underwear, my stockings, my shoes and my bag. With shaking hands, and with their laughter on the other side of the door still clanging like an alarm bell in my ears, I ran to the end of the corridor and got dressed.

Another woman could go to the police. She could verbally sketch out the image of the two white men with emotionless eyes and carnivorous grins who were her attackers. She could describe the number of curves and points that made up the serrated edge of the blade and how it felt pressed into her skin. She could explain the smell of fear that filled her nostrils. She could tell of the terror of thinking she was about to be raped and left with her throat slit in a small hotel in London. She could outline the horror of imagining the details of your life and your gruesome, sordid death factually noted in a small column in a newspaper. She could recall the disgustingly delicious mix of relief and humiliation as she ran to the end of the corridor and stood by the lift getting dressed as quickly as possible, and to still feel it when she finally got home.

But I wasn't another woman, I wasn't any woman. I wasn't a 'woman' at all, was I? I was a hooker, a whore, a prossie.

The police won't care that I got robbed. They would probably arrest me for soliciting; they would probably question me to find out if I was on drugs. In the grand scheme of things, the hierarchy of crimes, something happening to me would rank somewhere near the bottom rung. Even if I was murdered, who would really care?

X

17th February 1995

'Aren't you going to work?' Elliot asked me earlier.

I haven't been out to work in three days. I'm too scared. I can admit that here. I've been telling myself I don't need to work because I've already earned enough to get by this month, despite being robbed the other night, but in reality I am too scared to go out there. The reminder that no one would care if something happened to me added to my fear.

Elliot was out when I got in the other night so I had bathed and cried – the first time in ages – before I forced myself to go to sleep. It would be better in the morning, I decided. But I woke up in a sweat, panicked and terrified several times in the night, and felt heavy-headed and weak by the time the sun came up.

He hadn't noticed anything was wrong – not even that I'd taken

292

up smoking again. Now he noticed because I wasn't out there, earning. I often didn't work over the days of my period, but that was last week.

'No,' I said, simply, focusing on the television.

'Why not?' he asked, as if my job was a normal one, as if I was stupid to put it in jeopardy. As if he shouldn't mind what I do.

'Because three nights ago two men attacked and robbed me at knifepoint,' I said. Stating the cold hard facts of what happened sent a chill through my heart. *Did that really happen to me?* I thought. From nowhere, the time I was attacked outside Habbie's came into my mind. I'd stopped working for a few days after that, too.

'You didn't give them all your money, did you?' Elliot asked, his concern for the money so very touching.

'Yes, I'm fine, thanks for asking,' I replied.

'Well, you're obviously fine,' he replied, as if I was stupid. 'Did they get all your cash?'

'Why haven't you asked if they raped me?' I asked.

'Well, they can't can they?' he said with a casual shrug. 'You're a prossie. You can't rape a prossie.'

'Oh, fuck off, you wanker,' I said to him.

'What? You can't, can you?'

'No means no – whoever is saying it. When I went up to that man's room, I had agreed to have sex with him for money. If I changed my mind and didn't take his money, that doesn't give him the right to do it anyway.'

'Yeah, but—'

'Shut up. If you want to carry on living here and getting money from me, just shut up.'

I turned up the sound on the TV, pulled my legs up to my chest and stared hard at the screen. I had to get away from him, I realised. He was poison. If he hadn't stolen all my money, I would not be sitting here, disgusted with my body, unsure of who I am, desperate to be able to get out of this cycle I'm in.

I'm stuck again, of course. I didn't want to do this long-term, but here I am two and a half years later.

Things have got to get better soon, right?
Right?

Lady (ha ha) In A Mess

chapter fifteen

libby

'What would you like to get out of these sessions, Libby?' the woman sitting opposite me asks.

I am in a room in her basement flat where she works from. The opaque blinds that cover the large windows let in some light from the street, and the space is a delicate mixture of functional and comfortable. Two of the walls have bookcases filled with books on psychology, psychotherapy, counselling and trauma. The third wall, behind her head, and beside the door is taken up with her framed diplomas and qualifications. Beneath the window, behind me, is a large wooden desk, which is neat and orderly. She has also managed to fit in two large, squashy chairs that you sink into. Both have three cushions – excessive but probably necessary to create the illusion of comfort. Nothing like comfort is going to take place in here.

'I don't know,' I admit.

I want to get back to being me again, I want to go back to the part of my life where I thought Jack loved me and I only needed to give him time to heal so he could show me so completely. I want to stop having weird dreams. I want to have my face and my hair back. I want to understand how someone who seems as nice as Eve can get sucked into the world she did. I want a lot of things that are highly unlikely to come from just talking to this woman.

'That's a good place to start, believe it or not. You're probably more open to the process if you don't have any unrealistic expectations.'

I've been known to give the unrealistic expectations spiel to people who come to have a facial in the hopes it'll reverse the twenty years of sunbaking/sleeping in make-up/smoking/excessive drinking they've done. 'You're lucky to have a good underlying bone structure,' I used to say. 'A long-lasting, youthful complexion comes down to genes as well as taking care of yourself. I think a course of facials will help a lot, but I can't promise it'll reverse all the damage.' In other words, you have unrealistic expectations – the only way they would be realistic is if I had access to a time machine so I could go back, slather you in sunblock, slap the cigarette out of your hands, stand over you while you wash make-up off every night or send you home to bed after just a few drinks.

I'm sure this woman is saying the same thing because she heard briefly about my problems on the phone and probably thought I was a textbook case who she could talk and nurture back to health. In 3D, full Technicolor, she is now probably thinking the same thing I think when I see a sun-loving, booze-swigging smoker who wants to look like the young model on the front of a magazine: unrealistic expectations.

I say nothing to Orla Jenkins. Most people I give the spiel to accept that I am going to do the best I can while expecting a miracle. I am realistic enough to know that there will be no miracles from this process – I might be lucky and walk away feeling better about myself but with all the other issues still raging in the background.

'What's the most pressing problem you have at the moment?' Orla Jenkins asks.

I want to leave my husband. I'm obsessed with a dead woman. I still can't completely assimilate the horror of looking in the mirror and seeing someone completely different to the image I have of myself in my head. Leaving the house is like a hell where

I am being tortured in the most intimate ways. 'I can't get into a car.'

'How did you get here today?'

'I walked.'

'And how was that?'

'Not easy, since walking anything but a short distance is very hard.'

'Have you been in a car since the accident?' she asks.

'Yes, on the way home from the hospital. I couldn't get on the bus so it had to be in a taxi.'

'And that's it?'

'Yes.'

'How did it feel being in the back of that taxi?'

'Not good,' I say. 'It probably wouldn't be so bad if I was driving. I don't like the idea of sitting there passively and being . . .' My voice stops working.

'And being?' Orla Jenkins prods.

I shrug. 'I don't know,' I mumble.

'Being in control seems quite important to you. Do you like to be in control?'

Doesn't everyone? Aren't even the people who relinquish control to others constantly plagued with doubt that they're not doing the right thing? 'Yes, but I don't see that as anything unusual. Don't most people like to be in control?'

'But life is full of things and instances that are out of your control.'

I have been picking at my nails and manage to break a small bubble, to slip the edge of my thumb nail under it then lift away a flap of base coat, varnish and top coat in one go. It peels back across my nail like the lid of a yoghurt pot. It's gratifying enough to take away the sting of her words, a reminder that I am walking proof that most of life is random and out of control. That a man I have never met, who thinks he can make a dash for a small gap in traffic but misjudges it because he has his mobile hooked between his chin and his shoulder and isn't concentrating, can

299

change my life. I'm not going to say 'wreck my life' because it isn't wrecked. I still have my life, I can still walk and talk, I haven't lost anyone in the purest sense – Jack is an exceptional case – so my life isn't wrecked. Although I'll probably never go back to being a beauty therapist. Even with make-up and a wig until my hair grows back, I don't think I could do that job again. But despite that, I am still lucky. I know that.

'Maybe,' I say. 'But that doesn't change the fact I don't like to live my life in a state of chaos or anarchy. I like to be in control as much as possible.'

Orla Jenkins sighs. 'The thing is, Libby,' she says in that tone someone uses only when they're about to tell you off, 'I'm concerned that you seem to be intellectualizing a lot of what has happened to you. You're not allowing yourself to feel.'

Not allowing myself to feel? I feel a lot. I've cried, *buckets*. 'I've cried more in the past few weeks than I've cried my entire life,' I say to her.

'But you're not able to let go and cry properly, are you? You must be so angry and sad – I'm sure anyone would be in your situation – but you don't seem to be allowing yourself the space or permission to feel that.'

'What good would getting angry do apart from upsetting everyone around me?' I ask her. 'And who would I be angry at?'

'Who do you think you would be angry at?'

'The idiot driving the other car,' I say without conviction. For some reason, I can't think about him in terms of what happened after the crash. Whenever the police call to tell me what is happening, I can't talk to them and I ask them to speak to Jack instead. The first few times he tried to tell me he stopped talking after a few words when he realised I was staring at him with glazed-over eyes and had put my hands over my ears. I didn't want to know; I couldn't know, for some reason.

'You don't sound very sure,' Orla Jenkins says.

'Has it been an hour yet?' I ask.

'No.'

'Oh, well . . . Look, I'm sorry, you're very nice and you have fabulous skin, and I'm sure you've helped lots of other people, but I can't be here. This isn't my thing at all. I think . . . I think I'm just going to have to get on with it. You know? Stop being so pathetic. If I try to be more positive, focus on the things I've got, I think I'll be all right.' I stand, pull my hat further down my face and wrap my rain mac around myself again. 'Thanks, really. You've been great.'

'I'm sorry this hasn't been what you expected,' she says, standing too. 'But if you change your mind, you'll know where I am.'

'Thanks,' I say again. 'I'll get in touch if I need to.'

I won't. We both know that I won't.

But I know exactly what I'm going to do when I get home.

libby

When I get home, the door to the 'Eve cupboard' in the cellar is ajar and it is empty. It wasn't like that yesterday. I stand staring at it, a feeling of dread creeping through me. I hope he didn't do that for me. I hope he didn't dispose of her belongings because of me. I'm not worth it, not to him.

If he destroys or rids himself of her belongings because he thinks it will change anything between us, he will start to hate me for 'making' him do it, and he will hate himself for being weak enough to go through with it.

He can't help not loving me. No more than I can help still being in love with him.

'*It's all a bit of a mess, isn't it?*' Eve says, sitting with her legs pulled up to her chest and watching me with sympathy.

'For both of us,' I reply. 'And yes, I am aware that I have completely lost my mind – talking to my soon-to-be ex-husband's dead wife is probably as close to crazy as a person can get.'

eve

So, now I'm in Brighton.

That last conversation with Elliot was the wake-up call I needed to get out of the life I was living. The second he left the flat the next day, I packed my diaries, my dress, Aunt Mavis's rosary, my picture of my parents and me, and the cash I had hidden in Uncle Henry's kitbag. I took as many clothes as I could get into the bag in a short space of time, then I ran for it.

After speaking to him, realising how little he thought of me, how much he thought of the money I made from what I did, I decided that I had to put myself first. I splurged on a black cab to Victoria and with every street the driver turned down, the knot of anxiety and fear loosened because I was going to be away from him. I'd already decided to leave London. There was no point sticking around here when there was even the slightest possibility of bumping into Elliot. It'd be too painful, too awful.

Walking away from everything wasn't as bad the second time. Leaving my books, my clothes, my underwear, my crockery, cutlery, little knick-knacks was easier this time than it had been when I left Leeds. This time I knew what was important, what money couldn't replace, and that nothing could be as hard as walking away from my mother.

So, I am here in Brighton.

I spent the first few nights in a hostel, then I found a pretty two-bedroom flat to rent in a place called Kemptown. It's nice here.

I'm sitting in my clean living room, with seagulls wailing in piercing tones outside as if crying for some lost love, about to leave for my third admin interview of the day.

Since that birthday I spent in Brighton, I've always fancied living by the seaside. And now I am.

Fingers crossed I'll get this job and then my new life can really begin. All that other stuff will be in the past and I'll be worthy of my dress again. Fingers crossed, fingers crossed.

Eve (Yes, it's really me again)

21st September 1995

Six months in Brighton.

And this is what I have learned: the men you meet escorting are very different to the men you meet in hotels.

A lot of them have considered what they're going to do, I suppose: planned for it, booked a hotel room or made sure they're alone in their home for the night so they can get a girl like me over.

Towards the end of my stint in London, I'd lowered my prices because the men just weren't up for paying as much as they used to. I don't know why. Dawn muttered something about there being more supply than ever so the 'clients' got to be picky. Good old capitalism at work there. With this agency I've signed up with, I get much more money than I did, even after the cut they take (thirty per cent!). And they do checks on the men to make sure they are safe and legit. No more men waiting for me with knives.

Henrietta (don't think that's her real name but she calls me Honey, so there you go), the boss I had the 'interview' with, told me to get my hair done at a posh salon, to make sure I got regular manicures and facials, and that I bought some expensive underwear because

304

the men she sent girls to expected class. And I had a look of class about me . . . well, I could have if I got myself groomed. She reminded me of Ophelia a little: the same apple-shaped face, swept up greying hair, sophisticated clothes, and posh accent. But unlike Ophelia, Henrietta's accent dropped every so often and I was sure I could hear hints of Yorkshire in there. But I could be imagining that because I am so often knocked over by homesickness.

'It's all fanny at the end of the day, darling,' she said, 'but these men think the fannies they "visit" should be neat and groomed and smelling sweet. Totally unrealistic view of what women are all about, but what do I care? They can pay anything in the region of five hundred pounds per hour for the right girl, which makes me very happy.'

It isn't all about fucking, I soon found out. Some of them do actually want you to escort them to places – to events and dinners, shows, and even the cinema. Some of them want to take you to dinner first, to talk to you, to ask you questions, before you go back to their place. They like to have someone good looking on their arm while they are seen out and about, or they like to pretend they're on a date. Whatever the activity, it doesn't bother me – I'm getting paid by the hour so the longer they want to spin it out, the more cash I go home with.

Some of them don't want you to fuck them the first few times; they like to talk to you, they want a cuddle, they want to be held. They want you to verbally stroke their egos while you physically stroke their bodies. Some ask you to take your clothes off and to lie in front of them so they can touch you, they can try to pleasure you.

The bottom line is the talking: the men I escort almost always want to talk. And they are almost always married or attached, and keen to tell me how their wives or girlfriends just don't want to put out any more. They don't say it like that; they say their wives don't want to have sex, that they're too busy with children, or they feel they're too old for all of that, or they don't have as high a sex drive as he does and he's at his wits' end and in desperate need of that physical release.

305

I nod, because I can feel their pain, I gather them in my arms, I allow them to enter my body, I caress them better, I make sure they get that release they so desperately need.

Then I go home and become Eve and roll my eyes at the bullshit I have been spun. If I had not been a lap dancer, or the girlfriend of a drug addict, or worked as a prostitute in London, I might have bought all that nonsense. I might actually feel the empathy and understanding I showed them. But I have been all those things, so I know: if you're that unhappy you leave, do not hurt another person with lies and theft. I have to stop my thought processes there because if I think it through much more, I will start to feel guilty about taking their money and I would not be able to earn my keep.

I still go through my Honey ritual, just with more expensive make-up and more pricey clothes, because I do not want Eve to cry. It is more money, they are safer working conditions but it is still selling my body, it is still slicing off pieces of something precious and giving it to the person with the right amount of cash in his hand. So it is still enough to make me cry.

No one wanted me, by the way. In the four months down here I spent applying for admin and clerical jobs, no one wanted me. Those positions were going to graduates, or even people with A levels. They all liked me, they all thought I was bright and would throw myself into the role, but to them taking on someone who was a cleaner with ten O levels instead of someone who had at least A levels and usually relevant work experience was not an option.

'I once fucked the sales director of an international company for three hundred quid, doesn't that count as relevant experience?' I almost said to the last person to deliver the news over the phone. The ones who really liked me always phoned – and that was worse in some ways. Telling me I was nice but just not good enough was bad when it was written down, but when you were then forced to reply to them, to say that you understood, that was the nasty part.

And there I was again: someone who felt very small and scared and not good enough. So I went back to the way of making money that made me feel less small and less scared about being evicted. I still felt not good enough, but this way it felt better than having nothing to eat and bailiffs at the door.

I've totally fallen in love with Kemptown. It's dead easy to walk to the centre of Brighton from here, and to walk to the seafront. It's got lots of cool little shops, lots of wonderful cafés, trendy clothes boutiques and there are loads of second-hand bookshops, which feeds my addiction.

Speaking of addiction, I spoke to my old landlord from London a while back. From Victoria, before I got on the train, I had sent him an envelope with a week's rent in and a note saying I'd had to leave suddenly and I was sorry I hadn't given more notice. I said he should keep my bond as the final month's rent and that I was grateful to him for being so nice to me over the years.

I rang to double check it was all OK. Me being me, I felt guilty about leaving him in the lurch, and also I thought I would need a landlord's reference. It turns out the people down here are much more laidback about such things if you show them you've got the cash.

He told me he was sorry to lose me as a tenant but had already found a new someone to move in. That was within a week of me leaving. 'Who, Elliot?' I asked.

'Elliot?' he asked, confused. 'Is that name of idiot you live with?' (His English had not improved.)

'Yes,' I replied.

'No. I throw him out day I get letter. Any man who live off woman . . . he no man in my eyes. I know he won't pay rent. I no get into that sitting tenant nonsense. I have no time for it. I get some men, come over, pick him up, throw him onto street with his stinky drugs and stupid clothes.'

'How did you know he lived off me?' I asked.

'Evie, my lovely little lamb, I know what you do. I have friends: they talk, they tell me things. I know what you do to pay rent. I feel bad, but rent is business. And I know that man who can let his lady do that, and take money from her, he no man.'

In his own twisted way, he was showing me he cared. Not enough to leave my rent at what it was, or to not have suggested I fuck him to pay my rent before but few of us are perfect, after all.

It was an awful thing to realise that I didn't really care what had happened to Elliot. I had loved him and propped him up for so long, but that had been eroded over time. Eroded and corroded until there was nothing but the vaguest, flimsiest memory left of what our relationship was like.

I've started to write to my mother again. I can tell her about Brighton, and what it's like to live by the sea. I can tell her about the wonderful architecture, the salty air, the sound of the pebbles moving together under foot, the unique calls of the seagulls telling each other their latest adventures in high-pitched tones.

Still no reply, but that's not going to stop me writing.

That's where I am. Back to where I was, but a little bit further down the road. I'm not unhappy, I suppose that's main thing.

Me

7th December 1995

So, something happened tonight that was unexpected.

I got to a booking at a hotel in Brighton earlier than expected, and I saw there was a private party on. It's nearly Christmas, and the world seems to be celebrating, but I don't really have anyone to have a works party with, if you see what I mean. The concierge didn't look twice at me because I was dressed up, so I decided to slip in and have a look.

The ballroom was spectacular with a dancing area and tables with several chairs around them, and silver stars and fake snow and the biggest Christmas tree I've ever seen. Everyone was in their finery and drunk or on their way, dancing, laughing, talking – basically having a good time. I've never really been to one of these parties to have a good time, if I've gone it's as someone's escort and so I've been working. I stood at the back, by the door, keeping

308

out of sight so no one would throw me out until I'd had a chance to experience a little Christmas spirit, no matter how vicarious it might seem.

'You don't look like you belong here,' that was the first thing he said to me.

I immediately stood up straight from leaning against the wall, fearing I was about to be manhandled and thrown out of there. That had happened to me on more than one occasion in the hotels in London. Some concierges were nicer than others at turning a blind eye to your patronage of their bar.

'Oh, I'm sorry, I just heard the party and wanted to see – I'm sorry, I'll go. I didn't mean any harm.' I pushed my clutch bag under my arm and made to leave.

'No, no, no,' he said. 'I didn't mean it like that. I know almost everyone here apart from you.'

'That's because I'm a gatecrasher,' I said, uttering the last word in a stage whisper.

'I am, too,' he replied.

I was confused: he was dressed in a tuxedo and looked like he fitted in, but so would I in my knee-length black evening dress and shiny black stilettos. 'Are you?' I asked.

'Not technically, because I was invited and all that. I just don't really fit in with all these people.' And he smiled. He smiled and my chest expanded so much it was fit to explode.

'You look the part,' I said nonchalantly.

'Ahhh, looks can be deceiving,' he said, and smiled again. The second smile made my heart stop its erratic thumping, and allowed it to perform a little pirouette in my chest. Just as it settled down, the butterflies in my stomach did the same happy spin.

'They certainly can,' I said. I reached out and touched the spot on his face where his hair curled down from his head around his ear. 'It *looks* like you've been playing with white paint.' I'd had to touch him, he was far too good looking not to. Just that brief moment of feeling his skin under my fingertips warmed me through. I hadn't realised how cold I'd felt inside all these years until I touched a person who

309

was normal. It felt like I hadn't encountered someone like that – someone who had no idea of what I did – since that waitress in the café the day I bought my dress. His normalness thumped through me, warming every part of me it touched. 'Someone dressed like you doesn't usually have white paint on them. So, I can't help but agree that looks can be deceiving.'

He looked surprised, touched his face. 'Oh God, did I miss a bit?' he rubbed at his skin. 'Is it gone?'

'It's gone,' I confirmed.

'Gah!' he said, pulling a face. 'The pitfalls of renovating a house with your bare hands.'

'A house? You've got an actual house all to yourself?' I said.

'Yeah, it's mostly being held up by the wallpaper and layers of dust, but I love it. Does that sound crass? Saying I love a house?'

'No, not at all. It's good to have things that you love. They keep you grounded, make you realise how much you've got to lose.'

'I've never thought of it like that before.'

'It's good to love people. But if you don't have anyone you can truly give your heart to, then having something that means the world to you can often act as a good stand-in.'

'What's your stand-in?'

'Why do you assume I have a stand-in?'

'Because that theory wasn't formed by someone who has another person they can give their heart to.' He smiled again. 'And I'm more hoping than assuming that you not wearing a ring means you haven't given your heart to anyone else, so I might have a chance.'

In another life, in another reality, the way my stomach flipped and my heart pirouetted again would have been exactly what I wanted. But I couldn't do it.

'I guess that's going to be one of life's great mysteries,' I said to him. 'I think I'd better leave before people start to point at me, shrieking "gatecrasher" or whatever the posh people's equivalent is.'

His smile dimmed a little and I felt bad. 'Can I walk you out?' he asked.

'Yes, that would be lovely,' I replied.

At the door of the restaurant he reached into his pocket and pulled out his business card. 'Call me, if you ever feel like answering my question,' he said.

I took his card, and looked at his name. 'Jack Britcham,' I said carefully.

'And your name is?'

'Eve.' I'd almost said Honey. Almost, then realised I didn't need to lie to this man. He wasn't paying me, he wasn't watching me dance; he was simply being nice.

'Just Eve?'

'Just Eve.'

'OK.'

For a moment I thought he was going to lean in and kiss my cheek, but he obviously changed his mind, probably mindful of entering my personal space. I wanted to touch him again, to be warmed by him, but didn't dare in case I wouldn't be able to take my hand away.

I could see Jack Britcham quite easily becoming my drug of choice.

'Bye, Jack Britcham,' I said, my heart heavy at the thought of not seeing him again.

'Goodnight, Eve.'

I walked a way down the road and waited around the corner for a few minutes until I could be sure he would be gone. He was nowhere in sight when I returned to the hotel and I walked quickly across the foyer to the lifts.

The man in room number 301 opened the door then went to sit himself in the armchair by the desk and waited for me to enter.

'Hi, I'm Honey,' I said with the smile and the voice.

With a nod of his head he indicated to the white envelope embossed with the hotel's crest on the bed, and I picked it up, checked it had the money in it then slipped it into my clutchbag.

I turned back to him and smiled again – even though his face was mainly in the shadows of the room – the only light coming from the desk lamp and the open bathroom door – I could tell he was older,

311

distinguished; most of the men who could afford the agency's rates were.

'Take off your clothes except your shoes then sit on the bed with your legs open,' he said huskily.

'Of course,' I said, still smiling.

'I want to talk to you first.'

'As you wish,' I said. I – Eve – had already tuned out and Honey was in control.

In the bath later, when I allowed myself to slip back into being Eve again, I thought about Jack Britcham. I argued with myself, actually, about Jack Britcham. I wanted to call him. But how could I call him when as well as being Eve, the woman he met, I was Honey the hooker, too? How could I tell him that and expect him to want to go out with me?

Some of the other girls I had met along the way who did this job had boyfriends, and some of them weren't even their pimps. Some of them said their boyfriends didn't really mind the job they did – they loved them despite the fact they did it with other men for money. Others said their boyfriends didn't know, and that it wasn't their business. Neither of those options appeal to me. I didn't exactly respect Elliot for not minding what I had to do to keep a roof over our heads, and how could I lie to someone I was in love with and not tell them about this thing I had to do to so I wouldn't have to live on the streets?

But, God, it's hard to think about Jack, with that smile of his and the shape of his face, and the look he had in his eyes *without* wanting to call him. I've kept his card, but only because it's a little like the dress, the rosary, the kitbag and the picture I took from my mother's house. It's another thing in this world that Eve has, another thing to keep me grounded. Another reminder that no matter what I do to earn money, I am still a real person.

Eve (in honour of Jack Britcham who reminded me of that)

It's silly, I know, but I keep thinking I see Jack Britcham wherever I go.

Logically I know it can't be him, and that he can't be everywhere – on the bus, in the back of a taxi, outside a café, walking along the seafront, in the faces of the clients I 'service' – but every time I get a flash of honey-blond hair, or that curve of his nose, or his height, or his build, my heart skips happily in my chest, and does that little pirouette it did when I first spoke to him. It's a good feeling. Probably the best feeling I have at the moment. It's like having stardust sprinkled on you every day of your life. I always smile when I think of him and, when I see his doppelgangers I rubberneck to get a look, then allow myself to dissolve into a serene, secret little smile as that feeling takes over.

Is it possible to fall in love with someone you've only met for five minutes?

He seems to have become a part of my life and I'm disappointed if I don't see him. If I get to the end of the day without seeing someone who reminds me of him, I feel as if a dull shadow has fallen over me and the only way to remedy it is to get his card out and stare at it. Read his name and his number, commit them both to memory and wonder if it would ever be possible to become Eve Britcham?

Yeah, I know, get a life, huh? That's what people say nowadays to saddos like me. It's hard though. Cos thinking about Jack Britcham, playing that game where I see him or a bit of him every day, is kind of liberating. It helps me get through the day. And it reminds me that I'm twenty-four.

I would love to kiss him. I've only kissed two people in my life – Peter and Elliot. I would love to snog him as well. Peter and I would snog: we'd kiss and snog and hold each other. Even after we slept together, sometimes we'd just snog. Elliot and I were more sort of 'adult' about it all. We'd kiss hello and goodbye and we'd kiss as part of foreplay, but we wouldn't kiss just for the sake of it. Not when we got together properly.

I would love to snog Jack Britcham. I would love to inhale the smell

313

of him, feast on the scent of him, become intoxicated by him. And of course there is nothing wrong with looking at him. I would love to run my fingers over the lines of his body, touch him and see if I could absorb him through the pads of my fingers, have him enter my bloodstream and race through my veins. I would love to taste him. See if he tastes as good as he looks.

I don't know why he's got so far under my skin, but he has. And that's not a bad thing, I don't think. It gives me something to look forward to, I suppose.

Loved-up Saddo

15th March 1996

Went out tonight with one my regulars, a man called Caesar – that's really his name: I've seen the credit card he pays with and it has 'Caesar Holdings' on it, and the agency have that as his name.

That's not remarkable, noteworthy or unusual in itself, except what happened during dinner is.

I've been seeing him for three or four months now and he's always been a talker. The most we've done is me strip down to my underwear and us lie on the bed, hugging. He's one of those with a wife who doesn't want sex, so is craving affection and the touch of another person more than anything else. I don't mind men like him. It's nice to talk and be talked to as though I have interests and opinions, and it's nice to earn money without having to get naked. The downside, of course, is that I have to be careful not to let the lines between Honey and Eve become blurred. It would be so easy to let my guard down, and be Eve when I don't have to have sex, but the whole point, of course, is that clothed or not, fucking or not, I am still being paid to be somewhere I would not otherwise be; it is still a business transaction.

We were at a lovely restaurant out in Seaford, which was very near the water and so peaceful and calm at night. We'd eaten there a few

314

times before and this time I'd decided on the duck confit, even though Cesar said it was odd to have fowl in a fish restaurant. During the main course he sat back, and relaxed a little. Cesar is a lot older than me with brown hair and a healthy looking face, one that's not pale, but not artificially tanned. He has lines around his eyes and on his forehead, in the hollows of his cheeks, but they aren't, you know, proper lines. His face would look odd, unfinished, without them. He's what they call distinguished, because not only does he look good and dress smartly, he also holds himself well. He would sit upright and seemed to know the proper way to do everything – from testing wine to the right cutlery to what to tip even if the service hadn't been especially good.

'Do you have any ambitions, Honey?' he asked me, studying me very carefully.

I paused in slicing away a piece of my duck and smiled my Honey smile. I liked it when the men who didn't fuck called me Honey – it reminded me that I wasn't out socialising, I was working. 'Yes,' I replied. 'I'm saving up to go to college, and then to go on to university.'

'And what would you read?'

'Either English or Sociology. I'm fascinated by the workings of society. It's the most important thing about us as humans, don't you think?'

He said nothing, just continued to study me, and I wondered if I had gone too far, had said too much. Had crossed that line between escort who can engage and escort who pisses a man off by being too clever.

'I would have liked to read English,' he said. 'My father decided Law would be better for me. I came to agree with him in time.'

I smiled and nodded in understanding, desperate not to speak until I had a better handle on what he wanted from tonight's meal. Often he just wanted conversation and I was more than able to provide it: we would explore ideas together, challenge and tease each other. Other times he would want someone to listen to him and not interrupt or contribute too much, no matter how knowledgeable on the subject

315

I might actually be. Tonight I had thought it was going to be a proper conversation, but I was obviously wrong.

'I would like to make you an offer,' he said after a while.

I smiled, wondering what he could offer me.

'I will pay you thirty thousand pounds – enough to get you through college and university – if you become my escort exclusively for six months.'

That film with Julia Roberts – *Pretty Woman* – came to mind. I had seen it years ago, well before I started on this path, and I'd loved it at the time for being a sweet love story. Now I was on the other side, it was a different matter entirely. Even when she was walking the streets she seemed far too open and honest to be doing that. And, of course, he was a sleazebag who went with prostitutes – could you get anything more unromantic?

But here I was, being presented with something not too dissimilar.

'That's a very generous offer,' I said, 'but I can't accept it.'

'You didn't even consider it,' he said, sounding surprised and a little perturbed. Who could blame him? Aren't us hookers only in it for the money?

'I did. And it's not for me.'

'You haven't even asked what it would entail.' He was affronted now. I didn't want to upset him; he was a lucrative customer and I hadn't had to have sex with him yet. Men like him were rare.

'Sorry, sorry. What would it entail?'

'Just being my escort, and not seeing anyone else.'

'For six months?'

'For six months.'

'Thank you, it's such a wonderful, generous offer, and thank you for thinking of me but, really, I can't take you up on it.'

'Why not?' he asked, a little sternly. 'I would have thought that it would be the perfect opportunity for you to get yourself on track with your ambitions.'

'It is, it's a wonderful, generous offer, but it's just not for me.'

'Give me a good reason why and I will let the matter rest,' he replied. I could see upset on his face, well hidden although it was, and the pain of rejection in his eyes. But I still did not want to tell him why I couldn't do it.

I couldn't do it because I could not be Honey twenty-four hours a day for six months – no matter how much money was on offer. I would not want to lose Eve, and I would not want to have to rip myself away from who I was to slip into this role whenever he turned up. I would always have to be well groomed – no matter what time of the day it was. I would have to do some of the disgusting things Dawn told me about to be able to work during my period. In short, I would be selling the parts of me that were not – and never had been – for sale. I did not want to tell him that because that would be admitting that whenever I was with him I was playing a role, and he might well guess that, away from being Honey, I felt neither empathy or compassion for the men who I saw. I tried my best to feel nothing at all.

'Can't we just agree that it's not for me?' I replied, suspecting that I was going to have to give him back his envelope of money and would probably not see him again.

'Honey, I'll be honest with you – you not jumping at this offer is one of the reasons why I made it. You're not like other women I've encountered: you don't just do it for the money.'

I do, I thought.

'You seem to really enjoy what you do.'

I don't, I thought.

'You bring a special quality to this.'

I really, really don't. I'm just a better actress, apparently, I thought.

'I'll be even more honest,' he continued. 'I don't like the idea of you seeing other men. I don't like the idea of other men talking to you, and them participating in intimate activities with you.'

'That's very flattering,' I said, to stop him embarrassing himself any more. This had never happened – I didn't think it was possible – but it was sounding as if he was saying that he had feelings for me. That he was possibly falling in love with me when it would never be reciprocated: Honey wasn't capable of love, just sex; Eve was in love with a man she'd spoken to for five minutes, months ago. Love was

317

not on the agenda with me. 'And I feel so honoured that you feel that way. In the light of what you said, I really can't take you up on your offer. It wouldn't be fair to seem to allay your insecurities for a few months and then to have them start up again if I do decide to return to normal work at the end of it. That's the best reason I can think of. It just wouldn't be fair on you.'

His demeanour shifted and he seemed to shrink a little, to stop being the distinguished gentleman who I accompanied and he became vulnerable and disappointed, bruised even. He reached across the table, placed his hand over mine, his touch different to how it normally was. Normally, he would be seeking affection, trying to take it from me to replenish his diminished stores; this was a touch that was giving affection, a way to make a connection and show his feelings.

It wasn't unpleasant, but that wasn't the point, really.

'Please, Honey, just think about it. If you think it through and it really isn't for you, then I will concede defeat and I will not bring it up again. Will you do that for me? Please?'

'Yes, I will think about it,' I finally said to get him to leave it alone.

And so here I am, thinking about it. A little resentfully, actually. It's very clever of him to get me to agree to think about it, isn't it? Because now I'm doing something for him for free and as Eve. That sounds callous, but he only pays for my time when I'm with him – away from him, I leave all that behind.

Having said that, thirty thousand pounds is thirty thousand pounds. On what planet could I turn that down? He's married and he has a demanding career – I probably wouldn't have to see him every night. Also, from the way he was talking, I could probably take control of the situation and put some conditions in place such as only seeing him at night and him having to give me notice so I could prepare to become Honey.

It wouldn't take too much to strip the flat of anything that was Eve-like, but I would probably have to tell him my real name.

Then there's the agency: they would not be happy that I was taking on work behind their back. I would probably have to quit. But then, with thirty thousand in the bank, I could go back to cleaning while I studied for college.

I have no idea what to do, to be honest. But that saying, 'if something seems too good to be true, it probably is' keeps coming into my head. I think I should probably leave it, don't you?

Puzzled of Brighton

It's now forty-five thousand pounds for only three months because he brought it up again, despite promising not to – in fact it seemed to make him more determined.

How can I turn down forty-five thousand when it's for an even shorter time? It's a ludicrous amount of money. Does he even have it? When I asked him that, he said he would put it into a special bank account set up just for me that I could check on every day if I wanted, but would only be able to withdraw at midnight on the final day. In the meantime, he would give me enough cash to cover my rent, bills, food and other expenses and deduct that from the forty-five thousand at the end.

When I said that I had a life away from escorting, he said I could set the conditions, if I wanted. So I asked for some outrageous things:

1. No visits or dates during the day – no matter how desperate he might be.
2. No visits without at least two hours' warning.
3. No staying over – he always had to be gone by three o'clock.
4. No questions or jealousy about what I might or might not get up to.
5. No talk of love or any of those types of emotions.
6. No sex – if things were to become sexual – during my period.
7. Contraception *always*.

319

8. No quibbling if I need extra money for dresses or anything that is connected with going out with him.

He agreed to them all without hesitation, which left me stuck. What good reason did I have for saying no? I would have notice of when I had to stop being Eve – much like I did now – and I would only be having sex with one man. I suppose that could become dangerous in that I could form an attachment to him, but that was the sort of thing girls who weren't hookers did. Hookers knew that falling for a punter was more dangerous than walking the streets without anyone to look out for you – a punter is not someone you can trust your heart with, no matter how well meaning, kind, generous, hurt, loving and damaged they may seem. They will ALWAYS hold what you did against you. *Always*.

I'm not going to tell him my real name – that's for me more than anything. I need to be reminded that to him, to any person who pays me for sex, I am Honey. I will go with him to the bank and get a printout of the balance of the account. I can go and check that it is still there any time I want.

I seem to have all the bases covered. And at the end of the three months, I will be able to stop worrying about money. I will be able to be a cleaner but with a pot money behind me, and I will be able to give up Honey for ever. I will have my life back. I may even take a bit of time off and go visit my mother. She hasn't written to me yet, but it'll be very hard for her to ignore me when I am standing on her doorstep.

Looks like I'm going to do this, doesn't it?

It really is no different to what I am doing now, so why do I get the feeling – only a small little feeling – that I am going to regret it? But it's only a tiny, grain of sand of a feeling, and I'm sure it will go away when I get started.

Me

Haven't written in here because I have nothing to report. It has been two months into this agreement and you know what? I still haven't had to fuck him.

We lie together on my bed, and sometimes he asks if I'll strip to my underwear, but he doesn't seem interested in watching me take my clothes off. He simply likes to have me with bra and knickers on and lay his hands on me, not even in an overtly sexual way. He craves touching skin, it seems, and he snuggles close to me, and whispers in my ear his troubles like people do with worry dolls. He relaxes when I hold him and stroke his hair. But it never leads to sex.

I don't know if it's because he can't, if he fears it'll be over too quickly or if he doesn't want to, but he does get hard – I can feel it through his clothes.

He has started taking me to evening business meetings because he says it looks good having someone like me on his arm. Most of his business associates all have their 'companions' (it's obvious to all of us who the others are) too, while others bring their wives.

My cover story if anyone – not just the wives – ask is that I am thinking about majoring in Law so have been lucky enough to shadow Caesar on all aspects of his work. But no one asks. No one is interested. Every now and again some of them will ask what I think of the wine or the meal, but mostly they are more interested in themselves and their conversations and their businesses.

Last night we went to a dinner at the same hotel where I met Jack Britcham and my heart was in my throat, throbbing out the conflicting emotions in me, because I wanted to see him (not that it was likely he'd be there, but there's no reasoning with my feelings for him) and I also didn't because I didn't want him to see me with another man. I wanted to be able to say to him, 'I'm free!' When of course I wasn't.

At this dinner, there were at least three men – not at the meeting – there in the hotel that I had escorted. They all looked straight through

321

me, of course, which was fine but, if I were Eve, I would have wondered how they could have been so callous. They'd had intimate relations with me, had been naked with me, had probably all told me the same line about their wives – none of which looked 'past it' or 'not up for it', by the way – and they had needed me to make them feel better but now they could ignore me. Or, worse still, they could forget me.

I had slept with a lot of men – and I remember them all. I remember their faces, their names and I remember the type of sex we had. I have to: for safety, so that I don't put myself in a dangerous position if the man had unsettled me before; and for business reasons – men are flattered if you remember things about them, and they show their flattery through their wallets. Like I say, that's the sort of thing that Eve would never think. That's why it's a good thing that Honey is the one who does all this work.

It's nice, though, to not have sex. It's healing. He still uses my body to get the comfort and affection he craves, but he isn't doing anything more than touching my skin. I can live with that for another few weeks.

Me

27th June 1996

Three days to go and everything has changed.

Caesar came over last night, and seemed quiet and troubled.

'Are you OK?' I asked him.

'Yes,' he said with a desolate nod, 'I am.'

'Here, let me help you unwind,' I said, and undid his gold tie and unbuttoned his top button.

'I'd like to lie on the bed, if that's acceptable to you,' he said.

'Of course,' I replied. Inside I was feeling a little sad because his mood was starting to rub off on me.

'I'm aware of what the date is,' he said. He was pressed close to me and I could feel his erection beneath his clothes, pushing into my leg. His hand was working its way up the skirt of my summer dress with buttons up the front, and caressing my thigh. 'I have been fooling myself that the end of this wasn't going to come. I'm going to miss you, Honey.'

'I'll miss you, too,' I said, automatically, although it was true: I would miss him. It's been nice, calming, not to be always dressing up to go out and not knowing who I would meet, what they would want from me. It was nice to be in a pseudo-relationship without the emotional entanglements.

It took a moment for me to register that he was undressing me, was rather clumsily undoing the buttons on my dress. I was taken aback, but not horrified – this was, after all, what he'd been paying me for. He found the clasp of my bra – front-fastening – and opened it, and before I could brace myself his mouth was working rather amateurishly on my breasts. Then he rolled me onto my back and was tugging at my knickers. While I lifted my hips to let him get them off, I realised that he wanted to do this himself. He wanted to unwrap me himself.

Soon he was freeing his erection, which I didn't look at because I was reaching for the bedside table and the condoms. Before I could fully pull the drawer open, he was inside me. His eyes were tightly closed, his face scrunching and releasing in a strange mix of agony and ecstasy in time with his thrusts. In minutes his body was jerking as he came and I had barely moved. Like most of the sex I had as a prostitute, it was barely necessary for me to be there.

'I'm sorry about the condoms,' he said as he rolled off me. 'I needed to feel you completely.'

I said nothing because it was not OK. Thankfully I was on the Pill but I did not know where he had been, or who he had been with. But, after nearly three months of being paid by him and not having sex, it seemed a small thing to get cross about. I'd have to make sure it didn't happen again and I'd have to go for a HIV test sooner than I usually went.

'Was, was it OK?' he asked, sounding nervous. But if he hadn't

323

had sex with his wife in years, as he'd told me, then it was understandable for him to be nervous.

I thought about it: the act itself. Was it OK? It was more clumsy than expected. He didn't seem to know what he was doing, and he didn't seem very experienced, which surprised me about a man such as himself. His persona gave the impression that he was a man of the world, had bedded quite a few women – some of them probably prostitutes – and had become rather skilled at it. Maybe, I thought, with more than a hint of shame, he was telling the truth. Maybe his wife really was the love of his life and not being able to have sex with her, and her not wanting to hug and cuddle because they both knew it would lead to a failed seduction attempt, were a great source of pain to him. Maybe he was genuinely craving affection and had only crossed the line with me because it would feel like another loss when this came to an end.

'It was lovely,' I said to him.

And to my utter horror, he started to cry.

He's just left. After he cried, we lay curled up together on the bed. Then he got up, got dressed and left.

God knows what that's all about!

I'm a bit worried that he's not going to live up to his end of the bargain and let me go in three days. I'm scared that he's going to tell me he's in love with me or something and then I'll be done for. Because I can't force him to give me the money and, to be honest, I don't want his love. Whether he gets no affection or not, he is still being unfaithful to his wife. I can't get involved with someone like that – even if I was capable of loving him. And I couldn't be a kept woman, either.

Earning my own money, relying on myself, is the only thing that I've got going for me.

Urgh! Why has he done this? I could be wrong, but this changes everything and not for the better. Will just have to see how the next few days pan out.

Stupid Me

He's offered me another forty-five thousand if we keep the arrangement going for another three months. That, I wasn't expecting.

Part of me wants to go for it because the last three months haven't been that bad at all. But part of me doesn't want to get his hopes up or to hurt him. I said as much when he made the offer.

'You won't hurt me, Honey,' he said, with conviction. 'The other night I was a bit . . . upset about my wife. That's what she said the first time we became intimate. It was the first time for both of us and your words brought back the bittersweet memories of that time. I like your company, Honey, and what you have done for me, how you have brought me back to life, I cannot begin to describe, but I recognise now that anything I think I feel for you is what I feel for my wife. I'm so sad that our relationship is no longer physically intimate. I think that's why I want to keep this arrangement going – it is like having a little bit of my original relationship with my wife here. If you understand?'

I nodded, and felt a little better. But still . . .

I don't know why I'm writing this as if there's still a decision to be made. We talked and talked and talked and finally I agreed. He's going to show me the money in his account for me tomorrow, and then we're going to continue with our arrangement.

I might be mad, but if it's anything like the last three months, it really won't be any kind of hardship.

13th July 1996

On my grave, it will probably say Eve Quennox, The Most Stupid Woman on Earth. Or something shorter, snappier, and easier to chisel into stone.

That is what they call gallows humour.

But there was nothing humorous about last night. I just have to put it into context so that I do not go into the kitchen and take a knife and plunge it into my chest. Or start to scrape away at the top layer of my skin until the filth that is my body is changed for ever.

Last night, Caesar came over with a friend of his that I had met a few times on those business meetings I attended. We had barely spoken and he seemed a nice enough man, a little bumbling, a little foolish but not unpleasant. I was a little surprised because he hadn't mentioned on the phone that he was bringing anyone with him, but I led the way to the living room and they both sat on the sofa while I played the perfect hostess and made drinks, asked them if they would like to eat, sat in the armchair waiting for instructions from Caesar as to what to do next.

Like the men do when I go to their meetings, they mostly ignored me as they sat and talked and smoked cigars and drank the whisky I kept for Caesar. Then Arnold got up, asked for directions to the bathroom and then left us to it. Caesar sat in his armchair, holding his cigar in one hand and his short whisky glass in the other, ignoring me. This was not the man I had got to know over the last few months and it was unsettling.

'Come and sit on the sofa, there's a good girl,' he said suddenly, not looking at me, but at the table in the middle of the room.

I did as I was told, the uneasy feeling growing inside. He had sounded so cold and removed when he said that, I did not understand why. I did not understand what I had done wrong. Hadn't I been welcoming enough, had I somehow offended him?

When Arnold returned from the bathroom, he came back to the sofa and sat so close to me that our thighs were pressed up against each other. I instantly looked to Caesar, to see his reaction, if he had noticed what had happened. He was sitting watching me, watching us. He was still watching as Arnold reached out and put his hand on my knee, resting it there as though it was a piece of furniture he had just happened to lay his hand upon, not the knee of a person.

I looked at Arnold's hand: chubby and short, the tips of his fingers stained yellow. The palm of his hand was moist against my skin. My eyes flew up to Caesar again, expecting some sort of reaction from him now. Nothing except to lean back in the seat, raise his glass to his lips and stare down his nose at me.

Arnold's hand left a damp trail as he moved it under my dress, then he forced it between my thighs. I had a flashback to the way my mother's boyfriend would try and touch me, the way his hand had been unwelcome and disgusting on my skin back then. Arnold's hand was just as unwelcome, even though I had been touched there by so many men in the last few years.

Arnold clumsily moved his thumb up and down in his pathetic attempt at a caress. He leaned in close to me. 'I've been waiting to get close to you ever since you walked into that restaurant that night,' he said, his breath rancid and slurred with alcohol, as well as the whisky, and the cigar he had smoked. I locked gazes with Caesar, his eyes hard and unyielding, cold and expressionless. He was telling me, by his lack of reaction, what was expected of me.

I had not said this was out of the question in the agreement, had I? I had not said he couldn't invite anyone over whenever he felt like it and let them have a go. 'You wanted it, too, didn't you?' Arnold said, his grip on my thigh tightening, his thumb rubbing hard enough to leave friction marks.

Swallowing in one go the bile pool in my mouth and the disgust shivering through my body, I forced myself to focus on the man in front of me. I compelled my hand to reach out for the second button on his shirt; I made my face become a smile; I willed my body to unclench enough to do this; I forced my heart to stop crying.

'You want me to give it to you, don't you?' Arnold said not far enough under his breath for it to sound seductive. It sounded pathetic. Like he was. Like I was for going through with this.

Stop thinking, I told myself, *stop feeling, start being* her *again. Start being Honey, start being the woman who can do this.*

'I think we'll be a lot more comfortable in the bedroom,' I said, in Honey's voice. I had her make-up on, I had her clothes on, I had just forgotten to switch her persona on. I felt the smile deepen on my face. I stood up, taking my time, stretching my body so he could see.

327

I took Arnold's hand and I ignored the man who stood also to follow us out of the room, down the corridor and to the bedroom door. Still holding his whisky and his cigar, Caesar stood in the bedroom doorway, as if watching something on television.

'Take off your clothes,' I said in Honey's husky, sexy voice, 'and lie on the bed. I'll be with you in just a minute.'

Drunk and overtly desperate, Arnold was tearing at his clothes in seconds. I knew his sort well: he talked a good game about the young women who'd been begging him to fuck them, but he had clearly never been with anyone apart from his wife. Either that, or he was the type who had got away with sexually harassing a few secretaries in his time and thought that counted as being a 'ladies' man'.

I turned my back on him for a second, put my hand on the doorhandle and stared right at the man in the doorway. He was nothing to do with this.

I shut the door with a determined click, and then turned the key in the lock.

Then I spun back to Arnold, lying naked on the bed, his chubby, flabby-looking body pale and pasty, but strangely solid and unmoving, his face a picture of eagerness, his penis erect and ready.

He still wore his black socks and, from the way they were up to his shins, had probably pulled them up just before he lay on the bed.

Honey would find this one so easy.

But Eve was the one who was here. She was using Honey's voice, and she was using Honey's smile, but it was Eve who walked over to the bed and began to undress for work.

14th July 1996

Had to stop writing yesterday because I was reliving it all over again and I got scared that I would actually harm myself.

Caesar left two hours ago, and he came to tell me that I would do that with whoever he wanted me to, whenever he wanted me to.

328

Or there would be no money, and he would not pay next month's rent and he would hunt me down wherever I went and kill me. 'At the end of the six months – and yes, it is now six months – I will review the situation, see if I want to release you from your contract or not.'

There was something in his eyes that told me that he was not making idol threats; there was something in his cool, languid body language that reassured me that he would think nothing of carrying out his promise. He was certainly rich enough and powerful enough to do it, to kill me.

I looked at the man on my sofa and saw the shadow of a premature death all prostitutes knew stalked them, and I said nothing. What could I say? He has not given me the forty-five thousand from before – it was going to be a lump sum at the end – and I have nowhere to run to. I doubt the police would take me seriously, and my savings are very depleted from the months I spent looking for a proper job before I started escorting again.

'Is that understood?' he said to me.

I stared at him. By understood he meant, of course: you are going to accept those terms.

'I do not appreciate the silent treatment,' he said.

'Yes,' I said.

'For your sake, I am glad you've accepted.'

And then . . . then he showed me what he was really like. That clumsy, amateurish man pining for his lost relationship with his wife, who cried after that first and only time, is a lie. He does not exist.

Caesar is nothing like that. The real Caesar has left so many bruises on my body I can barely move. He has made me feel so degraded, I can barely think. The real Caesar is the devil incarnate. And I have made a pact with him.

Must go to sleep now, am hoping my body feels better tomorrow. It may recover quickly but what am I going to do about my mind?

Me

They're not all like Arnold, although I have had to 'see' him again.

Most of them are a lot worse than Arnold. A couple are as pathetic as him, but the rest . . .

You know, the worst part of all of this is that Honey has gone. She has left. I cannot access her any more; the mask does not stay in place. It's me doing these things. Always me. Eve.

I spend so much time in the bath, in the shower, crying, changing my clothes and changing the already-clean bedding. I don't sleep in the main bedroom, any more, either. I sleep in the smaller second room, so that I do not wake to be surrounded by the memories, the images that are almost solid, the feelings of what I have experienced.

Dawn told me to avoid pimps like the plague. 'They'll always bleed you dry, take everything you've got, then find someone else. Always.'

Look at me: not only do I have a pimp, I have probably the classiest, poshest pimp in town, who is bleeding me dry, but probably not looking for anyone else.

chapter sixteen

libby

'Now you listen to me, Butch, we both know that Jack walked you this morning, so if you're thinking I'm taking you out right now, you've got another think coming.'

Butch whines at me from his place by the door with his lead in his mouth, his big black eyes staring sorrowfully at me.

'Are you trying to emotionally blackmail me?' I ask him.

Another whine, this one longer, softer and more pathetic than the last, his head cocks even further to one side, his eyes become even larger.

'You are a disgrace,' I tell him. 'No one's going to fall for this.'

He whines in reply. Of course I'm going to fall for it. I fall for it all the time. Whenever he's done something bad and goes to hide under the kitchen table he'll then whine and simper until I forgive him.

'You see, the thing is, I haven't actually been out of the house since I came back from that counselling session. I've had no reason to go out and I don't like being out there. I feel safer in the house and people don't stare at me in here.'

He lays down and rests his head on his paws, his blue and silver lead clattering as it hits the wooden floor.

I can't believe this. I am being made to feel guilty by a dog. And it's not even my dog!

Butch sighs, rather dramatically for a little dog, I feel, but still it's had its desired effect: 'Come then,' I tell him. 'We'll head out the back door so I can brace myself for going out there again.'

He takes his time to get up, as if he's not sure if I really mean it. But then I know, as I go into my bedroom to change into jeans and to find a hat, that he's probably doing a little victory dance in the corridor.

I've made it to the side entrance of the house without any problem but here, at the threshold where the house meets the pavement, I am having trouble moving my foot from the boundaries of the house to the outside.

Obviously Butch has no such worries and sits on the pavement, his head cocked, staring at me. My hand is resting against the rough, cream render of the house as I hold myself up, the air I keep trying to get into my body is rushing in and out too quickly for me to breathe.

I can do this, I tell myself. *I can do this.*

My body will not move, though. My right foot will not lift itself off the ground and move forwards. My chest is rising and falling even faster than before.

I can do this. I can do this.

I force my gaze down, down to my trainered feet to see if they have somehow become welded to the concrete path. They haven't.

I can do this. I've done it twice before, I can do it right now.

BANG! suddenly rocks my body and I feel it through every cell as I'm violently shaken. I look out into the street, looking for the noise, for what is making that noise and BANG! again. I can hear the screech of car tyres, I can feel my body being swept aside, I can see the wall and the lamppost heading towards—

I stumble back, waiting for the collision that isn't going to happen, that happened nearly a month ago, that is in the past. But it feels like it is happening now and I feel myself hyperventilating.

Butch is sitting on the pavement watching me.

'*Come on, Butch,*' I manage to say. But I'm not making sounds. Like after the crash, I'm speaking with my mouth, but no sound is being produced. '*Butch!*' I say. Nothing. Nothing. They called it Aphonia. I put my hand to my throat and then turn away, hoping that action will tell Butch to follow.

The pain that has been mainly under control is gripping at my middle again, and I clutch my arms around my body as I force myself to move, to shuffle back to the safety of the house. Butch is by my side, suddenly, walking with me and looking up constantly in something that would look like concern on a human face.

'*It'll be all right,*' I tell him with my silent voice. '*When we get inside, it'll be all right.*'

Once I shut the kitchen door behind me, my body unclenches. 'Are you OK, Butch?' I ask him. The sound of my voice is a sweetness that I did not know my ears would miss.

Butch barks in reply.

'Good, that's good.' I move to the sink and turn on the cold water tap, splash water on my face, enjoying the chill of it on my skin as well as the ease with which oxygen is now filling my lungs.

'I'm going to lie down,' I tell him. 'And take some painkillers.' I've hardly needed them this past week or so, despite trying to get some more from the GP. But I need them now. I need them to completely kill this pain and to let me sleep.

Silently, Butch follows me to my bedroom. He waits for me to take two tablets, then to lie down on the bed. Once I am settled, he hops up and curls in close to me. He's been doing that almost every night since Jack started sleeping upstairs again. I should probably tell him to get down, to stop him getting used to the idea of sleeping on a human bed, but as the tablets take over and do their work I reach out and lazily stroke my fingers through his fur. The truth is, it looks like I am stuck in this house, and I feel so much better for having Butch here.

libby

Today, Eve is lying on her back with her eyes wide open, not moving. She looks as though the life has been sucked out of her. That there is nothing left to give.

'I'm sorry this happened to you,' I whisper to her.

And she turns to me and smiles. *'It's not your fault,'* she says. *'I'm sorry for what's happened to you, too.'* Then she returns her unblinking gaze to the ceiling, goes back to being almost dead.

eve

I went out today to do one of my favourite things – reading on one of the walls that separates the sea from the promenade. It's so wonderful to be able to spend as much time outdoors as I want during the daylight hours and I often lay back on the concrete, rest the book I'm reading on my chest and listen to the world go by.

It's calming for the soul, it's cleansing for the mind, and it is fortifying for the body. I always walk a little way down into Hove because there are less people there than Brighton.

I lay on my back and was devouring the pages of the book in my hand when someone said to me, 'I don't often see people reading Noel Coward.'

Jack Britcham. I knew I was going to look up and see Jack Britcham. And I was going to fall apart or burst into tears, or throw my arms around him as you would a friend you haven't seen in years.

I took a deep breath, closed my eyes and then opened them again just before I lowered the book and turned my head to the side.

A thousand angels started to sing as I saw him and I did none of the things I thought I was going to do. Instead I stared. I took another gulp of air, then moved the book to look at the cover, as if I didn't

337

know that in my hands I held my favourite play written by Noel Coward.

'Just Eve,' he said, when I looked at him again.

'Hello, you,' I replied, surprised that my mouth could work when it – like the rest of me – was overcome. That was the only word for it. Overcome.

I inhaled again and noticed that his chest, covered in paint-splattered builder's overalls, rose quite far as he inhaled and then fell as deeply as mine did. His hands were clean, but his hair and face were splattered with spots of white.

'*Blithe Spirit* is one of his best works,' I said. 'It's a bit crazy, but also rather compelling and cynical.'

I sat up, and I saw the way his eyes watched my hair fall into place around my shoulders. I often watched men watch me and he didn't have that look in his eyes that repulsed me about men. He wasn't looking at my hair and imagining his hands wrapped around it, pulling it, or hooking his fingers into it while I did something to him. Jack Britcham was watching my hair fall the way a person watches a waterfall – with fascination and awe. Almost reverence.

'I don't think I've read it,' he said. 'I know I haven't read it. I don't know why I said that.'

'For something to say?' I replied.

'You're probably right.'

We stared at each other for a moment and then both started talking at once. Then we both stopped. And started again. Then stopped. I'd never been in such sync with someone before. We both waited then I raised a hand and pointed to mean, 'You speak.'

He smiled and made all the butterflies in my stomach do that special pirouette before they fluttered their wings. 'I was going to tell you that since we met, I've been seeing your doppelgangers everywhere I go. It's silly, but I keep seeing you and then I realise it's not you. I actually thought I was going to be explaining myself to a woman who had no idea who I was when I saw you a minute ago.'

'I've been doing the same,' I confessed. 'Except I haven't actually approached anyone.'

'Really?' he asked, his eyes lighting up. Then they clouded over with confusion. 'So why didn't you call?'

Because I'm a whore, I said to myself. *Because most nights of the week, men I don't know and I don't like penetrate or degrade me for the simple reason that I sold my soul to the devil without realising that was who he was. Because you could never love a woman like me. Because I could probably never love the man you really are, only the man I want you to be in my head.*

'Just because,' I said.

Jack Britcham smiled and I died a thousand little deaths inside that he seemed so innocent and nice and I was anything but. Having said that, it could all be a front. Jack Britcham might be nothing like that. With Elliot, I overlooked his drug-taking, with Caesar I overlooked the whole visiting prostitutes thing, I wondered what there was to 'overlook' with Jack Britcham, what little clues to the darkness in his soul there would be that I would ignore.

It didn't matter at that moment in time because he was standing in front of me, smiling. And there was nothing I had wanted more all these long months.

I smiled back, like it was the most natural thing in the world. Then we both started to speak at once again, then stopped, then started, then stopped. I raised my finger and pointed at him again. He killed me all over again with his grin.

'Will you come for a walk with me?' he asked. 'Just up the seafront? I came out to clear my head.' He indicated to his clothes. 'I'm still working on my house – it's a big job – and I love to walk to Brighton and back. Will you walk with me?'

'Yes,' I said.

'You will?' he asked, surprised.

'I was about to say I was heading home because I've got an appointment later, and did you fancy a walk for a bit if you didn't have to rush back to work.'

'Really?' he asked.

'Yes.'

Another smile from him sent shooting stars up my spine. 'Wow. I could count on one finger the amount of times that's happened to me,' he said.

'Oh yes?'

'Yes.'

I slipped down off the wall, and he looked for a moment as if he was going to help but was unsure how I would receive his assistance. I liked that; I liked that he respected my personal space.

We walked slowly, meandering along the seafront, close enough to hold hands and it felt as if we should be holding hands, as if we had been together long enough to want to be clinging onto each other as we made our way through the world.

'I don't know what to talk about,' he confessed. 'All those times I've imagined running into you again and I had conversations lined up in my head so I would come across as erudite and witty, and I can't for the life of me remember a single one of them.'

'Me either,' I replied.

'We talked for five minutes last time.'

'I know.'

'But I couldn't stop thinking about you.'

'Me too.'

He stopped and turned to me, so I stopped and turned to him too. 'I feel like we should be kissing right now,' he said.

'I feel like that, too.' It was getting spooky how he was constantly saying what I was thinking.

He swallowed hard, looked as if he was going to step forwards and do it, when reality bashed me over the head. I was a whore who was basically trapped in a no-win situation that I wasn't sure how to get myself out of. I was not a twenty-five-year-old woman without a care in the world, free to have a relationship with any man who I met.

I stepped forwards. And so did he.

People walked around us, not even tutting or noticing like they would in London. Here, on the wide promenade, anything went. Our bodies touched and there was no spark, no ignition, no sudden burst of passion; it was far more beautiful than that. Touching him like that felt like he had reached into my being and put loving arms around my soul. I knew without doubt that I had met my soulmate.

The kiss, as lovely as it was, was pretty much inconsequential.

Eve

God, my last entry was gushing, wasn't it?

I'm not surprised, though, I just wanted to get down something nice that had happened to me. And kissing Jack Britcham on the seafront was pretty much one of the nicest things that has EVER happened to me.

The kiss, which was lovely, only lasted a minute or two before we both broke away, then stood staring at our feet, giggling quietly and shyly. It was all so silly and embarrassing – for both of us.

'What on Earth has come over us?' he said, still smiling at his shoes.

'Midsummer madness?' I replied.

'Would you like to come to dinner with me?' he asked. 'Do things properly.'

I had been to most of the best restaurants in Brighton, Hove, Worthing, Shoreham, probably most of Sussex, and to London, with some of the vilest men in the world. In the last two months, particularly, every time I sat down to dinner, there were at least two men at the table who had taken pleasure in hurting me while they fucked me and I'd had to pretend to find them scintillating company. The last thing I wanted to do was go to dinner with someone I liked. 'No, thanks,' I replied.

'Oh,' he said, dejectedly. 'Oh, right, right. Sorry.'

'It's not you. Going out to dinner just isn't something I like doing.'

'Oh, OK. How about a drink, then?'

'How about you show me around this house of yours that you're still working on?'

'You'd really like to see it?'

'I would.'

'Fantastic.' He was genuinely pleased. 'How about tomorrow night since you've got an appointment this evening?'

'Make it tomorrow afternoon and I'm in,' I replied.

He raised his eyes to the sky, thinking things over. 'I think I can move a few meetings around, how does three-thirty sound?'

'Perfect.'

'Can I have your number, in case I can't change the meeting?'

'No,' I replied. 'If you can't change the meeting then Fate is trying to tell us something. So, give me your address and I'll hopefully see you tomorrow.'

I'm on my way there soon.

I'm so excited, I can't tell you. Haven't been this excited since my first date with Peter.

Thinking about it, I was a bit dismissive of the kiss, wasn't I? Considering I haven't kissed anyone in years – actual *years* – I can't believe I didn't dwell on it more. It was lovely, and it was different from how I remember kissing. Maybe because, after a while, when I got to know him properly I didn't enjoy kissing Elliot all that much. With Jack, it was so different. So beautiful and pure, and gentle and giving.

I'd forgotten how much I loved kissing until Jack kissed me. It was better than I had fantasised it would be. Hope there'll be more kisses this afternoon.

Just kissing. I really don't want anything else.

Eve

15th August 1996

Caesar is buzzing at the door and I'm sitting on the floor of the small bedroom where I sleep writing this because there's a sufficient glow from the orangey streetlight in here to allow me not to put the lights on. I'm on the floor in case you can see my outline from the street if I sit on the bed. I don't think you can, but I'm not taking that chance.

I'll suffer for it tomorrow, because when I got back there was a message from him on my answer machine saying that he was coming over. 'Coming over' might have meant just him, but I couldn't be sure. But either way, after the afternoon I've had, I'm not willing to service anyone. How can I when I have the scent of the man I love on me and I do not want to wash it off?

Caesar can do what he wants tomorrow, and I won't care. Being alone tonight with my memories of Jack Britcham is all I care about. I keep touching my lips to find them tender and little painful from all the kissing. All that delicious, scrumptious kissing. There aren't enough words, I don't think, in any of the world's languages to describe what the kissing was like. I wish I could write it down, capture it on this page so that I can relive the sensations over and over.

The buzzing's stopped. I don't know if Caesar's given up or if he's trying to find a way into the building. Either way, I don't care. He'll have to break the door down to get in.

Jack Britcham's house was incredible to look at from the outside, a huge, detached building on one of those ultra-expensive roads that leads down to the seafront. The façade was faded by the salty air and the Sun, but it was still clinging onto its wonderful buttery-cream colour. The windows were beautiful old sashes with chipped paint and split woodwork, and the stone steps leading up to the front door were worn away with the footsteps of all the people who had come and gone over the years.

I wondered, as I walked up the steps to the front door, which was obviously new, how many people had been like me over the years: going up the steps to meet someone they were convinced they were in love with? How many times had love trod those weary stones and stayed?

He answered the door within seconds, and we grinned as we saw each other in that way we had on the promenade – I couldn't help myself and I don't think he could either. Jack Britcham just made me smile.

'You came,' he said.

'You were here,' I replied.

343

He was dressed as if for work – I guessed he worked in an office – and looked like he'd just arrived back from the way his briefcase sat by the door, and his suit jacket was hung on the banister. 'Did you just come home?' I asked.

'Yes,' he said, glancing at his black leather briefcase. 'I couldn't really move the meeting, so I had to feign an emergency to get out of it.'

'Do you think they believed you?' I asked.

'I'll find out tomorrow when I get in. Either I'll have my P45 or a cup of tea on my desk. I'll live with whichever one.'

He took me around the house, and each room was its own little world, its own little story. Some rooms were stripped bare – floorboards exposed, walls removed of everything except greying plaster and new red-brown plaster, freshly patched ceilings, single light fittings hanging crookedly from a ceiling that awaited its new intricate ceiling rosette and light. Other rooms were even more devastated, with huge holes and lines in the walls where the electric cables had been pulled out and replaced, parts of the floors were unearthed where pipe work was being re-laid, the walls still had parts of ancient wallpaper that had yet to be scraped away, skirting boards that were mostly removed, newly fitted radiators sticking out from where they had been placed, fireplaces that were dark gaping holes that threatened to suck you in. Yet other rooms were awaiting paint: they were perfectly put back together with the skirting replaced, the radiator in place, the ceiling rose and ornate period light fittings fixed, the floors clean and ready for carpeting after the painting, the walls all smooth with dry plaster, the fireplaces filled with their black iron surrounds and just waiting for winter so they could house a fire.

A few rooms – his bedroom, the main bathroom and the huge kitchen – were finished. They were obviously done so that he could live there while the rest of the work was being carried out. I walked around every room that I could go into, running my hands along the walls, revelling in the ability to touch history in such an intimate way. The flat I lived in was an old Victorian house that had been carved up

344

into apartments, but the heart had been ripped out of it and, along with it, the traces of history that it held. It was blank and white and beige.

This place, being so gently and carefully restored by Jack Britcham, was still teeming with history, with the lives that once dwelled there, the many, many stories that once played themselves out there. Under my fingers, the heart of the house seemed to beat and I so wanted to rest my head against the walls and listen to the heart, listen to any snatches of the past, taking it all in, so that those who had gone before would not be forgotten, they would be remembered.

That's silly, I know, but Jack Britcham didn't look at me as if I was mad – he simply took me from room to room, letting me touch the walls and stand for a while allowing myself to become a part of it.

'It's a beautiful place,' I said to him when we finally returned to the kitchen, where he went to put the kettle on.

'Thank you,' he replied.

'Although, beautiful doesn't seem a good enough word. It doesn't seem adequate.'

'That's what I think when I think about you. When I come to describe you in my head, I know you're beautiful but the word doesn't seem enough.'

I stared at him, startled. No one had ever said anything like that to me. It was so beyond a normal compliment and I was so stunned I didn't even have time to be flattered or embarrassed. 'Are you always so honest?' I eventually asked him when he simply stared back at me as though willing me to challenge him.

'Almost never,' he replied. 'I wasn't brought up that way. I come from a family where things are swept under the carpet and never talked about. I just can't help it with you.'

I continued to stare at him, again startled – but this time at my reaction. I wasn't as embarrassed as I thought I would be, I wasn't flattered, I was … it was the most natural thing in the world because from out of his mouth was coming most of the things I felt. In another person, one I did not have this attachment to, it would have been

345

gushing, clingy and embarrassing, from him it was like having a mirror held up to my soul.

'I don't know anything about you,' I said to him. 'Isn't that weird? And yet, I didn't think twice about coming to your house – when you could have been an axe murderer for all I knew.'

'You drink espresso-strong black coffee with three sugars,' he said.

'Four sugars.'

'You used to smoke a packet of mild cigarettes a day but gave up, but not for health reasons.'

'Yes.'

'You live alone in a two-bedroom flat because you lived in a one-bedroom place for so long that you need the extra space now you feel you can afford it.'

'Yes.'

'You're from Yorkshire originally.'

'Have you been following me?' I asked.

'No,' he said with a shake of his head. 'I just guessed all that stuff, apart from the Yorkshire bit because you've still got the hint of an accent. Those things just came into my head and I said them. Lots of other things came into my head as well, just in case you're wondering. Like, you're unhappily married to a man who is the deposed president of a small country. That you're an heiress coming into a huge pot of money someday soon. You're also a double agent on the run from people all over the world. That I can't believe you've been in my house for more than twenty minutes and I haven't even attempted to kiss you.'

'All those things are true, too,' I said with a laugh. 'Every word. And you . . . I think you went into your profession because your dad made you. You took a huge gamble buying this house and you're still unsure if you did the right thing. You prefer football to rugby even though you played rugby at school and college. And you're probably the youngest person to have ever reached your current position in your company.'

'Have *you* been following *me*?' he replied.

346

'Yes,' I replied.

And he laughed so much I started to laugh too. Then he was suddenly in front of me, pulling me into his arms and kissing me. And I was kissing him back and remembering again how much I loved this part of kissing. How incredible and innocent it made me feel.

I don't know how long we stood in the kitchen like that, because time seemed to stand still. And then by silent mutual agreement we were holding hands and heading upstairs. I know I wasn't meant to do that, but it seemed so natural with him. In his bedroom, we stood by the bed kissing again.

When I reached for his tie, I thought for a moment of all the men's ties I'd removed in my life, all the men I'd helped to undress, all the men I'd fallen onto a bed with and had tuned out with the second the sex bit started. Then I thought about the kissing, how that made this different. This wasn't just reaching for the tie of a punter, this was reaching for the tie of Jack Britcham. The man I'd been in love with for months. This was different. This was about him and me, and no one else. I would not let those men in here, I would let no one in here but Jack Britcham and me, and our perfect kisses. As I was letting myself relax into being with him, he stopped my hands and pulled away.

'I've never done this before,' he blurted out.

'What do you mean?' I asked.

He caressed my hands between his, and looked bewildered and scared. 'I've never,' he grimaced, then looked pained. 'I've never slept with anyone.'

'Ever?' I replied.

'I've been waiting for the right woman. I know it sounds pathetic, but I . . . I just wanted it to be right, the first time. Special.'

The whore and the virgin: how unlikely was that to happen? I should have told him there and then, but I couldn't. I was not that person when I was with him. 'Do you want to wait, then? Because we don't have to do anything. We can just lie together and talk.'

He kissed my hands. 'No, I want to. I really want to, if you still do. You might not enjoy it much because I don't really know what I'm doing … God, this is a conversation I never thought I'd have with someone whose second name I don't even know.'

'You do know my second name, it's Eve.'

'Eve?' he asked, puzzled.

'Yes. I told you, my name is Just Eve.'

He smiled at me and I felt my soul light up. I wanted to be with him more than anything. For selfish reasons. To be able to express what I felt for him, to be able to break down this barrier I had put around myself whenever I had sex. To be with him and know that it was possible – after all these years of not experiencing anything – to feel something for the person I was having sex with.

'If you want to,' I said to him, 'then I want to. It's that simple.'

In my mind, when he kissed me again, I shut the door to the men who had gone before. I closed my eyes and relaxed into the kisses of the man I was with.

It was dangerous, I know, but I let go of myself. I lay with him, I made love to him, I let him make love to me, and I did not resist in my mind, I did not allow the wall to build itself around me, I did nothing but allow myself to experience what being with Jack Britcham was like.

We held each other for a long time afterwards, not speaking, just being still with each other, occasionally stroking, mainly just being. I could be with Jack Britcham. I could be nothing and everything with him at the same time. I could simply exist.

I left when he fell asleep, getting dressed in the corridor outside his room so as not to disturb him. I stood at the bedroom door, watching him for a few seconds, sleeping with his head thrown back against the pillow, the sheet up to his middle, his eyes with their long eyelashes resting against his cheeks, his hair messy and sexy, the contours of his face so carefully defined and proportioned. It would take a lot to beat that sort of perfection. I put my lips together and pushed a kiss at him through the air, watching until I imagined it would land lightly on his lips before I turned to leave.

At the front door, I said goodbye to the house as well. It was so incredibly beautiful, so much a part of Jack Britcham that I felt sad suddenly that I probably would not be able to see either of them again. What I had done was selfish. I should not have slept with him when I knew how important sex was to him. It was important to me, too, but not in the same way. To me, it fed me and allowed me to not be homeless and a pariah in society. To him, it was something he had waited to do because it was more than just a physical act.

I searched in my pocket for a receipt to write a note on but instead found his business card. A talisman I had slipped into my pocket as good luck this afternoon. I wouldn't need it any more since I wouldn't be seeing him again, so I used the pen that had fallen off the telephone table in the hall to write:

Buying this house is the best thing you've ever done. I meant to tell you that earlier. X

Then I left, and caught a taxi home because it was getting late and I was sure Caesar would be around at some point.

I didn't immediately shower because I liked the smell of him on me. He was the only person who I didn't want to remove from my skin the moment I could. I loved the feel of him, the impressions his body had made on mine. I was hanging onto the thoughts of him, of what we did and how we connected. And my lips, so fantastically bruised, were there for me to touch to remember over and over again.

It was inconceivable that I could be with anyone else tonight. That's why I've been hiding and not answering the door. No matter what happens tomorrow, I've had a moment of perfect happiness and, because of that, I can put up with anything else that comes my way.

Eve

February 1997 (just an update)

I was already pregnant when I slept with Jack.

I had a little boy or little girl growing inside me while, for the first

349

time since I was fifteen, I understood what they meant when they called sex, 'making love'.

I did not know, of course, otherwise I would not have done it.

Being pregnant was also the reason I left Caesar. Once I found out, discovered that the sickness and the tiredness weren't simply down to hating almost every second of my life, I realised I couldn't do it any more. I could not let another man inside my body so that Caesar could get his kicks.

It was the crossover in Pills, you see. The doctor changed my prescription because I'd been getting debilitating headaches, and I'd been warned to use condoms in the crossover period, but not all of the men would. Unprotected sex, like all the other horrendous, sick things I'd priced myself out of with the hotels and the agency, was something I sometimes had to do. I took a gamble and I had been caught out.

On a Monday I took the test. I told Caesar on the Wednesday. For two days I had this little secret, something no one else in the entire world knew and it felt so good. It felt like I had been gifted something special. For the first time in my life, I had been given something that was just for me. I didn't care who the father was, all that mattered was who the mother was and that was me. I had to tell Caesar before Friday because Fridays were often the worst. They would go to one of their clubs and get stoked up on wine and port and spirits and cigars and they would come to the flat expecting service. Sometimes two at once. Sometimes the others would watch. I knew it was a good night when there was only one of them. I couldn't do any of that with a baby inside me.

'Get rid of it,' was all Caesar said at first. He didn't even wait that long to digest the news, he simply said that. Then he reached into the pocket of his discarded jacket for his wallet. From it he pulled out a small white card and a bundle of notes.

He placed the card and the notes on the table in front of me. I was sitting on the floor by his feet – his favourite position for me – and so could read easily what the card said. 'These people will do it discreetly and quickly with the minimum of fuss. This is all you'll need.

350

I expect it to be dealt with by the end of the week.' Friday. He expected me to get 'it done' within two days.

I don't know what I expected. I don't know if I had been secretly hoping that he would let me keep my baby.

His answer was clear, though. He did not touch me the entire night, did not undo the button on his trousers which usually meant I was to get up on my knees, unzip him and take him in my mouth. He stayed and talked as if nothing was wrong, nothing had changed, as if on the table in front of me was not the means and information needed to kill the baby inside me.

At two o'clock, when I was as sure as I could be that he was at home with his wife and would not be coming back that night, I packed up my dress, my diaries, Aunt Mavis's rosary beads, and my photo in Uncle Henry's kitbag, and left with the clothes on my back. It was stupid, probably, but I did not take the money – the one thousand pounds – he gave me.

After that night I did not answer the door to him, he made me get a key cut for him so he could come and go as he pleased. I wanted him to come over and find the money and the card there and to know that I didn't do as he had ordered.

So, in September, I left Brighton with little more than I had left London with. I caught a cab to Worthing, and then from a phonebox by the station I finally got the courage to call the number of a women's refuge that I had memorised.

They helped me. They found me a safe place to stay, way out in the Kent countryside, and they were nice to me, even when I told them I was a pregnant prostitute hiding from her pimp. They took care of me for a week, made me doctor's appointments, let me stay inside as much as I could in case someone saw me, and were so incredible to me. And, yet . . . it wasn't meant to be. That's what I tell myself. That's what I told myself then and that's what I tell myself now. It wasn't meant to be.

I have been through some horrors in my life, but that was probably the worst. I can't describe it, I can't relive it. I can only bear it by telling myself it was not meant to be.

After that loss, I decided I didn't care if he found me. If he dragged me back to the flat. If he did unspeakable things to me. I moved back to Brighton, I applied for benefits while I applied for any jobs that didn't need me to explain the holes in my CV, and before my benefits came in I'd found a job cleaning offices in the early mornings and late evenings, and another waitressing in the afternoons. Anytime I wasn't working, I was reading books I'd got from the library, and telling myself it wasn't meant to be. I was paid a pittance, so I had no money except to pay my rent, buy food and pay my bills, but it was better than the alternative. When I was cleaning late at night, while the others I worked with were complaining about what filthy pigs we had to pick up after, I would be smiling because I knew I wasn't going to be penetrated that night by a man I despised. I knew that cleaning a toilet was better than being used as one. I knew that some day I would maybe be lucky enough to experience what I had experienced with Jack Britcham.

Keeping myself busy, forcing myself to fill the waking hours with work and reading and not much else was a balm on my soul. It slowly helped to bring me back to myself. I was soon strong enough to think about the future, about applying for a college Access course so I could eventually do a degree, and so that I could start to put the woman I was before behind me. Every step forwards I took was another way of dismantling the changeling Eve, who had been an office assistant, then a lap dancer, then a prostitute, and then a sex slave.

Eve

libby

Today Eve is lying on her side, staring into space. She seems so broken and I'm not surprised. She went through all this and she was still someone that Jack loved and Grace liked. She was extraordinary.

eve

I suppose it was going to happen one day. Brighton isn't exactly the biggest place in the world. I live in a flat above an off licence right in the centre of Brighton. It is tiny, probably smaller than the place I had in London, but it's central and I can walk anywhere I like.

I don't pay too much in rent because I agreed with the landlady to decorate it for her while I live here. Best of all, it is two minutes from the café so I can be there and back in no time. And it's not that far to walk to the various offices around Brighton where I clean. I live a very ordered life nowadays and I like it a lot. So what was going to happen one day that happened today?

Running into Jack, of course.

I've stopped calling him Jack Britcham now because I called him that when I was so enamoured with him, when he was the fantasy man who had handed me his full name on a business card. Now, older and wiser, he's simply Jack to me. Funny how a change of circumstances can change how you see someone. I have no doubt in my mind at all that back then I was in love with him. The strength of those feelings wasn't fake or imagined, but it was not sustainable, I don't think.

I'd gone over to the table where he was sitting to fill the order –

354

strong black coffee – Clara had taken before she slopped off for a sneaky cigarette, and hadn't really looked at the man at the table. I'd stopped looking at the customers when I kept seeing men who looked like men I'd escorted. Some of them probably were them, but other men – innocent men – had the look of them that sent chills through me.

Also, I sometimes felt that the scars I had on the inside were visible on the outside so I had to hide myself away, to stop people staring, to stop people wondering, to stop feeling like a freak of nature.

No one cared about my scars – and they wouldn't even if they were on the outside – because people are too wrapped up in their own lives, their own loves, their traumas. You, especially if you are stranger, are too insignificant for them to notice. I know this, but I still hang my head, avoid the eyes of others in case their looks, however fleeting, exposes my scars and imperfections to the world.

'Just Eve as I live and breathe,' he said when I settled the cup on the table.

My eyes flew up to find his and our gazes collided.

'That rhymed,' he said. 'Did you notice that?'

I couldn't help but smile at him, and he grinned back at me.

'Jack,' I said. And I heard in my voice that I still had feelings for him, and I heard, too, that it wasn't the same. I wasn't the same, I suppose. Like I grew out of reading romance books, I'd grown out of being a fool in love.

'You said my name,' he replied, his voice was different too, he'd grown out of being that fool as well. 'You never said it after that first time we met.'

'That's because I always thought of you as Jack Britcham, not simply Jack, for some reason, and I didn't imagine for one minute you'd understand why I did it.'

'Why did you do it?' he asked, and I knew immediately what he meant.

I shrugged and shook my head. 'Just because.'

'Wasn't it good?' he asked carefully and quietly.

'It was fantastic, Jack, really. It couldn't have been better, but . . . it was what it was.' *It was the most incredible few hours of my life.*

355

'Even though Fate so clearly wants us to be together, I take it a drink is out of the question?' he asked.

'No, it's not.'

'You'll come out with me? On a date?'

'Yes.'

'Why?' he asked, baffled.

'Just because.'

'Can I have your number then?' he asked.

'Yes,' I replied, and the shock lit up his face again. He could have my number and I would go for a drink with him because I've been thinking a lot about moments of happiness. Jack featured in one of my biggest moments of joy. I only had a few, and I wanted to collect more. If there was even the smallest chance that he could be a part of another moment of happiness or even just of fun, then I was going to take that chance. I had nothing to lose and everything to gain. I was no longer going to martyr myself.

So, what began as an ordinary day became a good one. I had to go back to work and he sat and drank his coffee, and we kept looking at each other until he left. The tip he left – a fiver – was under a small square of white card. I knew what it was before I picked it up: it was his business card, of course. I turned it over and in my handwriting was the note I had written him all those years and lifetimes ago.

I tucked it into my bra and liked the feel of it there as I went back to serving customers (had to give Clara the fiver, of course).

Phone is ringing and I know it's going to be him.

Eve

May 1999 (another update)

I'd forgotten how lovely it is to kiss Jack. Truly, I had. And kissing him is out of this world. I think we do most of that, although we do a lot of the other thing and that is incredible, too, but it took us a couple of months to go back there. Yes, I wrote that right – months.

356

We both had our reasons for waiting. I guess his were because I'd run out on him after the first time and he hadn't done it with anyone else since me, which I was surprised at. But Jack seems to have remarkable self-restraint. While he likes the act itself, I'm sure, he doesn't feel the need to do it all the time whenever the chance presents itself to him. And I'm pretty sure it presents itself to him on a regular basis because women present themselves to him on a regular basis. It's odd that I didn't notice it before, but women do stop and look at him when we're out together. My self-consciousness about the internal scars that might be obvious and visible to others make me hyper-vigilant, but Jack is excellent camouflage because when I'm with him, I become invisible.

Women smile at him all the time, some say hello, others strike up conversation, and others still even offer him their number – even if he is holding my hand or has his arm around me. It doesn't matter to these women because most of them are posh, rich girls who know I am not one of them and know he is one of theirs and do not see me as anything other than his plaything.

I love that Jack always introduces me into the conversation, and has more than once turned to me and said, 'I don't know, do we want to take (insert posh girl's name) number?' It throws them because, I guess, he wasn't brought up to be so rude to one of his own. To be rude to a commoner like me, I'm sure they think nothing of it. But what I'm trying to say, of course, is that Jack could have had several women in the gap between our meetings, but he hasn't. I could tell from the way he was around me that he'd been hanging on to the hope of us meeting again. I wonder sometimes how long he would have waited.

It's obvious why I wasn't mad keen to do it again.

It wasn't Jack's fault, but after the loss I spent a lot of time trying to get in touch with my body again. I wondered constantly in the early days afterwards if that was the reason why it'd gone wrong. If not being in touch with my body completely because I had effectively separated it from my heart and mind for so long was what made it happen. I knew logically that wasn't the case, that there was very

357

likely something wrong with the baby – which I was meant to call an embryo – and that is why it didn't develop. Nature has its way of handling things, apparently. And maybe considering its conception, it might have been for the best. But that's all logical. The reality is, I thought of him or her as a baby, and I wanted them, I wanted someone to love and care for, and I lost them, and I had no real reason or explanation for it happening. It was something else I had to carry with me. Another scar that I feared people could see. And I blamed my body for it. What else could I do? When it came to something like this, 'just because' was not a good enough reason.

So I was not in a rush to have sex all over again, to take part in that act that had left me scarred. I don't give a damn what anyone says about getting back on the horse again as soon as possible after a trauma – the last thing you want to do is go back to putting yourself in danger. Yes, even if that means you might not want to participate in that particular activity ever again.

If I fell off a horse and was left feeling as I am now about the things I did, I would never go near a horse again. Not until someone could guarantee me that the horse I next approached – all those years later when I could put my fear of what happened into some kind of perspective – was one hundred per cent safe.

Jack was safe.

It took me a couple of months to work that one out. But the kissing was the best part, anyway. He told me that he'd kissed a lot of people, because it was what he had done instead of the other thing, but he hadn't realised how much he could enjoy it until he kissed me. Which sounds very silly written here, but at the time I knew what he meant.

I almost said (but didn't) that he wouldn't have to kiss anyone but me again, because I hoped I wouldn't have to sleep with anyone else but him again. I'm sure, if this doesn't work out with him, I won't be doing it again. Not the sex part, anyway. No matter how much I want a baby, I don't think I could face allowing another person into me.

Probably won't be writing much in here again for a while because Jack and I spend most of our spare time together. Every spare moment we have, we greedily claim for ourselves. I've only been able to write in

358

here now because it's Sunday afternoon and he has gone on a hunt for some food. We literally have nothing in the cupboards or fridge because we have not left the house, or really the bedroom, since Friday night. 'I'll go be hunter-gather,' he said, beating his chest. And I'd had to kiss him several times before I felt safe enough to let him go.

It's silly, but whenever we leave each other I have to tell him I love him and seal it with a kiss because I am scared that if we don't see each other again he won't know. I'm not planning on leaving or dying but sometimes I get an irrational fear that either Elliot or Caesar is after me and I think they will find me and kill me.

That doesn't scare me as much as the thought of Jack not knowing before I die that in this life of mine, I have only ever loved one man. I loved Peter, but he was a boy. In this life, I have only truly loved one man and Jack is that man.

So that's it, my update.

I don't think I've made it clear how happy I am. Happiness is an alien concept to women like me, I think, but I am happy. He makes me laugh, he makes think, we talk, we kiss, we sometimes even decorate his house together. I won't let him come to my flat because I think it's important not to let another man – no matter how safe, no matter how much I love him – into my space again. I need a haven, and that's why I keep the flat on even though I practically live here.

I am happy. I have my jobs, I have my Access course, and I have my Jack. So I am happy. That is all that matters in the end: I am happy.

Love,
Eve

22ⁿᵈ November 1999

Hello old friend, you're here again.

I like that you are always here, never judging, never leaving. No matter how long I leave you for, I always know where you are when I need you. And I need you.

What has happened now in the dramatic world of Eve? I have seen him again, that is what. Caesar. I have seen him again.

Last night, after much persuasion because I do not like to do the 'date' thing, Jack took me to the opera in London.

It was my chance to wear my dress. I haven't worn it since that day I bought it, and putting it on again was like being embraced by an old friend. I felt as wonderful as I did that day in the shop, and I was grateful to Jack for persuading me to come to the opera, for giving me a chance to wear my dress.

The opera, *Madame Butterfly*, was beautiful. I allowed myself to float along with the music, experience the emotions of the words, having read the story years before. I felt for Butterfly, so willing to do whatever she had to – including denouncing her faith – to be with the man she loved when all along he just wanted to get her into bed.

During the intermission, I went to join the ladies queuing for the loo while Jack went to get us some drinks.

In the mirror in the toilets, I noticed how different I looked. Not only because of the dress, but around the eyes, in the eyes, I was different because I was happy. I had no make-up on – make-up reminded me of Honey – so I never wore it now. But still, I was and looked happy.

Making my way back towards Jack, I saw him talking to a man. No surprise, really, since Jack seemed to know people everywhere we went. But as I drew nearer, I realised who he was talking to. *What* he was talking to.

I stopped walking as I took in the full horrific sight of him: Caesar.

Jack knew Caesar. My knees went weak as I stood still, staring at the pair of them. Their body language was formal, reserved, so they did not know each other very well. But then, I looked from Jack to him and their similar height, their similar build, the shape of their faces . . . No, no, I shook the thought out of my head. No. Simply no.

At the same time, I backed away, and then escaped the way I came, back towards the powder room, away from there. Inside the plush interior of the loos, I frantically scanned the faces of the women, looking for her, seeking her out among the posh frocks, expensive hairdos and heady perfume. And there she was: a cool, tall blonde with up-do hair, wearing a simple black sheath dress with pearls around her throat, expensive black shoes and bag, and immaculate make-up. Caesar's escort. Other women would not notice her, would think she was like them, and there for the music, ambience and experience, few women would know that she was working. More of the men would know, because many of the men here could probably afford her.

She glanced at me, having seen me watching her, and gave me a glacial, near-smile and I knew she could see it in me. She could tell what I used to be. Our eyes met and I knew she was nowhere near where I was towards the end. She was probably still telling herself that the money was worth it, that she was helping those men, that she felt empowered and liberated by what she was doing. She was probably pitying me for not being strong enough to go the distance and letting it defeat me. Stalking past me, she went back out there, and I followed, sticking my head out of the door, to see if I was right.

I was. As soon as she saw that he was talking to someone, she kept her distance, hung around, looking in her bag, playing with her mobile phone, and generally being invisible until he was free.

The bell ringing, telling us it was time to return to our seats, made me jump, and I pulled my head inside the powder room before Jack looked up and around to find out where I was. I stayed in the toilets, in a cubicle, until there was no sound from outside, and the second bell rang to tell people the rest of the performance was about to start.

I waited a few more minutes before I went out outside to find Jack standing alone, holding our drinks, our programmes tucked under his arm.

'Are you OK?' he asked. 'You were gone for such a long time I was about to send out a search party.'

'Sorry,' I said quietly. 'I just . . . I don't feel very well.'

'You do look a little pale,' he replied. 'And you're, you're shaking.' His gaze darted around, looking for the nearest flat surface. When he had disposed of our drinks, he came back and took my hand. 'You're freezing,' he said, concerned. 'Come on, let's get you home.'

'Are you sure you don't mind?' I asked him. 'Those tickets must have cost a fortune.'

'It doesn't matter, all that matters is getting you well.'

'Thank you.'

'You don't have to thank me,' he said. 'I love you. You look after the people you love.'

Outside, in the fresh air, I felt a bit better, probably because I was further away from *him*. I inhaled London, remembering how in love with it I used to be, how perfect the city had seemed when I first arrived. And how scary and hidden with unknown dangers it seemed by the time I left.

'You just missed my father,' Jack said. 'He was here at the opera. Should have known he'd be here. He tries to see every new production of *Madame Butterfly*.'

I barely heard the rest of what he said because the first part had forced me to turn to the nearest wall and bend double as I threw up.

Poor Jack was horrified. He took me in his arms after I had emptied my stomach, and then he held me until I'd stopped shaking enough to lean on his arm and walk with him back to the car. Later, he carried me up to bed and stayed awake until I had fallen asleep in his arms.

What do I do?

I have to finish things with Jack, of course. He'd been making noises about me meeting his family, but I hadn't been keen. I couldn't reciprocate, so I didn't want to do that. I liked our world of two, as well. Having it made us seem all the more special. I didn't like to let others in. And now I have more reason not to.

It was weird, thinking about it, how Jack and I never talked properly about our families. I knew he had parents and a brother, he knew my father had died when I was young and my mother lived in Leeds, but it was only surface information. Anything deeper hadn't seemed required.

I should finish things with Jack, but how can I? When I haven't been this happy in years, how can I be expected to just let him go?

It's not fair, this, you know? Haven't I atoned enough for what I did? Wasn't losing my baby enough punishment? Why does it seem I have to lose Jack, too? Why did Caesar have to be his father?

libby

I throw the book to the ground, desperate to get it away from me. I stare at my hands, looking for the grime and filth that must have rubbed off from Hector onto me.

He can't be Caesar, he just can't.

My body is very still, except for my panicked breathing. I look around the cellar, searching for her because she's gone. Of course she's gone. She couldn't stay here and face this.

I struggle to my feet, and start to pace, wringing my hands and fighting every urge in me to start screaming. How could she have lived with this secret? Did she tell Jack? She must have. But how could he have lived with it? Trying to force your son to have sex with a prostitute was one thing, but . . .

How am I going to face Jack after this? How am I going to talk to him like normal when I know? Hector not only enslaved a woman, that woman was the woman his son married.

Faintly, I hear a car pulling up outside, and then I hear Butch's scampering and barking as the car door shuts. Jack.

Working quickly, I wrap up the diaries and return them to their hiding place, then leave the cellar as quickly as possible. I make it into the bedroom seconds before the door opens and Jack enters the house. Butch's barking stops for a few seconds and then I hear his nails scraping along the wood floor as he runs back to his bed.

'Libby?' Jack calls.

'Yeah?' I reply from my place behind the door.

'I found a couple of waifs and strays on the way back who need feeding,' Jack says.

Angela and Grace. Oh, thank God. Thank God. They'll hopefully stay all evening so I don't have to speak to Jack and give away what I have just found out. I can work out how to deal with this.

I open the door and stick my head out, smiling as I do so.

'Hello, Liberty,' Harriet says.

'Hope you don't mind us dropping in like this,' says Hector.

'We were in the area and Jack didn't think it would be a problem,' Harriet adds

'It's not, is it?' Jack asks.

Breathing, breathing, breathing. I just need to concentrate on breathing. Not talking, not standing, just breathing. 'It's fine,' I say. 'It's fine.'

chapter seventeen

libby

Hector is sitting in our living room with a pre-dinner drink.

Eve's Caesar is our living room waiting to be fed.

I've busied myself in the kitchen since their arrival even though Harriet has been trying to get me to take it easy, to go and sit down and talk to them. Hector makes everything about me crawl, as if I am covered in creeping, sliming film. Every time I look at him, I see nothing but the man who was capable of doing those horrendous things to Eve. How many others had he done that to? How many women had he paid for sex? Paid. For. Sex. The thought of it was bad enough, but to know that once he handed over his money, he saw nothing but a piece of flesh he could treat as he wanted . . .

'What's the matter?' Jack asks me and I nearly drop the dish in my hands out of fright. I have been focusing as much as possible on dinner, on trying to put the things I know out of my head so I can eat a meal with the man in the other room, I didn't hear him approach.

Does Jack know? Does he know what Eve did for a living because she felt so trapped by poverty? Does he know about Eve and his father?

I turn to him and force a smile. 'Nothing, why?'

He reaches out to lay his hand on my arm and I flinch. His hand doesn't make contact, but hurt spirals into his eyes. 'You seem very nervous,' he says through his disappointment. 'We can tell them about the divorce if you want, so you don't have to worry about pretending, if that's what's making you stressed.'

Divorce? I think for a moment. *Who's getting a divorce?* Then I remember. We are. I am. 'No, no, it's not that,' I say. 'I just want things to be OK with the dinner.'

'Are you sure you don't want me to help?' he asks.

'Yeah, I'm sure.'

'You know, Libby . . .' he begins, then stops talking.

Acting on instinct, I step forwards and slip my arms around him. It feels incredible to touch him again. I close my eyes and rest my head on his chest, listening to the beating of his heart. Slowly, cautiously he wraps his arms around me. He cups his hand around the back of my head, holding me gently against him.

I love you, I think, hoping he can feel it through my touch, through my skin. *I love you so very much.*

'I won't let them stay too late,' he tells me. 'Maybe we can talk?'

We haven't done that, have we? It's been too painful, the end too inevitable to have those truths of how he really feels about Eve, about me, spelt out to me. But how can I leave when we haven't even talked it through properly? I haven't even asked him how he truly feels about me. I have just assumed. 'Yes, I'd like that.'

He's able to hold me closer then, to dare to breach the gap between us with a tighter hug, and I can feel his heart racing, matching the sudden racing of my heart.

'Libby, that was fantastic,' Harriet says, carefully placing her knife and fork on the plate side by side. I glance around at the plates, all empty – except mine. I didn't realise until I sat opposite him that I would not be able to eat in Hector's immediate vicinity. I'm finding it hard to talk as well, oh, and breathe.

'Coq au vin is probably one of my favourite dishes,' Hector says, cheerily. 'I'm now torn between whose I prefer – yours or my wife's.' He reaches out, places his wrinkled, veiny hand on Harriet's. 'No offence meant, my darling,' he says sweetly to Harriet.

She smiles, receiving her husband's touch with a grateful gentleness. 'None taken.'

Horrified, I look away and stand to reach for the plates.

'No, you are not clearing away after all that cooking,' Harriet admonishes and suddenly she is on her feet, taking plates and cutlery. Jack gets up to help and I can see what is about to happen: they're going to gather up the plates, they're going to take them into the kitchen and then they're going to load the dishwasher or wash up and leave me alone with him. And I'll have to talk to Hector.

'No, no, I'll help,' I say frantically.

'You'll do no such thing,' Harriet replies.

'No arguments,' Jack adds, 'you sit down and relax.'

When we're alone, Hector sits back in his seat and smiles at me. I stare down at the table. The contours of his face are imprinted on my mind, so not looking at him isn't even a respite. I can't imagine what it was like for Eve after everything.

'You're looking very well,' Hector says.

'Thanks,' I mumble.

'You must be ready to think about going back to work now.'

I shrug, listening to the scraping and clinking sounds coming from the kitchen, willing Jack and his mother to hurry up and get back, to save me from this torture.

Hector stops talking, stops trying to connect with me and we sit in an uncomfortable silence. 'Have I upset you?' he eventually asks.

My body freezes. What do I say to him? He hasn't done anything to me, but he did to Jack, he did to Eve. I feel sometimes that I went through what Eve did. But I didn't.

I shake my head at him.

'Will I be granted at least the favour of a glance and a verbal answer to that question?' he says.

My mind is such a mass of confusion that I am actually doing as he asks. I lift my head and, inhaling deeply, I say, 'No.'

His eyes, the same shape as Jack's, hold mine and I can't look away. I want to look as deep as possible into them to try and see the nature of the evil that lies in his mind, that lives within his soul; and I want to look away and never look at him again.

'*How* have I upset you?' he asks, reasonably, calmly – all the more menacing for it. The Hector I have come to know all these years is no longer in the room; the man who abused Eve is now sitting opposite me. I had no idea that they were so easily exchanged, so closely enmeshed. There is no point in lying to him.

'I know about you and Eve,' I say. 'Or should I call her Honey?' I sound more confident than I feel.

'What is it that you think you know?' he replies. The only thing that has changed in his expression is the set of his mouth – it becomes flatter, firmer.

'I found her diaries,' I say. And then I want to reach out and cram the words back in my mouth. He did it, he killed her. Of course he did. He killed her to get those diaries, to get the evidence she had on him.

And now I have told him that I have them, I have all but said: kill me too.

jack

I often wonder if my mother really has no idea what my father is truly like. Or if she knows and has decided to pretend it isn't happening.

After we came home from that trip to London on my fifteenth birthday, I walked into the kitchen to find my mother waiting with a birthday cake. It had fifteen candles and she said, 'I know it's silly, darling, and you're far too old for this, but I would love to hold on to you being my little boy for one more year.' I was almost mute from what had happened, and I wanted nothing more than to be her little boy right then. My father had gone off into his study, as he often did when he was annoyed.

I went to her and threw my arms around her, my mother. I'd always shied away from her constant need to baby me, to treat me like a little boy, but right then I needed her to comfort me, to be my mother. Startled, she put her arms around me. 'What's the matter?' she asked, concerned and confused in equal measures. 'Did you and your father have a row?'

'No,' I said, trying to keep the sobs out of my voice. 'No.'

'Come on, tell me,' she coaxed. 'Tell me, I know something happened.'

I looked at the watch on my wrist that he'd bought afterwards as a cover for what my real 'present' was. He'd practically thrown it at my head. 'I, erm, don't like the watch he got me,' I said, erasing the sound of my inadequacy and juvenileness. 'He got a bit cross.'

My mother hesitated, not sure whether to believe me or not, I realised. 'Thank you for the cake,' I said, stepping away from her. I had to behave like a man for the first time today, and not burden her with this. And how would I explain to her that I had seen him go off with someone else, when he had her at home? He had chosen someone so young to ... 'It's chocolate, my favourite. Can we light the candles?'

My mother stood very still for a moment, then she turned on the smile that I loved and went to retrieve the matches from the kitchen drawer.

'Make a wish,' she said, once all the candles were dancing with flames in front of me.

To never turn out like my father, I thought, and blew. The stream of my breath, thankfully, extinguished all the candles. *Thank you,* I thought to whoever was there. *Thank you, because I never want to be like him.*

'How is Libby feeling?' My mother asks me. I've always been envious of the way Libby so easily calls her parents Mum and Dad, the way she says, 'my mum' or 'my dad'. I've never been able to do that, I've never been that free with them. They are formal people to me, formal and removed. Eve never talked about her family, not until the night she told me everything about herself. And that became lost in the midst of what else she told me. I never found the right moment to ask her about it, another of those things I can chalk up to thinking I had all the time in the world.

'She's better. Still finds it hard to leave the house, but she isn't as ... wounded any more.' I think about the moment we shared earlier, I think I may have a chance. I may have another chance with her.

'She really is lovely,' my mother says.

'I know,' I reply.

We clean up in silence for a while and then my mother places a plate decisively on the recently dried pile and turns to me. 'I wish you were closer to your father,' she says. 'Things were never really right with you two after that trip to London on your birthday. What happened?'

'Which trip was that?' I ask, wondering if I can tell her now. I look at her: her hair, streaked with white is cut into a style that flatters the soft lines of her face. Her eyes, always so kind and understanding, are surrounded by a network of lines that show she has had laughter in her life. My mother is a welcoming woman, which is why I have always wondered why my father does it. What can he want out there that he does not get from her?

'Your fifteenth birthday trip to London,' she says calmly, obviously she has not fallen for my attempts to deflect this conversation.

'When we fell out over the watch?' I ask her.

'Jack,' she says, reaching out to stroke the length of my face with her hand, 'my little boy, you don't have to protect me. Tell me what really happened.'

If I don't protect her, who will? 'Mother; Mum,' I try out the word, it doesn't feel right on my tongue, but I repeat it, to see if I can get a proper taste for it, 'Mum, it was a long time ago. I've forgotten most of what happened that day. Hector probably has, too.'

She nods her head, and smiles at me, sadness in her eyes. 'I thought so,' she says. 'But, Jack, don't ever believe that. Your father never forgets anything.'

libby

I am sitting here, playing a game of visual chicken with the man who probably killed Eve.

And I know he is going to win. Because the calm certainty of his stare and the way he is unruffled by my revelation have confirmed what I realised microseconds after I revealed I had the diaries: he is cold enough to kill.

Feeling no shame in looking away first, I remove my gaze from his hypnotic stare and focus on my hands. Grace hasn't had a chance to redo my nails and I have been neglectful with the hand cream – my hands are going to get old before their time. That's ironic: my body will age normally, but the things that set me apart, my scars, will always be at least thirty-six years younger than the rest of me. By the time my body has renewed itself in seven years, the scars will be old but the rest of me will be older.

'Eve was a very troubled young woman, prone to fantasies and uncontrolled flights of imagination,' Hector informs me, in a measured manner. I am not surprised that Eve was too scared to run away until something more important than her own safety gave her the courage. I am unsettled, uneasy, probably bordering on terrified at this moment and I have a table separating us as well as two people in the other room protecting me.

'If you could show me the diaries, I could explain to you what she might have meant by the things she wrote.'

The day I met Jack, I remember smiling at the car salesman with my lips curled into my mouth and my eyes focused elsewhere because I found him so irritating, condescending and generally unpleasant. I give Hector another version of that smile because I do not want to say any more. I have done enough to dig my own grave for now. If I do not engage any more, I can maybe keep him at arm's length until the other two return.

'I don't appreciate the silent treatment,' he says to me, and frost snakes down my spine.

I keep my head lowered and say nothing. It is not a good idea to enrage him, but I do not want to engage either. How do you deal with the most dangerous man you have ever met?

'Coffee or tea?' Harriet says, entering the room in that space in time where I was about to be forced to choose my next move.

I immediately get to my feet. 'Harriet, you sit down, I insist. Jack and I will make the coffee, I need to talk to him any way.'

Harriet, ready to protest, opens her lips, but I am already at the door. Harriet looks from me to Hector but if she suspects something, it does not show on her face.

'Coffee for me,' Hector says, normal again, a father and husband again.

'Me too,' Harriet adds.

'Coffee all round,' I say then slip out of the room and into kitchen.

'Everyone wants coffee,' I say to Jack who is standing by the kettle, staring at its shiny surface, waiting for it to boil.

'You don't usually drink coffee this late,' he says to me.

'No, I don't. Actually, I think I'm going to go to bed. Do you mind if we talk tomorrow or something? I'm a bit tired.'

He's disappointed, but I do not wait to be touched by it, to be persuaded to stay and see the night out in the company of Hector.

As I undress, my mind keeps going to Eve's diaries. I need to finish them as soon as possible, to find out what happened to Eve. To find out if I really have just had dinner with a killer.

And if I'm going to be next.

chapter eighteen

libby

All day some fuckwit has been calling the house and hanging up when I answer.

I can't ignore the phone, either, because it might be important and since I spend all day down in the cellar and the mobile reception is dodgy enough in the rest of the house, I have to go and pick it up.

As soon as I do, the person on the other end stays there for a few seconds then hangs up.

I hope they get bored and find someone else to bother, soon, because I really can't be bothered going up and down the stairs all day.

'Butch, are you coming with me?' I ask. He's been a little quieter than normal today. I didn't even realise until I got into bed that he'd slipped into the room with me. He jumped onto the bed and curled up beside me. I'd stroked my fingers through his fur and had felt so much calmer, *safer* with him beside me. I could do with that influence now.

He barks happily, and jumps out of his basket and darts down the stairs ahead of me.

eve

I haven't finished with Jack. And I haven't told him I know his dad. How could I?

I know, I know: too many secrets. Secrets are not good, they are not healthy in a relationship. Especially when he has been making overtures towards marriage. I could be imagining it, but he has been having conversations relating to the future, relating to us, asking me what I think about the décor in this beautiful house. More than once he's asked me to move in permanently, to give up my flat and move in; more than once I've turned him down saying it's too soon.

It's not too soon – it's too scary. If I say yes without telling him about my past then I am not a good person. If I still have one foot out of the door, out of the relationship, then I can fool myself into thinking that I have not lied too much to him. I have not given myself completely to this relationship, which means I do not have to tell him everything.

Jack is hurt by it, but he would be more hurt to know what sort of woman I am. Something is going to happen to bring it to a head, though, I can tell. All it will take is for us to run into Caesar in the street.

Then it would be a matter of waiting to find out if he would come himself, or if he would destroy me by destroying Jack and telling him that the woman Jack was sleeping with was a prostitute. I do not know.

Things would be simpler, of course, if I didn't love Jack so much. I know I have calmed down a lot from the early days, and the loss has made me cautious, but I can't deny what I feel for him. I can't deny he is the man I want to spend the rest of my life with. But that is selfish, isn't it? Would I be the woman he wants to spend the rest of his life with if he knew? I doubt it. I truly, truly doubt it.

This is killing me.

Eve

25ᵗʰ January 2000

He's just been round.

Hector, Caesar, Jack's dad – whatever the hell he's called. He's just been round and put me straight.

I suppose I have antagonised him. I have worn red in front of the bull that is his personality so I should not have expected anything else. It all began at the weekend, when Jack finally insisted that I meet his parents. I've been avoiding it all costs, as I said before. I've made excuses, feigned illness, even begged to be called into work. But this weekend Jack wouldn't take no for an answer, and I could tell in the way that he asked that it was important to him. My evasiveness was causing him pain; making him wonder if I was ashamed of him when of course it was the other way round.

I dressed as simply as possible: a cream, flowery dress, my hair loose, and flat shoes. As he drove us over there I kept cycling between mini panic attacks where I could hardly breathe, to gulping back retches. 'I know you're nervous,' Jack said to me at one point, 'but there's no need to be. I'm sure they'll love you.'

'Jack, about—' I began several times, and each time the words got stuck in my throat, wedged themselves there and would not

381

move. How did I tell him his dad was once my pimp? That I slept with his dad before I'd slept with him?.

'It's all right,' Jack said after the fifth or sixth time, 'once my parents meet you, they'll see how beautiful, kind and generous you are.'

'I doubt that,' I said, trying to be jovial, feeling the swirling of anxiety inside. 'Only you see me like that. No one else does.'

'Everyone loves you,' Jack said.

I watched his hands, remembering how gentle and loving they'd always been when they touched me. Even in the heat of the moment, if we were consumed with passion, his hands, his body, his everything was always gentle with me. Gentle and loving. Despite all that I had seen and experienced, I knew that real men were like this. Most men were like this. They cared and were gentle and did not want to hurt anyone. They were nice because it was in their nature and they didn't demand to receive it back; they were passionate without being cruel; they were nice without being manipulative. Jack reminded me of that.

He was so different from his father.

When Jack got out to open the car door for me, I almost slid across to the driver's seat to hot-wire the car and drive away. Only problem being, of course, I did not know how to hot-wire a car. I did not even know how to drive.

We all shook hands in the corridor. I could not lift my eyes to meet Hector's fully. I looked slightly to the side of him, so I would not look into the soul of a man who had been in control of my life for so long. Is that how slaves used to feel? Once they had freedom, once their former masters could not control them any more, did they feel defiance and independence inside, but could not show it because the memories of the beatings, the chainings, the abuse were still so strong?

I wanted to be defiant, strong, proud, to hold my head up high and act all 'Look at me now, I made it despite what you did', but I couldn't. I'm sure most people couldn't. I'm good at pretending, but not that good.

He shook my hand warmly, and so did Harriet, his wife. We had tea in the living room, Jack and I sitting side by side on the sofa, making small talk. Jack's mum, Caesar's wife, was nice enough. Cool, though. Reserved. I guessed she would be like that with any woman dating one of her precious sons.

Jack held my hand and smiled a lot and told jokes that we all laughed at, but the atmosphere was still there and I could not look at Caesar – Hector (I must remember to call him Hector) for any length of time – I felt sick every time I tried. I wanted to vomit because I could remember his hands on me, his body next to mine, him dominating me, him renting me out.

I try not to feel like a victim, but sitting in that living room, knowing this was where he would come after being at the flat with me, where he would pour himself a drink, where he would sit some evenings and read the paper with his wife, maybe even make love to her in front of the fire, it made me feel nauseous.

Eventually it was over, and we could leave. I had been inspected, lightly questioned, primarily approved. I knew this because at the door Harriet said, 'The two of you must come back again for dinner very soon. Then we can spend much more time getting to know each other.' Maybe she could see how much I loved Jack so she was inviting me back. I wouldn't go, but having the invite meant a lot to Jack. I could feel him grinning beside me. I was about to smile in return when I saw from the corner of my eye Caesar stiffen, a warning that I shouldn't even think about it. That was why I did it. A small little fuck you to the man who thought he could control everyone. I smiled at Harriet, took her hands and said, 'Thank you, thank you so much for the invite. We'd love to come back. If your cooking is anyway half as delicious as those scones, I'm sure I'm in for a treat.'

Harriet smiled back and I felt Jack's grin grow wider. *And fuck you, Caesar,* I thought, *fuck you*.

He would not leave that unanswered, of course. No one swore at him and got away with it. He used to tell me about the young upstarts who worked at the firm where he was a partner who thought they could sideline him. Thought they could find a way to the top via him. He *always* stamped on those people. *Always* made sure they were there less than six months, and that he made them virtually unemployable with any good firms by sabotaging their reputations. I remember one business associate of his once left a mark on my face from where he'd hit me to get himself off. When I told Caesar who it was, he quietly erupted. I saw it in his eyes, and in the way his body almost solidified with rage. Yes, Caesar had set it all up, but he hadn't sanctioned this, and he was not happy. Caesar told me a few weeks later that the business associate was being divorced by his wife, who had evidence that he had slept with his secretary, he was also being investigated for tax evasion and had lost his job. Caesar said it casually, as a by-the-way in conversation to let me know that anyone who crossed him would be dealt with. A reminder, too, that he would not hesitate in stamping on me if I even thought about leaving.

It shouldn't have been a surprise, then, when I opened the door earlier today to find him on the doorstep. All six foot of him, solid and ominous in his dark suit and black overcoat, black gloves on his hands.

Before I could react, his hand was around my throat, choking me, as he pushed me through the porch, into the hallway, kicking the door shut behind him and slamming me against the wall.

'Don't test me,' he snarled. 'I will think nothing of snapping you in two, you cheap little *whore.*'

Breathe, I can't breathe, I was screaming inside, clawing at his hand to try to get it off my throat. *Can't breathe, can't breathe.*

'You get out of my son's life, and you stay out,' he continued to snarl. 'I don't care what you tell him, or if you tell him nothing at all, but you leave him. Today. And don't come back. I won't ask again.'

He took his hand away and I collapsed to the ground, spluttering, trying to get air into my lungs, while holding my throat and shaking.

'No,' I said. Even though I was still gasping for air, my eyes were filled with tears, my face felt like it was on fire, I still found the words to defy him. 'I'm not leaving him.'

'WHAT DID YOU SAY?' he shouted.

'I said "No. I'm not leaving him." There's nothing you can do.' I looked up at Hector, from my place on the ground, seemingly subservient, feeling anything but.

His fingers curled into the palms of his hands and I knew he was going to hit me. He could do a lot of damage with a punch, but that was no reason to do what he wanted or say what he wanted to hear. I had realised something the moment he stepped over the threshold, something that had never been as real a possibility as it was now that he had shown his hand. If he was so much in control, if he could get out of this unscathed because no one would dare leave or censure him, then why hadn't he told Jack or his wife? If he was as powerful as he liked to make me believe, then why bother coming to threaten me? After all, I am a cheap little whore, I am not someone of consequence.

'You have more to lose than I do,' I said. 'You hurt me, I will tell Jack everything. And then you'll lose your sons, your wife, and I know the people you work with might turn a blind eye to what you do but not if it was made public. And you can kill me. It's all written down. I've got dates, names, places. And you'll never find my diaries before Jack does. So go ahead, do your worst, it'll be you that suffers the most. Being a *whore* comes hand in hand with suffering: I can take it.'

'If you ever breathe a word,' he said, seeming to get taller and wider in that instant.

'I won't if you won't, *lover,*' I said. That was the sort of thing Honey would normally say. Not me. But I wasn't Honey any more. Or was I? Had I been fooling myself all these years that she was a persona I had adopted? Or was she really just me?

'You be very careful, little girl,' he snarled again, baring even more of his perfect, even teeth. Then he was gone, slamming the door with a loud, heart-stopping bang.

I stayed slumped on the floor for ages, fingering the part of my throat that he had crushed, wondering how I was going to explain it away to Jack. Maybe it wouldn't bruise too much, even if it went a little red. I'd wear a scarf or a polo neck for a few days, and it would be fine.

385

I know Jack's dad will be back. Maybe not physically, but he will find a way to get at me, to get rid of me – it is just a matter of time. He might have more to lose, but he won't let this go. He's not that type of man. After I left, I always wondered if he came after me. I wondered if he thought I'd be back, or if he used those contacts he always boasted about to try to find me. I doubt it. I might have been his possession, and he might have had a cursory look, but there were plenty of other *whores* out there to take my place. And if he did have someone look, they can't have looked very hard because they didn't find me. It's not as if I went very far away. Effectively, I was hiding in plain sight, if I was hiding at all.

He might have let me be if I had not hooked up with his son, if I was not in his life again. And if I hadn't threatened him. What's done is done, though.

I know it's stupid, but I'm actually more scared by discovering that I might actually be more like Honey than I thought. If that's true, then . . . all those things that I did in the past, I did them because I – EVE – was capable of doing them. I hadn't stepped outside myself to do them; I hadn't worn a mask to protect myself from the horrors of it all.

I, Eve, had been a prostitute.

I was dirty, grubby, and disgusting.

I was desperate, trapped, and afraid.

Those things were not in the past, they were in the present because Honey is in the past and Eve is the person I see when I look in the mirror. And if it was Eve who did those things, then she isn't gone. She is in the here and now.

I am Eve. And I am a prostitute.

Me

14th February 2000

This is what happened this morning.

Jack lay next to me in bed, watching me sleep until his probing gaze was enough to stir me from a rather deep and satisfying slumber.

'Morning,' he said, leaning up on one arm and staring down at me.

Coffee. I could smell coffee. It was usually me who got out of bed and stumbled my way downstairs to get the fancy machine working and brought two mugs back to bed.

'Hmmm,' I said, knowing instantly that it was too early for niceties and too early for coffee. He was in one of his mental moments where he'd want to do something fit and healthy that was good for the body and mind, while I wanted to lie in and not think about anything until midday.

'I've made coffee,' he said.

'Hmm-hmm?' I replied, which was me asking, *What do you want, a round of applause or something?*

'And I've got you a present,' he said.

'Hmmm,' I replied, thinking, *Can't this wait? At least until it's properly daylight.*

He placed the 'present' on the pillow in front of me. 'There you go, princess.'

I prised open an eye, and there on the white pillow lay a gold and diamond ring. Both of my eyes flew open and I stared at it, startled and slightly afraid.

My line of sight moved from the ring to his face, which was grinning at me. He was wide awake and his eyes were dancing.

He raised his eyebrows. 'Well?' he was asking.

I found my smile, looked back at the stunning diamond cluster and then returned my gaze to him.

I bit my lip as I nodded.

'Come here,' he said, gathering me his arms, knocking the ring somewhere into the bed.

'No, you come here,' I replied, submitting in his arms, but placing my hands on either side of his face and drawing him close so we could kiss and kiss and kiss the morning away.

Eve

387

The phone keeps ringing and then being hung up the second I pick it up.

It only happens when Jack isn't here, and the silence at the end of the phone is so unnerving. I would prefer it if he told me what he wanted, what he wanted to do to me, that he was going to kill me. I would prefer that to the silence. Because it feels like it echoes into the house when I replace the receiver. It makes this place, my home, feel so unsafe. I stand very still and look around, searching for shadows that should not be there, listening for sounds that tell of an intruder, waiting for something to come out of nowhere and do me harm.

It's Hector, of course. He started it since we announced the engagement. He wants me gone, he wants to scare me off. He does not want me to marry his son. His tactics are working, though: I am becoming more and more nervous. I don't like being here alone now. It probably wouldn't be such a problem if the place wasn't so big, and constructed of so many small, intimate and scary spaces.

He's rung ten times this evening. In the end I unplugged the phone. But I have to plug it in again when Jack comes home, and taking it off the hook feels like I've let him win. He knows that he's got to me, scared me, unnerved me so I have to take measures to freeze him out. If I answer it shows that I am not that bothered. If I unplug the phone, it just rings and rings for him and he can't be sure that I'm not too busy to pick it up.

Sometimes I wish he'd just come over and do it, would finish me off rather than torturing me. But he likes torture, doesn't he?

I wish there was a way to tell Jack without it being the end of everything.

Me

libby

The phone is ringing upstairs.

The phone is ringing and ringing and ringing. It has been ringing for most of the day and the person never speaks when I answer.

It's just a coincidence, isn't it? It's just a coincidence that Hector used silent phone calls to threaten Eve and now, when he has reason to threaten me, I have been receiving silent phone calls.

I blot the ringing out of my head and concentrate on the diaries.

It's just a coincidence, just a coincidence, just a coincidence.

eve

The day I've dreaded and hoped for all these years has come.

A letter from Leeds arrived earlier and I haven't dared open it. I wrote to my mother in February and told her of my engagement to a lovely man who I would like her to meet one day, and I, of course, heard nothing.

But now I have a reply, it seems. The address and my name is typed, but it's postmarked Leeds and since contact has dwindled to nothing with all the other people up there I used to write to, it can't be anyone else.

It must have been telling her I was engaged that did it. Maybe she thought that I would now be OK with her having a relationship with Alan because I finally understood grown-up love.

I'm scared to open it, though, in case she is cursing me. She is telling me that she hopes I never have a daughter that does to me what I did to her.

Can't believe I haven't opened it already. Any time before now I think I would have torn it open, but now I am too afraid.

I will open it later. When Jack is here and in bed. I need his presence but I do not want to tell him if it is bad. Later, I'll do it later.

Eve

I made sure Jack was asleep before I slipped out and went into the room that is Jack's office, and opened the letter. My hands were shaking, of course, because this was the first contact with her in so long.

It was one sheet of paper and on it, in neat handwriting, was everything I needed to know.

I'm sorry, I can't write any more. I thought I could, but I can't.

'Are you having an affair?' Jack asked me, when I came home today.

I had tried to creep in, to not wake him, but I needn't have bothered, he was sitting on the third step of the staircase, waiting for me. It looked like he'd been there a while.

'No,' I said, a bit sad that he thought me capable of that.

'I don't believe you.'

'I can't help that, but I haven't done anything to make you think I've been unfaithful.'

'Well, the secret phone calls and getting all dolled up to go off to secret locations and coming back hours later than you said, suggest an affair to me. Plus I saw your friend from your English course. I asked her why she wasn't on the day trip to Brontë country, she had no idea what I was talking about. When she realised you'd lied to me, she tried to cover for you by saying she'd been off sick so couldn't really afford to go on the trip.'

'Why do you think she was covering for me? She has been off sick,' I said rather lamely, wondering why I was trying to keep this charade going.

He nodded. 'Which friend am I talking about?' he asked.

I stared at him in silence.

'So, I'll ask you again, are you having an affair?' he said.

I stared at Jack, wishing it was as simple as an affair. Wishing that

391

it could be something as fixable as an affair. I shook my head in answer to Jack's question.

'What's going on?' Jack asked. 'Your silence is scaring me.'

The corners of my mouth turned down and the strain of the last few days came spilling out, shivering through my body, making me weak and insubstantial; I did not know what was holding me up because my body did not feel as if it was strong enough to be defying gravity at that moment. 'If . . . if I tell you, I'll have to tell you all of it. I can't see how I can't tell you all of it. And if I do that, you'll wish I hadn't told you. You'll wish that it was something as simple as an affair.'

'You can tell me anything, Eve, I thought you knew that.'

I managed to stop myself laughing at him. Laughing at my poor innocent Jack. He had no idea; nothing in him could conceive of my life so far. I liked that about him, loved that about him. It repulsed me a little, too. How could someone so close to me not have even the slightest clue what I had done? Was I really that good an actress? Had I truly buried it that deep? Did the world really see me as Eve Quennox, erstwhile waitress, part-time student, loving fiancée and nothing else?

'Tell me, Eve. Where were you today?'

'I was . . .' I was holding up a knife to throat of the image of the current version of Eve Quennox. And the next few words would carve up her visage, and then would draw the knife across her throat, murdering her in the eyes of the man I loved. 'I was in Leeds.' The knife plunged into Eve's flesh, hacking away. 'At my mother's funeral. I haven't spoken to her in seventeen years.' Eve's face was almost unrecognisable now for the knife wounds. 'Not since I told her that her boyfriend had been trying to rape me since I was fourteen and she didn't believe me.' The knife wounds were almost comforting, the pain expected. 'She died last week in her sleep.'

'Eve, why didn't you tell me? I could have come with you. I could have supported you.'

I was bewildered by his concern, it had no place in this.

'Because, Jack, I . . . I . . .' I shook my head, trying to clear it, trying to make him understand. 'I have done some terrible things because I had to leave home that early. I loved her so much, and because she chose him over me, I dropped out of school and didn't finish my A Levels, I moved to London and I tried to make contact so many times over the years but she always ignored me.'

'None of that is your fault. I'm just astounded that you were forgiving enough to go to her funeral after all that.'

'She's my mother. Of course I went. I love her. She was the most important person in my life.'

'I still don't understand why you couldn't tell me this. None of it is your fault.'

The knife, having hacked away at this new improved Eve's face until it was in ribbons, was back at her throat for the final slaughter. 'But everything I did after that is.'

'I don't understand.'

'After I came to London, I had a job, but I was made redundant so I . . . erm . . . I eventually started working,' I paused, amassed all the courage I had, 'in a lap dancing club to earn money.' The knife bit into the flesh of Eve's throat, going deep, drawing blood.

'Behind the bar? There's nothing wrong with that.'

'I was seventeen, Jack, they check your ID if you want to work behind a bar, make sure that you're old enough so they don't lose their licence. If you want to work as a dancer, they generally just take your word for it that you're over eighteen.'

I saw the horror of realisation dawn on his face, his eyes growing wide with shock. 'But . . . but you needed the money. If you had no real qualifications or work experience, then you obviously needed the money.'

'Yeah, I needed the money. And it's for the same reason, a few years later, when my druggie boyfriend's habit almost bankrupted us, I started to sell my body to make ends meet.' The knife was drawn smartly across Eve's throat – no fuss, no mess. Just over.

Jack's eyes narrowed in suspicion, wondering if I was making it up. 'What?' he asked. 'What are you saying to me?'

'I'm saying that until the end of 1996 I was a prostitute.'

393

I don't know how I expected him to react, what I thought he would do, but I was still surprised when he sat and stared at me. Every passing second, though, saw him draining more and more of colour, saw the healthy glow he had disappear until his face, his lips, his hands were grey-white.

His eyes were trawling through his memories, trying to work out if anything had told him, if there'd been any clue. 'But you can't have been,' he said, lifelessly. 'You can't have been. The summer of 1996, me and you . . . You didn't ask me for money. I didn't pay you. You can't have been.'

'I was. When we . . . I was.'

'So, my first time, I . . . *with a prostitute*?'

His body started to convulse as though holding back retches. 'Have you been laughing at me all this time? Was that some kind of sick game, bagging a clueless virgin? Then helping yourself to the cash from my wallet while I was sleeping?'

'No, Jack. God, no! It was nothing like that. I didn't take any money from you. Remember how you felt at the time? I felt exactly the same way. If you had any idea how much that meant to me . . . I've had sex with a lot of men, but you're the only man I've ever made love to. If you believe nothing else, please believe that.'

His body convulsed again, holding back another retch. Then he was suddenly on his feet and, without saying another word, he turned and climbed the stairs, walking as though there was lead in his shoes; moving as though there was lead in his bones.

I stood where I was, wondering what I should do. I still had the keys to my studio, so I could go back, but everything was here. I wasn't sure what he wanted me to do. I could sleep in one of the many spare rooms, but would he want me to leave and never come back? Minutes later, he reappeared on the stairs wearing running shorts, a T-shirt, socks and trainers. He walked past me as if I wasn't there. I spun on my heels to watch him open the front door, exit, and then shut it behind him.

That was two hours ago. He's still not back.

I don't know what to do.

I've been sitting on our bed, in my funeral clothes, since then.

I don't know what to do. Or how to check he's all right.

I've ruined everything, again. By telling another person I love the truth, I've ruined everything.

Me

It's been an odd, unsettling few days and I don't think either of us has any real idea what is going on.

That night I told Jack almost everything, he went out for a run and didn't come back for hours. It was nearly midnight when he left, so he stayed out until four or something like that.

I must have dozed off at some point even though I didn't think I could sleep. My head had been buzzing with all the stuff that people had said to me at the funeral: how my mum had been so proud of me going out there to London on my own and sticking it out in an accountancy firm, then moving to Brighton and starting work as an administrator for a group of solicitors. Mum had made up this whole life for me based on my letters that she read, kept, but never replied to.

And then when I got engaged, she was so excited about the wedding we were going to have. How it would be beside the sea and she would have to travel down for it.

Bea, Mum's best friend from the bingo, took me to one side later because she knew the truth about why I left. She told me that Mum threw Alan out after my first postcard from London. Apparently, the fact I had moved so far away from her made her realise I'd been telling the truth. She knew, Bea said, I would never have gone if I was making it up or if I was mistaken, as Alan had convinced her I was.

'But I called one time and he answered the phone,' I said.

'So that *was* you. She was so sure, but we tried to tell her not to get her hopes up. No, lovey, that wasn't him – it was Matthew, my husband.'

'What do you mean, "get her hopes up"? She didn't reply to my letters, so why would she be hopeful about the call?' I asked.

'You know how it is, lovey, a letter is one thing; speaking to someone is another. Shame's a terrible thing. Your mother was so ashamed that she didn't believe you, that she didn't see what was staring her right in the face. She never forgave herself. Many's the night I held her while she sobbed over how she had let you down. She often said your father would have been ashamed of her for not protecting you. I tried to tell her to contact you, to try to make things right, but she wouldn't listen. You know what your mum was like, she was so hard on herself. But she could not have kept her distance and kept on punishing herself if you were on the end of the phone or on her doorstep.'

Oh my God, oh my God, I thought. If I'd just spoken . . .

'I would have come back if I'd known he was gone.'

'I tried to tell her,' Bea explained. '"Even send her a birthday or Christmas card," I said, but your mother thought you were happy. In your letters you were always happy and you didn't seem to need her.'

I collapsed where I stood. 'That's not true,' I replied. 'That's not true. I needed her. I needed her so much. So many times in my life I just wanted my mum.' I started sobbing then, couldn't stop myself. Until that moment, it hadn't seemed real, it hadn't seemed possible that I would never speak to her again. And it hadn't mattered as much because I thought she still considered me a liar. But if I had been honest with her, if I had told her just once how horrible my life was and how much I wanted her to help me fix it . . .

Bea hugged me, and tried to console me. That's why I was so late back. I just couldn't move from where I'd collapsed and I couldn't stop crying so I missed my train. Everything had gone wrong when I left Leeds, and I wouldn't ever have the chance to fix it now because I'd done so many awful things, and my mother was not here to comfort me, to make it all better.

'I've never seen her as happy as she was when she heard you'd got engaged,' Bea kept saying as she held me. 'She was so happy now that you had someone to look after you.'

In the wake of what I'd told Jack, I'd been picking through all these things, wishing as I had done on the train back from Leeds that Mum had just called me, talked to me. At some point I must have fallen asleep.

When I woke again, Jack was standing in the doorway, staring at me. He was all sweaty, his clothes sticking to him, his usually muscular body looking diminished and drained. His hair was almost black with perspiration and his face was pale. I didn't know how long he had been standing there, staring at me, but his presence, his demeanour, wasn't malevolent considering the emotions he must have been going through.

'Jack?' I asked.

Without saying anything, he turned and walked down the corridor to the main bathroom. A few seconds later, I heard the shower come on. I sat on the bed, waiting, not sure what to do.

Eventually he returned, a towel wrapped around his waist, and he went straight to the wardrobe, took out a bundle of clothes then went into the en suite bathroom to get dressed. I pulled my legs up to my chest and wrapped my arms around them. I was still dressed in black, still dressed in the clothes I'd worn to my mother's funeral. It was quite appropriate, really, given that another relationship – killed by my truths – was about to be buried.

When Jack re-entered the room, he didn't look as vacant as he had a few minutes earlier. Now he looked as close to normal as I guessed he was going to get. Normal, clean, cleansed.

He sat carefully on the edge of the seat of the leather armchair by the dressing table, and then reached out and turned on the sidelight, even though the day was creeping in through the open blinds and we would soon be starting Saturday morning proper.

'Tell me,' he said. 'I need to know everything. Please tell me. I want to know. I'm going to try to listen without being judgemental, but I think it'll be easier if I know it all.'

'Are you sure, Jack?'

'Yes. I don't know how we're going to get over this if you don't tell me everything, otherwise I'll just imagine it is worse than it is.'

397

'So you think we can get over this?'

He stared at me, and slowly nodded. 'Yes. I hope so. It's what I want more than anything. So please tell me.'

I told him. I stepped outside of myself and I told him: about the lap dancing, about Elliot, about leaving London, about trying to get a job in Brighton, about the escort agency. I told him about Caesar, but I did not use that name. I said I met a man who seemed nice and who eventually became my pimp but never gave me any money and made me go with lots of different men until I ran away. I did not tell him, either, about the baby, about the loss.

'The only time I stood up to him was the afternoon I spent with you. I couldn't even think about letting another man near me after I'd spent some of the best hours of my life with you. I hope you believe that. And that's it. That's everything.'

Jack had not interrupted, he had listened, he had flinched and he had held back his retches as much as he could. It hadn't been easy for him, but he had done it. Was that what love was about? Doing something like that because you love the person so much?

'I can't imagine what it must have been like for you,' he said quietly. 'I'm sorry, so sorry you've been through all that. I don't know how you survived.'

'I'm sorry I didn't tell you before.'

'It's not an easy thing to talk about.' He got up. 'I'll be honest: I'm struggling, but I don't want to lose you. I need some time by myself right now. I'll sleep in the spare room. But only for the rest of tonight. Tomorrow, if it's what you want, we can go back to normal, OK?'

I nodded.

'And we won't talk about it again.'

'If you think you can do that.'

'I'd really like us to try, if you would?'

'Yes, I'd like that very much.'

'Goodnight, Eve.'

'Night.'

*

That was a week ago. And he was as good as his word. The next day, we went back to normal. It is normal. But not the same. Can it ever be the same? Ever?

Yesterday at college a woman called Michelle was talking about her relationship with her ex-husband.

I can't even remember what got her going on the subject, but she's really loud and talkative, always chatting about really personal stuff that most of us don't talk to our best friends about. I was only half listening but then she said that they'd split up a long time before they actually physically separated, which got my attention.

'We didn't start arguing or anything, it was just over for such a long time before I had the guts to go.'

'Why, what happened?' someone asked. I wanted to ask, but I didn't want her to think I was that interested. Because if there's one thing Michelle likes more than talking about herself, it's getting other people to talk about themselves – personal stuff she'll keep asking you about until you give in and tell her to get her off your back. I try to keep under her radar, so I was dead glad when someone else asked the question.

'I don't know for sure,' Michelle said, 'but I think it was after I was sexually harassed by someone I used to work with. It was all sorted out, at work, I mean, and the guy was actually sacked because it wasn't only me he'd been doing it to, but after that, I don't know, he kind of withdrew from me. He was supportive and made all the right noises at the time but, afterwards, it was as if a barrier of Clingfilm came over him and we were never really close again.

'He'd hug me, kiss me, give me special little pats on the bum, we'd watch telly all snuggled up, we had sex, but all of it was like he wasn't completely there for it. You know, on paper he was the same loving, caring man I'd married, but in reality it felt like it was his body doing it; his mind and heart never really engaged.

399

'It's hard to explain if you've not been in a situation like it, but it kind of kills you slowly but surely. What's that saying about death by a thousand cuts? That was so it.' I sat listening, knowing that I'm in that situation with Jack.

'What do you think caused it?' someone asked.

'The sexual harassment stuff, I think,' she said. 'He was on my side, but I guess a little needle of doubt stuck in his head. He couldn't be quite sure that I hadn't encouraged this man, flirted or whatever – basically brought it on myself. I reckon in his head it was sort of cheating. He thought I'd cheated on him, but not completely, so he could still be with me, but I suppose the image of me and this other man wouldn't go away. It drove a huge wedge between us.

'I thought I was going crazy, for a long, long time. I thought it was me and it wasn't until I asked him what had changed and he kind of shrugged and said he didn't know, but something had. I suggested counselling, but he wasn't up for that. Most men aren't. Don't think he wanted to admit to himself or me or a stranger that he blamed me. So we split.'

I listened to her and knew that I wasn't going crazy. Jack has been lovely since that night. Asking me how I am, asking if I want to talk about my mum, making me cups of tea, cuddling me, kissing me, telling me he loves me. But it's all done robot-like. As though he is acting on the memory of what it is like to do those things rather than actually doing them because he feels them; he's been pretending – with the biggest pretender of all. I thought it was me, I thought I was the one being overcautious, imagining things, seeing a withdrawal in him that wasn't there. But it wasn't me. He had done it.

And how can I blame him? I've lived my life and I still can't handle it, how is he expected to? Sex was so important to him. He'd been waiting for the perfect woman and that woman, the one who he'd finally had sex with, was someone who sold sex. She was a *whore*. I hate that word, it is so cruel, so dirty, so demeaning. I feel subhuman whenever I hear it – even if the person using it is talking about someone else, even if I'm using it about myself.

It still makes me feel like a fourth-class citizen. When a man would whisper it in my ear, would tell me to say I was a dirty little whore and I liked what he was doing to me, it used to kill me a little inside; it used to remind me that no matter how many times I showered, how much money I made, how I managed to get out of this business, I would always be subhuman and dirty; no one would ever respect me because I was a whore. I was someone who cheapened themselves, and cheapened sex by doing what I did. And here I was with a man who thought a lot of sex, who had taken his time and considered who he would take that step with.

The knowledge of what I had done must be killing him. He has been acting so normally, when he is probably disgusted by what I am and what I have done.

Again, is that what you do for someone you love? You put aside your feelings and do what you think is best for them?

I hope so, because I do love Jack. Which is why I've done this. I've left college early today and I've packed up my things. I was meant to be writing him a note, but I ended up writing in here instead – trying to organise my thoughts. I don't know what to say. Unlike Elliot and Caesar, Jack doesn't deserve to have me simply disappear. But whatever I write will sound as if I am blaming him, and it is not his fault. It is mine for not living a better life; for becoming a whore.

I didn't think doing what I did could rob me of anything else, once I left Caesar, but now it's robbed me of the chance of a normal life.

Time is ticking on. Maybe I should just go and then send Jack a note later. He'll probably be relieved that the pretence is over and that he can go out and find himself a decent girl.

Because decent is the last thing that I am.

Me

16th June 2000

Leaving Jack didn't exactly turn out how I planned. I'd actually taken more clothes as well as everything that I usually took with me when I moved on, but I got to the bottom of the stairs to find him waiting for me.

He'd guessed that I was going to leave. GUESSED! Can you believe it? He obviously knows me better than I know myself because it wasn't until that morning that I'd decided what I was going to do.

'Please don't leave,' he said, quietly, staring at Uncle Henry's kitbag with his eyes scrunched up as if he was in pain and could hardly see, when it was because he was holding back tears through sheer force of will.

'I'm trying, I'm trying so hard to put it out of my head. And I know it was before we . . . but it was also during the first time. And my father tried to make me go with a prostitute my first time . . . I . . .' He was shaking from trying so hard not to cry. 'I couldn't. I couldn't and then there was you. I didn't know you but it felt so right so I did . . . And then . . . I can't get the image of you with other men out of my head. I know it's not fair on you, this is my problem, but please don't leave. Give me some time. I just need some time. I'll try harder, I promise.'

'I can't let you do that,' I told him. 'Jack, when you love someone like I love you, them being hurt is far worse than any pain you could possibly suffer. What I've done to you . . . I'm sorry, I'm so sorry. I don't know—'

In three strides, he'd crossed the distance between us, and without hesitating he put his arms around me, then kissed me. I took a moment or two to respond, to drop my stuff and to kiss him back. I probably shouldn't have. I probably should have stuck to the plan to leave, but it felt so good to do it.

It felt even better to make love right there, on the floor of the hallway. To tune out every doubt, everything in the world, and to strip away the words that weren't enough to explain how I felt about him.

Afterwards, everything felt different, a little better, a little closer. I knew I wouldn't be leaving, and I was hoping against hope that somehow, with me having a break from the Pill, we had made a baby.

Eve

The phone calls are driving me insane.

They stop for a while, then just as I've started to relax, started to forget all about them, they'll start again. He knows how and when to get to me. But then I know how to get to him, too.

Earlier this month, one of the calls wasn't silent. It was a voice – not his voice, but a male voice – telling me if I left I would get ninety thousand pounds. Basically, the payment from those months back in '96. I didn't even consider it for a second, and hung up.

That was the first and last of the calls that someone spoke to me.

Then, two weeks later, Jack and I were sent a cheque by his father for that exact amount. I felt nauseous when Jack showed it to me, knowing what that money represented, what it meant. Hector was trying to infect my relationship with the things that had happened in the past. Jack didn't know what to do: he's conflicted about taking money from his father, because of the control his father likes to have, but Jack knows giving him and his brother money is one of his mother's ways of maintaining a relationship between them all.

I KNOW YOU'LL USE THIS WISELY, his father had written.

So, I told Jack we should give the money to a women's refuge (the one that I went to for help) and a homeless charity. Jack was more than willing. Wish I'd been there when Hector found out.

The phone calls started again the very next day. Probably my own fault for antagonising him, but I hate feeling so weak and defenceless.

No baby, and am back on the Pill.

Just sighed then. It's painful sometimes how much I want a baby. I want a girl and I want to call her Iris after my mum. That'll help. That'll help with the huge pit of unhappiness that still lives inside me every time I think about Mum and the time we lost.

I think that's partly why I want a baby, as well. I want someone else to love. But I don't want to rush Jack. Only just got things back to normal, don't want to rock the boat.

Me

One of my favourite people of recent times is Grace Clementis.

She's one of Jack's oldest and closest friends along with her husband, Rupert, and she has been so nice since I met her. She's one of those rich girls who has lots of designer labels and seems to have had everything handed to her on a silver platter, but she's incredibly warm and friendly too. I thought, when I first met her at a dinner Jack arranged for the four of us, that she was going to be a problem. Snide and condescending, but she was all smiles and hugs when we arrived at our table and she started to talk to me like she'd known me for years. As she teasingly questioned me about how Jack and I met, and what I thought of the house, and why I'd disappeared from his life for so long, I got the impression that she wouldn't be doing it if she didn't want us to be together. By acting as though we were old friends and any subject was 'fair game' she was telling me that I was part of their inner circle; they'd keep in-jokes to a minimum because I was now one of them.

'Do you know the amount of phone calls I fielded from Jack asking me why I thought you'd just disappeared?' she'd said.

'Grace . . .' Jack had warned.

'What?' she'd replied, all wide-eyed innocence. 'It's true, isn't it? My favourite was that you were on an undercover mission and shouldn't have got involved with him.' I'd grinned and she'd said, 'Oh, yes, he really said that.'

At the end of the dinner, she gave me a hug holding me close like an old friend, and said to me, 'I'm glad you're back,' as if she'd known me before, 'I hope you're here to stay.'

Tonight, she was a lifesaver because Jack was in one of the foulest moods I've ever experienced. He was fine as we got ready to meet them, and looked dashing in his navy blue suit with waistcoat and red tie, while I wore a simple, matching red dress. That wasn't intentional, it was just what we both came up with while we were getting dressed.

We laughed and joked as always on the way to the restaurant, and

404

things were fine until the main course. After the main course was placed on the table, his demeanour changed, his face – usually so open and relaxed – closed in and he seemed to be silently grinding his teeth as he stared down at his plate. Roast lamb was a favourite of his and it didn't seem too well done or too rare, while his potatoes and vegetables all looked delicious. The wine was fine, but he wasn't drinking because he was driving. I didn't understand the change in him. I reached out, put a hand on his leg to ask if he was OK, and he unsubtly shifted himself away from me. The message was clear: don't touch me.

I didn't understand what I had done or what was wrong. Feeling sick and a little scared, I returned my hand to my lap and stared at the plate in front of me, unsure if I could eat my meal or not, waiting for tears to start dripping down into the tomato sauce over my pasta. I glanced up and caught Grace's eye, then had to look away in embarrassment because she had obviously seen what had happened.

'What's wrong, Britcham Boy?' Grace asked across the table.

Jack raised his line of sight to her and the look he shot her was deadly.

'Ohhh, if looks could kill,' she said.

'Shut up, Grace,' he snarled.

'And a bon appetite to you, too,' she replied.

The atmosphere at the table was deteriorating and I knew it was my fault, but not why.

'Well,' Grace said suddenly and decisively. 'I vote that if Jack doesn't cheer up really soon, we steal his wallet and then all leave him here to do the washing up to pay for the *very* expensive bill.'

'Jack won't mind, he's good at washing up, aren't you, old boy?' Rupert said.

'What would you know about washing up?' Jack said suddenly, seeming to come out of his mood. 'You've never done a day's hard work in your life.'

'Make no mistake,' Rupert replied, 'supervising is extremely hard work.'

I pushed out my chair and then made as dignified an exit to the toilets as possible, while Rupert and Jack continued to banter. I walked around the empty room, ignoring my reflection in the mirror as I tried to breathe in, calm down and – most importantly – not start crying.

A few seconds later, Grace appeared in the loos and came straight to me, put her arms around me. 'It'll be OK, you know,' she said as I melted against her. It felt so good to have her hold me, it felt so wonderful for my soul. I didn't want to start crying because I didn't want to sit through dinner with red eyes as well as a heavy heart.

'Jack can be an arse sometimes,' she said, stroking my back and holding me tight. 'But he does love you.'

I nodded.

'Come on now, let's go out there and get absolutely smashed, that'll teach him.'

'OK,' I replied and willingly followed her outside, where my unfriendly fiancé was waiting.

I found out later, of course, what the problem was. We were barely through the front door back at home when Jack turned on me and said, 'Is there a man in Brighton you haven't slept with?'

I took a step back at what he had said and at how nastily, venomously, he had said it. 'What?' I asked. 'Where did that come from?'

'There was a man in the restaurant, tonight, that you've escorted, wasn't there?'

Yes, one of them had been there. But I didn't know how Jack could possibly know that, so I said nothing.

'Do you how I know?' he asked to my silence. 'You get this look on your face when you see one of them. No wonder you don't like restaurants: it always seems to happen in those sorts of places. One minute you're fine, the next minute you're glassy eyed with a fixed look on your face, like you're trying to remember the details.'

'That's not what I'm doing,' I replied. I never realised it was obvious on my face, that anyone outside of the old client in question and me could tell what had happened.

'What are you doing?' Jack spat through the nasty sneer on his face.

'I'm trying to pretend it never happened. I'm trying to erase his face and everything about him from my memory so I don't go into shock every time I see him.'

'How many of them were there?' he asked.

'I thought we weren't going to talk about this again?' I replied.

'No, we weren't, but I can't handle it sometimes. We have this huge secret, and most of the time it's not so bad. But at the same time, I'm scared to go out with you to places in case we run into one of them and you get that look on your face. The second I know he's one of them, the movie of it starts playing up here.' He pointed to his head. 'I imagine you with him and I—' He stopped talking and horror blossomed in his eyes, then slowly tugged down his face until he was opened mouthed with whatever new nightmare that had upset him.

'Have you "escorted" my father?' he asked in a tight voice. 'Have you done it with him?'

I stared at him. My beautiful Jack who would hate me for ever when I answered that question.

Don't make me answer that question, Jack, I thought. *Don't make me do this to you or me.*

'Have you?' he asked again.

I closed my eyes because I could not watch the devastation I was about to cause. 'Yes.'

I whispered it, said it as quietly as I could so maybe he wouldn't hear and he wouldn't be hurt. But of course he did. And in response, there came a sickening thud as he hit the wall, coupled with the crunch of bones cracking, and I knew he'd probably broken almost every bone in his hand.

Standing still in the corridor, with my eyes closed, I wanted to go somewhere else. I wanted to be somewhere else, be *someone* else. I did not know that when I started having sex for money it would devastate the person I loved. How could I know? I was not thinking of the future, I was living day to day, trying not to end up homeless and even lower than I was already. How could I know that at some point

407

in the future I would be happy, I would be without a druggie boyfriend, and that I would be properly in love? 'I'm sorry,' I said quietly. To him and to myself. I was apologising for making the mistakes that had brought us here today.

Grains of plaster rained down onto the floor as I heard him remove his fist from the wall. Then I heard him sink to the ground, and slowly he began to fill the space around us with his crying.

I had broken him.

I could not imagine what he must feel because no one had hurt me as much as I had just hurt him. Not even my mum not believing me about Alan because I found out later that she did believe me, and that was a little bit of relief from the pain of having to leave her. Nothing can relieve this pain for Jack. I've been fucked by his father. I will not call it sex or 'sleeping with' because it was meant to be a business transaction that he twisted and abused. He made it personal, he made it a living nightmare.

'I'm sorry,' I said again, louder this time.

I didn't know what else to say. It wasn't an affair; it wasn't something I enjoyed; it wasn't something I ever wanted to repeat. And if Hector would just leave me alone, it would be something that I could forget.

Jack eventually stumbled to his feet, bracing himself against the wall with his good hand. The other hand was a bloodied mess. I wondered how he was going to get around and work with a broken hand.

'You should have lied,' he said to me, his puffy, tear-stained face trying to look strong.

'Yeah, I know,' I said to him. *And you shouldn't have asked*, I thought. *If you didn't want an honest answer or, at least an answer you knew you couldn't live with, you shouldn't have asked.*

'I'll call a taxi to take you to the hospital,' I said to him.

He shook his head. 'I just want to be alone,' he said, and walked out of the front door.

I stood and watched him go to his car and get in, then lean over the steering wheel. He's still out there now. I don't know if he's going to come in or if he intends to spend the night out there.

Like an idiot, I gave up my studio flat so I have nowhere to run to. I

408

don't expect he'll make me move out straight away, in any case. He's not like that. I'm sure he'll let me stay in one of the spare rooms until I get myself sorted. He kept telling me I didn't need to work, that he made more than enough to support us both, but I wasn't going to do that again. I wasn't going to rely upon someone else to take care of me financially, so I do have a bit saved and I could find somewhere to live. Not sure if I'd want to stay around here, though. Not when there'd be the possibility of bumping into Jack and the woman he ended up with.

Part of me wants to ring Grace, to tell her what's going on and tell her to come over to take care of Jack. I couldn't tell her the whole truth, though. One person being disgusted with me is enough for a lifetime, I couldn't have anyone else look at me and see a dirty little scrubber instead of the real me.

I am flawed, I am imperfect, but I am not a prostitute any more.

How many times have I said this in my life: I don't know what to do. Is that what life is like for people like me? Is life just a series of events that lead you to various crossroads, where you have a choice to make? Is life just a series of moments when you find yourself in impossible situations and ask yourself what to do? That's what mine seems to be.

Me

18th December 2001

After eight weeks, Jack's hand is out of plaster, and we're getting married tomorrow.

We have agreed to not talk about it. By which I mean, after he returned from the hospital the day after our latest big revelation, he told me that he's known for a long time that his father uses prostitutes and he hates him for it, but doesn't distance himself from his father because of his mother. He doesn't know what she would do if she were to find out the depth of his betrayal.

I longed to ask if any of it was true, if she had indeed withdrawn sex and affection from Hector, because she didn't seem like that when I met her – but you never know what goes on behind closed doors, what 'happy family' front people put on for the world.

Jack told me that he lost respect for his father a long time ago, and he hates himself for being able to ignore what his father did. Does.

'But you love your mother,' I reminded him. 'I remember thinking more than once I should have just stayed and let my mum's boyfriend do what he wanted to me because I loved my mother so much. We will do almost anything for the people we love.'

'Did my father recognise you?' Jack eventually asked. 'Has he ever said anything to you about it?'

I glanced at his hand and knew I couldn't tell. 'I don't think so. But men who visit prostitutes don't generally see us as anything more than walking vaginas so it wouldn't surprise me if he didn't.'

'Please don't say "us",' Jack said quietly. 'You don't do that any more.'

'No, I don't,' I replied. 'I really don't.'

He nodded at me. We stared at each other, seeing who we were when we first met and experiencing who we are now.

'Let's get married as soon as possible,' he said. That was his way of telling me we were not going to talk about it any longer.

'All right.'

'Grace and Rupert can be witnesses,' he said.

I nodded.

I had no one to invite – except possibly Dawn and since I hadn't heard from her in well over a year, I had decided not to investigate the possibility that she had become one of the vast number of prostitutes murdered every year that we knew nothing about. I told myself she was busy and had no time for me. 'Is it OK if we don't invite anyone else?' I asked him. I could tell he wanted to say it, too, but didn't want to in case I took it the wrong way. Or rather I took it the right way but was hurt by it. Jack did not want to risk having anyone at the wedding who I might have been an escort for.

Jack looked down at the table, sadness upon him. 'Are you sure that's what you want?'

'As long as you're there, and I'm there, we really don't need anyone else, do we?'

'No, we don't.'

I reached across the table, covered his damaged hand with mine. 'This is what you want, isn't it, Jack? We don't have to do this if you're at all uncertain.'

Suddenly, his face became a sunshine smile that tripped up my heart and had it tumbling in my chest. 'Eve, I don't think I've ever wanted anything as much as I want to marry you. Everything in life is just background noise to the joyful song my heart sings over you.'

That's one of the most beautiful things I've ever heard and I knew then that we really wouldn't talk about it again.

Grace will be here soon because Jack's gone to stay at theirs for the night. I've unplugged the phone and will plug it in again when she arrives. The phone calls are getting more intense, more frequent – I think he's trying to warn me not to be there for Christmas dinner. We won't be there this year because we'll be on honeymoon in Hove. (In bed, in the house.)

Grace has been dying to see my wedding dress, but I said I'd only show her it the night before the wedding. She's going to be surprised as anything.

I'm really excited about tomorrow. This is something I've waited for since I first met him. It's my dream come true.

19th December 2001

I am Mrs Eve Britcham.

Can I say that again?

I AM MRS EVE BRITCHAM.

Jack cried when he saw me walking up the aisle and we held hands throughout the whole thing. Grace cried and even Rupert had wet eyes.

I was choked as we said our vows, the enormity of what we were doing hit me at that point, but I was so excited to be able to do it.

The sun came out and Grace threw confetti and Rupert took pictures.

Jack carried me over the threshold and we lay in bed drinking champagne and giggling about how fabulous our lives were going to be together.

I can't believe how happy I am.

Forever in love,
Mrs Eve Britcham

17th March 2002

Jack and I talked about having a baby today. We've been talking about it in a vague way – we both know we want children – but today was the first time we actually discussed when we would.

I want to now, of course, I'm ready, I think he's ready, so what are we waiting for? I'll be able to take time out or defer my college course for a year while on maternity leave, and I'm never going to get maternity pay with my jobs so I will have to rely on Jack for that period of time. Besides, I really want to have a little Jack – girl or boy, I really want to have another little part of him to love.

He wants a baby, too, but wants us to wait. He said maybe in a year or so because we haven't had much time together to do things like go on holiday and get to know each other as a couple.

He's right, of course, and I understand what he's saying, but I still wish, you know? I would love to be pregnant again and to have tried to get pregnant this time round, rather than . . . Rather than how it was last time. I would love to be a mother. It's not easy, I know, but the thought of having Jack's baby just fills with me with such joy.

But it's only twelve months or so to wait until we start trying. I'll probably be really grateful for this time when our baby finally arrives and we don't get another full night's sleep ever again!

Things are really good between Jack and me at the moment. It'll take something huge to shake us. We seem to have fallen back into that state of our relationship where we want to take any time we have for ourselves. Where we want to talk and laugh, and hold each other in our own little oasis while the planet carries on around us. If we didn't have to go out to work and college on a regular basis, I think we'd happily become hermits, living together in a harmony that we don't get when the real world creeps inside.

The house is finally finished. Every room decorated and 'dressed' with furniture and soft furnishings. It's been an epic task, most of which has been undertaken by Jack, but it has been worth it.

I often walk around, stroking the walls, rubbing my toes into the carpet, inhaling the scents of each room, luxuriating in what we've achieved. It does feel like my house, too, now. I was incredibly lucky to be able to pour some love and attention into the place alongside Jack. We've painted the walls in a white that has hints of green, which makes everything look far less stark than it did before. I've encouraged Jack to have splashes of colour in each room to warm it up and, most importantly, there are photos in every room. I missed having those around all these years, so in every room there are pictures of a younger Jack, and me with Jack. There are a few of me on my own, which are cringe-worthy, but in the main it's fine.

In the living room we have our wedding photo. It is one of us stepping out of the register office, a shower of confetti around us and Jack and me holding hands, grinning at the camera but also secretly looking at each other.

I have a version of the picture of my parents and me, the only one I took from Leeds.

We won't be having children immediately, but our house is ready, we are ready, so unless something BIG happens in the next year, we should be on our way to parenthood soon. I can live with that. As Jack said, 'What's the big rush? It's not like we're going anywhere.'

Lots of love,
Eve

This is going to be my last diary entry, ever.

It's too dangerous to keep getting them out, writing in them – I need to hide them permanently. I could burn them, but I don't want to destroy them because that would be like destroying my life, as flawed and strange as it is.

Yesterday I was mugged. In broad daylight someone grabbed me from behind while I was walking that last bit from Kingsway to our road, and dragged me into the doorway of the block of flats at the bottom of our road. He was taller than me and broader than me, but because he was behind me the whole time I could only tell because he was holding me so close to his body and the outline of him easily dwarfed me. He had gloves on and the stench of sweated-into leather made me gag as he held his hand over my mouth and nose; he also smelt of that pungent, almost sweet mixture of sweat and weed – how Elliot used to smell on the days when he couldn't be bothered to shower.

I thought for a moment it was Elliot, that he'd found me and that he was going to kill me. I started to struggle, kicking out, trying to scream against the cloth covering my mouth – trying anything to get free.

'Mr Caesar says hello,' the man whispered into my ear. It was the voice from the telephone. 'And this will be a lot worse next time if you don't hand over those diaries.'

His hand that was around my body reached down and ripped open my jacket, causing the large black buttons to fly off in all sorts of directions. I watched the buttons scatter and a new type of terror tore through me. Apart from Caesar, I'd been attacked twice before but this was different, this was personal and felt all the more deadly for it. The person delivering the threat would clearly do as he was told; the person who was sending the message would think nothing of ending my life. I'd seen that capability in his eyes when he told me he would kill me if I left, back in '96.

The man who had been sent to do his bidding shoved me

forwards with enough force to leave me on my hands and knees, while ripping my bag off my shoulder at the same time. Shaking with terror, I watched as he unzipped my bag and emptied it over my head.

Laughing, he walked away. I couldn't move until I had heard his laughter and footsteps fade. And as I was waiting for him to leave, I kept thinking about how he could have had a knife, could have sliced it across my throat or plunged it into my side. Trembling and trying not to cry, I scooped some things into my bag, then gathered the rest in my arms and ran home as fast as I could move on shaky legs.

I had been only a few feet from home and I had almost met my end.

I was still quivering when Jack came home, and I told him I'd been mugged but the person had run off without taking anything. Jack immediately called the police. They were very nice and gentle, and took a statement about what had happened. I couldn't tell them much because I hadn't seen his face, I could only tell them about the smell of the leather gloves and the fact he also smelt of cannabis, but nothing else. I couldn't tell them that it was a warning, that the man who had once pimped me out to his friends, who had intentionally hurt me every time he had sex with me, was now out to kill me. I could not tell them that I was starting to fear my days were numbered.

I almost told Jack once the police were gone. While he was rocking me and holding me and reassuring me that the world wasn't a bad place, just that people occasionally did bad things. It almost all came spilling out. But then I remembered his broken hand, his tears at finding out I'd been with his father. Could I really do that to him? Could I really tell him everything in order to break his father's hold over me?

If it was anyone else, I would tell in an instant. Because it was Jack, someone I loved so much, I could not hurt him with another big revelation. I'd had my chance and I let it slip away. If I did it now, I would hurt Jack, I would destroy his family and he would never look at me in the same way again.

I could hand over the diaries but that would essentially be signing my death warrant. Caesar is only threatening me because he can't get them. Maybe I should fight back. Maybe I should tell him that if he continues to threaten me I will show my diaries to Jack. If he leaves me alone he has nothing to worry about. Why have I been so passive in all of this? Why have I let him do this? He is acting out of fear; I can act because I have nothing left to lose.

That is what I am going to do. I will hide these well and I will take the fight to him.

But I must say goodbye now. You've been the most faithful and enduring friend I have had, always listening, never judging. I will miss you. Maybe when I am an old woman I will get these out and read them and find something to laugh about. Maybe age will allow me to look back on this time with cool and generous eyes, and I will be able to tell Jack all of my secrets without the fear of losing him.

Thank you for all you have done by being here, for stopping me from going crazy by giving me an outlet. I will miss you.

Love, always
Eve x

libby

'Oh my God, Eve, what did you think you were doing?' I say to the book in front of me because the vision of Eve has permanently gone. 'Going up against him when you know what he is capable of? Are you mad?'

I know she felt she had no choice but she must have been mad to ring him to threaten him. He definitely did it, didn't he? And he let Jack be arrested for it rather than come clean. His own son. The man is a psychopath. That is what is so disturbing about all of this: he seems so sane and normal – you would never know that underneath he is a card-carrying psychopath.

And the silent phone calls when Jack isn't here keep coming, keep interrupting my day. He's definitely after me now.

Ding dong, intones the doorbell.

My heart stops and across my mind flashes, 'Do not ask for whom the bells toll, they toll for thee.'

Butch is already up the stairs and barking at the door.

Ding dong.

The doorbell goes again and I hurriedly wrap up the diaries in the cloth, then the plastic bag and shove them back into the fireplace. Finally I pull the plate into place.

Ding dong.

Whoever it is is not going away. I move as quickly as I can up

417

the stairs, and pause to shut and lock the door behind me. I tuck the key into my pocket.

Ding dong.

'I'm coming, I'm coming,' I call as I head towards the door.

Ding dong.

I open the door, and it is only as I swing it open that it occurs to me that it could be Hector. Didn't I just think two minutes ago that he was the one making the phone calls, that he was out to get me? And now I am blithely opening the door without finding out who is on the other side.

'Harriet,' I say, relieved that it isn't Hector.

Her usually friendly face is set, her mouth a grim line, her eyes focused and unblinking. There is not a hint of the usual warmth that surrounds and exudes from her. She is, in fact, quite frightening. Fear, the kind I had the moment of the crash, spirals inside. I'm going to die. I know it now as I knew it then. Harriet is a killer.

She places a Harriet smile upon a murderer's face. 'Liberty,' she says. 'I need to talk to you about Hector.'

'I . . . I, erm . . . I need to go out,' I stutter. Upon hearing the tremor in my voice, Butch races back to his basket and all but puts his paws over his eyes.

'Not until we've talked,' she says firmly and takes a step forwards, forcing me to step back. 'Don't worry, I'll make the tea,' she continues as she forges ahead into the house. 'I am, after all, very good at making tea and being mother.'

I have my mobile in my pocket, and my hand on the dial button.

While Harriet was bustling around the kitchen as if it were her own, gathering things together to make tea, I put 999 on the screen then slipped it into my pocket.

I'm hoping I'd be able to fight off a woman of her age, but I can't be certain I will because I don't seem to have as much strength as I had before the accident. But being able to dial 999, if she does attack me will give the police time to trace me, I hope. I have a lot riding on this. I remember Angela saying that she was amazed at how much people relied on mobile phones. They acted as though they were weapons that would get them out of a deadly situation. 'I am a woman: and I am safe because I have a mobile phone,' she said. I'd agreed with her that it was ludicrous, that people with mobile phones got mugged, raped and murdered every day. Now I was being forced to rely on one.

Why I didn't tell Harriet to leave, I don't know. I seemed incapable of being rude to her, even though I suspected her of something heinous and of intending to do me harm.

We have settled on the sofas in the living room. I am as far away from her as possible. I have taken my mobile out of my pocket and put it on the sofa beside me, out of sight, I hope. I can't sit on the sofa with my hand in my pocket.

'Coffee instead of tea,' she said, holding out the cup to me. I am shaking as I reach for the cup and saucer, and they rattle together noisily. Harriet's eyes, the same green as Jack's, stare at the clanging crockery, then move up to my face. 'Are you all right?' she asks.

'Fine, fine,' I say. I shift myself back across the sofa, leaving her on the edge of the other one. 'Why wouldn't I be?'

After carefully making her tea – adding milk and no sugar – Harriet takes a couple of dainty sips. I watch her hands, watch her lips, wondering if it took too much effort to push Eve down the stairs, or if those lips were twisted in rage, shouting as she did the deed.

'That's better,' she says with a sigh. 'I find driving such thirsty work.' She carefully places the cup on the table, then returns her attentions to me. I am trying not to look intimidated or scared, but I am both. 'Now, Liberty – Libby – I'm going to ask you a question and I would appreciate an honest answer.'

'OK,' I say with a nod.

'Are you sleeping with Hector?'

I stop moving, close my eyes so I can hear what she said again without any other distractions. When I open my eyes my face is creased in disgust and disbelief. 'No,' I reply. 'Emphatically, absolutely, NO! Why would you even ask such a thing?' I shudder, trying to shake off the very idea from clinging to me and contaminating me.

'You wouldn't be the first of Jack's wives to do so, would you now?'

A stillness surrounds us as I stare into Harriet's eyes and she, unabashed, stares back at me.

'You know about that?' I ask.

'Of course, that's why you think I killed Eve, isn't it?'

'I ... I ...'

'It's perfectly fine,' Harriet says. 'If I were in your position, let's just say it would occur to me.'

'How do you know?'

She smiles a bitter smile. 'We're not stupid or blind, you know, the wives of the men like Hector. We are not oblivious to the failings and indiscretions of our husbands, we simply have to weigh them up against what we have to lose.'

I could not reply because I could not see myself staying with a man I knew to be cheating on me. I was struggling as it was with the fact that Jack was still in love with a dead woman; if I thought he'd had sex with a woman in the here and now ... I would not be able to stand it.

'I see you don't understand. Let me tell you a little about my life,' Harriet says. 'Years ago, I would attend many more functions with Hector than I do now. We would also go out for meals with friends or just as a couple. When you have two independent, grown children, it's easier to do things together. I noticed, though, that more often than not, there would be a woman at these things who would almost petrify at the sight of Hector. She would look first at him, then at me. Sometimes she would look at him with fear, then she would look at me in bewilderment. Other times, these young women, whoever they were, would look at Hector with such compassion in their eyes and at me with disdain and disgust.

'I grew tired of their looks, wondering what they were whispering to their friends when out of earshot, until I had the opportunity to run into one of those girls – a waitress – in the corridor of a restaurant. I took her to one side and asked her how she knew my husband. She tried to deny it, but I threatened to have her sacked if she did not tell me.'

Bitch! I think. *Over-privileged, monied bitch! Threatening someone who probably needs that job to get what you want, is . . . bitch!*

Harriet sees the look on my face and replies, 'I'm not proud of myself for doing that, but you must understand I could feel the whispers about Hector and myself and I had to understand why. In many ways, I wished I had put up with the looks and the whispers. She eventually told me that she had worked in a brothel and that's where she knew him from.'

I stare at Harriet, thinking at the back of my mind I should feign surprise, but I don't because I can't be bothered.

'I see that this isn't news to you,' Harriet says sadly. 'She told me that at first he was very nice and spoke about how his wife – I – had rejected him, had put an end prematurely to intimate relations, and how he wanted affection more than anything. She said the first few times they simply talked, and sometimes she held him. Then she told me how he started to cry one night about his failed relationship with his wife and, as she comforted him, he overpowered her and took her . . .' Harriet's matter-of-fact tone falters, but then she finds her voice and continues, 'without any form of protection.' Her eyes fill with glossy tears as she stares at the plain teacup on the table in front of her.

How could I have thought her a murderer? I must have been insane.

'We were still being intimate at that time, so he could have put me at risk of catching something, but it didn't seem to matter to Hector. She also told me that he regularly came back and changed his name every time so he could see her again. With every visit he became worse, more violent, more depraved. And although he left a bigger tip each time, by the fifth visit she was terrified of him. The people who ran the brothel didn't care that she was being brutalised by him because he was paying them over the odds to be let in to see her. After his tenth time, she had to leave because the stress of not knowing if and when he would return became too much for her.'

Her eyes still focused on that no man's land between then and now, the space where we all go to think things over, Harriet brusquely brushes away a tear that is sliding down her face.

'I knew she wasn't lying. And I knew my husband was a monster.'

'So why didn't you leave him?' I ask.

'Leave for what?' she replies. 'Do you think for one minute Hector is the type of man who will allow someone to leave him? I was a housewife and mother for most of my adult life. I haven't worked outside the home for years. Hector decides when things are over; he would never let me leave unscathed, and he would do his best to keep me tied up in legal knots and to distance me from my children. I did all I could – which was to leave his bed, and to make plans. I have been putting aside money for a long time. I should have enough soon to be able to leave and weather any legal battle without suffering too much.'

'But you could leave him tomorrow and come and live here. We have plenty of room.'

Firmly, Harriet shakes her head. 'No. I have two sons, remember, and while I fear Jack may know more about Hector than I'd like, I do not know what Jeffrey knows and I cannot risk alienating him until I have properly left and properly talked to him.'

I can't understand why she would stay with a man who so clearly revolts her, who has humiliated her over the years, and who she doesn't respect. To save face? I don't think I could do that, not even for my child because my fear of damaging them, of unintentionally showing them by example that such behaviour is acceptable, would outstrip everything else.

'Why did you think I was sleeping with Hector?' I ask.

Harriet is sipping at her tea and I can tell by the way her

jewel-like eyes stare into the mid-distance that she is choosing her words carefully.

'After I understood why those young women – and they almost always were young – were looking at me like that, I had to cut down on the amount of socialising I took part in with my husband. Encountering those looks was intolerable. Instead, I spent more time with the wives of his friends and I watched them, all of them looking at each other knowingly while we all battled to contend in our own ways with the knowledge of our husband's infidelities. I wasn't alone, I discovered, far from it. Other wives put up with these things too. That made me more confident in my decision to sit and wait.

'One day, Jack, my beloved boy, brought home the woman he wanted to marry. I was so pleased that he had finally decided to settle down, but imagine my horror to see that look of fear in her eyes, and to know that she had been brutalised by Hector, too. During the lunch I came to the conclusion that it had been worse for her, something far more intense and personal had happened. I knew at the time that Jack had no idea so I had to keep my peace, but it was a terrible thing to have to live with. It was one of the hardest things I had to do, but I chose to avoid seeing my son to prevent her going through that again.

'I cried for two days when my suspicions were confirmed by them choosing to get married in secret. I couldn't be there for my son's wedding because of what Hector had done.'

And yet you put up their wedding picture in your living room, I think.

'I still don't see what any of this has to do with you thinking that of me and Hector.'

'You have the same look in your eyes, Libby. It wasn't there the first time I met you, and it hasn't been all these years, but the last two times we have seen you that fear and loathing was in your eyes … I've been terrified that he has taken advantage of you since your accident. Used your vulnerability against you.'

My gaze drifts to the phone on the sofa beside me, its screen black. Underneath the blackness is 999, my chance to ring for help. Help is what I need right now. How much do I tell her of what I know? On the one hand, if she knows then maybe I won't be in as much danger from Hector. On the other hand, how do I know I can trust her? How could she have not removed herself from the vicinity of a man like Hector the second she knew the truth? How do I know she hasn't got a form of Stockholm Syndrome? She may well have killed Eve at his bidding; she could be here fishing for information to take back to him.

'I found out that he went with prostitutes and it's made me lose respect for him,' I say. 'I'm sorry, but it makes me nauseous thinking about what he's done.'

'And Eve?' she asks. 'How did you know about Eve?'

'I kind of worked it out. Once you know a bit about Eve's background and the poverty she was living in, coupled with how Jack is about his father sometimes it's not difficult to put two and two together.'

'Jack knows about Eve and his father?'

'I think so,' I say. 'I've never asked him directly.'

Pain, raw and frightening, claws through Harriet's eyes and across her features. I want to go to her, hold her, let her know she can cry on me and I will understand. That would be intolerable for her, though. It would be a loss of dignity she could not stand on top of everything else.

'I will leave you in peace,' she says. 'I've taken up enough of your time and your good will.'

I can't let her leave like this. I would never forgive myself if something happened to her on the way home. 'No, Harriet, please, stay,' I say to her. 'Please stay the night.'

She is confused, probably only slightly more than I am because I hadn't intended to ask her to stay when I opened my mouth.

I smile at her and shrug. 'Stay. Go back tomorrow. A night away from Hector will do you good, and I would love the human company.'

She still does not say anything.

'We won't talk about all that stuff again, we'll just enjoy being here together, watching television, reading, having a couple of drinks.' *Like you never got to do with Eve.*

'That would be lovely, Liberty,' she says and through her agony she manages a smile. I can't begin to imagine the loneliness she has felt all these years, how she has withstood it.

I smile at her and get up to go and put the kettle on again. Her eyes alight on my mobile phone, sitting next to me on the sofa and then they turn to me. We both know why it's there, but it's fine now. It really is. Because I know in my heart of hearts that Harriet isn't capable of murder.

'Let me help you,' she says, picking up the tray, and I feel for the first time that I could really get to know this woman I've always liked.

chapter nineteen

libby

I'm resting in bed, thinking about Eve, of course, when the phone starts ringing. It's three o'clock, the time that Jack usually rings to tell me what time he'll be home and ask what I would like for dinner.

The phone calls stopped the day that Harriet came to visit. She'd picked it up without thinking and said hello into the receiver and the person hung up a lot quicker than they usually do.

I told myself that it was a coincidence, and that I had nothing to worry about.

Jack has been trying to engineer a conversation between us since the night his parents came to dinner and I have been avoiding him. I don't want him to know that I know, and I'm scared every time we speak or see each other that something might slip out.

Moving stiffly, because some days it feels like I've only just had the accident, I move across the bed and pick up the receiver.

'Hello?' I say.

Silence.

'Hello?' I repeat.

Silence.

'Hello,' I say cautiously. There is someone there, I know it. They are there and they are not speaking.

'Last chance,' I say brightly because I do not want them to know they have unsettled me. 'Hello?'

Silence.

'OK, have it your way. Goodbye.'

I replace the receiver with a hand shaking so badly it takes a few seconds to get it correctly into its cradle.

Pulling my knees up to my chest, I stare at the phone, willing it to ring. Willing the person to do it again to prove to me that I have something to worry about, not that my imagination is running wild because of Eve's diaries.

The phone stares belligerently back at me, unwilling to be goaded into anything it doesn't want to do. Wrong number; long distance call that did not connect; person who realised too late they had misdialled are all plausible reasons for that call. It wasn't because of Eve or Hector. It was my imagination.

Ring ring, the phone replies.

I stare at it.

Ring ring, it repeats.

My heart is galloping and a pulsating ache begins where my rib was fractured, hurting in time with the phone's ring.

Ring ring, the phone insists.

I snatch up the receiver.

'Hello,' I say firmly.

Silence.

'Hello.'

Silence.

'Hello.'

Silence.

I throw the receiver down and hug my legs closer to my chest, my heart still beating in triple time. I stare at the television instead of the phone, trying to calm my breathing, trying to ignore my fears. Each deep, laboured breath causes pain to shoot from my previously cracked rib. I push my hand on that area, trying to hold it together, physically and emotionally.

Logically, I know I should call the police, I should tell Jack.

430

But what will I tell them? That I've found Jack's dead wife's diaries and I think Jack's father killed her because he paid her for sex and allowed other men to use her body? That I made the stupid mistake of telling him I had the diaries and now he's trying to intimidate me too? I can see them all saying, 'Yes, Libby, we can see how your recent trauma hasn't twisted your perception of things, and yes, of course, we believe every single thing that is written in these diaries. We don't think they are the delusional imaginings of a very disturbed young prostitute. Let's arrest noted solicitor and pillar of the community Hector Britcham straight away.'

What was that noise?

My eyes dart to the door, because I'm sure I heard a creak and then a thud somewhere outside this room. It's an old house and it creaks all the time, but this time I'm sure it sounded more purposeful, less random than that. My racing heart accelerates.

Maybe I should call Jack and ask him to come home. I'll tell him everything. I'll explain about the diaries; I'll tell him that I know about Eve and Hector; I'll say that I think Hector is out to get me like he was out to get Eve. And he'll say . . . he'll say . . .

I can't even begin to imagine what he'll say.

What could he say? What will discovering the full extent of what Hector did to Eve do to Jack? He clearly already struggles with the idea of her having been a prostitute, what will knowing about the abuse she suffered at the hands of his father do to him? He loved her – *loves* her.

Ring ring! starts up the phone.

I stare at it. I don't want to answer, but each time I do and I get the silent treatment is validation that I am not mad to be worried about Hector. It is also a reminder that he could murder me like he probably did Eve and get away with it if I don't tell.

Ring ring! it taunts.

I continue to stare.

Ring ring!

Ring ring!

431

I snatch up the receiver.

'Hello?'

Silence.

'Hello.'

Silence.

I throw the receiver down, tears moving my body.

Immediately: *Ring ring.*

Ring ring.

I snatch up the receiver again. 'If you call me one more time, I'm calling the police,' I say.

'Libby?' Jack asks cautiously. 'What's going on?'

Hearing his voice is such a sweet relief, I break down, my body racked with sobs that I can't control. 'Oh God, Jack,' I manage between sobs. 'I think someone's trying to kill me.'

jack

Libby isn't the hysterical type, so when she said someone was trying to kill her while *crying* down the phone, I took her seriously. I left work immediately and came back. I take the stone steps two at a time and slip my key into the lock, and almost knock Libby off her feet. She is standing there, behind the door, in bare feet with her mobile phone clutched in her hand. Just like Eve used to.

My heart turns over in my chest, seeing Libby looking as relieved and terrified as Eve did when I would walk through the door at night. Was someone trying to kill Eve? She never said as much, not even after the mugging. I constantly asked her why she was so jumpy but she always said it was because she'd stupidly watched a few horror movies, and had swapped ghost stories with the women at work and college. But for Libby to be doing the same thing after what she said on the phone . . . Maybe Eve *was* murdered.

Right, Eve, murdered. Why would anyone murder Eve? She left all that stuff with her past way behind, my father did not recognise her as woman he had been with, so no one had any reason to harm her. Besides, murder is something that happens to other people, other families. Accidents happen to people like me.

Libby flies into my arms, clinging onto me tight, holding on for dear life in a way she has never held me before. I never noticed before that Libby has never clung to me; she has never shown that she needs me to be strong for her. Not until now. My heart flips. 'It's OK, it's all right,' I say to her, stroking the soft contours of her head. She is shaking all over, her heart is speeding so forcefully in her chest I can feel it against my body.

'What's happened?' I ask her.

'I need to get out of here,' she says, panicked, terrified. 'Now. Take me away from here, now, please.'

'You're barefoot,' I remind her. 'Let me get you—'

'No!' she insists, her hysteria rising dangerously like a high tide, ready to gush over into something uncontrollable. 'I need to get out of here, now.'

'Right,' I reply. I glance at Butch, who is watching us with wary eyes from his basket, obviously aware that Libby is having some sort of breakdown. I open the front door and she cringes from the full light flooding in from the outside. As I suspected, she hasn't been leaving the house – not even to go into the garden.

She inhales deeply, stares at the outside world, then casts a look back over her shoulder at the inside world. Tentatively, she takes a step out, flinching at the cold stone underfoot.

'Do you—' I ask, reaching for her.

'No,' she replies, pushing me firmly away. 'I can do it.' She stares at the world ahead. 'I can do it,' she repeats, this time a little quieter, a little more uncertain.

Trembling, holding onto the rail with both hands, she navigates herself down the steps. I watch as a parent watches a child walking for the first time: horribly torn between wanting to swoop in and help to spare them any pain from possibly getting it wrong and falling, while knowing I have to let her do this for herself. I don't know what terror there is in the house that has driven her outside, but I am grateful to it.

At the bottom of the steps, she pauses, still clinging to the railing, her eyes slowly taking in her surroundings, the sharpness of the sea air, the magnitude of the sky, and the details that make up the world we inhabit. Taking another deep breath, she leaves the railing behind and moves towards the car.

'Take me somewhere,' she says, staring at the handle of the car door, her face quivering with fear.

'Are you sure?' I say.

She nods, even though I can tell most of her mind is reminding her she doesn't want to get into a car again. 'Take me anywhere that's away from here.'

Her hand reaches out for the handle but can't seem to connect, can't seem to get past the barrier. I wait to see if she can do it, if she can leap that final hurdle of fear, but she can't. Her hand remains frozen in the air, a monument to intention, a testament to failure – the perfect example of mind over matter.

She begins to gulp air as I open the door and she takes a step forwards. I want to stop her, to tell her she doesn't have to do this, but that is the last thing she needs to hear. If she decides that she can't then she can't, I mustn't be her excuse not to try. Shaking, gulping in air, she tries to move her foot towards the car again, but then she is backing away, shaking her head.

She backs away until she is at the steps, and she sits, staring at the car, trembling. 'I can't do it, I can't get into a car.'

I take a seat beside her.

'What's going to become of me, Jack?' she says, suddenly breaking down into tears, the first I've seen since the hospital. 'I can't do anything. I can't leave the house, I can't stay in the house; I can't get into a car, I can't face the world looking like this. I can't work. I haven't got anything. One stupid bastard on a mobile phone in a car has ruined my life. It's not fair. What did I ever do to him?

'I know I'm not perfect, I know I've made some stupid decisions in my life, but what will he care about what he's done to me? He gets to walk away from his mistake. He gets to look at himself in the mirror every day and not see *this*. And what have

I got at the end of it all? Because I got into a car with my husband one day, everything is gone.'

'I'm sorry,' I tell her.

'I wish I was stronger, I wish that I could just look in the mirror and feel fine about all of this. I wish I could turn this into a positive, but I can't. I can't. I can't. I can't.'

Every one of those sobs rips through me like a chainsaw through silk.

I cried like this over Eve. I cried like this over myself losing Eve. The realisation that no matter what I did, I couldn't change what had happened and there didn't seem to be any point to living, to carrying on. Not when we were so mortal and finite and the whole thing was pointless and cruel. Yes, I actually believed life was cruel for playing this joke on us. We find someone and we fall in love and then that person is ripped away from us. Why did we have to fall in love if it is only going to end? Why did we have hearts for feeling if they are always going to end up broken?

Libby has lost herself; she is grieving for the life she had and the woman she was and the person who she was going to become. I know how she feels, how the terror of having to carve a new self out of the ruins of what you once had can seem insurmountable. But she can do it. I know she can.

Libby allows me to envelope her with my arms, with my body, with the love I have for her. She doesn't need to hear what I have discovered, what her decision to end our relationship made me examine and realise. She just needs me to be here and to hold her and to listen to her the way a best friend should.

chapter twenty

libby

'I'm glad you came back,' Orla Jenkins tells me as we sit in her office.

'I'm not,' I say quietly.

'Why not?' she asks.

'Because it's like admitting defeat, isn't it?' I say. 'This is like saying to you and the world that I'm not strong and I am weak and I do need help. I don't like to feel like that. I don't like to feel powerless.'

I can relate to so much of what Eve went through. The constant worry about money, feeling trapped, the inability to know what to do when what you want seems so far removed from what you can actually get.

Like this situation with Jack: what I want is him. Especially after the last two days, where he has taken time off work to be with me. To sit and hold me and listen and let me cry. It's not fair on him since I'm the one who finished our relationship, but I haven't been able to do anything else. I've needed him. And I still want him. I know he probably isn't capable of loving me, but that doesn't stop me aching for him. Longing to still be with him. I keep thinking I should ask him if we could try again. If we can start again, now I know why he can't talk about Eve. But can I do that and not tell him about Hector? Can I do that when I can't be sure that Jack has ever completely loved me? I just don't know what to do. Like Eve, I feel stuck in a no-win situation.

Of course the phone calls have stopped since Jack's been there all the time, but that has seemed secondary to realising that I haven't been coping at all.

On many levels I knew I wasn't, in some ways I did try to 'move on', but it was easier to focus on Jack's obsession with Eve, and then on Eve's diaries and then on Hector than it was to admit that I needed help. I needed to look at myself inside and out and then start to rebuild my life.

'Everyone needs help at some point in their lives,' Orla Jenkins says kindly and calmly.

'Yeah, I'm sure they do.'

Orla Jenkins sighs. 'You're going to be very difficult, aren't you, Libby?' she says.

'Yes, probably,' I reply.

'Well, that's good. It shows that there's some of the old you still in there, doesn't it?'

libby

The phone is ringing as I open the door. I don't run to answer it because I know who it'll be. I spoke to Jack on the way back from the counsellor's place and Grace and Angela are coming over after work to see me. They are the only people who would call my house phone first. Them and Hector.

'Butch?' I call as I shut the front door behind me. Nothing, not even a bark. 'Oh God, what have you been up to now?' I call to him, heading for the kitchen – his favourite hiding place when he's chewed something or left an extra special pressie in one of our shoes. He'll lay under the table, giving us the big eyes treatment until we discover what it is that he's done, by which point he hopes the big eyes and sorrowful look will have won us over. And it usually has.

'If you've pooed in Jack's trainers again, I don't think he's g—'

Hector is sitting at the kitchen table holding Butch very close to him. Unlike Benji's hugs, Butch doesn't look like he's enjoying this hug. He looks stifled and scared, exactly the same things that I am feeling.

'Hello, Liberty,' Hector says. 'You weren't taking my calls so I thought it best to use the spare key we have for emergencies to check you were OK.'

I want to step away, run back the way I came and escape this house and this man, but the way Butch's furry little neck is caught between Hector's huge, glove-covered hands makes me feel sick and scared. One sudden movement and . . .

'*Or maybe her neck was broken and she was thrown down the stairs to hide it,*' Jack says in my head.

'Sit down,' Hector orders.

'No,' I reply.

'Don't test me,' he says, tightening his hands around Butch's neck.

I pull out a chair and take a seat, my eyes fixed on Butch.

'I want those diaries,' he tells me.

'OK,' I reply.

He blinks at me, suddenly uncertain that it's been so easy. He is used to people doing as he tells them without question, but he was expecting more of a fight from me, obviously.

'You have to answer some questions, first.'

'I don't have to do anything,' Hector states.

'Did you kill Eve?' I ask, ignoring his reply.

He stares at me for a moment, then shakes his head. 'No. I came here to look for those diaries but she came home and caught me. I must have been close because instead of taunting me that I would never find them, she turned and ran. Then tripped and fell down the stairs; broke her neck on the way down.'

'And you didn't think to call an ambulance, to maybe spare Jack the horror of finding her?'

'She was already dead, what good would me being questioned by the police do? It was her own fault. If she had given me those diaries—'

'You would have killed her sooner,' I cut in. 'And me? Are you going to kill me?'

He fixes me with his eyes, the way he did over the dining table the other week. 'Or course not,' he says with his mouth.

Of course I am, he says with his eyes.

A wide, ice-cold chill runs the length of my spine and I sit

442

back to distance myself from this man. How could he have made a son like Jack? While Jack is gentle and flawed and intrinsically honest, this man is poison.

'Liberty,' he says carefully, 'there really is no need for all this unpleasantness. Give me the diaries and we'll say no more about it.'

My mobile starts to ring in my pocket and I automatically reach for it.

'Please don't do anything silly,' Hector says to me with his cold smile.

'That's Jack's ringtone,' I tell him. 'If I don't answer, he'll come home to see if I'm all right – that's if he hasn't called out the emergency services by then. Since the accident, he gets worried if I don't answer the phone.'

Hector stares at me while the phone keeps ringing.

'Don't say anything stupid, remember your precious little Butch and what could happen to him,' Hector eventually concedes.

I answer the phone and with a heart that is beating out a staccato beat, I say 'Hello,' into the receiver. I sound normal, calm. My eyes stay locked on Hector's so that I can't see poor Butch's terrified face.

'I forgot to ask you what you wanted for dinner, tonight,' Jack says.

'Oh, I don't know, anything. You decide.'

'Fine,' he says laughing. 'But no complaints when it's not what you want.'

'I promise, no complaints. By the way, your father's here. Do you want to speak to him?'

Hector's face darkens and I brace myself in case my gamble hasn't paid off and he snaps Butch's neck. This was the only way I could think to save us both.

'What's my father doing there?' Jack asks.

'Wanted to check that Butch and I are OK, I suppose. Here, you speak to him.'

I hold out the phone to Hector, who glares at me.

'Hello?' Jack's voice comes out of the mobile. 'Hello?'

Reluctantly, Hector releases one hand from Butch to take the mobile, Butch immediately wriggles free, jumps onto the table and leaps into my arms.

'Hello, son,' Hector says into my mobile, his eyes wide with rage, his face white with anger. He is sweating he is so angry. 'Yes, yes, fine. Was just seeing a client in the area and thought I'd see how Liberty and the dog were getting on. Yes, yes, she's fine. Everything's fine. Yes, will do, will do.'

'Oh, Jack,' I call loudly as Hector is about to hang up. 'Sorry, Hector, I forgot to ask Jack something, can I have the phone, please?'

His anger mounting, Hector starts to take bigger and deeper breaths but hands over the phone anyway.

'Jack, I forgot to tell you what else Orla Jenkins said,' I say, my heart a knot of fear, my stomach spinning with terror. 'Sorry, Hector,' I say casually, into the phone, 'do you mind if I show you out? This could take a while, and it's rather personal. You didn't want anything else, did you?'

He stands and turns into a Goliath in front of my eyes. I stand too and follow five paces behind him to the front door.

He gives me a murderous look as he opens the door, and I know he isn't done with me yet. He won't be done with me until I am dead.

The second I shut the door behind him, I put the bolt and the chain on, then go to the back door to check that it is locked, too. Then I sink to the ground and hold Butch close.

'Are you OK?' Jack asks.

'I'm fine,' I say, 'I'm fine. I just needed to get rid of Hector then. He looked like he was settling in for a long chat and I can't face that right now.'

'Oh, right.'

'Look, when you come home, I'd like us to have that talk we were meant to have.'

'Yeah?'

'Yeah. I want to talk to you about us, and . . . there's lots of things I'd like to explain to you. I'll see you later.'

'I'd like that,' Jack says. 'I'll try to get away as soon as possible.'

We both say goodbye and hang up.

I hold Butch close, thinking about Jack and how he has had to deal with Eve's death – and her life – all these years, all alone. He could never tell anyone the full story, so it wasn't surprising that he shut down whenever I tried to get inside.

He must have been so lonely, so ripped apart. Maybe telling him the truth will alleviate his guilt about her dying alone? And, maybe knowing that there is someone else out there who knows about her life will make it easier for him to talk about it and start to deal with it. He might hate me for being the person who finally destroys the image he has of his father, and who tells him everything there is to tell about Eve, but at least he'll be free. At least Jack will be free of his father and free to let Eve go, too.

And for my own safety I have to tell Jack and show him Eve's diaries. I do not want to hurt Jack, or to be the reason that he re-examines every moment of every second of his life with Eve, but I do not want to end up murdered, either. Hector will be back and he will keep on coming back until he gets what he wants. And what he wants is to get away with murder.

Two hours later, Jack calls me again. His voice is shaky and thin as he wrestles with his fear and anxiety to tell me he won't be home straight after work. 'It's my father,' Jack says. 'He's had a massive heart attack, and they don't think he's going to last the night.'

445

jack

When I was fifteen, my father took me to a brothel and tried to make me choose a woman to lose my virginity to. After I refused, he decided to treat me as a failure. When I was twenty-nine, I found out my wife had once slept with my father when she was a prostitute. When I was thirty-three, I wondered for a second, for the briefest of seconds, if my father had killed my wife. It was ludicrous, a thought that came from nowhere and went nowhere, but I had always thought that my father was capable of murder. Especially the murder of someone he saw as less than human – someone like an ex-prostitute, for example. But it was a transitory thought, one that had no basis in fact nor ever led anywhere. Because thinking someone might be capable of murder doesn't mean they would *actually* do it.

Now I am sitting outside his hospital room, wondering if I will soon be thinking when I was thirty-eight my father died and I felt the loss more for my mother than I did for myself. I saw on a daily basis how devastated Eve was by her mother's death, I don't think I will feel the same. My mother is in the room with them now, and I am waiting here for Jeff, my brother, to arrive from Scotland.

I sit on the chairs and rest my head back against the wall. It seems like minutes ago that I was doing this, waiting for news on

Libby. It seems like minutes ago that I was too scared to pray in case God answered me the same way he did last time. Praying hasn't even occurred to me with my father.

'How are you doing?' Libby asks.

I open my eyes and clamber to my feet; is she really here?

'Libby? What are you doing here?'

'You sounded so scared on the phone, I had to make sure you were OK.'

'How did you get here?' I ask.

'In a taxi.'

'You got in a car?'

'Yeah, I got in a car. And I clung onto the handle with my eyes closed and I prayed and hyperventilated, and nearly screamed a few times, but I got here, eventually.'

'You did that for me?'

She nods. 'Is there any news?' she says, trying to dismiss the enormity of what she has done. I remember Eve once said that when you love someone, them being hurt is worse than any pain that you could suffer. Libby got in a car for me when two days ago she'd had a breakdown at the very thought.

'Nothing, yet,' I reply.

We sit down side-by-side on the seats, staring at the door in front of us.

'She was never my friend,' I say to Libby and she turns her beautiful face and her shaved head with its light covering of newly growing hair towards me to listen. 'Eve was never my friend. I loved her, passionately, I can't deny that. But I can't deny that I love you passionately, too. And that I also love you rationally, completely, as a friend, as someone I can rely upon one hundred per cent.'

She takes my hand, links us together by sliding her fingers between mine.

'And after the crash, when I was begging her not to die because I thought you were her, I did that because I never had the chance with her. When I came around properly and I realised

447

that it was you and not her, I felt so guilty all over again that I couldn't remember if I'd told her that I loved her the day she died, so I stopped myself from telling you, either. I'm sorry. And I'm sorry for lying to you. I was being selfish. I didn't want to lose you. I was trying to be fair when fairness doesn't come into it in that kind of situation.

'You've helped me to grow up, to become a better person, and I haven't been completely honest or open with you. There are a lot of things about Eve that I find hard to talk about. She had so many secrets that I've spent so many years trying to forget. But I'll share them with you. I don't think she'd mind, and I want you to know everything so we can move on from there.'

'You have no idea how long I've wanted you to say that,' Libby replies. 'But, no. I don't need to know anything. If you want to talk about her then do, I will willingly listen; but if you don't, then we never have to talk about her again.'

'Are you sure?'

Libby nods.

'I've put Eve's things into storage because I'm not ready to get rid of them yet, but I removed them because I want the house to feel like our home. All of it.'

Her smile deepens and without saying anything else, she rests her head against my arm – Libby's way of telling me we're going to try again.

harriet

The Internet is a wonderful thing.

Women like me can find the things they need, buy the things they want and not have to worry too much about people seeing them. They can also find out what they need to do to achieve certain things.

I think it's fitting that a man who has shown over the years to have very little heart but is very focused on the face he presents to the outside world, has once again been attacked by the organ he has most neglected in his life, and as a result he looks weak to the outside world. He may well survive this but his life will always be limited because his heart is irrevocably damaged. He will always need someone to take care of him, and of course that task will come down to me. What else would a loving, devoted wife do?

'How are you?' I ask him. He is pale and visibly shaken as he reclines against his nest of pillows. He is diminished. This man who was always so powerful is stripped of his dignity and strength; he now lays in this hospital bed, trying to make sense of it.

'Better,' he says.

'Good, good. I'm glad.'

He reaches out to me and I take his hand. It is wrinkled, more wrinkled than mine; weathered, aged. He is an old man. He should really have eased off on his activities years ago.

'I love you, Harriet,' he says. I know he does, in his own way. In the only way a man like him can love – selfishly. He needs to say this now because he is weak and vulnerable. He needs to ensure that I will not leave him now he needs me to give more than just respectability to his outward façade.

I will not leave him. I do not love him, but I will not leave him. Leaving was originally my plan, but, the more I thought about it, the more I wondered why I should be the one to go. That was my house, my home, my life. Why should I walk away when I had done nothing wrong?

When I found out from eavesdropping on a conversation between Jack and Grace that he had taken Jack, and Jeffrey before him, to a brothel, trying to make them into reincarnations of himself, trying to instill in them his sick vices, I knew I could not leave. I would not leave when I could do this instead.

Hector has always relied on me to run his life for him. And that includes filling his prescriptions and putting the tablets into a daily pillbox. The Internet is a wonderful thing. You can buy all sorts of things. Say, for example, the right medication in a substantially lower dose. It would take time to work, but it would work. And it has worked.

'I don't ever want to lose you,' he says. Hector needs me. And I need him to pay for what he did to my children and for how he has humiliated me.

'Don't worry, Hector,' I say to him, curling my hand around his. 'I am not going anywhere. I am never, ever going to leave you.'

He smiles at me in gratitude and relief, and I smile back at him feeling grateful for my patience all these years and for the invention that is the Internet.

chapter twenty-one

libby

The diaries catch fire quickly, the sparks lapping greedily at the paper until it goes up in blue flames that dance and twist, becoming a myriad of colours along the orange spectrum. I watch them burn with my heart racing in my chest, knowing that I'm doing the right thing. It's what she wanted.

Eve died so that Jack would never find out what sort of a monster his father is and now I know that I am safe it is not my secret to tell. It's not for me to stir up the waters of their relationship, to make Jack reassess the love that they shared. The horror of Eve's Caesar is at an end now – he is so ill he will never hurt another person again. I know that is what Eve really wanted, so she can now rest in peace.

Once the flames have died out, I sit and wait for the barbecue to cool. It's a bright, clear day with the sun shining down upon me as if there are no cares to be had anywhere in the world. The ashes cool quite quickly, allowing me to scoop them out and scatter them around the garden. I found out how much Eve loved this house, so it seems fitting that what is left of her is placed here to become a part of this house's history. The garden is quite small for such a large house, so I manage to leave a little of the ash, a little of the essence of Eve, around most of it.

As I wash my hands, I glance out into the garden and there she is. Standing in the middle of the lawn, almost transparent in the bright, brilliant sunshine. She's wearing her dress, and she has trainers on her feet, just like she wore the first time she bought it. Her face lifts in a smile, crinkling her beautiful indigo eyes and softening the lines of her face. She raises her hand and waves at me.

Without thinking, I wave back.

She says something, and even though she is there and I am here, and I know it can't be real, I hear her voice in my head. It is different from the voices I've conjured for her before.

It is soft and plain, ordinary – it's the voice of any woman on the street. 'Thank you,' she says to me.

'Thank you,' I say back to her.

Behind me I hear the front door slam. 'Libby, are you ready? If we don't leave now, Butch will miss his Scottie girlfriend.'

'I'm coming!' I call back to Jack, my eyes still fixed on Eve. 'And you say that like Butch will do anything more than stand and drool in her general direction.'

Eve shoos me away with her hand, telling me to go and get on with my life. Her smile becomes a grin and, as I wave again, she fades away until I can feel with every fibre of my being that she has finally gone to a better place.